THE COURTNEY ENTRY

Aviation in the mid-twenties seems, to most people, to have little commercial value beyond air circuses and stunt flying. Yet there are some who believe that it has a practical future: a successful flight across the Atlantic would provide the boost that is needed. The Orteig prize of 25,000 dollars for the first man to fly non-stop between Paris and New York is, so far, still unclaimed, though many have died attempting it. Among those who are still ready to face the awful hazards of such a long-distance flight is Ira Penaluna, a hard-bitten war veteran from Cornwall. Ira discovers that the Courtney aeroplane he is to fly requires drastic design modification, but increasing financial pressures jeopardise its safety. The news that there is another challenger on the point of departure forces Ira to take off in perilous conditions. His struggle to cross the Atlantic against storms, with unreliable instruments and without a radio, makes compelling reading. He has no means of knowing the progress of the competing airman—a young man named Lindbergh. . . .

Also by
JOHN HARRIS

★

THE LONELY VOYAGE
HALLELUJAH CORNER
THE SEA SHALL NOT HAVE THEM
THE CLAWS OF MERCY
GETAWAY
THE SLEEPING MOUNTAIN
THE ROAD TO THE COAST
SUNSET AT SHEBA
COVENANT WITH DEATH
THE SPRING OF MALICE
THE UNFORGIVING WIND
VARDY
THE CROSS OF LAZZARO
THE OLD TRADE OF KILLING
LIGHT CAVALRY ACTION
RIGHT OF REPLY
THE MERCENARIES

THE COURTNEY
ENTRY

*

JOHN HARRIS

THE
COMPANION BOOK CLUB
LONDON AND SYDNEY

This edition, published in 1972 by
The Hamlyn Publishing Group Ltd,
is issued by arrangement with
Hutchinson & Co. (Publishers) Ltd.

THE COMPANION BOOK CLUB

*Made and printed in Great Britain
for the Companion Book Club
by Odhams (Watford) Ltd.*

SBN. 600871444

3.72

Part 1: The Challenge

CHAPTER ONE

THE SIKORSKY had seemed a magnificent machine, and years ahead of its time. A huge biplane, its lower wing had been well above the heads of its crew as they had clambered into their seats. Its upper wing had been supported by enormous struts and had towered over three times the height of a tall man.

To Ira Penaluna, as he stared at the picture that was being indicated to him in a thick glossy magazine held out from among the pile of assorted luggage alongside him, the harsh mid-west voice of its owner, a cheerful Nebraskan describing the machine from first-hand knowledge of it, drove into his consciousness with the mercilessness of a mechanical pick.

'That's just how she was, son,' the Nebraskan was saying in slow tones heavily larded with drama, as he jabbed a finger at the folded pages. 'She sure looked good. All metal. Windows down both sides. I guess she was the most beautiful bit of machinery I ever saw. I looked inside her, too. Lots of us did. At Roosevelt Field. She had a fifteen-foot-long cabin furnished like a parlour, and they'd got some interior decorator guy to give it a colour scheme of red, gold and silver. Mahogany finish, too, and panels of Spanish leather. Looked like something out of a millionaire's vacation house.'

Ira stared at the illustration again. Originally built for two great engines, a third had been added to the huge Sikorsky to give it extra lift, and the result was a picture of concentrated power as the bunched cylinders crowded round the cockpit in circles of stabbing exhausts. Clearly its pilot, René Fonck, had been satisfied because it was he who had advocated the extra thrust. And he was a man who knew his subject. A thirty-four-year-old Frenchman, he was one of the most famous pilots of the recent war against Germany, a man whose precision flying and attention to detail were well known, a man credited with destroying perhaps a hundred and twenty-seven German aeroplanes.

'Smart guy, he was,' the Nebraskan said, manoeuvring the stump of a wet cigar from one corner of his mouth to the other.

5

'Pudgy, though, and kinda little. Dressed in leather leggings and a blue uniform. He talked about what they were going to do when they got to Paris, and some guy gave him a box of French croissants. A symbol of American-French unity, they said.'

The Nebraskan was a cheerful pale-eyed man wearing a stiff collar that sawed at his ears, and on the back of his head a hard straw hat with a patterned band. He was an ardent supporter of President Coolidge and prosperity, his business was real estate, and he believed firmly in money and security, and as the subject that was occupying his attention just at that moment concerned none of them, he was out of his depth, confused and very puzzled by the failure of what should have been a good American product.

'They called her the *New York–Paris*,' he said. 'Mayor Walker was at the christening ceremony. They broke a bottle of soda pop or sump'n over her. They couldn't have champagne because of Prohibition, I guess.'

Ira turned the crumpled pages of the magazine slowly, studying the photogravure illustrations with a shrewd eye. The Nebraskan watched him, still puzzled.

'They say she cost over a hundred thousand dollars,' he said, as though that alone ought to have guaranteed success. 'The most goddam expensive airplane ever built.'

Though he didn't say so, Ira knew the story as well as the man from Nebraska. He'd read the reports—more carefully than his companion ever had, and with better reason. But he had other things to think of just then than the crash of the big Sikorsky at the beginning of its attempt to fly the Atlantic the previous September. The time would come when he would study the reports again, but, for the moment, he was more concerned with what he saw about him from the station entrance in this soft Southern city of Charleston.

Newly arrived in the United States, he had decided, fascinated, that there were more motor cars about than he'd ever seen in his life before. And what motor cars! In New York, which he'd left the previous night, there'd been Chevrolets, Franklins, Fords, and a dozen other makes he'd never even heard of; sedans, limousines, roadsters, coupés; all high and heavy and all equipped with vast yellow headlights like glowing eyes; all clattering and roaring and backfiring so that the streets between the steel, brick and concrete skyscrapers were blue with smoke and acrid with the smell of burnt petrol.

6

When Ira had last been in England the motoring craze had hardly caught on. Here in America it had long since swept across the country like a prairie fire, and on a young man almost exactly the age of the century it had had a remarkably exhilarating effect.

The voice of the Nebraskan broke in on his thoughts. 'Hand-picked, that crew was,' he said, persisting in his theme and jabbing a broad finger at the portraits that accompanied the picture of the Sikorsky. 'Co-pilot was an American naval officer. The radioman was a Frenchman, and the mechanic was a Russian immigrant. They say he was one of the best friends of the designer himself. And no guy's going to send his best friend up in something he don't believe in.'

Ira gazed at the pictures under the broad finger again. He was an even-tempered young man but by this time he was beginning to grow a little tired of the Nebraskan's tirade. He had seated himself next to Ira in the club car in New York and had struck up a conversation from which Ira had been trying on and off ever since to extricate himself. He had started on the theme of aviation in Richmond and, knowing nothing of Ira's professional and private interest in aviation, had been repeating it ever since and still showed no sign of coming to a stop.

'She did all right in her trial flights,' he said. 'With a light load, I guess, though. I saw her myself once. I was always in New York. All silver, she was. Like a goddam great bird. They say Sikorsky lavished every care on her.'

Though he didn't know it, in Ira's suitcase alongside his feet was a report on exactly what he was telling Ira now, a report, moreover, that was far more technically perfect and covered far more than anything the Nebraskan could know. Ira had already read it so many times he knew it off by heart. With favourable weather and a French machine already lifted from Paris to Persia, a distance of three thousand two hundred and twenty-nine miles, the Sikorsky's chances of flying the Atlantic had seemed extremely good.

'They said it couldn't fail,' the Nebraskan continued. 'They'd got the best pilot and Sikorsky had even built a kind of auxiliary detachable undercarriage under the tail. To support the weight, they told me. He did everything a guy could do.'

Except one thing, Ira thought, with an expert's knowledge of what *could* be done. Except *one* thing.

The Sikorsky's three great Gnome-Rhone engines had been

warmed up in the early dawn light, and the vast machine, loaded with nearly two thousand four hundred gallons of petrol, had been shoved off by straining mechanics to go lumbering slowly down the runway, watched all the way by the huge crowd of spectators who had turned up to see it take off.

'I was in New York on business,' the Nebraskan went on. 'I thought I'd go see 'em off. I didn't know nothin' about airplanes, and I still don't, but I guess half the crowd who were watching didn't either. I could see right there and then, though, that something had gone wrong.'

And so should Fonck have done, Ira thought with a cold professional detachment. It shouldn't have been too hard.

He had been unable to get the tail off the ground and, roaring over the unlevelled service roads that crossed its path, the great machine had begun to bounce, lurching awkwardly like some runaway juggernaut under the shifting weight of the enormous cargo of fuel.

Then the auxiliary landing gear built to support the tail against the tremendous overload was seen to be shedding parts in a terrifying manner. A wheel broke away, bouncing high into the air, and the machine began to yaw. Then, as the auxiliary gear was hastily jettisoned by the co-pilot in an attempt to regain control, the tail dropped with a crash and another piece of undercarriage was flung up to damage the rudder. The cloud of dust that rose had half-obscured the machine.

The cheers of the tense crowd had long since died to anxious murmurs and as a watching pilot near the designer cried, 'Lift her, for God's sake, lift her!' in an agonized voice, a woman began to scream hysterically, the sound cutting across the howl of the great engines.

'But it didn't stop,' the Nebraskan said in bewildered tones. 'It didn't stop. It just kept right on going.'

Although the chances of a take-off had long since faded, the thundering juggernaut had continued to pound down the airfield and, without even lifting its wheels from the grass and still trailing a vast cloud of dust, it had swooped into a twenty-foot-deep hollow at the end of the runway and vanished.

The Nebraskan searched Ira's face for signs of horror. He seemed startled not to find any. 'Guys began to run,' he said in shocked tones. 'And automobiles began to pull out of the

8

crowd. I guess some of 'em drove faster than they'd ever done before. I got a lift with one of them. But, hell, long before we reached the dip there was a thud and a "whoosh" of gasoline going up, and a goddam great column of red flame and black smoke went up into the air. Straight up. Like it was an oil tank caught fire. When I arrived two guys had gotten clear. One of 'em was Fonck. The other was the co-pilot. Fonck said something to me, but I couldn't say anything back. I was still getting my breath back, and I guess we were all shocked some. But not as much as those two guys. They looked like some guy had socked 'em between the eyes. The radioman and the mechanic were still in there. *They'd* been staring at a funeral pyre.'

As Ira handed back the magazine with its grim story of the previous autumn's disaster, he looked round at the chubby-faced American who had come to meet him at the station and was now juggling with the throttle control of a heavy open tourer by the kerb. The American was engrossed in his task and Ira's gaze went beyond him to the skinny young man in tweed jacket, military breeches and laced-up ankle-boots who had travelled with him and was now staring round him in awe at the busy street. He was hoping that one or the other of them would rescue him from the Nebraskan, but they were both absorbed in what they were doing, and the voice of the Nebraskan came again, troubled and still overlaid with the memory of the shock.

'I was there, son,' he was saying heavily as he folded the magazine and slipped it under his arm. 'I saw it happen. I saw it fall apart.' His voice rose. 'I saw it burst into flames! I saw those two guys die!'

A cab appeared and he jerked his cigar from his mouth and waved it urgently at the driver. He was too late, however, and as someone else reached it first he turned again to Ira.

'They were going to fly to France,' he said. 'France, for God's sake, son! France!'

Ira didn't answer. France was almost four thousand miles away and out of his thoughts just then, while the United States was a living pulsating thing that transferred its vitality to its visitors as no other country he'd ever visited before had done. In his short life he'd seen quite a few—Europe, Russia, India, Africa and China—and he knew what he was talking about, and he wished, as he'd been wishing for some time now, that the talkative Nebraskan would leave him alone with his impressions and go about his business.

The Nebraskan had no such intentions, however. He'd got his teeth well into his subject now and he was determined to make sure that Ira was aware of his views.

'It just can't be done,' he said. 'Flying the Atlantic? New York to Paris non-stop? It's a great idea, but, gee whiz, who's going to do it?'

'Alcock and Brown did it,' Ira said mildly. 'Eight years ago.'

The Nebraskan gazed round him for another cab and shook his head. 'Newfoundland to Ireland, son,' he pointed out gently. 'One thousand nine hundred miles. Not four thousand. *And* they crashed.'

'They landed in a bog,' Ira said.

The Nebraskan was waving now at every wheeled vehicle that appeared in the station entrance and Ira began to hope he'd been forgotten.

The air about him was warm, quite different from the crispness of New York, and it was possible already, without going beyond the station, to sense something of the difference between the Northern and Southern States of this great new land. Here there was none of the brashness or the uncomplicated drive of the North that was symbolized in the tall buildings that shouldered the stars, and the girders, stark against the sky, which showed where new ones were still going up. Yet, despite the change and already aware of the vast complicated differences of America, Ira felt he'd never been so much alive before and he wanted to savour the experience.

But the man alongside him continued to interrupt his mood. He seemed determined to make his point before they parted company.

'They'll never build an airplane to fly *that* distance, son,' he insisted. 'Not in one hop. The future of air travel's with airships.'

Ira said nothing. Airship disasters had become far too predictable for prophecies of that sort. And from what he'd seen of aviation in America in the short time he'd been there public interest was certainly not lacking, whatever official policy might be. His first sight of the new continent, in fact, had been the manoeuvres of a small yellow biplane which met his ship far out of reach of the Californian coast and had circled and dipped and done delirious half-rolls in the clear blue sky above the masts, to the amazed delight of the passengers crowding the rails. From then on he'd seen aircraft everywhere—none of them new or original in design, to be sure, because some blank spot in the official mind seemed to have kept America behind Europe, but enthusiasm was nevertheless implicit in the gay colours of the Orioles, Wacos, Swallows and Jennies and the dozen and one other kinds of machine he'd seen, which at least gave the impression that there were a great many eager young men trying to wrest a living from building them.

A cab drew up alongside at last and the Nebraskan began to thrust his luggage aboard.

'It's just a stunt,' he said. 'To get folks talking about airplanes. So they can peddle some of that old wartime junk the government had to get rid of.'

'It's just that everybody wants excitement,' he ended, his head through the window as the cab began to draw away, 'everybody's gone excitement crazy.'

He finally disappeared with his nasal mid-western voice and his cheerful lacklustre theories which were the firm beliefs of everybody who flew aeroplanes from the depths of club armchairs. Men like him would never be converted by the acrid odour of acetate and nitrate dope or the smell of hot oil. Staring round at the approaching cabs, their horns barking as though they were some new kind of animal, Ira hardly noticed his departure.

Only three and a half short weeks before, he had been in the walled cities of Hunan and Kiangsi in China, and looking on the swiftly flowing stream of the Yangtze-Kiang; and he still found it hard to believe. Stepping into the daily life of the United States was like stepping into a different century. China had only just made the first hesitant move forward into the twentieth century and its cities were still dark unlit medieval villages, but his first impression of the United States had been one of light—glaring gaudy light that covered the hillsides and islands of the Pacific coast. San Francisco Bay had glowed with spectacular electrical displays, the city blocks glittering with a myriad points of gold. Even the station, by the standards of every other country he knew, looked as though it had been built to house an emperor, and the luxuriously appointed Pullman cars in which he had travelled across the continent had made him realise just how far ahead of the Old World the New World was in ideas, style, simple know-how and what the recently departed man from Nebraska had chosen to call 'git-up-and-go'.

'There's a lot wrong with this country of ours, I guess,' he had announced with sombre foreboding. 'Girls with skirts above their knees and bobbed hair and painted faces. Bootleggers. Politicians you can't trust.' His eyes had brightened suddenly. 'But there's one thing that ain't wrong, son,' he had added, 'and that's business. Business is booming because we've begun to realise it's not less dignified to make money than to be in any of the other professions. You can even take a course on it at college these days.'

For all his narrow views, the Nebraskan had hit on a substantial truth, because the consciousness of prosperity seemed to have taken hold of this vast new nation and shaken it into a remarkable state of alertness and impatience. Even the newspapers Ira had read in the train had had the same blaring excitement the streets displayed, as they screamed the latest scandal and disaster at the tops of their voices— 'LAWYER'S LOVE-NEST EXPOSED—STUNT FLIER CRASHES INTO CROWD'. Yet from the middle of all the violence that was implicit in the foot-deep headlines, middle-class solidity shone like a beacon from the pinched Vermont face of President Coolidge who seemed to direct an acid gaze on the nation he led, as though he disapproved of everything it did.

In spite of its size and the over-gaudiness of everything, there was a strange naiveté about it all, too. America had a newly acquired world importance after generations of isolation, and Americans, finding that what they said and did was suddenly important in other parts of the globe, were enjoying their importance as much as they were enjoying their prosperity; and it was this as much as anything else that appealed to Ira as he stood sniffing the warm perfumed air of history-haunted Charleston, so different from the shiny spanking newness of New York, absorbing it all with the excitement of a child at a circus.

He was a squarely built young man sweating in the humid Southern heat in a tweed jacket and trousers, his clothes ill-cut and creased as he stood guard over the pile of threadbare luggage on the pavement. Considering how far it had travelled, there was remarkably little of it.

'This is quite a country you've got,' he remarked gravely to the man with the tourer. The American looked up. He wore belted trousers marked with oil-stains, scuffed shoes, a lopsided bow-tie and a voluminous flat cap resting over one ear.

'Yeah,' he said solemnly. 'Quite a country.'

He studied Ira warily, as though he were still a little dubious of foreigners, as though, even, he weren't sure that the job Ira had arrived in the States to do couldn't be done much better by an American.

Ira was aware of his unspoken distrust. He was hardly used to the idea of why he was there yet himself. He had been approached in a bar in the Bubbling Well Road in Shanghai by an American businessman he knew, speaking on behalf of a mutual friend in the States; a contract had followed, and then he had been hurried aboard ship and set in motion towards the United States. He hardly seemed to have drawn breath between the preliminary bout of talks and his arrival in Charleston.

The tourer's engine caught with a roar and the American hurried to the steering wheel to adjust the throttle, then he stared round him, frowning and bewildered.

'Where's your buddy gone?' he demanded. 'He's wandered off again.'

His brows down, he set off towards the thin youngster in the breeches who was staring open-mouthed at a two-horse carriage with a fringed awning and a black coachman, waiting nearby. His thin neck protruded so that his Adam's apple stuck out like a promontory, and his beaky nose seemed to jab at the sunlit sky.

'O.K., Mr. Shapiro,' the American said, touching his arm. 'The auto's going. You can get in now.'

The beak nose swung round quickly and a pair of fierce black eyes glared up at him. Ira grinned. No one—no one in the whole world—pushed Sammy Shapiro about. Even Ira had learned to tread warily in his dealings with the hot-headed, prickly personality inside the frail frame.

Sammy was not very old, but he had long since decided that Samuel Amos Shapiro was master of his own fate and captain of his own soul—now, in the future and for ever more, amen.

He stared up at the taller man holding his arm, his gaze direct and baleful.

'That's a dangerous thing to do, Mr. Woolff,' he said gently, his face expressionless. 'I once shot a bloke dead for doing that very thing when I wasn't expecting it. Four-five revolver. Blew his brains all over the wall. Name of George Cluff.'

Ira laughed outright. It was an unblinking and outrageous lie and George Cluff had been a partner in an airline he and Sammy had once tried to run in Africa, until he'd grown despondent at their lack of success and walked out on them. But it was symbolic of the cool cheek that had got Sammy where he was. He had walked into Ira's life seven years before as a skinny youngster in shirt and shorts and had eventually almost taken over his business affairs. It had been Sammy's curiosity that had led them to China, where they'd run into the contract and the offer of a job in the United States.

Woolff was looking dubiously at him now, finding it hard to associate the virulence of his threats with his small frame and smooth cheeks. He glanced at Ira uncertainly.

'Say, how old is he?' he demanded in a heavy aside.

Sammy heard him. 'I'm seven,' he snapped. 'It's just that I'm big for my age.'

He moved to the car alongside Woolff, his walk a confident strut. 'I think I'm going to like this dump,' he decided aloud.

Woolff almost choked. 'Dump!' he said. 'I guess we'd better get you guys to your hotel before somebody hears you!'

Sammy eyed him equably, quite unperturbed. Nothing ever intimidated Sammy. The only person he deferred to, the only person his independent temperament would accept as his acknowledged superior, was Ira, whose judgment he accepted in everything except the care of the aeroplanes which were his pride and joy. In his knowledge of these—largely self-taught though it was—he would defer to no one.

'Don't get your bowels in an uproar,' he advised Woolff. 'It's a compliment. Where we come from, they rolled the pavements up at ten p.m. *If they had pavements.*'

Their belongings were strapped to the back of the quivering car now and they climbed eagerly aboard. As they moved from the shadow into the bright white sunshine, Woolff tried to start a conversation, speaking hesitantly as though he were a little shy and diffident of his own capabilities.

'You guys are English, aren't you?' he said.

'Yep,' Sammy nodded.

'This is a great country to work in.' Woolff's manner was cautious, as though he were proud of his own land but unwilling to force it down anyone else's throat. 'Courtney told me to meet you with the automobile. He's in Philadelphia fixing some business.'

Sammy turned from watching a Negro girl leading a couple of children across the road, her dress the sort of vivid flame-purple only a coloured girl could wear.

'Is he really a millionaire?' he asked.

Woolff grinned, an unexpected spontaneous friendly grin that broke down the barriers of his shyness. 'Not so's *I've* noticed,' he said. 'I guess he did all right with those autos of his, but Chevrolet decided he's dangerous and they're paying for the sort of ads he can't afford. He'll be back tomorrow, full of ideas same as always, straining like a dog after a bone. He's O.K.,' he ended in mild tones, as though he regarded Felton Courtney with a great deal of affection and amusement.

He moved the gears of the big throbbing tourer and released the brake, and they headed through the town between a strange mixture of mechanical and horse-drawn transport. The sun was already hot and the shadows between the buildings were dark slashes like huge hatchet strokes across the glaring brightness.

Heading down King Street towards the harbour between antique houses with lacy iron balconies, Woolff stopped the car near the Battery in the shade of old oaks hung with Spanish Moss. Among them they could see the silhouetted shapes of ancient guns pointing out to sea. Beside one of the guns a squirrel squatted on its haunches, its forepaws to its mouth.

'Thought you'd like to take a look,' Woolff said shyly. 'Civil War started here.'

From a nearby house they could hear the wail of a dance-band saxophone on someone's radio and the hiss of wire brushes on a snare drum coming through the palmetto flags that hung still and dusty in the sunshine.

'Kinda like this place,' Woolff pointed out. 'Nice and slow and easy. 'Course, it has its troubles. Workers ain't so expert as they are in the North where I come from, but you get 'em cheaper, I guess. Come on. I'll get you to your hotel.'

He started the car again and they headed along the shore and crossed the Ashley River to turn west into an area of swampland.

Woolff gave his vast cap a push so that it skidded to a point over his right ear. 'One thing,' he observed, 'it's flat around here. O.K. for flying.'

15

The sun on the open car made them perspire and Ira jerked off the heavy tweed jacket he wore and tossed it on to the seat beside him.

Woolff noticed that his shoulders were broader than he'd thought.

'What's he like, this Courtney?' Sammy asked.

Woolff shrugged. 'He's O.K.,' he said again. 'He likes aviators. He was in France with the Lafayette Squadron.'

'I met him,' Ira said. 'How is he? He was shot in the chest. Did he get over it?'

Woolff nodded. 'I guess so. Left him with a tricky heart, I suppose, but he's O.K. He told me about you. He thinks you're the best flier he ever met. He's a great guy for airplanes. He started on autos after the war but he's decided now he'd like to try his hand at selling to the airmail companies. That's why he moved down here from Boston. Labour's easier. Land's cheaper. We've got an airfield out at Medway. Part of an old plantation. Had to take up the house 'n' everythin' else with it. Slave quarters. Everything.' He looked up from his driving as they moved through a patch of sun-splashed shadow. 'I'm factory manager and chief mechanic. Not that that means much. We've hardly got goin' yet.'

Ira looked at him quickly. 'Do you build many aeroplanes?' he asked.

Woolff gave him a shy grin. 'Some,' he said. 'Takes some doin', though, gettin' started. Everybody's building planes these days. But I guess we'll be O.K. when things start movin'. Especially now *you've* arrived.'

'Yes,' Sammy said. 'Now that we've arrived.'

'You'll have a lot to do,' Woolff went on.

'Sure.' Sammy's interest was still on the palmetto leaves that pierced the shadows and the slow-moving Negroes along the fringe of the sun-hot road. 'You can't get ready for a thing like this in five minutes.'

Woolff glanced at him. 'No,' he agreed. 'Not a thing like this.'

They were both skirting the subject in their minds. Woolff was anxious to talk and so was Sammy, but they were both wary. Woolff looked at Ira and went on in a sudden burst of confidence. 'We'll do all we can,' he said quickly. 'All we can to help.'

His willingness, his sheer friendliness, struck a chord in Sammy and he grinned warmly in return. 'We'll need it,' he said. 'Everything you've got. Even angels if you can fix 'em. You don't fly the Atlantic without help of that sort.'

Woolff's plump face grew abruptly sober as Sammy spoke. Though he wasn't a pilot himself, he'd worked on airfields long enough to know something about the risks of flying. He was aware of its mystique, that knowledge of bright sky and dazzling cloud and solitariness of spirit—and a certainty of danger!—that people who never left the ground would never fully understand. He knew enough about aeroplanes to feel proudly that the men who handled them, smelling as they did of dope and the other unfamiliar scents of their profession, were a race apart, men not quite of the earth. It seemed to Woolff—a humble, honest, sincere young man who knew his trade and entertained no delusions about it—that they took their lives in their hands every time they lifted their wheels from the grass of the cow-pastures from which they flew, that they possessed a special knowledge denied to all other men. They knew exactly what their fragile, weather-dominated machines of wood and fabric could do and how far they could be pressed in an emergency. Yet in 1927, because nothing was certain about flying, they were still sometimes terribly wrong enough to die.

He even knew about aviators' deaths—a jolting ride, as often as not, under a stained tarpaulin to the back door of a village store somewhere out in the sticks, and a screwed-down coffin hastily made by a local carpenter. Aviators' coffins were always hastily made and always screwed down and the relatives were never allowed to see inside.

Woolff's round good-humoured face was grave as he took his eyes from the road ahead and glanced obliquely at his passengers with an expression of bleak honesty and unreserved admiration. They seemed surprisingly untouched by the implications of what Sammy had said, apparently accepting the dangers as part of the way they earned their living. As they gazed unconcernedly around them, Sammy's eyes were dark, Ira's blue with the deep tints of Cornish sea, and Woolff nodded slowly.

'I guess it *isn't* every day a guy gets picked for that,' he agreed. 'France is a long way away and you'd need twice Orteig's twenty-five thousand dollars to get *me* to try it.'

CHAPTER TWO

WHEN RAYMOND ORTEIG, the French manager of a group of New York hotels, had made his original offer of twenty-five thousand dollars to the first man to fly non-stop between Paris and New York there had been no takers. With the world still drawing its first relieved breaths after a devastating war, this was hardly surprising since no one had yet managed to build an aeroplane of sufficient range and power for such a journey. The distance was too great and, with the machines that then existed, there was no margin for error. Under the best of circumstances the odds were overwhelmingly against success.

Machines *had* been lifted across the Atlantic, of course—in easy stages just after the war—two American round-the-world Douglases and a Navy Curtiss flying boat. But there had originally been *three* Douglases. And the NC boat had been the sole survivor of four. Despite the biggest headlines since the war and the battleships stationed at intervals all the way across, one of the flying boats had been battered beyond repair at her moorings by a gale before starting, and two had had to give up before they had even reached the Azores.

And this wasn't the end of the story. Locatelli, the Italian, had been forced down by fog between Iceland and Greenland; Raynham and Morgan had crashed on take-off; and Hawker and Mackenzie-Grieve, despite a flight of over a thousand miles, had still had to ditch in the sea. Only Alcock and Brown had successfully made it non-stop between the two continents, and even their flight—only across the narrow northern neck of the ocean between Newfoundland and Ireland—had been through fog and storms so violent the sleet had chewed pieces out of their faces and at times they had hardly known which way up they were flying.

By the time the offer was renewed for a further five years, however, things had changed considerably and there had been an immediate rush to take part by men with reputations made in the war against Germany. The first to register had been Paul Tarascon, a crippled Frenchman, whose chosen partner was François Coli, a one-eyed expert on Atlantic navigation and meteorology. Close behind had come two more Frenchmen, Drouhin and Landry, with a Farman Goliath in which they had already set up an endurance record of more than forty-five hours' non-stop flying.

During a trial flight, however, Tarascon's big Potez had crashed in a storm and Tarascon had barely escaped with his life. As an economic crisis in France had drained away the backing for a second try, René Fonck, perhaps the greatest name of all in French aviation, had decided, following a visit to the United States, that only there was money likely to be available for an attempt on the Atlantic. What was more, he had realized that, since the prevailing winds blew from west to east, New York, not Paris, was the obvious place to start.

He was not alone in his conclusions and a group of investors in America had already persuaded an émigré from Russia, Igor Sikorsky, to build a big two-engined machine which was at once offered to Fonck. A former stunt pilot, Clarence Chamberlain, had also indicated that he was looking for a machine for the attempt, and the commander of the Massachusetts Naval Reserve Station at Boston, Noel Davis, had said he would enter the competition with a tri-motored machine built by Anthony Fokker, the chubby Dutchman who had constructed warplanes for the Germans and had managed to smuggle not only his fortune but all his left-over machines, engines and spares into Holland just in time to prevent them being seized by the victorious Allies as reparations. Though neither of these last two ventures had come to fruition, Fonck had actually reached the point of take-off when his attempt had ended in tragedy and death.

Thus, the year 1927 had begun with the broad Atlantic still unconquered, while the competition had a new and evil reputation that seemed ready-made for those newspapers that preferred scandal to fact and bloody crashes to solid achievements. The dangers had become better known than the aims, and the failures more publicized than the solid advances in technology and skill.

Nevertheless, the New Year had brought a fresh batch of contenders, all of them undeterred by the horrifying end to Fonck's attempt and Alcock's stories of ice, frozen sleet and fog.

In France, the one-eyed Coli now had a new partner in Charles Nungesser, a wartime contemporary of Fonck's, a man with seventeen wound scars and thirty-nine decorations and a reputation as a pilot second to none. In America the competitors ranged from Clarence Chamberlain, Lieutenant-Commander Davis and an unknown airmail pilot, to Richard Byrd, whose experience included the almost incredible feat of flying over the North Pole. Despite the crashes and the casualties, the Orteig competition was still very much in the news and very much the centre of controversy.

For some time nobody spoke, as though they were all avoiding the subject. They all knew that, despite the enthusiasm and the new contenders, the prospect of success was still a bleak one. A sea obscured for long periods by fog and storm and the business of getting off the ground the vast load of petrol that would be needed for such a tremendous flight were problems that had not diminished with the passage of time.

As the big car left Charleston behind them, Woolff was silent and seemed to be concentrating on his driving, as though it were essential that he prove to Ira and Sammy that in this at least he had a skill equal to theirs.

He handled the heavy car easily, holding it tightly to the inside of every corner and changing gear skilfully, threading in and out of the traffic without losing speed.

'She's an English Sunbeam,' He broke the silence almost reluctantly, but as though he felt it was his duty to make his passengers feel at home. 'Or she was until I redesigned her. She's O.K. but she's sometimes hard to start. I've even had to drip ether into the cocks of the cylinders. Sometimes I guess it would be cheaper to take a cab. I used to do some racing once. Indianapolis.'

He became silent again, squinting into the sunshine. 'Never was any good,' he went on shyly. 'Always thought too much of what I was doin' to the engine. Then I got the flyin' bug and went in for designing airplanes instead.'

They roared through a village of shabby tin-roofed houses once painted white with gingerbread lace fretwork round the eaves. The coast at this point was already spoiled by filling stations, chicken-dinner restaurants, camping sites and crowded colonies of tiny shingled shacks, labelled with sentimental names like *Bide-a-Wee* and *Dunroamin*.

'Goddam builders,' Woolff said, without real bitterness, however. 'Spoilin' everything everywhere.'

Alongside the road just beyond the village, an air display was taking place, and several elderly Jennies, painted in gaudy colours, stood in a row. Another one was just taxiing away from a flag-enclosed area near the hangar, and Woolff halted the car for them to watch. Nearby a man in a straw hat and tan boots was hanging notices on a fence. BUCK

'Hot air!' Woolff said. 'He has a strap round his chest under his clothes.'

The Jenny that had taken off was climbing over the end of the field now and another machine was just being swung into wind by mechanics in the roped area. A patch of undoped fabric rippled in the slipstream, the skeleton of the spars showing through; one wing tip looked like a bandaged toe; and there were several tears along the fuselage which had been crudely sewn up. The pilot walking towards it wore a tight-fitting helmet with fluttering ribbons sewn to the crown, big bug-eyed goggles, a leather jacket, army breeches and puttees.

'This is why we have to fly the Atlantic,' Woolff said. 'People think *this* is flying.'

'Do they make much money?' Ira asked, squinting into the sun towards the crowd.

'Doing this?' Woolff shook his head so violently his plump cheeks quivered. 'Hell, no! Some of 'em are only as good as they talk, though I guess a few of 'em make some dough smuggling booze. You can pick up a Jenny for around three hundred dollars, but I guess they're not very reliable. Most of 'em have pieces of picket fence held in place with baling wire for the spars they've broken, and use rubber hose and adhesive tape to feed the carburettor.'

A band, their hard straw hats on the backs of their heads, their jackets discarded in the heat to show coloured sleeve bands, was playing 'Hail, Hail, the Gang's All Here' and a few people were sitting, nervously expectant, in flivvers and horse-drawn buggies to watch the display, gnawing on chicken bones and cold fried chops and scattering their newspapers and wrappings to let the breeze do what it willed with them. A few more cars stopped, their occupants in holiday mood, hot little families of six and seven, like all crowds eager to see something happen—the more dangerous the better.

The beribboned pilot had stopped by the second Jenny now and, as the mechanic climbed from the cockpit, a large female figure emerged from the crowd and began to argue with him.

'This is the stunt man,' Woolff said in a flat unimpressed voice. 'This is a regular. The crowd always swallows it.'

The 'woman' was insisting on climbing into the plane now,

still arguing with the pilot, and as he tried to stop her she gave him a push and he fell backwards off the wing. At once the engine roared and the aeroplane began to roll forwards.

The pilot picked himself up and began to chase after it, shouting, while the crowd screamed in alarm as the 'woman' in the cockpit waved her arms and the machine began to zigzag across the field. As it headed towards the parked flivvers and trucks, people began to scatter, but at the last minute it swung into the wind and made a perfect take-off, climbing steeply. At the top of its climb it stalled and dived, then went up into a loop. A series of Immelmann rolls followed, then one half-roll after another until it was in position below the machine which had taken off earlier. The 'woman' passenger was standing on the wing, now.

'He's going to change planes,' Woolff said, frowning. 'They do no good to aviation, and if he missed his grip and fell, nobody would give a good goddam. Tonight they'll be flying around in the dark trailing roman candles. No wonder we're way behind Europe. We encourage trapeze artists, not aviators.'

He waited until the Jennies had landed and the barnstormers' officials were moving among the crowd, trying to persuade the laughing farmers to try a flight, then he started the big Sunbeam's engine again and they moved off through a cloud of drifting dust.

'They'll be off again tomorrow,' Woolff said. 'To put on another show at Walterboro or Fairfax. They scrape a livin'.'

Passing along a stretch of twin-rutted road among the trees, the Sunbeam began to labour through deep sand, vibrating violently as the big wheels jerked and shuddered.

'Damn' road,' Woolff said shortly, his round face gloomy. 'It's enough to shake the fillings outa your teeth.'

They finally reached a small town of one-storeyed houses among the chinaberry trees. There was a cinema, an all-night restaurant and a billiards hall, and a hotel with towers, wide piazzas and limp flags where Woolff stopped the car.

'Guess you'll want to wash up,' he said.

Despite its turreted towers and flags, the hotel was a bare sparse place without much comfort. Opposite was the old jail and a weathered harness store that had been there since the Civil War, the bark of its hitching rail nibbled off years before by tethered horses. Its clock tower had painted hands and in its shade gaunt-shanked old men, who looked as though they'd once ridden with Jeb Stuart, sat with their dogs at their feet in the dust, chewing, smoking and spitting, arguing in their slow Southern way, and eyeing the hotel as though its erection had spoiled their peace with the coming and going of the cars it attracted.

Not that it seemed to attract many. Its beds had long since begun to sag from the weight of wayfaring humanity and the walls were thin enough to make it possible to know without straining exactly what was going on in the next room. There were cuspidors everywhere and dust lay thickly on the blades of the fan, among the wickerwork of the chairs and in the lace of the curtains at the windows.

'Isn't much,' Woolff said apologetically. 'But I guess it's all Medway runs to.'

'It's O.K.,' Sammy said generously and entirely without truth. 'It's got class. I'm all for class. Good for tick at the grocer's.'

Woolff gestured. 'There's no bar or anything like that,' he said. 'We've got some goddam funny laws over here about drink just now but I could get you a bottle of something if you want one. We make our own.'

Sammy grinned widely. 'I like to hear men talk like that,' he said.

He already had his head in his suitcase and was throwing out, with a fine air of disinterest, clothes that looked to Woolff as though they'd been around for far too long. Ira was by the window, staring thoughtfully out at the dusty street below. They seemed surprisingly at home already, Woolff decided, well in command of themselves and certainly not in need of his ministrations.

As he brushed his unruly hair before the mirror, Ira's mind was busy. His eyes rested on a set of typewritten sheets that lay propped up against the side of the mirror, catching an angled ray of sunshine.

It was a dossier on all the previous attempts on the harsh, unpredictable Atlantic, and it wasn't exactly a story to inspire confidence.

Judged by the short history of aviation, the story was already a long one, well marked with wreckage and illuminated by the sacrificial efforts of young men who believed in the future of the aeroplane. There was nothing in any of the previous attempts to suggest that the next one, whenever it

23

took place, would achieve more than had been achieved already.

He leaned forward, his eyes on the folded sheets of paper, aware of Sammy whistling in the bedroom behind him. Despite the tune, there was a tense nervousness about Sammy and had been all morning, and the brittle gaiety of his manner didn't delude Ira. He had known Sammy long enough to know that the chirpy enthusiasm he was showing for everything he did hid a deep uncertainty about what was ahead of them.

'There'll be some opposition, Ira.' Sammy's words came loudly over the rattling of a newspaper. 'It's all in here. All written up like a prophecy of doom. Chamberlain's saying he's got a plane now and so's that chap Davis, and Sikorsky's rebuilding for Fonck.'

Ira nodded at the mirror. He knew the details as well as Sammy.

Sammy was still whistling and rattling the newspaper, a curious mixture of boastfulness and unease. Once started on a project, Ira knew, nothing in the world would make him throw in his hand if he believed in it, but Sammy was far from being an inexperienced pilot and was unlikely to accept unnecessary risks without question.

His next words confirmed Ira's beliefs. 'How keen are you on this business, Ira?' he asked, putting his head round the door. The words were spoken casually but Ira knew a lot of heavy thinking had been going on behind them.

Ira turned from the mirror. 'Dead keen,' he said. 'Who wouldn't want to be first across?'

'Nobody,' Sammy said. 'If it can be done.'

'Why shouldn't it be done?' Ira asked. 'The Yanks got their flying boats to Lisbon.'

'One,' Sammy pointed out bluntly. 'Out of four. And that stopped at the Azores on the way.'

Ira shrugged. 'I'll bet you my salary for the month someone gets across *this* year—non-stop.'

'Maybe.' Sammy paused, not entirely convinced, because he, too, had read Ira's typed notes. 'You ever get nervous, Ira?' he asked.

Ira's face became as sombre as Sammy's. Despite his enthusiasm, he had never blinded himself to the dangers of what they were proposing to do. 'I get nervous all right,' he said.

24

Sammy paused. 'What do *you* reckon of our chances?'

Ira hesitated before answering. Their chances depended on so many things—high among them chance itself.

'Depends on the plane Courtney's building,' he said. 'It's not just luck that that prize of Orteig's hasn't been collected yet.'

Still trying to force the mop of black hair into some sort of order, he crossed to the window and stared out over the dusty little town. Over the sea to the south-east, thundery dark clouds were now building up so that the sun shone through in lurid rays with a strange sort of menace, as though the heavens were full of evil.

'There must *be* a chance, though,' he said. 'Or experts like Fonck and Nungesser and Byrd wouldn't be thinking about it, too. We're not exactly novices ourselves, either. There was never much in Russia or Africa or China to pick out as landmarks. Our chances are as good as anybody else's if we take the right precautions.'

Despite his words, however, he was aware of how little they really knew of ocean flying, and Fonck's crash the previous year had been a salutary lesson to anyone with too much ambition. Setting out to fly farther than any man had ever flown before, he hadn't even got off the ground. Suddenly Ira remembered the man from Nebraska who'd plagued him on the train south.

'Why go in for airplanes?' he'd said cheerfully. 'They're building airships these days big enough to carry fifty passengers and crew. What airplane'll ever do that?' His contempt for heavier-than-air machines had been clear, Ira remembered. 'Sure, this guy, Byrd, flew over the Pole, but that's not to Paris, and this Chamberlain, hell, he's just a barnstormer, son —a stunt man! And look what happened to Fonck last September! This Orteig's sure got his nerve!'

Perhaps he had, Ira thought as he carefully knotted his tie. Perhaps the man from Nebraska had been more right than he realized and they were all a little mad to think of lifting an aeroplane across the Atlantic.

Woolff, who had disappeared to fill the Sunbeam with petrol, returned as they were snatching a puff at a cigarette. He tossed a New York newspaper down as he entered the room.

'Found this downstairs,' he said. 'Thought you might like to see it. It's about the Orteig competition.'

25

Ira reached for the sheets which were folded back at the story. Most of it concerned Coli and his new partner, Nungesser, who were to fly a new type of Levasseur designed for the French Navy.

'They've got a watertight hull,' Woolff said slowly, his brows down in a puzzled frown as though he were trying to work out the intricacies of the design. 'So they can jettison the undercarriage after take-off and float on the sea when they land.'

His eyes caught Ira's and Ira grinned. To Ira the idea of an aeroplane full of highly inflammable fuel so rejecting the earth as to give up, by dropping its wheels, its chances of returning to it in safety in the event of something going wrong seemed an extraordinary line of thinking. It was probably daring enough to succeed, however, he decided, because he'd long since come to the conclusion that it would require daring—and innovation—to get a fragile machine across three thousand six hundred miles of ocean where there would be no landmarks, nowhere to put down in case of engine failure, and precious little good weather to help it along the way.

Woolff watched him as he laid down the newspaper. So far, Sammy had done most of the talking but Woolff guessed that it wasn't because Ira hadn't any views of his own. There was too much intelligence in his face to lead Woolff into thinking that, and behind the craggy look that came from a scarred chin and a broken nose—relics of crashes during the war—there was a shrewd sensitivity that probably explained his silence.

Woolff had worked around airfields long enough to know that most people thought of aviators simply as lusty, noisy young men in army breeches who had a tendency to drink too much; but studying the keen-faced quiet young man opposite him, he knew that he was looking at a professional, and that the real professionals spent their time less on drink than over a work bench in a hangar jotting down figures on a scrap of paper, or labouring far into the night on some piece of recalcitrant machinery on which their lives might depend.

'That crash of Fonck's didn't put anybody off,' he said. 'There are a couple of Frenchmen and a German crew with a Junkers somewhere, too, to say nothing of all the oddballs who want to get in on the act—this airmail-pilot building in California, for instance.'

26

Sammy looked startled. 'The sky'll be black with aeroplanes,' he observed.

Ira was studying Woolff carefully. 'What does Courtney expect out of this flight?' he asked.

Woolff shrugged. 'Publicity, I guess,' he said. 'Having his ship first across'll produce more publicity than all the billboards you could ever set up. Like us all, I guess he hopes it'll prove flying has a future.'

'It has,' Ira said.

Woolff stared at him. There had been many times in the past when he hadn't thought it had, because most aviators, good, bad and indifferent, still flew antiquated aeroplanes—not from choice or devilry, but because governments couldn't see to the next milestone, let alone beyond it.

'Yeah,' he agreed. 'It has.'

'What's Courtney's plane like?' Sammy asked unexpectedly.

Woolff gestured. 'Different.' He didn't seem impressed, somehow. 'He's planned to have two engines slung from the top wing. She'll cruise at around a hundred and she'll hold enough fuel for four thousand miles.'

Ira rubbed his nose. 'Will she lift it?' he asked.

Woolff looked up, frowning, his eyes troubled, and when he didn't answer at once, Ira went on quickly.

'His aeroplane could be fast as greased lightning,' he said. 'But it wouldn't make much difference if the ratio between her weight and her power were wrong.'

Sammy nodded agreement. 'It'd be handing it to Isaac on a plate.'

'Isaac?'

Sammy gestured. 'Isaac Newton. Gravity.'

Woolff frowned again. Unwittingly they had touched at once on the one thing that had been troubling him. 'I wondered about that,' he said. 'According to Courtney, it will.'

'What do *you* think of it?' Ira asked.

Woolff shrugged. 'I don't think,' he said. 'I just build it. When a guy as decent as Courtney sets his heart on an airplane you don't start off by telling him what's wrong with it.'

'*Is* something wrong with it?'

Woolff evaded the question again. 'I guess if there is you'll soon spot it,' he said.

Ira and Sammy exchanged glances. They had never flown particularly for the thought of reward and they had always undertaken the dangers of flying as part of their profession,

27

and it had never been in their minds as they struggled to improve on the ancient machines it had been their lot to fly that they were furthering the progress of aviation and the grand design into which they and their small achievements might fit. They were simply trying to wring a living out of something they enjoyed, and could think of no other way of life, so that they never considered themselves martyrs and certainly never thought of themselves as brave. Nevertheless, they *were* professionals and as professionals they believed in taking every possible precaution against disaster.

Woolff was obviously aware of what they were thinking and he flashed a glance at Ira that was bleak with honesty.

'You'll have to ask Courtney himself about it,' he said at last. 'Or Alix.'

'Who's this Alix bloke?' Sammy asked.

Woolff grinned. 'It's not a "bloke". It's his daughter.'

'I didn't know he had one,' Ira said.

'Sure.' Woolff's expression softened. 'She's O.K.'

'What's she like?'

'O.K.,' Woolff said again, as though afraid of putting them off with too much praise. 'She's quite a dame. Drives a goddam big Pierce Arrow. Flies her Pa's plane.' He pulled a wry face. 'Sort of headstrong. Maybe she's had her own way too much—his wife died some years back. She's O.K.'

Ira gave him a searching look. 'How much does she know about aeroplanes?' he asked.

'Plenty. She was married to an aviator.'

'Was?' Sammy asked.

'It didn't work out.'

'Is she a partner or something?'

'Yeah, I guess so.'

'You mean Courtney says "Do this", "Do that" and she raises her hand and says "O.K., Pop, let's"?'

Woolff grinned. 'Not on your sweet life I don't mean that,' he said. 'Girls don't do as Pop says anywhere these days. Alix Courtney does as Alix Courtney wants, and says what Alix Courtney thinks—even if the Old Man don't like it. She's waiting at the house for us. You can drive straight on to the field out of the back door.'

Sammy eyed him thoughtfully. 'Good-looking?' he asked after a while.

Woolff nodded enthusiastically and they guessed he was probably a little smitten.

28

'French blood,' he said. 'Courtney's wife was from New Orleans. Black eyes. Dark hair. She's . . .' he searched for a word to describe her and ended lamely with the same words as before, 'she's O.K.'

Sammy grinned. 'Fine,' he said. 'If she's as O.K. as all that, what are we waiting for? Let's go.'

CHAPTER THREE

AS THEY DROVE out of Medway, Ira noticed that among the old Fords and farm trucks parked in the shade there were still a lot of horse- and mule-drawn vehicles. Men in bib-fronted overalls moved among them, straw-hatted, thin-limbed and slow-speaking.

'Hick town.' Woolff jerked the words out in his shy awkward way. 'I like it.'

The Courtney house was set back off the Charleston road down a dirt track between high dark trees whose leaves hung heavily in the heat, and they turned into a wide gate and down a long shadowy avenue set with a double line of oaks on either side. The Spanish Moss hanging from the branches barely moved in the still air.

'*Magnolia*,' Woolff said. 'Some guy built it around 1846.' He didn't seem over-impressed by the age of the house. 'Went down some after the Civil War. Falling apart now, I guess.'

Ahead of them now they could see rusting wrought-iron gates and, beyond, a white building and a row of crumbling brick huts.

'Slave quarters,' Woolff said indifferently, gesturing with one hand. 'In the days when there were slaves.'

Lopsided wooden stables and a disused cotton gin appeared on their right, then they were through the wrought-iron gates and Woolff was braking on a dusty drive where grass sprouted between the crushed pebbles. An elderly Negro pushing half-heartedly at a hoe stared at them disinterestedly. Apart from him there appeared to be no one else about the house, though they could hear a radio blaring jazz through an upper window. As they climbed from the car, they saw that the house was unkempt and lacking paint, and the brickwork showed in places through the whitewash.

Woolff led the way on to the high front porch and through the pillared portico, and they found themselves in a shabby green-painted hall. Opposite them was a winding white staircase devoid of carpet and to their left, down a set of wide steps, a huge library whose shelves were almost bare of books.

'In here,' Woolff said.

Above the fireplace there was a photograph of a man in a khaki uniform wearing the pale blue képi of the French Army. Beneath were other framed photographs of the same man wearing the leather coat of a pilot, sometimes with a helmet and goggles, sometimes without. He stood in front of a whole array of long-vanished aeroplanes—Caudrons, Moranes and Nieuport Bébés—sometimes surrounded by faces that Ira recognized. There was a model of a Spad hanging on a bracket on the wall, a Hotchkiss machine gun, an engine plate bearing the mark of the Johannisthal Works in Berlin, and a strip of canvas marked FOK EII 179 in Gothic lettering.

'That Courtney?' Sammy asked, indicating the photographs.

Ira nodded. 'That's him. He's a lot older than me.'

Woolff crossed to the bookshelves. From among the magazines, newspapers and broken-spined books, he produced a bottle of whisky. 'It's real,' he said. 'Sometimes you can get it. It makes a change from making your own.'

He was obviously at home in the house and seemed to have been in the habit of coming and going as he pleased.

He handed them glasses then he went into the hall and began shouting up the stairs. 'Alix!' he yelled. 'Hi! Alix!'

Upstairs they heard the harsh tones of a radio announcer cut off in mid-sentence and there was an indistinct answering call from somewhere above them in a high-pitched woman's voice, then Woolff reappeared. A moment later, they heard heels on the bare wood of the staircase, and Alix Courtney entered. She was frowning as though she had a headache.

To Ira's surprise, after Woolff's glowing description of her, she was not as beautiful by accepted standards as he had imagined, because her face was angular and her mouth was almost too wide, but the jetty hair and the black eyebrows that defied the prevailing fashion of plucking and pencilling made it striking. She was younger than he had expected, too— startlingly young—and, as they rose to their feet, she regarded them warily with a cautious expression that for a fraction of a moment made her look like a schoolgirl.

Then the expression vanished as she smiled warmly at

Woolff. 'Radio just announced that one of those stunt fliers at Thomsonboro killed himself,' she said.

Woolff's eyebrows shot up. 'He did?' He didn't seem surprised. 'We sure saw 'em trying. How?'

'Wing collapsed.'

'I guess it wasn't rigged right. They never are.'

'He had a guy from Medway as passenger. They're fishing 'em out of the sea this minute.'

For a moment she seemed to have forgotten Ira and Sammy, then she appeared to become aware of her neglect. 'Pa'll be here tomorrow,' she said. She spoke quietly but there was no shyness in her manner. 'He's negotiating a loan. He needs capital for his new braking system.'

She offered the information as though it were in parenthesis, something that was quite unimportant, and crossed towards a sagging settee, her eyes all the time on Ira.

She wore a yellow shirt and well-worn but neatly fitting oil-stained jodhpurs that managed to show every curve of her slender figure. In spite of her garb and the short hair bobbed around her ears, however, there was nothing boyish about her. Ira eyed her cautiously, noting the liberal application of lipstick and make-up.

She saw his eyes on her. 'I don't wear this get-up all the time,' she pointed out aggressively.

'Good thing,' Sammy said with a grin. 'It was always the women who wore the trousers in China. It never seemed to do 'em much good.'

Her head jerked round. 'I've even been known to wear evening dress,' she said. 'Such as it is. We don't wear as much as we used to, these days. We've found men won't dance with us if we do.'

Ira said nothing. They'd met girls like Alix Courtney in Shanghai. Despite their youth they had been surprisingly mature. They could hold their drink like men, knew all about sex, and hid their intelligence behind a frantic search for excitement.

'I expect we'll handle it,' he said.

She seemed a little relieved that they weren't nervous of her imperious manner and eyed them for a while longer, then she rose, lit a cigarette and poured herself a gin that was stronger and larger than any Ira had ever seen a woman drink before. As she sat down again, she stared at Ira with a blank, frankly curious gaze.

31

'You'll be Ira Penaluna,' she said.

'That's right.'

'My father told me about you. He met you when he was in France.' She frowned. 'You're not what I expected,' she ended.

He raised his eyebrows. 'What *did* you expect?'

She ignored the question. 'Pa's never stopped talking about you,' she went on. 'You went to Russia, didn't you? Flying against the Bolsheviks. Then Africa and China.' She gazed at him steadily. 'What was it like to kill all those men in the war?'

The question took him by surprise. He hadn't thought about the war for years. When it had ended he'd been little more than a schoolboy with a gift for survival and his youth had saved him from too many scars and too many memories.

'I can't remember,' he said shortly.

'Or don't want to remember?' she asked.

'If you like.'

'All those planes you destroyed, though. There weren't many better at it.'

'That wasn't flying.' Ira frowned, aware of a troubled look on Woolff's face and Sammy fidgeting restlessly, and conscious that the conversation was getting a little out of hand.

'This aeroplane of yours,' he said before she could continue. 'I understood we could ask you questions, because you knew all about flying.'

She gestured with her cigarette. 'Of course you can. The biggest thrill there is for me is lifting an airplane off the ground.'

Despite her poise and the faint, barely hidden hostility in her manner, she appeared a little in awe of Ira's reputation and her clumsy attempt at impressing him seemed to make her all the younger.

Sammy's eyes flickered. 'The biggest thrill for me,' he said, 'is getting it down again—in one piece.'

She looked up sharply at the sarcasm and for a moment the inky-velvety eyes were bright and keen and angry.

'Bully!' she said slowly. 'Only I don't believe you!'

'No,' Sammy agreed equably, pleased with the effect he'd produced. 'There's more to it than that. But that's important.'

She ground out her cigarette, her ennui gone in a new brisk manner. 'What do you want to know?' She had shed the uninterested manner completely now and become as forthright as they were.

32

'We've come a long way to fly this aeroplane of your father's,' Ira said. 'He's paying us a lot of money to do it. So far, though, we don't know much about it. We want to know what it'll do. How fast it flies. How high. How much it lifts. We're going to try to fly it for nearly four thousand miles non-stop on a route where if it fails us there won't be much chance of us coming out of it alive. We're interested in how safe it is.'

She stared at him for a while, then she sat bolt upright. The frown had vanished and she looked alert and intelligent.

'It's a Courtney,' she said.

Ira nodded. 'Up to now that's the first we've been told about it. I gather it's a biplane.'

She flung a glance at Sammy, faintly distrustful and wary after his tart sarcasm.

'Yes,' she said in a flat voice. 'It's a biplane.'

'Biplanes are out of date,' Sammy pointed out bluntly. 'Everybody's building monoplanes these days.'

She frowned heavily, glancing at him again as though she resented his presence and his brusque observations. 'Biplanes have been proved reliable,' she said, a sudden sharp edge of irritation in her voice.

'And not so strong,' Sammy pointed out.

She seemed to feel they were being unnecessarily critical. 'You'll not find much to complain of in that department,' she said sharply.

'How big is she?'

'She'll have a forty-five-foot wing-span and she'll be twenty-eight feet long. She'll weigh around three thousand pounds.'

'Unladen?'

'Unladen.'

'And laden?'

'Do you want it exactly?'

Ira nodded. Yes,' he said. 'We've got to lift it off the ground and every pound'll count. What's the wing area?'

'Enough. Do you want to see the plans?'

'Have you got them?'

'Somewhere, I guess.'

'How about having a go at digging them out?'

'Now?'

'Why not? It'll be as well to know a few things about her, otherwise we might find ourselves going down the runway at eighty miles an hour without a cat in hell's chance of getting off.'

She gestured with her cigarette, faintly irritated by their persistence. 'We could put a bigger wing on her if you weren't satisfied,' she said.

Ira refused to be put off. 'How's she powered?'

'Two Gnome-Rhône Jupiters.'

He said nothing and she looked quickly at him. 'What's wrong with that?' she asked sharply.

Sammy gestured, his dark eyes fierce. 'There are better engines than Gnomes these days,' he pointed out. 'These new Wrights burn only two-thirds what Gnomes burn.'

She frowned, a little taken aback by his firmness, and Ira interrupted, trying to take some of the tension out of the interview. He could see Woolff's face growing longer and he was moving awkwardly on his feet, obviously disturbed by the marked hostility in the air.

'There *are* better engines,' he agreed. 'Engines that go for days without stopping. Engines made here in the States.'

She glanced at Woolff but he refused to be drawn into the argument and she turned back to Ira. 'You're asking a lot, aren't you?' she said roughly. 'They're new. They cost money.'

'They might cost us our lives,' Ira said quietly. 'What happens if an engine cuts?'

'You have another.'

Ira nodded. 'Will she fly on one engine?' he asked.

'Yes.'

'Have you tried her?'

'Yes.'

Ira was suddenly beginning to enjoy himself. 'With the full amount of fuel aboard for the dead engine?' he said.

She paused, frowning again as though this point had troubled her, too. She looked quickly at Woolff once more.

'I knew you'd ask that one,' she said. 'Perhaps the engine *won't* fail.'

Ira leaned forward. 'If it did,' he pointed out, 'the other one might not be enough for the extra fuel and the crew.'

She sat silently for a moment, seeing that neither he nor Sammy was likely to be talked into giving ground. She moved restlessly on the settee, fingering her cigarette case and toying with the frayed turn-ups of the jodhpurs, then she glanced again at Woolff, who looked down abruptly, and back at Ira.

Abruptly she swung her feet to the floor. 'I guess we're not getting very far.' Her voice was brisk and cold and unrelenting. 'We'd better go see the ship.'

CHAPTER FOUR

SHE LED THEM through the back of the house and out on to the lawn. It was shaded by a gnarled oak so vast that even on the hottest day the garden remained cool. The air throbbed with the mourning of doves, and nearby they could see cane brakes and a gleam of water, and a few white birds among the reeds. The drowsy honk of water fowl came from the river that meandered behind the house, the old cotton route to Charleston, and they could see a jetty built of heavy timbers where a rotting flat-bottomed barge was moored.

Beyond the magnolias and the over-grown banks of azaleas there was a small graveyard among the cannas and moss-garlanded oaks, where all the names—every single one of them —were the same. The dates stopped abruptly at 1867.

'This is a beautiful place,' Ira commented.

'Magnolias and moonlight,' she said shortly. 'The romantic South.' She shrugged. 'It's falling apart.'

Certainly the garden was overgrown and the grass was uncut. Hedges encroached on to the paths and the neglected fences had fallen down.

'Damned house,' she went on bitterly. 'Never enough people around to do anything. I sometimes look forward to going back to New York. I've got a house on Long Island.'

Beyond the tufty lawns there was a wide spread of longer grass that stretched in flat folds to the horizon. In the distance they could see the roofs of Medway and a few large sheds among the trees. 'Those are the hangars,' she said.

A red Pierce Arrow that looked as big as a destroyer stood on the edge of the field. She slapped the bonnet affectionately.

'Drive her,' she said. 'She's got a standard shift.' She turned to Woolff. 'You'd better take Mr Shapiro, Hal. You can talk about motors.'

Woolff nodded and he and Sammy disappeared through the bushes to where he had left the Sunbeam. As Ira felt for the gears of the Pierce Arrow and moved the throttle and choke levers on the steering wheel, Woolff's car roared round the house, lurched on to the field, rolling on its springs, and set off across the grass towards the hangars, swaying and bouncing over the undulations in the ground.

'Better follow him,' Alix said.

Ira let in the clutch and the Pierce Arrow jolted forward. 'She's fast,' he commented.

She shrugged. 'She'd be faster if she were new. You can borrow her until you can hire one of your own. You'll need an auto. Everybody has an auto.'

For a while she was silent as they bumped across the field, then she half-turned in her seat to look at him. 'How did you get into flying?' she demanded unexpectedly.

Ira paused, his hands gripping the quivering steering wheel. Though his grandfather had been a sea-captain plying out of Fowey in square-riggers for Australia, for his father excitement had come not from stately sailing ships but from the fragile new-fangled string-and-wire contraptions that were beginning to claw their way into the sky. When one of them had finally sent him to his grave with a broken neck in 1913, the particular strain of Cornish Penaluna that ran through Ira's veins had put the sea behind it for ever.

'My father built aeroplanes like the Wrights,' he explained. 'But the Wrights were cleverer than he was and made it first. He was killed when one of his engines failed. I used to help him. *That's* how I got into flying.'

For a moment she said nothing, then she gave him a little twisted smile. 'I just wondered,' she said. 'Because there are a lot of phoneys in this racket. Wise guys, all hot air. I know. I married one.'

She looked barely old enough to have been married and seemed to have remarkably little affection for aviators. Her voice was full of contempt. She tossed aside a dead cigarette and lit another.

'What about the money?' she asked bluntly. 'Are you in it for sport or for cash?'

'I'm a professional flyer,' Ira pointed out with equal bluntness. 'I have to be. It's the only thing I can do. And the better I am at it, the better it is for me and the people who employ me. I earn what I'm paid.'

She seemed to feel he was resentful of her questioning. 'Don't get so edgy,' she said sharply. 'We need people like you over here. Flying in this country so far's only produced a lot of crazy fools who've made it an attractive form of suicide. They stunt second-hand wartime planes. Half the excitement comes from not knowing what'll happen next. A lot of 'em kill themselves like that guy at Thomsonboro—because their ships are old and badly serviced—and people have gotten around to associating flying with lunatics. That's not what the Wrights intended when they got their Flyer off the ground.'

36

It was a long speech, quite unexpected after her earlier taut comments, and it was a shrewd enough summing up to show that she knew what she was talking about. Ira began to regard her with considerably more respect.

'Growing pains,' he said. 'That's what it is. Flying has growing pains like everything else. It'll improve.'

She was watching him carefully now also, drawing thoughtfully at the fresh cigarette. 'When you arrived, Captain Penaluna,' she said slowly but without animosity, 'I'd have been quite happy to see you cut into strips and fed to the hogs. I was in Charleston last night, dancing, and I got myself a little plastered on home-made gin. Everybody gets blotto on home-made gin these days. I still feel a little this-side-up-handle-with-care.'

Ira grinned and she looked at him again with sudden interest. 'Doesn't the thought of such hostility worry you?' she asked.

'I've made a few mortal enemies in my time,' Ira said.

She paused, then went on earnestly in a way that made her seem very young again. 'My mother died when I was a kid,' she said. 'I brought myself up. Did Hal Woolff tell you?'

'Some of it.'

'I'm a walking lunatic asylum,' she continued in the same crisp breathless way, as though she were still trying to impress him but was uncertain which line was likely to be most effective. 'A nut. I'm a psychological fireworks display.'

Ira grinned. 'I'm used to explosives.'

'I'm a malcontent. Didn't Hal warn you?'

'He did. It doesn't matter. We need a few more of those in this world.'

The engine of the huge Pierce Arrow roared as they rolled sedately after Woolff's Sunbeam and she jigged up and down under the vibration in the corner of the seat, the ends of her mouth lifting in a small cold smile. 'It worries most people I meet,' she said. 'What were you doing before my father got hold of you?'

'I was trying to be a businessman, I suppose.'

'And were you succeeding?'

'I'd just gone bust.'

'I'm sorry.'

Ira shrugged. 'It wasn't as painful as I expected.'

She stared at him, and as he glanced at her he saw now that her gaze was direct and fearless. 'Better call me Alix,' she suggested briskly. 'Most people do. Where'd you get this name of yours?'

'It's Cornish functional. "By Pol, Tre and Pen, ye shall know the Cornishmen." '

'You married?'

Ira hesitated. He almost had been once. 'No,' he said.

'Neither am I. I'm a spinster again. I spin like hell.'

He glanced at her quickly and her expression as she returned his look was as wary as his own. For a while they each waited for the other to speak, two young people each aware of being in the presence of someone rewarding to look at and potentially exciting to meet, but under the circumstances that had thrown them together, both unwilling to commit themselves to any great show of interest.

'I think,' she said after a while, 'that this time my father's hired a good one. He's bought enough stumble-bums in his time.'

She drew her feet up under her on the seat and looked up at him under a wing of dark hair.

'Aren't you scared?' she asked. 'By what's ahead, I mean.'

'Not so much by the flight so much as by what it involves.'

'What *does* it involve?'

'Dealing with your father. Dealing with you.'

'You think I'll be difficult.'

'All women are difficult!'

The smile that was more like a grin twisted her face again. 'I'll do my best to oblige,' she said.

She continued to stare at Ira as he drove, as though he puzzled her. Once or twice she seemed on the point of saying something, then, as though aware that he was watching her from the corner of his eye, she gestured abruptly at the Sunbeam bumping and rolling on its springs just ahead of them, with Hal Woolff bolt upright at the wheel, the big white cap over one ear, as though it were in danger of sliding off his head altogether, Sammy bouncing up and down alongside him.

'That Woolff,' she said, changing the subject abruptly. 'He's as bald as a coot. But you'd never know because he never takes his cap off. I think he's got a dirty word tattooed on his skull. Step on it and pass him. He'll chase you. He can never resist the chance to show how well he can drive.'

The Courtney hangar was plank-built with a flattened peak roof with the word 'Medway' painted across it, and as they roared up to it, lurching and rolling over the uneven ground and shouting across to the grinning Woolff and Sammy, Ira was surprised to realize it had obviously seen better days. Swinging round on two wheels, throwing up the dust, he noticed even that several planks were displaced, and that the hutments alongside were shabbier than he'd expected. He felt a curious sense of depression, as though the high hopes of the job he'd come to do might possibly have been misplaced.

Alix Courtney seemed to be aware of his thoughts. 'Flying's in a mess over here,' she said as she climbed from the car. 'I mean—look at *this*. The town airfield. Gosh, the size of this country could show the whole world just what flying could do, but I guess automobiles have kind of got in the way. When you can drive like a maniac on the ground at sixty miles an hour, nobody's going to risk his neck in the air at not much more than the same speed.'

There was an elderly De Havilland Nine standing outside the hangar and, as he climbed out of the car alongside it, Ira ran his hand affectionately over the fuselage, catching the strong familiar smell of petrol and dope.

'We use her to fly to New York,' Alix said, appearing at his side. 'You can use her if you like. You'll maybe need to get your hand in. She has the best attention.' She jerked her head to the hangar door where Hal Woolff was now drawing to a stop. 'Come on. Let's go see the plane.'

The fuselage of Courtney's plane stood on horses at the back of the hangar, welded steel tubing partially covered with fabric. Already alongside it there was a mock-up of the undercarriage complete with wheels and mudguards waiting to be fitted. It was a solid-looking aircraft, thick-bodied and with the wing-frames of spruce spars already in place.

Woolff jerked his head so that his cap, which had slipped even further over his ear during the wild drive across the field, looked about to fly off into space. 'That's her,' he said.

Ira said nothing and walked down the starboard side of the half-built fuselage. There was something in the way the frames for the two engines hung below the wings that was unattractive and made the fuselage look top-heavy, and the design seemed somehow to indicate the machine would be slow on the controls.

As he appeared under the port wing, he found himself face to face with Alix Courtney.

'Well?' she said. Her tone was almost aggressive.

39

He said nothing and she hurried on nervously, as though feeling he needed convincing.

'Pa decided on a biplane,' she said. 'Because of the two engines.'

'One'd be enough,' Sammy observed quietly. 'If it was big enough.'

She heard him and turned. 'Byrd used three when he flew over the Pole,' she said. 'He's using the same kind of plane for the Atlantic. Davis is using three. *He*'s being backed by the American Legion. They've got plenty of fliers in their outfit and they went into it carefully.'

Ira still didn't speak. He was standing back now, studying the lines of the fuselage. Courtney's dimensions were sound but he remained curiously unconvinced. There was a strange sluggish look about the half-built machine.

Alix Courtney was still eyeing him anxiously. Behind her Woolff stood, watching as Sammy stared with hostile eyes at the undercarriage.

'She'll have a radio,' she went on. 'And a crew of three.'

'Why not a crew of just two?' Ira said.

'You need a radio-man. You'll have to have a radio.'

Ira shrugged. 'I'd rather have petrol than a radio,' he observed. 'And *more* petrol instead of the man who's going to operate it.'

She gazed at him for a moment unblinkingly, as though he had made his point. 'Makes sense,' she agreed. 'If your navigation's O.K.'

Sammy looked at her pityingly. 'If Ira uses navigation,' he said, 'it'll be O.K.' He jerked a hand at the heavy mudguards on the wheels of the undercarriage. 'Those shields'll knock ten miles an hour off the speed,' he observed. 'Quite apart from the weight. Can't we do without 'em? They won't stop her flying.'

She stared at him. 'Pa wanted to streamline,' she said.

Sammy didn't reply and she went on in the same hostile tone, though there was something in her manner that indicated she was unsure of what she was saying and had to be all the more forceful because of it.

'You don't like his design, do you?' she demanded.

'Some of it,' Ira said.

'You think your ideas might be better than ours?'

Ira shrugged. 'Doesn't follow,' he admitted. 'But I've been flying a long time.'

'Pa's hoping to sell her to the mail-carrying companies.' She was talking quickly again in a sharp uncertain way. 'She could carry mail or two or three passengers in addition to the crew.' She paused, still hostile. 'What would *you* do?'

Ira smiled. 'I'd design for getting across the Atlantic, and nothing else,' he said. 'If we made it, he'd sell her to the mail companies all right—even if she flew backwards. I'd think in terms of a crew of two, do away with the radio and use the space and the weight for petrol. And to make things even easier, I'd do away with two engines and make sure I had one good one.'

She glanced at Woolff again—almost as though they were conspirators—and when she spoke once more her aggressive-defensive manner was less pronounced.

'Pa's worked hours on this thing,' she said unhappily.

Ira smiled. 'Let's hope it's better than I think,' he said, 'and he hasn't wasted his time.'

Her chin lifted and her eyes flickered. 'You think he has, don't you?' she demanded.

Ira stared back at her, sizing her up, wondering if she had the character to accept disappointment. He decided she had. 'Fonck had three motors,' he said. 'And he didn't even get off the ground. I'd hoped it was a single-engined machine.'

Her eyes narrowed and he went on firmly. 'What's wrong with one engine?' he demanded. 'You don't have to have half a dozen engines just because you're flying a long way. There've been plenty of long-distance flights on *one* engine and until we know more about multi-engined flight it's as safe—perhaps safer. As far as I can see, three engines only mean more petrol and giant aeroplanes to lift it. In the end you're no better off. One engine'd be cheaper and less complicated. The weight ratio wouldn't be much different and the cruising radius could be larger.'

She stared at him, and he knew all her friendliness had gone, all the laughter they'd had in the wild drive across the airfield obliterated. Yet at the same time he still couldn't throw off the feeling that the disagreement sprang more from a loyalty she felt she had to show towards her father than from any real conviction about multi-engined biplanes.

'I guess you wouldn't understand what it means,' she said. 'But my father spent months working out figures. So did I. I helped him. He spent every minute he could from making autos on the idea. He's got it half-built. It's designed for two engines. It's O.K.'

41

Woolff moved restlessly and Ira got the impression that *he* didn't agree with her, either.

Her eyes flashed as they moved from Ira's face to Sammy's and back again. 'O.K., she said. 'I guess the wing *could* be rebuilt and the fuselage *could* be adapted to take a motor in the nose.' Her brows came down and her chin lifted angrily. 'But my father hasn't time to rebuild the goddam wing! *Or* to adapt the fuselage! He wants to fly the Atlantic, not change everything he's done!'

Ira drew a deep breath, not enjoying himself very much. 'It's three thousand six hundred-odd miles to Paris,' he pointed out quietly. 'With nowhere to put down if something goes wrong. It might be worth while forgetting whose design it is and how long it took, and spending a bit more time to make sure we've got the best there is.'

CHAPTER FIVE

COURTNEY'S ARRIVAL later the same day was heralded by the ringing of the office telephone and the appearance of Hal Woolff with a long face.

'The Boss,' he said gloomily to Ira. 'I'm fetching him from the station. You'd sure as hell better get something straightened out before he arrives because he'll be as friendly as a timber wolf when he hears what you've been sayin'.'

He drove off in the old Sunbeam, swinging in a tight circle in front of the hangar to bump on to the road and disappear in a cloud of dust towards Charleston. Alix Courtney was watching from the office door as he vanished, and Ira and Sammy saw her glance at them, then quickly turn away.

The discussion over the plans she'd finally unrolled for them in Woolff's office had ended in an acrimonious argument that left Ira still feeling she was defending something she didn't entirely believe in. Her protests had been too firm and her objections too long, as though the doubts in her mind had increased as he talked.

Sammy saw him frowning towards the hangar, and there was a hint of compassion in his voice as he spoke. 'I reckon we gave her a bit of a jolt,' he said uneasily.

Ira nodded. 'We weren't very co-operative,' he agreed. 'But somewhere, somehow, someone's got to make sure this thing gets pulled out of the sphere of Mom's apple pie and shoved into the region of technology.' He managed a faint smile. 'She wasn't exactly co-operative herself, was she?' he ended.

Sammy glanced over his shoulder. 'The way *she* looks,' he said warmly, 'I'd forgive her anything. What happens now?'

Ira shrugged. 'God knows,' he said. 'You've seen the plans. Do *you* think it's any good?'

Sammy pulled a face. 'Tell you better if I saw it flying,' he said. 'But *I* reckon it'll waddle up into the air like a hippopotamus and hang in a turn like a truck with wings. We might never get her up to five thousand feet and that's the least we'd want for safety. As for climbing above a storm'—he shrugged —'I thought this Courtney knew about aeroplanes.'

Ira grinned suddenly. 'It seems he's better on motor cars,' he said. 'Perhaps he hasn't the small-plane mentality. He always favoured big planes. He used to talk of building machines to bomb Germany.' He paused, staring at the hangar where they could see the fuselage of Courtney's machine through the open doors. 'To fly the Atlantic,' he ended, 'all you want is a good engine screwed to the biggest petrol tank it can lift, and fitted with wings. *And that's all.*'

They heard Woolff's Sunbeam minutes before it swung on to the apron in front of the hangar, the deep-throated throbbing note from the wide exhaust echoing off the sides of the hangar almost before it was in sight down the long straight road from Charleston.

As it stopped, Courtney leapt from it and covered the distance to Ira in three huge strides.

'Ira Penaluna!' he roared in a deep booming voice that came oddly from a slight frame. 'My God, you old son of a bitch, you haven't changed a goddam bit! Me, I'm an old man!'

He began to pound Ira's shoulder, talking at the top of his voice all the time. 'Pills with every meal,' he said. 'Medicine before I go to bed. And no more flying because the pill-roller says I'm not well enough. It gets to be a hell of a life.'

He was a lightweight like Alix, but bursting with the same nervous energy. He had a commanding nose and greying red hair stood up wildly round his head as if it had received an electric shock. The dark business suit he wore was rumpled with too many papers stuffed anyhow into the pockets so that the material was pulled out of shape against the buttons. He had snatched off his hat as he had leapt from the car and sent it skimming over Woolff's head in a wild gesture of delight and he was now pumping Ira's hand with a noisy enthusiasm.

'My God, those were the days, weren't they?' he was saying. 'Remember Bar-le-Duc? Remember the day Nungesser came? They're printing pulp magazines over here about us these days, did you know? And did you hear Tony Fokker was in New York now?' He paused to draw breath and swung round. 'Where's Sam Shapiro?'

Sammy was pushed forward, had his hand pumped, and retired hastily to the background flexing his fingers.

'You've broken about forty fingers,' he complained loudly.

Courtney hooted with laughter and indicated another man climbing out of the car behind him. 'Meet Lavery Boyle,' he said. 'He calls himself a lawyer and out of sympathy I let him work for me.'

Boyle was a stumpy, elderly man with a sun-brittled face like a walnut. He wore a rumpled suit, boots with shiny lace-holes and a straw boater with a sweat-stained band. He looked like a cynical gnome.

'Lay off, Felton,' he growled, his face devoid of humour. 'I'm as good a lawyer as you are a businessman. And if you were a good businessman you wouldn't have me for a lawyer.'

Courtney roared with laughter and swung round again to Ira. 'Nobody was more pleased than I was when I heard you were coming to the States,' he said in that vast iron voice that came so strangely from his small figure. 'I'm darn privileged to sign you on.' He slapped Ira's shoulder once more and looked at Boyle. 'This guy's one of the greatest fliers that ever sat in an airplane, Lave,' he said earnestly.

Alix Courtney had appeared from the hangar now, still wearing the oil-stained jodhpurs, and stood on the edge of the group, as unsmiling and unmoved by her father's enthusiasm as Boyle. He didn't seem to notice it.

'Hello there, hon,' he said gaily. 'You know that? You heard what I just said to Lave? I told you about Ira, didn't I?'

'Yes,' she said in a flat voice. 'I heard about him.'

She seemed untouched by her father's gusto and was watching him with the same wariness with which she regarded everyone.

'How do you feel, Pa?' she asked.

'O.K., O.K.!' Courtney waved a hand in an energetic gesture. It didn't seem to impress her much.

44

'You look as though you could do with some sleep,' she said. 'Did you get your loan?'

Courtney paused just long enough for Ira to get the feeling that there were other things on his mind besides the business for which he'd appeared in Medway.

'Not yet,' he boomed in his huge voice.

'You've been trying a long time, Pa.'

Courtney grinned. 'You bet! They took about three days to tell me "No". I reckon if God built the world in six, with a day of rest on Sunday, they ought to be able to turn me down in six minutes, don't you?'

He put his arm round Ira's shoulder and tried again to move towards the hangar, but Alix's voice came once more, flat and suspicious.

'Pa, if you didn't get the dough, what are you going to do?'

He beamed at her. 'Don't let it worry you, Alix,' he said. 'She thinks too much,' he explained to Ira. 'That goddam mind of hers has been a plague to me ever since she was a child.'

'Pa!'

Courtney stopped dead and, from the expression that sped fleetingly across his face, Ira saw that her insistence bothered him.

'Banks are all alike, Alix,' he explained in a pained, patient way. 'Always ready to bite the hand that feeds 'em. I'm still negotiating. We aren't broke. I only want capital to expand. That's all. I can always see Joe Hughesden. I've worked with him for years.'

'Joe Hughesden'll swallow you alive if you give him a chance,' Boyle growled, his voice rasping and fretful. His eyes rested on Courtney as though he were a frivolous child.

'Joe Hughesden's an honourable man,' Courtney said.

Alix snorted. 'To Joe Hughesden, honour's a matter of taste, and *his* taste isn't mine.'

Courtney stopped dead. 'For God's sake, Alix!' he said. He still wore a wide smile but somehow it seemed to hide an old irritation, as though he felt she spent too much time sitting in judgment on him. They both seemed a little on edge, Courtney because of his failure, Alix because she was obviously not looking forward to the discussion on the new aeroplane that would have to take place before long.

For a second there was a pause and Ira had a feeling that

45

there was a greater gulf of disagreement between father and daughter than Courtney allowed to be obvious. Then Courtney fished in the pocket of the coat he was carrying and held up a bottle of whisky, grinning all over his face. 'Get some glasses, Alix,' he said. 'Let's have a drink. It came from Bermuda. Or so the guy said, though it could just as easily have been Chicago. Let's go into the office.'

They followed him towards the hangar and Courtney thrust a bundle of mail towards Ira. 'Came to my place in Boston,' he said. 'It's for you.'

Ira thrust the letters into the pocket of his jacket without looking at them and Courtney put an arm over his shoulder again.

'This is going to be the biggest goddam celebration that ever was,' he announced. 'This is going to beat Armistice Night and the Fourth of July and the end of the Civil War all rolled into one.'

'It isn't celebrations *you* want, Pa,' Alix said. 'It's sleep.'

Courtney ignored her, talking to Ira as if he were trying to pretend she didn't exist. 'I sure am sorry to drag you from your business, Ira,' he went on. 'But when I heard from that guy in Shanghai that you were in China, I just had to have you. Did you sell your business? Oriental Air Carriers, they told me. I guess I haven't heard of them.'

Sammy grinned. 'Not surprised,' he said. 'They died young.'

Courtney didn't hear him. He was carrying them before him, herding them almost like a sheepdog, moving them all towards the hangar with little pushes from behind, impatient, eager and enthusiastic. 'I heard you'd been in Russia,' he said. 'And I knew you'd been in Africa. Any guy who can fly round places like Russia, Africa and China ought to be able to fly across the Atlantic.'

He swept them through the hangar doors. 'You seen the machine?' he asked.

'Yes,' Ira said carefully. 'I've seen the aeroplane.'

'She's a great ship, isn't she?'

Ira intercepted the glance Alix flashed at Hal Woolff as her father spoke, but Courtney was enthusiastically crossing the hangar floor now towards the half-completed fuselage on the horses at the back. His vast strides seemed so out of place with his small frame he seemed to be making a series of leaps.

He stopped in front of the plane and ran his hand over the undoped white canvas, and the workman busy over it with

46

thread and curved needle stepped back with a grin as he had his back slapped.

'Best plane in the U.S.A.,' Courtney told him noisily. 'I put a lot of work into that, Ira.' He was pushing them towards the office now. 'Courtney airplanes will be making the Atlantic look like a bus route five years from now. Nobody can say the United States hasn't stepped out of the days of the pioneers at last, eh, Lave?'

The old man looked round him from where he was dragging up a box to sit on. 'Well, we aren't still fightin' Indians,' he said.

Alix had produced glasses by this time and Courtney began to slosh whisky into them. Woolff followed him round with water from a bottle filled from a tap in the hangar.

'Here's to us,' Courtney said with a wide grin. He swallowed the whisky at a gulp and filled the glass again.

'You should lay off that stuff, Felton,' Boyle growled.

Courtney grinned. 'Glory be to Moses in the bulrushes,' he said, 'this is a special occasion!' He lifted his glass again. 'Here's to beating the lot of 'em—Byrd, Davis, the whole goddam gang! What do you think of her, Ira?'

Again he didn't wait for an answer but crossed to the office window and stared out into the factory where the workmen were moving leisurely about the half-built fuselage and wing.

'I came down here,' he said, almost as though he were offering a company report, 'to keep it cheap. So we had more money to play with. So we could get the very best for her. And so the goddam newspapers don't get nosing around too soon. When she's ready I want her to burst on the public like the sun coming up out of the sea. I want 'em to see her and think, Goddam, *that's* the one that'll do it!'

He swung round to face them, beaming, and Ira was unhappily conscious of the frozen faces of everyone else. Courtney still failed to notice, however.

'She's a great-looking ship, isn't she?' he said.

He turned, his manner intimidating in its directness, and jerked a hand towards the half-built machine. Immediately there was a silence as Ira sought for words that would be critical without being hurtful. Clearly, Courtney had staked a lot on his creation.

He saw Alix glance again at Woolff, then Woolff lit a cigarette slowly and looked at Sammy.

Courtney became aware of the silence. 'Well, *come on*!' His

47

face was puzzled now, the ghost of the broad grin still hanging on his lips. 'What do you think of her?'

Ira took a deep breath, thoroughly unhappy in the role that had been assigned to him. 'I think we need to talk about her, Felton,' he said.

Courtney's face fell. '*Talk about her?*' he said. 'Hell, you make her sound like two cents rotten. I've wrestled with that goddam thing too long to want to talk about her.' The smile made an attempt to return, and he looked at his daughter and Woolff. 'Well, good grief,' he ended, '*come on*! What're you kicking about, Ira?'

Ira stared at him, suddenly aware that there was a puffy look about his eyes that he hadn't noticed at first, and he realized that, despite his nervous energy, Courtney was far from fit. Too little exercise, too little fresh air, and the strain of too much business worry had taken their toll of him over the years since they'd met during the war, and his features were covered with a thin sheen of perspiration over an unexpected sallowness. Boyle was watching him with alert narrowed eyes, sitting on a box and hugging an attaché case full of papers to his chest as though he thought one of them might steal it. Ira was conscious of five pairs of eyes on him.

'She's unorthodox,' he managed at last.

'Sure she's unorthodox!' Courtney boomed. 'She'll need to be unorthodox to fly that far in one hop. You thinking of those engines slung under the top wing?' He moved about the office eagerly, obviously not really concerned with Ira's ideas. 'Seaplane construction. Used on PN-9s, Boeings and the NC boats.'

'*They* flew a lot slower than we're hoping to fly, Felton.' Ira managed to break in at last. 'I think she'll need some modifications.'

Courtney's eyes flicked from one to another of them, finally resting on Boyle's face as though hoping he might draw encouragement there. But the lawyer was obviously out of his depth and unable to help. They were all in a half-circle round the desk now as though they were holding a wake, and suddenly Courtney's manner was hostile.

'O.K.', he said sharply. 'Let's have it! Let's have the bad news! What did I do wrong?'

Ira struggled again with his words. 'I think perhaps you approached it wrong,' he said.

'How?' Courtney's words were clipped and short now, and

all the enthusiasm and gaiety had gone. Ira could see Alix's face was miserable and full of concern for her father.

'O.K.,' Courtney urged. 'Let's start from the bottom up. Is the undercarriage wrong?'

I wish that were all that was wrong, Ira thought.

'It'd be all right for a bicycle, Felton,' he said slowly. 'We're going to have to lift a heavy load off the ground, probably from a rough field. It's not strong enough. I don't like that concertina shock absorber.'

'O.K.' Courtney waved his hand, and he looked faintly relieved. 'That's nothing! We can fix that soon enough!'

He sloshed whisky into his glass, as though he half-expected that they'd cleared the hurdle of their problems. He sloshed more into Ira's glass, too, and looked up with a smile, then he caught the grim look in Ira's eyes.

'There's *more*?' he said.

'There's more,' Ira admitted. 'You've planned for a radio. I don't want a radio.'

Courtney looked puzzled. 'How the hell will you know where you're at if you don't have a radio? Byrd's got a radio. You *need* a radio.'

'I'd rather rely on my navigation. Radios are big and heavy. I'd rather have petrol.'

Courtney seemed about to protest but Alix interrupted.

'He's got a point, Pa,' she said and, after the hostility between them earlier, Ira was surprised to find her taking his side so readily.

Courtney's eyes flickered round them and Ira studied him, wondering how close this project of getting an aeroplane non-stop across the Atlantic was to his heart. Then Courtney was talking again. 'O.K., he said. 'But before you go any further remember I got my plans checked by one of the best men there is. Frank Mulroy. He came over from the West Coast to do it. He has all the latest ideas.'

'He'd have been wiser to recommend a single-engined machine,' Sammy said bluntly, 'for the size you've planned for.'

The real basis of their objections was out now and Courtney's head jerked up. 'Byrd's got a three-engined plane,' he pointed out sharply. 'Davis's got a three-engined plane.'

'Fonck had a three-engined plane,' Ira said quietly.

Courtney was clearly shocked by this attitude and his manner had suddenly grown cold and distant. 'That all?' he asked.

'Not really,' Ira said slowly. 'I think the basic point is that you're making a mistake building a biplane for record-breaking. Monoplanes are the planes of the future, Felton. Biplanes have a built-in drag.'

Courtney's face was grim. 'Anything else?'

Ira gestured helplessly. 'I think that'll do for now,' he said miserably.

For a moment, Courtney stared at him, his hand straying to his waistcoat pocket. He extracted a small tin and took out two purple pills which he popped into his mouth and washed down with a gulp of whisky, then, as though it had been boiling up inside him during the nervous movement of his hands, his anger burst out of him in a shout.

'For God's sake,' he said bitterly. 'Anybody'd think I was a damned amateur! This isn't the *first* plane we've built. Courtney aircraft are flying all round the United States. Two of 'em are carrying mail already. So will this. I planned to sell 'em for mail and I'd put my whole organization behind this project! I was prepared to stake everything, and that goddam plane's costing me a mint of money. Mulroy didn't take his fees in trouser buttons!'

He had an aggressive, pained attitude now, as though he felt he'd been badly let down by them all. 'We designed her between us, I guess, from my ideas, so she could be adopted for mail or passenger-carrying later. For God's sake, why *shouldn't* a passenger-carrying airplane cross the Atlantic?'

'Why shouldn't it?' Ira agreed. 'So long as it's the right one.'

'And this isn't? For God's sake, Ira'—Courtney lost his temper completely—'I didn't pay your fare all the way from China to tell me what was wrong with my ship! This is *my* plane and I only hired *you* to fly it.'

Unyielding independence had driven past generations of Cornish Penalunas out of the narrow creeks between Polruan and the Gribbin to do battle with the wide Atlantic in every capacity from naval man and excise official to plain honest-to-God pirate, and the unswerving rigidity of generations of nonconformist sailors whose only weapon against the sea had been their own black stubbornness showed in Ira's face. He had been tinkering with aeroplanes ever since he'd been a schoolboy and flying them from not very long afterwards, and he had the confidence of sheer experience.

'You've got to decide what class you're in, Felton,' he said quietly. 'Whether you're among the big stuff or the small stuff.

The three-engined giants have got a lot of money behind them. The private concerns are going for small machines. They've both got equal chances. You're somewhere in between with this machine. If we have three engines and one cut, maybe two might pull us out of danger. If we have two and one cuts, one engine'll never get her across the Atlantic with a full load of petrol for two.'

'Neither will *one*, if that cuts,' Courtney snapped.

'With one engine,' Ira said, 'if it cuts, your chances are still as good as if one of two cuts, and the whole thing'll be less complicated.' He paused. 'And I think you can get better engines these days, Felton, than Gnome-Rhônes.'

'What do you want? Maybachs?'

Sammy snorted. 'Water-cooled,' he said. 'Too much plumbing. You're spouting steam all over the sky all the time. And these German motors burn benzol. It's too wasteful. You'd have to change your wing design for 'em, too. We should go for air-cooled radials.'

Courtney seemed almost to be choking on his indignation by this time. Alix watched him with a white face, her eyes anxious. Boyle sat on his box, still clutching his glass in one hand and his attaché case in the other, his expression watchful. Woolff looked wretchedly unhappy, as though he wanted to agree with Ira and Sammy and couldn't because of a long-standing loyalty to Courtney.

'Goddam!' Courtney managed at last. 'I picked on you because I thought you were the greatest flier I knew, Ira. *You* were the one guy I thought could get my machine across the Atlantic.'

Ira gestured awkwardly, aware of Courtney's rage and disappointment. He had obviously set great store by his design and their comments had shattered him.

'Flying your machine across the Atlantic's the one thing I want to do, Felton,' he said.

'My God, it looks like it!' Courtney gestured, his face red. 'All fliers are only stunt men when all's said and done,' he snorted. 'And this Atlantic thing's just the biggest stunt of 'em all. Maybe you don't have the guts . . .'

'Pa . . . !' Alix's yell of protest stopped him dead. She had leapt to her feet and lifted her hand as though she were going to bring back her arm and deliver a haymaker, and Ira suddenly realized that in their haphazard life together there had probably been times when she had.

'For God's sake . . . !' she choked.

Courtney stared at her and, as she dropped her hand, he picked up the half-empty whisky bottle and swung on his heel towards the door.

'Come on, Lave,' he said bitterly to Boyle. 'Maybe I hired the wrong guy. Maybe I should get a *real* flier to prove there's nothing wrong with my ship.'

He stopped at the door of the office. 'I'll take the Pierce Arrow,' he announced to Alix in an unsteady voice. 'You'll have to get Hal to bring you home.'

The door slammed behind him, and they saw him crossing the hangar in those vast comical strides so that Boyle was having to run to keep up with him. For a while, as he disappeared, there was silence, then they all moved uncomfortably, embarrassed and awkward, and Woolff let out his breath in a long whistle.

'That sure was warm while it lasted,' he said.

Sammy drew a deep indignant breath and Alix turned to Ira, surprisingly angered by her father's intemperate words. She seemed lost for something to say and, as her jaw worked, trying to force something out, there was another silence.

Ira smiled. 'This is what's known in literature as a pregnant pause,' he said.

Her eyes flashed and she looked as though she were about to choke with embarrassment. 'For God's sake,' she said. 'I don't know what to say. He said you were yellow!'

She stared at him for a moment, searching for words, then she reached for her coat and, flashing another glance at Ira, she disappeared. Woolff stared helplessly at the quivering door, his plump round face unhappy.

'Hell,' he said slowly. 'I thought it was going to be a lousy deal for the Old Man but I didn't think he'd take it like that.'

'What happens now?' Sammy asked.

Woolff shrugged. 'He'll go for the bottle, I guess,' he said. 'I'm sure glad Lave Boyle's around.'

He jerked at the peak of his vast cap so that it slewed round on his bald head like a skidding car on an icy road, and slouched out of the office, his hands deep in his pockets, his shoulders hunched, the picture of dejection.

Sammy stared after him as the door slammed for the third time. 'I reckon we've started something, Ira,' he said. He paused, his face troubled. 'You don't think you were too hard on him?'

The tough independent look appeared on Ira's face again. 'No,' he said. 'I don't. It had to be said, Sammy. I've been flying long enough now to know when a plane's a dud.' He stared, frowning, through the door towards the sunshine, where Courtney had disappeared. 'There's something funny about him I don't understand,' he said slowly. 'I thought he was the sort to listen. Perhaps he's got business worries. Or perhaps he's not well. You heard Alix. But we were right to stick out. You don't arrange to fly four thousand miles over sea unless you think you've got a chance of succeeding.'

Sammy said nothing and Ira went on hotly: 'He's got to make up his mind which class he's in. It's no good compromising by setting up another class somewhere in between.'

He jerked out a cigarette and lit it. 'For God's sake, Sammy,' he said angrily. 'I want to fly this bloody plane for him! I think it's a tremendous idea. Who wouldn't want to be first? But it's got to be the right machine. The wrong one would only end in a fiasco and probably a messy death for me and you. That helps nobody at all. It just stops everything in its tracks.'

He gestured awkwardly, struggling with his emotions. 'There's nothing I want to do more than pull this off,' he went on. 'I like Courtney. I liked him when I first met him—when I was still a kid in France.'

'I bet he's changed,' Sammy said shrewdly.

Ira paused. 'Yes, he has,' he said thoughtfully, staring at his shoes. 'He's older and I reckon he's got a lot on his mind. But don't take any notice of all that blowhard stuff. He's an honest man and a decent man. That's just nervous energy and disappointment—because he isn't as sure of himself as he seems. I still like him. I like Hal Woolff.'

Sammy grinned. '*I* like Alix,' he said. 'She's got all the right things in all the right places. Handled right, she could be worth knowing.'

Ira looked up and grinned. 'You thinking of trying it?'

Sammy gave him a sidelong glance. 'I'm not in the same league,' he said quickly.

Ira drew on his cigarette for a while, then he crossed to the window and stood staring into the hangar. As he stuffed his hands into his pockets he remembered the letters Courtney had handed to him.

He took them from his pocket and opened them slowly, reading them in the empty light of the hangar. There were three from Shanghai, two of them from girls who'd endeavoured to make their last days in South China more cheerful, and one from the Chinese who was looking after the last old aeroplane they still owned out there. There were also a couple of small bills and a letter from Canada.

The writing seemed familiar and he tore it open hurriedly. Sammy looked over his shoulder and Ira turned.

'It's from George Cluff,' he said.

'That bastard,' Sammy said shortly. Sammy had never had much love for the partner he'd replaced in the failing airline in Africa. He'd had too many good looks and too much success with girls to gain any of the prickly Sammy's affection.

'He's in Canada,' Ira said.

Sammy gestured at the envelope. 'How did he know we were here?'

Ira shrugged. 'All that guff in the papers when we arrived. TOP BRITISH ACE VISITS U.S. You remember it. He must have seen it somewhere.'

'What's he doing? Running an ice-cream stall?'

Ira grinned at Sammy's cynicism. 'He's flying again. He's been doing some airmail carrying and now he's talking of a long-distance attempt.'

Sammy's eyebrows shot up. 'He'd never make it,' he said at once. 'He wasn't the pilot to start off with, and for another thing, he'd never have the patience. Grab the first thing with a propeller, chuck a suitcase in it, fill it up with juice, and off we go. That's Cluff's method. It always was and it always will be. If he goes in for anything like this he'll end up dead, sure as eggs.' Ira wasn't listening. 'He's near Toronto at the moment,' he said. 'With a Canadian called Pelletan. They're doing long-distance flights. He says we'll be surprised.'

'Disgusted, more like.'

Ira grinned again. A lot of what Sammy said was true. Cluff had never been a stayer, never a man to face up to odds, and certainly never a man to be bothered with careful preparations. The first thing he'd always asked about were the girls and the drink.

His nostalgic thoughts were interrupted as Sammy nudged him. He was gesturing at the hangar. The men who'd been working round the half-built Courtney had stopped and were now gathered round Hal Woolff, who was clearly explaining that unexpected snags had arisen. There were a few soured glances in the direction of the office.

'They're calling us Limeys out there,' Sammy said flatly.

Ira chuckled. 'Limey *bastards* probably,' he agreed.

Sammy shrugged. 'One thing,' he said. 'If Cluffy's got a plane to fly, he's one up on us. We haven't.'

CHAPTER SIX

FOR ALMOST A WEEK they hung about the town and the airfield waiting for a decision.

The days were hot empty oases when they got up early, as they'd always been used to doing, but after the colossal breakfasts of ham, potatoes, hominy, biscuits and coffee that always seemed to be put in front of them, they found that that was the end of their daily activity.

Work on the Courtney had come to a complete standstill and they were given bitter looks by the workmen, as though they alone were responsible for the absence of any encouragement. Woolff was always about, plump, amiable, his cap askew, but he seemed depressed, and there was no sign at all of either of the Courtneys.

They soon grew tired of fried Southern food, especially as the flies that filled the dining room of the hotel were of a rare physique and a quite remarkable determination, and the only flying they saw was by a little Oriole which appeared over the town to stop the traffic while it wrote 'Lucky Strike' in the sky in smoke. Once, remembering Alix Courtney's offer, they climbed into the old De Havilland, wondering whether to take it up. The clouds had sprinkled an unexpected light rain during the night so that the dusty earth smelled sweet and Ira sat for a moment catching the familiar scent of dope and experiencing the momentary thrill that never failed to affect him when he climbed into a cockpit. He stared round him at the patched and varnished fabric and polished metal and saw the greasy stains on the padded leather by his shoulder, then he checked the instruments and moved the ailerons, elevators and rudder, frowning slightly in concentration. But the hard stares from the group of mechanics by the hangar seemed to preclude the possibility of taking off, and they quitted the airfield without leaving the ground.

Since the meeting with Courtney, which had broken up so

abruptly and with such embarrassment, Ira had thought a great deal over what he had stood for so firmly. Despite what he had said, he was still aware that a fierce clean breeze was beginning to blow through American aviation, for all the mistakes that were often made by people such as Courtney who had more enthusiasm than knowledge, and it couldn't help but affect a man like Ira who had lived all his life by aeroplanes and for aeroplanes, and he found himself often wondering if he'd been too severe. It wasn't given to every pilot in the world to have the opportunity of making an attempt on such a vast peak athwart the progress of aviation as the ocean that lay between the New and the Old Worlds. It was an enormous challenge and such a flight could only be backed by ambitious men, and it was probably impertinence on his part to be too critical.

Yet, on a flight of nearly four thousand miles, they could not avoid considering the elements of safety and, while they waited, he studied again and again the reports on Fonck's crash he had dug up during their brief stay in New York.

'I don't want a three-engined giant,' he said slowly to Sammy, more confirmed every day in the belief that he'd been right. 'Or even a two-engined machine. If you're a flier, you've got to believe in something apart from just flying, and I think they're building engines these days that will carry us all the way without trouble, so long as we screw 'em in the right numbers to the right fuselage.'

Lying back on the bed, his feet hanging over the end, Sammy slowly turned the sheets of typewritten paper and the sheaves of press cuttings they'd gathered.

'Suits me, Ira,' he said. 'There seem to be a lot of elements hanging round Courtney's project that hung round Fonck's and I don't want to end up like *him*. This stuff makes horrifying reading.'

Read in cold blood, it *was* a grim story, terrifying in its implications, and as Sammy tossed the papers to the bed, his eyes were direct and sober. 'What went wrong, Ira?' he asked.

Ira gestured angrily. 'The Sikorsky was too damn heavy,' he said simply. 'They couldn't lift it off. It was overloaded.'

Sammy shrugged. 'They had to carry the juice for the trip,' he pointed out.

'But not the drawing room and the dining room and the furniture and the hot meals.'

Sammy gestured. 'They must have known what it would do.'

'I doubt it. They didn't fly enough load tests. Fonck wasn't ready. He ought to have put it off till this year.'

Sammy stared. 'Why didn't he?'

Ira shrugged, his fingers toying with the cuttings. 'Publicity,' he said. 'They'd talked so much of getting off in 1926 they not only couldn't postpone, they even had to rush the preparations —cutting corners just as Courtney wants *us* to do.'

Sammy frowned and Ira went on quickly. 'They didn't even pay any attention to the runway,' he said. 'They hadn't time. And, God, Sammy, that plane weighed over twelve tons! It had short- and long-wave radios and special flotation bags in case they had to come down in the sea. And four men! *Four*, Sammy! With special meals on board all ready to celebrate the end of the flight.'

He tossed the cuttings down. 'And while they were wheeling it out, the tail skid fell off the dolly and damaged the centre rudder and the auxiliary gear, and by the time they'd done all the repairs the wind had changed from head to tail and they were trying to take off with a relative speed of around fifty miles an hour. No wonder they didn't make it.'

Sammy was frowning heavily now. 'Why didn't they cut the engines, Ira?' he asked in a slow bewildered voice. 'When the auxiliary wheel came loose. They must have had plenty of time.'

'Fonck said it would have thrown the machine out of control. He said there were so many people watching he'd have hit them. The coroner agreed to call it an accident.'

Sammy pulled a face. 'Four men's two too many to fly a plane *anywhere*,' he said firmly. 'And flotation bags—for God's sake, he was going to *fly* the bloody thing, not sail it! You've got to take a chance somewhere.'

Ira nodded. 'Yes,' he agreed. 'You've got to take a chance somewhere. But not in building the machine or getting it off the ground.'

The weather remained hot and stuffy, and out of sheer boredom Sammy went overboard for everything American. Outlandish ties and extraordinary socks began to take the place of the stiff collars and waistcoats he'd always previously worn, and to his wardrobe he added brown and white shoes, a bowtie and a large cloth cap like Hal Woolff's with a broken peak as big as the blade of a shovel. It made him look like a third-rate gangster, especially as chewing gum appeared in his mouth with the Americanisms he'd taken to using. Finally, to his delight, he found that with a great deal of winking, nodding and conspiratorial whispering he could buy bootleg gin in a dark office behind a saloon at the end of the main street that looked like something out of a Western film.

'Prohibition doesn't seem to prohibit much,' he grinned.

Although the notice on the swing doors said the place sold only soft drinks, in the room at the back there were four round tables and an unmistakable smell of liquor, and after a great deal of pantomime at the door, Sammy tried pushing his way in as though he'd been buying illicit spirits all his life. The gin tasted like petrol, they found, but it helped to relieve the monotony, and the fact that it was illegal gave it a little extra zip to make up for the taste.

Then he found that the man who ran the town store had a daughter with whom he had more in common than he thought and took to disappearing to the beach after dark in the hired Ford sedan he and Ira shared, and not returning till the early hours of the morning.

'She's not very bright,' he grinned. 'But she's interested and she thinks I look like Rudolf Valentino.'

Sammy's young life had contained more than its fair share of drama and he'd long since left his youth behind, and he suffered now from an aggressiveness towards women—as though, even while he enjoyed them, he didn't believe in them much any more. Like Ira, he'd opted for living for the day and didn't question too much what made it up.

He was somewhere in the darkness with his girl among the trees near the beach when the owner of the local newspaper stopped Ira in the hotel lobby.

'Name of Nestor, Captain,' he introduced himself. 'Robert E. Lee Nestor. I run the *Medway Examiner*.'

He was a huge man with a vast paunch that hung over his belt, a round, moon-shaped face as pale as death and shining with sweat, and the reek of prohibition whisky hanging round him like an aura. 'Thought I'd look you up,' he said. 'My job's to find out what goes on around the town. Yes, sirree.'

Ira nodded, remembering the shabby little newspaper he'd read, a drab sheet full of misprints and folksy chat and almost entirely devoid of news.

'Seen you around the town,' Nestor went on. 'Made

enquiries. Any new faces, people talk round here. Everybody's kin in Medway, see? Scratch any guy you like, you'll find he's a cousin. Hear you're quite a flier.'

Ira grinned. 'When I learned to fly,' he pointed out, cheerfully, 'you looked over the side and found the ground had gone, so you had to do something about getting down or kill yourself. They were lousy instructors.'

'Yeah!' Nestor didn't seem to understand his leg was being pulled and he greeted Ira's words with a straight face.

'Some folk *are* like that,' he said. 'Like one family's all mean and another can't none of them carry their liquor.' He paused and eyed Ira with a damp pale eye as expressionless as a suet pudding. 'I hear they're building a new plane out at the airfield,' he ended.

'That's right.'

'What for, Captain?'

Ira hesitated. 'Just to fly, Mr Nestor,' he said cautiously.

'Anything special about her?'

'Not so's you'd notice.'

Nestor seemed disappointed, but he didn't pursue the line of enquiry. Obviously he wasn't a technical man.

'I hear things,' he said. 'I heard it was a long-distance plane.'

Ira smiled. 'Lots of people are building long-distance planes these days, Mr Nestor,' he said. 'Every mail plane that flies has to be a long-distance plane. Four hours' flying time's around five hundred miles. That's long-distance.'

'Sure.' Nestor nodded. 'Sure, I get you. I heard they'd stopped work on her.'

Ira lit a cigarette to give himself time to choose his words. 'Temporarily, Mr Nestor,' he said. 'Just a hold-up.'

'Nothin' permanent?'

Ira shook his head. 'Not on your life. Aviation's still in its infancy. You have to stop now and then to argue things out.'

'Yeah.' Nestor nodded solemnly. 'I guess you're right. But the rumour got around. Medway folk wouldn't like to see work stopped. Work's hard enough to find around here best of times. When them Yankees came down to Medway after their cheap labour we got to expectin' big things. Medway folk'd be worried if work stopped. They got no love for Yankees, and them Courtneys come from up North. Do we get to see this plane?'

'Eventually, I expect. When it's finished.'

'Swell.' Nestor nodded. 'Me, I'm strictly a horse-and-buggy

59

man, though I drive a Model-T these days. What are *you* doin'
here in Medway?'

'Let's say I'm a test pilot,' Ira suggested.

Nestor seemed satisfied. 'I jest like to know, Captain,' he
said. 'You-all ain't sore at me askin'?'

'No. Not at all.'

'Fine. Anythin' crops up, I'm always interested.'

He hadn't been gone long when Woolff appeared, dragging
his vast cap over his eye in a shy violent gesture that left it
looking as though some strong wind had caught it and spun
it round on his bullet head.

'Hello there, Ira,' he said embarrassedly.

After the high feelings at the airfield Ira was pleased to see
him.

He tossed Nestor's pasteboard visiting card on the bed and
produced a bottle and two glasses. 'Sammy got it somewhere,'
he said. 'It's not too bad, apart from the taste.'

Woolff eyed the bottle dubiously, but he accepted a drink.
'I got a good recipe for gin,' he said. 'You can borrow my
bathroom if you want to make some.' He cautiously tasted the
drink and looked up. 'Saw Nestor downstairs,' he went on.
'Owner of the local sheet. He's a troublemaker—a real cheap
skate.'

'So I guessed.'

'He ought to be suppressed by the Vice Squad. What did he
want?'

'He wanted to know what's going on out at the field.'

'Tell him anything?'

'Nothing that you wouldn't have told him, too.'

Woolff seemed relieved. 'He don't like us,' he said. 'Because
we come from up around New York. They don't like foreigners
down here. He'd like to see us in trouble.'

He paused, eyeing his drink suspiciously. There was a long
silence. He had clearly not come for the drink, or even to
talk about Nestor, but Ira didn't hurry him. Woolff was a
heavy-bodied, slow-moving, deep-thinking young man who
didn't like to be rushed, and he was handicapped always by
his shyness.

'Courtney's gone back north,' he said after a while. 'Left
last night.'

'Did he decide anything?'

'Not so I've heard.' Woolff shook his head. 'He won't budge,

60

I guess. That's bad. You guys came over here to fly and I wouldn't like to see you looking for a job.'

'Nor me,' Ira said gravely. 'Twenty-five thousand dollars is a lot of money to let slip through your fingers.'

Woolff's sad face twitched into what passed for a smile. 'You've a long way to go before you get that far,' he said.

'Around four thousand miles to be exact. Without touching down.'

'Sure.'

There was another long silence while Woolff weighed his words, then he looked up, his eyes full of honesty and innocence. 'I been thinking,' he said.

'Go on, Hal,' Ira encouraged.

'All that stuff the Boss gave you—about how many planes we've built. We only built four, Ira.'

'Four?' Ira's jaw dropped. 'Is that all?'

'Sure. We sold two to a mail-carrying company, and two privately. They've done nothing but bitch about 'em. I guess the design wasn't so good.'

'Who designed them?'

'Courtney. Mulroy helped. Before I came.' Woolff paused, staring into his glass, his brows troubled. 'You were right, I guess. About that ship of his. She *is* a bastard. She's neither one thing nor the other. I guess they neither of 'em really knew what they wanted. Maybe they both wanted different. They just drew a few lines on a drawing board. You don't build airplanes like that these days. It was all right once upon a time but we know enough about aerodynamics now to work it all out beforehand.'

Ira studied him carefully.

'How much do *you* know about it, Hal?' he asked.

Woolff shrugged, as though he were vaguely ashamed of the admission. 'Some, I guess,' he said. 'I've been to college and read it up.'

He looked so bashful at the confession, Ira smiled. 'Hal,' he said, 'you could probably lead us all by the nose, I bet.'

Woolff made an awkward embarrassed gesture. 'I guess I know about as much as the Boss,' he said. '*And* Mulroy. Maybe more.'

Ira paused, remembering some of the things that had puzzled him. 'Hal,' he said slowly. 'How big is Courtney's organization?'

Woolff smiled again. 'I'll level with you,' he said. 'It isn't

61

so big. If it was, I wouldn't be chief mechanic, factory manager and spare designer all at the same time.'

'I was thinking about his other business,' Ira pointed out. 'Making motor cars.'

Woolff shrugged. 'He's made a bit of money, I guess,' he said. 'Everybody's making money these days. You'd have to have a wooden head not to make money—or be in farming, mining or cotton. That's why he moved here, of course. Thought he might absorb a bit of the labour that's lying around loose.'

'How about capital?'

'He's got some.' Woolff stared at him and scratched his nose thoughtfully. 'Or maybe I'd better make that "He's *had* some". Maybe he's still got it. I don't know. He's certainly made it in his time.'

'Why is he after borrowing more, then?'

Woolff stared at his drink. 'I've heard he wants to expand.'

'Then why can't he get the loan? A successful man oughtn't to have difficulty. Not these days.'

Woolff seemed to feel he was being disloyal and wriggled in his seat. 'Maybe the bank wants him to make up his mind,' he said. 'Whether he wants to build automobiles or airplanes. Maybe it's something like that.' He looked up sharply. His eyes were alarmed. 'You reckon he's *not* sound?'

Ira gestured. 'I don't know, Hal. I hope so.'

Woolff swallowed his drink, tossing it back with a nervous gesture.

'He's no millionaire outfit,' he admitted. 'He did well after the war. Those guys who flew with the Lafayette outfit *all* came back heroes. Rickenbacker went into automobiles, too.' He paused, thinking. 'Maybe that's why he's so goddam adamant,' he said slowly. 'Maybe he thinks he's sunk enough in it. Alix told me she'd tried to make him think again but he wouldn't change his mind.'

'She did?' Ira looked thoughtful. The news was unexpected, to say the least. 'Go on, Hall. You're making sense. Why did you come here? Not just to tell me Courtney's design was wrong.'

Woolff gave one of his slow shy grins. 'Hell, *I* don't mind one engine,' he said. 'I guess that's what I'd have done if I'd been asked. Only—well, you know Courtney—he moves so goddam fast, he makes up his mind without thinking much. We could soon convert what we've got, if he'd let us.'

Ira was leaning forward now. 'We could?'

'Sure we could.'

'Could you produce specifications?'

Woolff gave another shy awkward smile. 'Sure could,' he said. 'I've got plenty ideas. I've even got some drawings.'

'How about time?'

Woolff's eyes brightened. 'We've got the men and all the tools. We could hire more help and hurry it along if we had to.'

Ira rubbed his nose thoughtfully. 'How about talking about it?' he suggested.

Woolff gave him a grin. 'We can do that for nothing,' he said. 'Come round to my place. Bring Sammy with you. I guess we've all got ideas and if we're going to make changes it might be good sense to pool 'em.'

CHAPTER SEVEN

WHEN SAMMY RETURNED, starry-eyed, in the early hours of the morning, Ira was sitting at the table by the window of their room, a notebook in his hand.

He looked round as the door crashed open. Sammy stood in the entrance, his hat—a little misshapen as though it had been sat on—pulled down over his eyes, then he began to stumble round the room, groping in front of him as though he couldn't see. 'It's all dark,' he was saying in a doom-laden voice. 'I've gone blind!'

As Ira laughed, he pulled off the hat and tossed it into a chair, grinning, then he turned and shut the door with a meticulous care which indicated that he wasn't entirely sure of his actions, and it was only then that Ira noticed the baggy pantaloons that encased his thin legs. They were a mottled shade of pink and purple and he wore them over checkered stockings in green and white.

'What in God's name are you wearing?' he demanded.

Sammy gazed down at himself. 'Golfing pants,' he said enthusiastically.

'You don't play golf.'

'It doesn't matter. They're all the rage over here just now. Just the thing for flying, don't you think?'

Ira stared in amazement. 'Doped, you could cover a wing with what you're wearing. Where did you get 'em?'

Sammy grinned. 'The store found 'em for me,' he said. 'Natty, eh?' He disappeared noisily into the corridor, leaving the door wide open and singing softly:

'*Chase me, Charlie, Chase me, Charlie, lost the leg of me drawers.*
Chase me, Charlie, Chase me, Charlie, please will you lend me yours.'

There was a sound of running water, then he reappeared. 'Lor', Ira,' he said in ecstatic tones. 'These American girls! Do they move fast!' There was lipstick on his cheek, Ira noticed, and a gleam in his eye. 'We went to her home for supper. Behind the store. That's where I acquired the pants. You should see the way they were making gin in the bathroom. It was enough to peel the enamel off your teeth. We had it in lime juice to kill the taste.' He grinned again, his eyes a little uncertain of their direction, and made a movement with his hands to indicate a female shape. 'If it wasn't that I was well brought up . . .'

'You aren't well brought up.'

Sammy chuckled reflectively. 'No,' he agreed. 'So I found.'

He sat on the bed and began to take off his shoes with a secretive smile. 'I'll have to watch it a bit,' he said with a slow grin. 'I discovered her uncle's sheriff of this place. Puts a crimp in your style.'

He became aware that Ira's attention wasn't entirely on what he was saying, and his smile died.

'What's up, Ira?' he demanded.

Ira rose and lit a cigarette, then he grinned. 'Nothing's up,' he said. 'We might be in business again, that's all. I had a call from Hal Woolff. It seems he agrees with a lot we said the other day. We're going round to see him.'

'When?' Sammy looked alarmed. 'Tonight?'

Ira laughed. 'Tomorrow,' he said. 'And—you'll enjoy this —it seems *he's* pretty hot on bathtub gin, too.'

The main street was empty as they went out to the old hired Ford the following evening but there was a large square of light in front of the store. The turret of the old jail stood out against the sky and the old men outside the harness shop were still sitting in the warm darkness, talking in low voices. The cinema down the street was advertising a film about 'pleasure-mad daughters and sensation-seeking mothers', its posters surrounded by winking bulbs that drew groups of youngsters like moths to the light.

They drove to the saloon that Sammy had found and entered it warily. It was full of the faded gilt of the 1900s, with a marble-topped counter and sawdust on the floor. It smelled of the dead decaying ash of ten thousand ancient cigars.

Sammy tossed down a coin. 'Soda pop, bud,' he said to the bartender, and as the two bottles and glasses were thumped to the counter in front of them he added quietly: 'We'd like some gin. A friend of the Boss's sent me.'

The bartender was new and looked at him, outraged. 'You got the wrong place, bo',' he said. 'Only soft drinks here.'

Sammy's eyes flashed fiercely. 'Then how the hell did I manage to pick up a bottle here a week ago?' he demanded.

The bartender stared at him. 'You did?'

'Sure I did.'

The bartender's face showed no expression. 'I'll go see,' he announced.

Sammy grinned at Ira as a young man appeared from the back room, a young man with well-used eyes that seemed as though he'd got them second-hand somewhere. He took one look at Sammy then he jerked his head towards the back room and they followed him and sat down at one of the round tables there. A tired-looking girl making coffee nodded at them, then the young man with the old eyes reappeared with a brown paper bag containing something wrapped in newspaper.

'Mouthwash,' he said with a twisted expression that passed for a smile. 'Cost you six bucks.'

Woolff lived alone down a dirt lane off the Charleston Road near the edge of Medway. It led to a small Negro settlement some five hundred yards further along, where the plank walls of the cabins were supplemented by sheets of corrugated iron and the roofs were shingled with flattened tins. The air was full of the smell of fried chicken and bacon and the coal oil from the lamps that yellowed the open windows, and there was the low sound of a man singing a song about Jesus among the trees.

Woolff's house was only a shade less tumbledown than the Negro shacks. It looked like a large box among the pecan trees, its tin roof, as unpainted as the house itself, still shimmering from the heat of the day's sun. There was a deep porch and shutters hanging askew with neglect, and the fence sagged and rain-rotted shingles drooped over the eaves of the verandah. Lopsided gates led to a back yard where grass and rabbit tobacco grew along the fringes, and the azaleas in the entrance had rusty-looking leaves and broken twigs, as though Woolff clipped them with the old Sunbeam every time he parked it. The bell didn't work and to attract his attention they had to hammer at the door so that the coloured glass panels rattled in their lead sockets.

The living room was a shabby place, full of all the detritus of a bachelor life, and looked as though Woolff had never found time to decorate it. There were a few photographs of aeroplanes attached to the walls, but they were all out of date and more than one was crooked. The shades were pulled down against the night but they hung lopsided and dusty. Books lolled on the shelves and were stacked on every available surface, and rolled plans littered a table that also carried a dirty coffee cup, a steel alarm clock that ticked like a Ford engine, an empty bottle used as a paperweight, a cylinder, a spanner, and a group of valve springs.

'Sorry about the mess,' Woolff said apologetically, rubbing moist palms on the tight trousers that encased his thick legs. 'I never seem to have time to clean up.'

He jerked a pile of books from an old armchair. 'Try this one,' he suggested. 'It's probably the best. How about a drink? I've made some fresh gin. It's not too poisonous.'

When they were settled, he twisted his plump legs round the tall stool on which he worked at the high drawing board under the window and gestured at them. 'I guess I'll just put up ideas for you to knock down,' he said.

Ira sipped at the gin he'd been given. It had a nightmarish flavour. 'What are you aiming at?' he asked.

Woolff jumped from the stool and dragged at a roll of paper which he spread out on the floor between them. 'Take a look at this,' he suggested. 'This is my idea. I worked it out when Mulroy left. It's for a monoplane. It's got a tubular-steel airframe and it fits the one Courtney built. With a few modifications we could still use it.'

Ira looked up quickly. 'For a *monoplane*?'

Woolff smiled. 'Sure. I measured it up. He's designed for an enclosed cockpit with the mainplane resting on top of the cabin. What's wrong with doing away with the lower wing, strengthening it all up and making her into a monoplane?'

66

'Could we?'

'I guess so'—Woolff looked up shyly. 'Maybe it'd be better to build a new fuselage, but we can worry about that later.'

They all leaned over the drawings, holding down the corners of the paper and studying the specifications and the lists of figures.

'We both planned for outsize fuel tanks,' Woolff pointed out. 'So she's not as slim as she might be. But she could sure carry a lot of gas. There'd have to be a pump, of course, because I planned for a gravity feed from the centre section, and you've got to get the gas up there.'

'We'd need a hand pump, too,' Sammy suggested. 'In case it stopped.'

Woolff nodded. 'Courtney allowed for that. A wobble pump'd only weigh a couple of pounds.'

'How about weight generally?' Ira asked. 'Would it be lighter than Courtney's design?'

'Sure would.'

'Light enough over-all for the amount of petrol we'd need to carry?'

'Look'—Woolff's hand swept across the paper again—'I was thinking in terms of a long-distance aeroplane and nothing more.' He smiled his friendly, gentle smile. 'This business of getting across the Atlantic's been obsessing a whole heap of people over here for a long time, including me. It could be sold to the passenger or mail-carrying companies later but that's where Courtney's plan's wrong. His machine'd cost too much to operate. No company carrying mail in single-engined De Havillands would go over to a fleet of two-engined ships, because the gas consumption and maintenance would push passenger fares sky-high.'

Ira leaned forward. 'What's the wing area?' he asked.

'I planned on two hundred and eighty square feet, but, like Alix said, we could work in another six feet of span to give us extra lift. After all, we're going to have to get a ton and a half of gas off the ground.'

'You're talking sense, Hal!'

While Ira studied the drawings, working out calculations on the corner of the sheet with a pencil, Woolff went on with a curious sort of diffident eagerness.

'It wouldn't be difficult,' he said. 'We can use the same spars and ribs. I could work it out. We can arrange the wing-loading for take-off, which is most important, and we'll put the oil tank

67

behind the engine for a fire wall. I can reshape the fuselage some, so we could get extra lift from that—as if it were an extension of the wing area.'

'What about instruments?'

Woolff gestured at a list written on a corner of the paper in pencil. 'All the usual, plus maybe a drift sight, and a turn-and-bank indicator for bad weather. That's necessary. There were times when Alcock and Brown didn't know which side up they were. Two compasses and a fuel level. Courtney's got some arrangement with the Hughesden Instrument Company in Boston.' He gestured with his glass enthusiastically. 'They supply him with ammeters, gas gauges and speedos. They make fuel pumps, too, so maybe they'd come up with one for us.'

For a long time they were all silent, staring excitedly at the sheet of curled paper between their feet.

Ira looked encouragingly at Woolff. 'How much would it cost?' he asked.

'Around ten to fifteen thousand dollars start to finish. That's single-engined, of course. I've not been ambitious. I was aimin' at a flivver ship and no more. Something under a ton, even with the engine in. She'll waltz some in a high wind when she's on the ground but a full tank'll cure that. The cost's a lot less than Courtney was planning on and we won't have wasted much. We'd need around five thousand more. That's all.'

'When would it be ready?'

Woolff rubbed his nose. 'Well, hell,' he said slowly, 'I've been reading all these reports about the other teams. They all talk about being ready but I guess they're not. And they won't dare start till the spring's well along and the weather's settled. We've got time.'

'That's the one thing we want,' Ira said, lighting a cigarette. 'How long?'

Woolff paused to consider. 'Record time,' he said after a while. 'The boys at the field'll do all they can. They have to. If we fold they might be out of a job.'

'Can you give us a definite date?'

'Two months. Less if we hire more men. We'd have to take 'em off normal work for a while, of course. I don't know whether Courtney'd like that.'

'Perhaps we could work on him. Would it hold much up?'

Woolff grinned. 'We only have orders for three machines on

the books, but I think we could stall around some, because nobody's pushing. *They're* supposed to be powered with Pratt and Whitneys and there's a hold-up there. We could probably think up some good alibis.'

'What about these modifications?'

Woolff gave a deprecatory gesture. 'Well, hell,' he said. 'Courtney's older than I am but he's not a college man and maybe I've picked up a few things that slipped by him. Maybe his fuselage could be shorter. He's playing too safe and going for *too* much stability. After all, if the weather's right, flying a straight course's not going to tax a pilot too much. And I think he miscalculated on the landing gear like you said. He talked of running the axle all the way across but I said it would cause too much drag. It's still not tough enough. I think it would need an upright strut here.' He moved his hand over the drawings and jabbed with a plump forefinger. 'I guess he's always too optimistic about undercarriages.'

'I'd like a gear that goes right up to the wing root,' Ira said.

Woolff nodded. 'Why not? One single long strut with a good solid trombone shock absorber and molybdenum steel for the axles. They take around twenty thousand pounds to the square inch. We'd have to make 'em specially, of course, and clean 'em up with balsa-wood streamlining, but it could be done.'

They were all eagerly leaning over the plan now, watching Woolff's pencil.

'We'd need a wider wheelbase, too,' he said. 'Maybe seven foot, because she could be a little unstable across the ground and we wouldn't want her wandering like Fonck's Sikorsky did, if the gas swilled about. If she hit a bump she might be difficult to hold. A ton and a half shifting position can be dangerous. Cockpits for the crew behind the engine.'

'That puts the main tank behind the crew,' Sammy pointed out. 'If she came down with a bang we'd get it right in our necks.'

'Perhaps we *won't* come down with a bang,' Ira suggested. 'If we get her up, she ought to stay up.'

'You'll be lifting a hell of a load,' Sammy said sombrely. 'How about fixing some brakes?'

Woolff stared at him. 'Brakes? On an airplane?'

'To hold her with the throttles open until she can build up a bit of power—so we can get off to a fast start.'

Woolff considered for a time. 'Won't she nose over?'

'Not with the stick well back.'

Woolff frowned. 'Suppose they jammed in the middle of the run? She'd go over, then, sure as hell.'

'And we'd have a ton of petrol on top of a hot engine.' Ira grinned. 'Let's forget brakes for the time being.'

Woolff frowned. 'How about a ramp?' he said. 'We could build one. Winch her up and cut the cables with the engine revving.'

Ira chuckled. 'Sounds worse than brakes,' he said. 'What about range?'

Woolff gave a shy smile. 'I haven't worked it all out completely yet.' He reached to the table and dragged a map of the world on to the floor and laid it over the drawing. 'But I went into Charleston and talked to a ship's captain down there. We reckoned it was around three thousand six hundred miles. I could give you fuel for three thousand nine hundred. That's three hundred to spare. If you had a tail wind and a little luck, it could be as much as five hundred.'

Sammy looked up. 'Suppose we run into head winds?'

'That's a chance we have to take,' Ira said. 'How about the motor?'

'Wright,' Woolff said immediately. 'Wright Whirlwind. The Wasp's maybe better but you can't get 'em. The Navy's grabbed 'em all. But everybody's using Whirlwinds these days. Air-cooled, nine-cylinder two-twenty-horse jobs. Lightweight aluminium alloy. Economic fuel consumption. Good range. The new ones are probably even better because they've got enclosed rocker arms and the bearings are fed with grease from a magazine while you're in the air. I'm told they'll do nine thousand hours without failure.'

They all sat back, smiling at each other. The job appeared to be done. It was Sammy who brought them down to earth.

'Well,' he said, 'we've got the aeroplane we want. The exact one. All we want now is the O.K. to build it.'

They looked up at him with sheepish grins. In their enthusiasm they had been crossing their bridges before they'd come to them.

Ira stared at Woolff's specifications for a moment. 'Has Courtney ever seen these?' he asked.

Woolff grinned shyly. 'You know how fast he moves,' he said. 'I never got chance to get it on the desk. I thought of it some, but I guess I'm not the pushing kind.'

Ira frowned. 'Perhaps we ought to do some pushing for you, Hal. You ever spoken to Alix Courtney about it?'

'Some. Not much. She thought the same way as me, I think, but they were too taken up with their own design for her to give it much thought.'

'How much influence have you got with her?'

Woolff blushed. 'None. Maybe you would have.'

Sammy looked up. 'Sure,' he said quickly. 'Why not?'

Ira nodded. 'Hal,' he said. 'Get on that telephone, and get her over to the airfield. Now.'

CHAPTER EIGHT

ALIX COURTNEY arrived within half an hour, wearing a skirt for once and a shapeless green sweater, her face pale and strained. She was in an unpredictable mood and looked as though she hadn't been to bed. Her hair was wild after the drive across the field and she eyed them warily as she lit a cigarette. The hostility of their last meeting was gone but she was still hesitant and cautious.

They were waiting for her in the hangar, a cavernous place in the high-slung lights, shadowy in the darkness and echoing and empty without the movement of the workmen. They had rattled out of town in Woolff's old car, trailing a cloud of dust, Sammy bouncing about in the rear seat like a pea in an empty pod.

'You ought to do something about this bloody car,' he had yelled over the noise of the engine to Woolff. 'It's no advertisement for Courtneys!'

Woolff set the ball rolling as soon as they entered the office. 'You heard anything from your Pa, Alix?' he asked.

She shook her head. 'He's been probing around,' she said. 'I heard him on the telephone to Waco in Ohio and Travel Air in Wichita.'

Woolff looked startled. 'He's not aimin' to buy, is he?'

She shrugged. 'He's thought about it. He's written to Sikorsky and Lincoln and Laird and Breese and a few others. He even tried Bellanca but the only machine available there's gone to the Columbia Corporation. They bought it for airmail work but the way they're talking now, Chamberlain's going to have it for a try at the Atlantic. The only other Bellanca's owned by the Wright Corporation and they won't be drawn

71

into competition with manufacturers who're likely to be customers for their engines.'

Woolff glanced quickly at Ira, obviously disturbed by this unexpected turn in events. Sammy summed up the feelings of all of them.

'He'll sell no Courtneys flying a Bellanca,' he said shortly.

'No.' Alix looked up and shook her head, her eyes worried. 'He won't. But he was so set on the Atlantic, I guess he'll try anything. Maybe he's just trying to save face.'

Woolff screwed his cigarette out in an ashtray made from a piston. 'Alix, where's he getting the dough from?' he said. 'I thought he was already after a loan?'

Alix moved her head nervously, as though she'd already spent too many nights thinking about that. 'I guess he's worked it all out,' she said. 'I sure hope so. He's done some damfool things lately. Maybe wanting to fly the Atlantic's the stupidest.'

Woolff looked at her closely. 'Alix, he's looked lousy lately. Is he fit?'

She shook her head. 'No. I wish he'd slow down. He's all on edge. One minute he's up. The next he's down. Maybe it's the pills he's taking.'

Woolff gestured. 'Well, I sure as hell hope he doesn't waste his money on something nobody else wants. He won't get any-thing worth having—even if it made sense to buy, which it doesn't. They're all involved in some attempt themselves and they won't go into competition with themselves.'

She moved her shoulders nervously. 'He even talked about that place over in San Diego, but they're building for this airmail pilot who wants to have a try.'

'Alix,' Ira said. 'Whatever he's after, he's wasting his breath. Hal's got something right here that could beat the lot.'

She stared at him dubiously but her manner was not hostile for once, and she watched silently as Ira laid the specifications and plans of the Courtney in front of her and explained its shortcomings, then she listened carefully to what Woolff had to say.

'It seems to me'—Ira took up the argument as Woolff came to a halt—'that a committee-designed machine using the best ideas everybody can offer's a much better proposition than going ahead with something we can't agree about.'

'He won't O.K. it,' she said at once.

'Why not?'

'Money.'

72

'Alix'—Woolff gestured—'he's been talking of *buying*!'

'He won't buy, Hal! He can't afford to.'

'Couldn't he back it with some of the profits from the auto plant in Boston?'

She gave him a quick look, then shook her head. 'I guess not,' she said.

Ira smoothed the plans in front of her. 'It doesn't matter much, anyway,' he said. 'The way we've worked it out, it won't cost much. And we thought that if everyone's here to throw in suggestions we can build into it everything we want as we go along. And because we know how it's built we'll also know how to treat it when we come to fly it.'

She lit a cigarette slowly and looked up at Woolff. 'How much would it cost, Hal?' she asked.

Woolff's eyes lit up at her show of interest. 'Twenty grand altogether,' he said enthusiastically. 'Maybe a bit more, including engine and instruments, but most of that we've budgeted for already. We'd need around another five. That's all.'

She made no comment and they discussed costs for a while, then she rose and began to walk about the office, her arms about herself, her face grave and unsmiling, deep in thought.

They watched in silence, then she stopped and turned towards them. 'How long would it take you to set things up?' she demanded. 'I mean, if you got down to work on it, how much of it could you have ready to show him when he comes?'

Woolff considered. 'We can get the men on it right off. We're not selling much, Alix. In fact, if we *don't* go ahead, we'll have to fire some of 'em. . . .'

'*How much?*'

The question stopped him dead in his tracks. He blushed. 'We could use your Pa's airframe,' he said. 'Maybe we could have the undercarriage ready and make a start on the wing.'

'That ought to be enough to impress him.' She considered for a moment, staring ahead of her and blowing out cigarette smoke. 'O.K., Hal,' she said. 'Go ahead. I'll talk him round.'

'Suppose he says no?' Woolff was still hesitant. 'We'll have to account for the work we've done.'

She crushed out her cigarette. 'I'll pay for that myself right now,' she said. 'I'll put two and a half thou in. If he doesn't like it, we'll find the rest elsewhere.'

They had already begun to make progress when Courtney

reappeared unexpectedly. Woolff had produced drawings which he'd hung up on an easel in front of Courtney's fuselage, alongside which he'd arranged a new undercarriage and wheels, and work had already started on the new wing. He had been at his desk eighteen hours a day to get everything finished and they were all pleased with what they'd achieved.

They were warned of Courtney's approach by a telephone call from *Magnolia*. It was Alix.

'He's just arrived with Lave Boyle,' she said. 'They came down overnight. He's on his way over in Lave's auto.'

'O.K.,' Ira said. 'We're ready. Get over here yourself, too. We'll need you.'

'For heaven's sake'—she sounded panic-stricken—'I was in Charleston last night dancing. I haven't got up yet. I've just jumped out of the tub. I'm in my birthday suit.'

Ira grinned. 'That's all right,' he said. 'Don't stand on ceremony. Come as you are.'

When Courtney arrived he was walking so fast, in his huge strides, Boyle was having to run to keep up with him. He slammed open the side door of the hangar with such force that Boyle, who was close behind, had to jump aside as it rebounded off the wall.

All work stopped as Courtney strode towards the office. A workman welding a steel tube in place on the skeleton of a fuselage paused to watch, and winked at the other men scattered about splicing cables, crouched with screwdrivers and spanners or bent over the big sewing machines that worked the heavy cotton fabric. At the far end of the hangar Sammy was standing with Hal Woolff examining a wing plan alongside a group of men who were fitting and gluing ribs to smooth pale spruce spars and brushing dope on to the smooth curves of a wing surface.

He turned as he heard the door bang and watched Courtney heading for the office.

'Looks as if the in-fighting's started,' he said.

Ira was in Woolff's office, bent over Woolff's plans, when Courtney appeared in the doorway. He seemed more unkempt than ever as he stood in the entrance.

'Ira . . .' he began.

Ira looked up and Courtney managed a half-smile.

'First of all,' he said in brisk no-nonsense tones, 'I guess I owe you an apology, Ira. What I said the other day was uncalled for, unfair, and quite untrue. You've got the guts all right. Nobody more. And there aren't any better fliers.' He looked embarrassed and angry at the same time. 'I hope that's O.K.' he ended awkwardly.

'Of course.' Ira smiled. 'I always fall for an apology, Felton. It takes a good man to make one.'

Courtney seemed to relax. Boyle was standing beside him, his eyes on Courtney's face, reflective as an old cat's.

Courtney drew a deep breath. 'But I'm still going ahead with my own plane, Ira,' he went on. 'I put a lot of work into that design. I want to use it. That's the one I want used.'

Ira rose to his feet. 'Not by me, Felton,' he said. 'If you're going to insist, you'd better count me out.'

Courtney paused, his eyes on Ira's face, and Ira could see he was a sorely troubled man. He began to walk up and down the office, all his restless caged energy showing in his taut, impatient manner. He stopped dead and stared at Ira. 'We've got to make up our minds, Ira. It's my job to provide the ship. It's yours to fly it.'

Ira shook his head. 'I think you've got it wrong, Felton,' he said. 'Producing an aeroplane for a job like this isn't something you can do from a motor-car plant in Boston. You do it here, where the factory is, and where the airfield is.'

Courtney eyed him for a long time, wondering how to reply, and he was just drawing his breath to continue the argument when the side door of the hangar slammed open and they saw Alix's lean shape heading across the factory floor in her long tigerish stride, watched with interest by the grinning workmen. Sammy put down the plan he was holding and jerked his head at Woolff. 'Come on, Hal,' he said. 'We're in this, too.'

The office door burst open. 'Hello, Pa,' Alix said. 'I only just made it.'

Courtney had turned to her. 'Only just made what?' he demanded.

Alix gave Woolff a quick grin as he appeared behind her with Sammy. 'I want to know what's going on,' she said.

Courtney gestured. 'Ira's bowed out,' he told her. 'We don't agree about the ship.'

'I know.'

Courtney's jaw dropped. '*How* do you know? We've only just decided.'

'Give me chance to speak and I'll tell you.'

Courtney held on to his impatience with difficulty. 'O.K.,' he said. 'Spill it, Alix.'

75

The jetty eyes flashed. 'When I'm good and ready I'll spill it!'

'You're wasting breath already.'

'Don't holler at me, Pa! It's my breath. You've not bought it. I've been doing some thinking and I've decided I agree with what Ira said about the plane. I think we should change the plans.'

Courtney stared at her, frowning. 'I budgeted for a fixed sum for this aeroplane,' he said. 'I'm in no position to change the plans.'

She stared at him angrily. 'For God's sake, Pa, don't be so stubborn! Surely you're not prepared to kill someone just to save a couple of thousand dollars.'

Courtney looked weary. 'Alix, when I went into this thing, I went into it to make a profit. To get publicity to help us sell airplanes. I didn't want to get so involved I have to keep pumping dough into it.'

'Pa, it doesn't involve much!'

'I've put all I can spare into it, Alix! I'm finished!'

Before they could present him with the model they'd built, Courtney swung round on his heel and flung the door open. They watched him stalk across the wide floor of the hangar again, followed by Boyle, and eyed all the way by the workmen who had halted what they were doing to watch the drama of the quarrel. For a while there was a disappointed silence, then Woolff spoke, despair washing over him.

'He didn't even look at it,' he said.

Alix was staring after her father, her eyes angry. 'I've offered my two and a half,' she said. 'I'll stand by it. Maybe we could raise the rest and build a new plane from the ground up.'

'*Twenty grand!*' Woolff gave way to an agony of apprehension. He thrust his hands in his pockets and stared through the window, a baffled defeated expression on his round face. Then he turned and looked at Alix, as near to being angry as they'd ever seen him.

'There isn't a bank in the State that'd give us that sort of money for an airplane,' he snorted. 'They're still driving two-horse buggies round here.'

There was a depressed silence in the office for the rest of the morning and they ate a gloomy lunch in the diner outside the gates of the airfield. Woolff seemed to be trying to eat and chain-smoke at the same time. Occasionally, Ira caught Sammy's eye, but Sammy showed no sign of what he was thinking and munched steadily, apparently unperturbed by the tensions below the surface.

Nobody seemed able to do much work when they returned to the hangar, and although they bent over Woolff's plans, their minds were entirely on Courtney. During the afternoon, the telephone rang. Ira picked it up and handed it over to Woolff.

It was Boyle and his voice was quite distinct in the silent office.

'Lave Boyle here,' he said. 'The Old Man's on his way down to the works. He'll be there in half an hour. Stay right where you are.'

Woolff's eyes flew to Ira's face and he clapped his hand over the mouthpiece of the telephone. 'He's coming down again,' he said. 'Maybe he's thought it over!'

Boyle's voice came again, rasping and suspicious. 'What have you lot been up to?' he demanded. 'That newspaper guy, Nestor, was on the telephone and Felton's been prowling about here ever since, like he ate something didn't agree with him. Nestor said you were building a new plane.'

Woolff's eyes widened and he glanced at Alix.

'That's not so, Mr Boyle.'

Boyle's voice came again, deep, harsh and vaguely threatening. 'Because, get this straight, Hal, Felton's not got any dough to throw around on new airplanes. He hadn't when he started this damn project and he sure as hell hasn't now.'

Woolff replaced the receiver slowly and put the instrument down. 'He's on his way,' he said nervously. 'Boyle said Nestor had been on the telephone. Maybe he's said something to make your Pa change his mind, Alix. What do we do?'

Alix glanced at Ira and Sammy. 'Take it as it comes, Alix,' Ira advised. 'Find out what it's all about first.'

They went on checking Woolff's figures while they waited, but Woolff was unable to sit still. He stared frustratedly at Ira and Sammy, then at Alix, but she sat silently in his chair, smoking, in a pool of isolation, offering no consolation or encouragement, her eyes occasionally flickering to Ira's face.

Courtney was alone when he returned and he seemed strangely subdued, standing in the doorway, his short legs in tight, badly creased trousers, his hat over his eyes as though he'd tilted it there to keep the sun out of them while driving across the field.

'That guy Nestor,' he said immediately. 'He was on the

77

telephone.' He tossed his hat on to the table. 'He's a punk. I don't like him any more than he likes me.'

Woolff swallowed, his eyes flickering towards Ira, aware that as an opening gambit this could be encouraging. 'Sure,' he said. 'He's poison, Mr Courtney.'

Courtney pulled a chair towards him with one foot and sat down, then very deliberately he lit a cigar and blew out a few puffs of blue smoke. There was a long silence in the office as they waited and Ira and Sammy quietly went on checking figures.

Courtney stared at them for a moment, then he sighed and drew a deep breath, his eyes on the glowing end of the cigar.

'He told me he'd heard you'd already started work on that new plane,' he said.

Woolff shook his head. 'He's got it wrong, Mr Courtney. Nobody's started anything.'

'He said there was the danger of a strike if I stopped you. Because it would be throwing Medway folk out of work.' Courtney paused and ran his fingers through his hair. 'You think there'd be a strike, Hal?'

Woolff, who was watching him like a rabbit petrified by the presence of a snake, came to life with a jerk. 'Hell, no,' he said. 'The boys are right behind us, Mr Courtney! Give 'em the work, they'll not complain.'

'That's what I thought.' Courtney jabbed at the air with the cigar, his eyes roving over Alix and Ira and Sammy.

He was silent for a moment and they could see the effort he was making by the way his adam's apple worked in his throat.

'He said you'd got something sensational,' he went on in a low voice. 'Has he got *that* wrong, too?'

Woolff coughed, looking uncomfortable. 'We could have, Mr Courtney.'

'*Could have?*'

'I'm only thinkin' about it up to now.'

Courtney stared at him coldly. 'How the hell are we financing it?' he demanded.

Woolff drew a deep breath. 'We don't need dough, Mr Courtney. 'Least, not much. We could use a lot of your own design.'

It was a stroke of genius and Courtney's expression changed at once, as though, as Alix had suggested, he was badly wanting to change his stance but needed something to save his face. Nestor's nose for the folksy chit-chat he liked to print in his

78

drab little newspaper had given them the break they needed and Woolff's ingenuous words seemed to have turned the trick completely in their favour. Courtney's eyes were suddenly gleaming.

'You can?' he said, and as he spoke, Alix's eyes flickered to Ira's and he saw Sammy's mouth twitch.

Now that he'd recovered from his surprise, Woolff was becoming confident and more enthusiastic. 'Sure we can use your design, Mr Courtney,' he said cheerfully. 'It'd only mean reshaping the nose and the leading edge. Maybe we'd need a little more wing area as well, of course . . .'

And maybe a new undercart, Ira thought grimly. And different tanks. And perhaps even a new fuselage in the end. You couldn't change step as easily as all that.

'She's a committee-designed ship, Mr Courtney,' Woolff went on and Courtney frowned.

'Committee-designed? What the hell's that?'

'Pilot, navigator, designer, works staff, backer, all putting in their ten cents' worth. All watching the details as they go along. She could be ready in a month.'

'A month!'

They were all round the table now, and Courtney eyed them, unable to hold back his excitement any longer. Woolff went on eagerly.

'It'll take no longer than the other one and it'd work out around the same price, Mr Courtney,' he said. 'I've totalled up the cost. We ought to be able to do it easily for that.'

Courtney sucked at his cigar in silence, as though he felt somewhere he'd been cheated.

'Carbon-steel tubes,' Woolff went on quickly before he could argue. 'Spruce spars and ribs for the wing. Wright engine. Around two thousand pounds unladen.'

'Two thousand! That's featherweight.' Courtney took the cigar from his mouth, his eyes a little startled. 'You got plans for me to see?' he asked.

Before he'd finished speaking, Sammy was unrolling the sheets of stiff paper in front of him. Woolff bent across the table, his hand running over the lines he'd drawn.

'Monoplane, Mr Courtney,' he said. 'We've got over the problems of making the wing strong enough these days.'

'Two sets of wings look safer,' Courtney said, frowning.

'Birds manage with one,' Sammy said laconically.

Courtney turned swiftly, his eyes flashing, but Sammy's po

face met him, expressionless and innocent, as though the words had been conjured out of the air.

'I'd run struts from the base of the fuselage up to the wing.' Woolff's hand was gesturing at the plan again. 'That'd help keep it stable. The fuselage'd have to be strong at that point, anyway, because we'd have to fit the undercarriage there, and it'd have to be able to carry the load. I've worked it out. She'd hold enough fuel for forty hours' flying and she'd lift it off the ground, too!' His enthusiasm burst out of him uncontrollably. 'Hell, Mr Courtney, this is the plane of the future! If we could pull this thing off, you'd sell 'em like hot cakes in winter to the airline companies.'

'You reckon so?' Courtney sucked on his cigar for a moment longer, his eyes gleaming, then he nodded.

'Maybe I was wrong. *You* think I was wrong, Hal?'

Woolff swallowed. 'Yes, Mr Courtney. I reckon you were wrong.'

Courtney stared at him, startled by the firmness shown by the mild-mannered Woolff.

'You do, eh?' he said. 'Hell, I must have been *way* out.'

He got to his feet stiffly and began to walk about the office with his hands in his pockets. Alix watched him silently. Ira glanced at Sammy and caught the hint of a wink, then Sammy's face was frozen again. Woolff was fighting to get out the fact that they already had the new machine started, when Alix gestured and he became silent.

'Money's a problem,' Courtney said hesitantly. 'It isn't that I'm broke, but my dough's tied up.'

'She'll be worth anything we spend.' Alix jerked the words out. 'She'd be built specially for the job.'

Courtney was still frowning, clearly troubled. 'How much would it cost?'

Woolff grinned impulsively. 'Five grand,' he said.

Courtney looked up, startled. 'Five grand!' he said. 'That's not much. I guess I could raise *that*.'

Alix shifted in her chair. 'You're too late, Pa,' she pointed out, staring at her father with the confidence of a steady-eyed cat with a twitching tail. 'I'm in it for two and a half already. If there are the sort of profits to be made that Hal says there are, *I'm* having some of 'em.'

Courtney stared at his daughter for a moment, then he nodded again. 'O.K.,' he said. 'I'll put up the rest.'

He looked round them, frowning, then his expression relaxed

and he began to smile. Alix smiled back and Courtney's smile became a grin. 'Daughter,' he said, 'you're a cheap chiseller. Where is this goddam plane?'

'Right there, Mr Courtney,' Woolff said, pointing. 'Right there in the hangar.'

Courtney stared through the window in the direction of Woolff's pointing finger. 'You're working on it,' he accused. 'You said you weren't.'

'Just a bit, Mr Courtney. Just experiments, that's all.'

Courtney's eyes were glowing. 'I'll be a son of a gun!' he said. 'It looks good, Hal. Hey, Ira, doesn't it look good?'

Despite himself he was clearly impressed.

'We'll call her *Dixie*,' he announced. 'It'll be built here in Dixie and it'll be good business to let people know. The folk in Medway'll like it and, if she's as good as you say, we might be expanding any time and needing more labour. Sure,' he ended. '*Dixie*. That'll be a good name for her.'

Followed by Sammy, he vanished with Woolff into the hangar, leaving Alix and Ira alone in the office. She looked over her shoulder at him and grinned, then she whirled round and flung her arms round him and planted a spontaneous noisy kiss smack on his mouth.

'We did it!' she said.

Then she suddenly became aware that they were standing with their arms round each other, and she broke away abruptly, jerking awkwardly at the heavy green sweater and frowning suddenly.

'For heaven's sake,' she said a little breathlessly. 'We've got things to do!' And she whirled on her heel and vanished after her father into the hangar.

Part 2: Trial—and Error

CHAPTER ONE

WITHIN AN HOUR, Courtney had assembled the workmen round the skeleton of the new machine and explained the need for urgency, and, without hesitation, they all agreed to throw everything they had into it. The idea of building a machine to be the first to fly non-stop to Paris appealed to them all and their interest was stirred.

With the project under way, Ira turned his attention at once to the problem of navigation. Beneath him he would have a brand-new aeroplane capable of flying four thousand miles without refuelling, and a dozen new navigational aids that he'd never had a chance to use before, but neither the plane nor the navigational aids would be of any use if he couldn't first plot a course and then fly accurately along it. The Atlantic was a stormy ocean, noted for its fogs and its contrary winds, and there were two thousand miles of it in which he could be blown off course with nothing below him to fix his position. There'd be no beacons and the only lights would be the moving lights of ships, so that he'd have to make his changes by the angle of the minute and hour hands on a clock, working out his position by theory and time instead of by external visual aids.

He could shoot the sun from a sextant, but he suspected that, from a cramped and overloaded aeroplane, using a sextant wouldn't be easy, and as the navigation that he'd picked up in the ten years of his flying experience filtered through his mind, he remembered that he'd never before flown for long distances over water and that all his navigation had been done with the help of landmarks with which he could check his route. Watching whether the junction of railway tracks faced north or south, how lakes fitted into the curves of the hills, how a river looped across a plain—these were the things that had always helped him fix his position on a map, but the sea was not only without landmarks but its surface was always shifting and would show only his own shadow.

'You could fly by the Azores,' Alix suggested. 'And get a fix there.'

'Too far off the route,' Ira pointed out. 'We'd be flying on our last drop of fuel before we picked up the coast of Europe.'

She seemed eager to press the point of safety. 'Shipping could help you.'

'If I carried a radio. I'd rather carry fuel. And if we fly the direct route via Nova Scotia and Newfoundland, the shipping lanes'll be too far south.'

Sammy's face was sombre. 'Newfoundland's a long way north, Ira,' he pointed out slowly. 'Bad-weather country.'

Ira shook his head again stubbornly. 'Alcock and Brown used it,' he said. 'Besides, we could get a fix at Halifax and again at St John's. That would tell us how the compass was behaving. We could be over St John's before dark, and that'd enable us to pick up Ireland in daylight the next day.'

'How about going down to Charleston?' Alix suggested. 'I guess the shipping offices'll find you a captain who'd help. I don't suppose navigating by sea's all that different from navigating over water by air.'

In a block of offices, in a flat-fronted yellow-washed building in East Bay Street, Ira found the name of a ship undergoing a major overhaul in one of the dry docks among the oil tanks and cranes, and the shipping manager sent a young Negro with him to indicate the way. Her captain, a young man by the name of Ziegler, wore a yellow shirt and looked more like a holiday-maker than a ship's officer, but he caught on at once to what Ira wanted. 'Great-circle navigation,' he said. 'The shortest distance between two points on a sphere.'

'How much knowledge of mathematics does it need?' Ira asked.

'Not more than you've got, I guess. You can handle it if you work at it.' Ziegler looked sideways at Ira. 'Why don't you cross in a ship?' he grinned. 'It'd be more comfortable and a hell of a lot more certain.'

He pulled out a flat drawer in the wheelhouse and extracted two wide sheets, almost entirely covered with pale blue. 'These are what you'll want.' His hand gestured at a square of small print. 'You'll find instructions on 'em and you'll also need a time-zone chart and a chart of magnetic variation, and I guess it would help to know the prevailing wind for the period when you aim to make the crossing.'

He looked up, then fished a pipe from his pocket and began to fill it slowly.

'How far will this airplane of yours fly?' he asked.

'Four thousand miles.'

Ziegler scratched a match and began to puff smoke. 'Ought to be enough,' he said, though he sounded doubtful. 'Make sure you've got the wind behind you, though, when you start. If you run into a head wind, you'll be in trouble.'

'How about weather information?' Ira asked. 'Can your ship give warning of storms from mid-Atlantic?'

'Sure, We all do. You can pick it up from the New York Weather Bureau. They're hot stuff. They get it through the Radio Corporation of America. If you had the weather for the day you left, you could fly round any storms there were.'

They talked for a while and Ziegler gave advice on instruments, then Ira found a shop in Calhoun Street where he was able to buy a sextant and all that Ziegler had advised. A visit to the public library produced a list of books, then he drove back to the hotel in Medway.

It was dark by the time Sammy returned to the hotel, and when he arrived Ira had the charts spread across the floor of his room. The weather had suddenly changed and it was hot enough for him to have switched on the fan and the room was loud with the click-clicking as some faulty mechanism caught as it revolved.

Sammy had his arms full of plans and graphs and he stood staring down at the curved line Ira had drawn across the Atlantic, his eyes interested.

'It's a hell of a way, Ira,' he said thoughtfully.

He watched for a while, then squatted on the floor alongside.

'Ira,' he said. 'I just had an idea. I talked it over with Alix and we've been sitting in the office working it out. According to the papers, Nungesser and Coli are supposed to be busy with an idea for an undercarriage they can drop when they take off.'

Ira looked up, frowning, and Sammy went on eagerly. 'Hawker and Mackenzie-Grieve had a detachable undercarriage,' he pointed out. 'As long ago as 1919. And they almost made it. That was a hell of a flight for those days.'

Ira said nothing and Sammy began to unroll the plans under his arm. 'Why don't we think along the same lines?' he asked. 'It'd weigh a bit more than an ordinary one, but without it we'd cut down the drag in the air and get extra range.'

'What about landing?' Ira asked. 'What's Hal say?'

Sammy grinned. 'Hal hasn't said much at all today. He's been trying to telephone Courtney in Boston to twist his arm a bit. He hasn't delivered the money he promised yet and the bills are piling up.'

Ira gestured at the plan. 'We'd need some sort of metal skid underneath,' he said. 'And a strengthened fuselage.' He moved his hand along the plans. 'Here. Or here.'

'You'd be landing her with empty tanks.'

Ira studied the drawing. 'How much extra weight would have to go into the strengthening?' he asked.

'A few pounds, Hal says.'

Ira frowned. 'He's already got to strengthen the undercart to get the load of fuel off the ground,' he pointed out. 'Wouldn't this bring the weight up *too* much?'

'There'd be no drag.'

'No. But we're streamlining the undercarriage already. And suppose we found ourselves facing head winds and had to turn back with a full tank and no undercart.'

'Couldn't we fix something to jettison the petrol?'

'A dump valve's O.K. We could fix that.' Ira paused and grinned. 'Let's stick to the conventional gear, Sammy,' he said. 'We shan't have much chance to practise landing without wheels, shall we?'

Sammy rolled up the plans. 'Probably you're right,' he said. 'It was just a thought. How's the navigation coming along?'

Ira shrugged. 'You'll pick it up easy enough. It's practice on instruments we need, and I'd like to make it the real thing.' Ira was frowning. 'Sammy, how long would it take us to fix some sort of hood over the cockpit of the DH?'

'Hood over the cockpit?' Sammy stared. 'You wouldn't be able to see!'

'For a lot of the way across the Atlantic we shan't be able to see either. It'll be dark and we'll be flying on instruments. You could sit in the rear cockpit and correct me if I went wrong. It's an idea the Air Force's beginning to use. Hal told me there's a chap over here called Doolittle working a lot on it.'

Sammy frowned thoughtfully. 'I reckon we could do it,' he said. 'You'll want some sort of folding device like the hood of a kid's pram, that you can push back when you've finished.' He considered for a moment, then he nodded. 'It'd be easy enough with some steel tubing and canvas.'

Ira was drawing a rough diagram on the edge of the chart, then he looked up at Sammy.

'Why don't we go along to see Hal Woolff about it?' he suggested. 'We could talk to him about this detachable under-cart idea of yours at the same time. Besides'—he grinned—'perhaps he'll have made some more gin!'

The weather had grown suddenly hot as the early Southern spring edged towards the heat of a long dry Southern summer. Round the airfield, the trees drooped their leaves in the heat and the scattered clumps of conifers, stark against the brassy sky, took on the dusty colour of the red earth.

As the sewing machines and the planers and sanders clattered in the stifling tin-roofed hangar, the Courtney began to take shape quickly as Woolff's workmen translated his drawings into a gleaming white fuselage and wing. The whole factory was working overtime now to make sure they'd have plenty of time for the final details, and Sammy and Ira were often busy for twenty-four hours at a stretch. With the drawings finished, Woolff was concentrating on performance figures and rarely left his office for the shop floor. It was Sammy and Alix who watched progress.

They had long since telegraphed their application for entry to the Orteig competition officials, and with the machine at last emerging from the plans, they were able to concentrate on the details hedging the flight. The pace was increasing now and as the game warmed up, it seemed that there were would-be entrants all over the world.

Fonck was still in the running, it seemed, backed this time by an aeronautical corporation, and was biting his nails as Sikorsky struggled to build him his new machine in time. Over in France, Nungesser and his navigator, Coli, were said to be ahead of everyone. Aeroplanes and crews were also reported in England, Italy and Germany; and Junkers, Farman, Bernard and even Savoia-Marchetti in Italy were said to be getting in on the game. Only one team in America appeared to be anything like ready, however. Noel Davis and his navigator, Wooster, had already taken delivery of their new tri-motor Keystone Pathfinder and were testing it in Pennsylvania prior to heading for Mitchel Field, Long Island, for the take-off for Europe.

'Seen the price?' Sammy asked glumly, gesturing with the newspaper. 'Hundred thousand dollars. Bit more than *our* effort.'

'It won't be any better,' Woolff promised. 'It's only a Huff-

Daland with a new name. Though I'm told Davis is a red-hot navigator and this guy Wooster he's got with him's supposed to be pretty hot stuff, too.'

He moved a pile of bills on the desk thoughtfully. 'Talking about dough,' he said uneasily, 'I wish the Old Man would hand over that two and a half thou he promised.'

Ira looked up. 'Hasn't it arrived yet?'

Woolff gave a little gesture of embarrassment. 'It will,' he said. 'I guess he just forgot.'

'Does Alix know?'

'She's tried to telephone him, like I have. She's not been able to contact him.' Woolff shrugged. 'I guess he's just too busy right now. Maybe the press are chasing him. They're beginning to get in on the act.'

Certainly the newspapers carried regular articles on the competition that they studied eagerly, trying to assess how they stood against the other competitors, trying to pick up tips that might have slipped past them despite the regular conferences in Woolff's office and the notes they all made for discussion and decision.

'Who's this bird down in San Diego?' Sammy asked, staring at the small print at the bottom of the page. 'He's keeping quiet and he's flying alone, he says.' He gestured. 'Who's going to do the navigation while he flies the thing?' he asked.

'Perhaps he's got two heads,' Ira suggested.

The fuselage and wing of the new aeroplane were completed now and the workmen were brushing the acid-smelling dope on to the fabric. Ira watched them at work whenever he could, knowing how important to him it would be that it was well done. Together, these two components, deliberately kept as fragile as possible to save weight, had to carry Sammy and himself across the Atlantic, had to lift them, with the weight of the aeroplane, its engine, and a ton and a quarter of petrol, from ground that might well still be soggy from spring rain.

They had already talked long into the night about what equipment they should take and had finally decided to do without parachutes.

'How about a rubber raft?' Alix asked, still obsessed with the idea of safety. 'You could stow it on top of the tank.'

'Byrd developed a good one,' Woolff pointed out. 'It weighs only twelve pounds.'

'All right,' Ira said. 'Let's try to get one.'

'How about food?'

'It won't do us any harm to be on short rations for a couple of days.'

Alix looked concerned. 'Are you sure you won't consider a radio?' she said. 'You'll probably be trying to find Le Bourget in the dark.'

'They've got beacons all the way from London,' Ira pointed out. 'We ought to be able to line up on them.' He grinned suddenly. '*If there's no fog*,' he added.

'If there's no fog,' Sammy repeated. 'Beacons are fine when you can see 'em. When you need 'em, though, you never *can* see 'em.'

For a moment, they were all silent, knowing how easily the unexpected advent of fog could bring disaster, then Ira changed the subject.

'Let's plan on being ready around June 21st,' he said. 'The weather'll be best then and the nights'll be shortest.'

They sat up late in their room with a bottle of bootleg gin from the saloon, poring over charts and books and performance figures. Woolff joined them from time to time, his round face growing grey from overwork as he tried to improve his graphs. His estimate of the range had gone up to four thousand two hundred miles now and he thought they ought to be able to land in Paris with over forty gallons of fuel still in their tanks.

'That's enough for anybody,' he said. 'So long as we find the correct throttle and mixture setting, and we can do that in tests.'

Sammy jabbed at the newspaper. 'One thing's for sure,' he said. '*Somebody* ought to pick up that twenty-five thousand dollars this summer.'

Now that the aeroplane was approaching completion, there seemed to be plenty of time for planning. Sammy worked with Alix at the factory over every detail of construction, while Ira laboured again and again at the navigation or sat in the library in Charleston, reading all he could find on the coastal areas of Nova Scotia, Newfoundland, Ireland and France. A Fowey man, he hardly needed to read up the iron coast of Cornwall to check his landfalls. When he wasn't studying, he sat with a notebook on the beach, staring at the sea they were proposing to cross, and trying to decide all the minor questions which had to be resolved before take-off. When would he have to turn back, if the decision were forced on him? When would it be wiser to push ahead instead of turning back? How heavy could he expect the weather to be and how much ought he to endure before he felt there was no chance of succeeding? How much headwind and for how long? He frowned at the charts of the Atlantic and the wind roses with their blue arrows, working out his chances in a take-off when he might have to risk heavy ground conditions simply because the weather over the sea was expected to be good.

He had struggled with the charts for some time now, going over again and again the course he was drawing off on them, transferring points on a straight line between New York and Paris on to the Mercator's projection, indicating on each one the change of course to the next one. Since Woolff expected the aeroplane to travel at around a hundred miles an hour, he worked at hundred-mile intervals and when he had finished he took the course along to Ziegler's ship.

Ziegler was beginning to grow excited now. He had turned out to be an expert on spherical mathematics and they talked for a while about gnomonic projection before he started to lay out a second route across the sea, using trigonometry to find the courses.

'You're bang on the button, Captain,' he announced. 'There's nothing wrong with your workings. I've followed it all the way across and you haven't been more than a degree out anywhere. You'll be O.K. on *that* course, and even if you're a little out at the other end you ought to be able to hit Europe somewhere between the north of Scotland and Gibraltar.'

Having found out how to plot a course, they now began to study how to fly it.

Woolff had constructed a black fabric hood to go over the pilot's cockpit of the De Havilland and had installed a second compass in the rear cockpit.

'She's yours, Ira,' he said when he'd finished. 'See what you can do with her.'

'O.K., Sammy,' Ira said. 'Let's go.' He spread a chart on the lower wing and indicated the triangular course he'd marked out. 'This'll do for a start: Charleston–McCormick–Savannah–Charleston. That's just under four hundred miles and near enough her full range. We'll get up to five thousand feet for safety and fly at a hundred, then I'll close the hood and use instruments. O.K.?'

Sammy nodded. 'O.K.'

'All you have to do is keep your eyes open for other aircraft and watch the turns. If I go off course or don't turn at the right time, waggle the stick. If I fly one wing low or nose down, the same. If we're in real trouble, keep on waggling and take over and I'll shove the hood back.'

'O.K., Ira. I've got it.'

Alix was waiting by the wing-tip as they settled themselves into their seats. Behind her, Courtney waited with Lavery Boyle, while Woolff prowled round the machine, his eyes on wheels, rigging and fabric. Courtney's face was thin and tired. He had arrived by train the previous day with Boyle but had put in only a brief appearance at the hangar before returning to the house with the excuse that he had work to do. Alix's eyes had followed him anxiously and they had heard that he had spent half the night at the dining-room table poring over papers with Boyle.

As the propeller turned, there was a splutter and a strangled cough from the engine, like a metal animal stirring in its sleep, then as Ira eased the throttle, the big Liberty crackled to life at the second pull, with a rich roar of exhausts. Listening to it, his head on one side, Ira sensed the machine quiver under his touch. As the propeller whirled into invisibility, he opened the throttle, feeling the machine surge against the chocks, catching the flexing of its muscles through the soles of his feet on the rudder bar as he listened to the thundering resonance of the exhausts which seemed to belong to something more alive than mere wood and steel could ever be, more vital than mere pounding pistons.

As he lifted his eyes from the instruments and adjusted his helmet there was a bang on the fuselage alongside him and he looked round to see Alix standing by the cockpit, her hair plastered flat to her small neat skull by the blast. She looked serious and concerned.

'Good luck!' she shrieked above the din of the engine.

'Thanks.' He grinned. 'If I end up over Cape Cod, we'll know we're miscalculating somewhere.'

Her grave face broke into a crooked grin.

'You'll not end up over Cape Cod!'

Ira lowered his goggles and lifted a gloved hand and, as the mechanic pulled away the chocks the machine began to lurch forward.

It was some time since they'd been off the ground and it

was an exhilarating feeling to be in the air again—the same sort of eagerness any craftsman has for the feel of the tools of his trade—and Ira settled into the cockpit behind the big Liberty, catching the tang of hot oil and metal and watching the ripple of fabric above the wing spars. At once, as they lifted into the emptiness above the crowded land, the spaciousness of the sky—a thing which never failed to surprise him, no matter how often he flew—struck him again and he drew a deep breath at the views and the distance about him, more overjoyed to be back in his element than he'd have thought possible.

Under the bright sun, the earth had an ashen, worn look about it, but every road, every river and patch of swamp land, every tree, was sharp in the harsh light and they were able to pick out every individual homestead and barn. The big Liberty pulled them up through the hot humid air and at five thousand feet, with Charleston spread below them like an arrowhead between the Ashley and Cooper Rivers, and the swampland bright green and glinting with water on either side, Ira signalled to Sammy, and, pulling the hood into place, locked it firmly.

Inside the cockpit it was dark enough now to see the phosphorescent marks on the instruments and Ira began to fly on the altimeter, turn-and-bank indicator, compass, and rev counter. At first he found it was easy, but as the minutes passed, he found his instincts were telling him that the instruments were faulty and that he was flying left or right wing low. Tempted to correct, he was reassured, as the stick shook in his hand, that there was nothing wrong and that he must have absolute faith in them and force his mind to ignore his instincts. They had worked out what little drift there was before they'd taken off, and, unless the wind changed direction, the course he'd written down in the notebook strapped to his knee was the course he had to fly. If he kept the ball in the centre of the turn-and-bank indicator and the compass and altimeter needles steady, and turned at the right time, he ought to end safely back over Charleston.

Watching the hands of his watch, he set his new course after an hour and thirty-three minutes, keeping the bubble of the turn-and-bank indicator central. It was noisy and growing warm under the hood by this time, in spite of the height and the blast from the propeller, and working with his head down he began to wish he had donned less clothing. His turn was cautious and, watching the bubble carefully, he tried to ignore the feeling of his senses that told him he was sliding off his bank. Setting the new course, he noticed there was no response from Sammy and he assumed he'd taken up the new direction successfully.

With a feeling of pleasure, he decided he was doing very well, then he remembered that there had been practically no breeze to blow them off course and decided, as he watched the compass settle, that he'd try it next time with a strong wind.

At the end of another eighty-seven minutes of flying, he turned again, swinging from south-east on to an almost north-easterly course. Again, there was no response from Sammy and he assumed he was safe and apparently the right way up.

Fifty minutes later he unlocked the hood and thrust it back. The sun dazzled him for a moment, then he saw Sammy grinning at him and pointing over the side. Below him and just ahead, pointing to the south like a wedge, was Charleston, blue under a haze of smoke, the Ashley and Cooper Rivers curving northwards in the sunshine, the broken fragments of land between Folly and Morris Islands and James Island lying like a disturbed jigsaw, the tacky scrub of the land glaringly green alongside the blue water that threaded web-like between the chain of pools and tidal creeks.

Below them the Courtney house stood out clearly, circled by the necklace of the river curving through the marshes towards Charleston, and they came in low over oaks draped with long folds of parasitic moss. The field was long and wedge-shaped, set on a strip of hard earth between the swamps, and they made their touch-down across its narrowest part.

Alix came running across the grass towards them as the D.H. swung round in front of the hangar, the rudder fishtailing, the propeller blowing up a great cloud of yellow dust.

'Bang on the dot,' she said, as the propeller jerked to a stop. 'I timed you myself. You're not more than five minutes out. I bet you peeked.'

Courtney appeared behind her. 'How did it go?' he demanded.

'I thought of setting course for Paris,' Sammy said, his eyes enormous in his goggles. 'Then I thought we ought to come down and get some grub.'

Alix gave him a wide eager smile. 'This calls for a celebration,' she said. 'Let's all eat out!'

Courtney shook his head. 'Not tonight, Alix,' he said. 'I've got to go north again.'

Alix swung round, her pleasure forgotten in a worried frown. 'For God's sake, Pa! Already? You only just arrived!'

Courtney shrugged. 'Problems,' he said vaguely. 'I'm still after that loan. I've got to see Joe Hughesden.'

Her eyes narrowed. 'Pa, you're not making a deal with Joe Hughesden, are you? Just to raise dough?'

Courtney smiled. 'Don't you believe it,' he said.

She didn't appear to trust him. 'I heard Lave on the phone with him, arranging something.'

He patted her arm. 'Joe Hughesden makes parts for my cars,' he said. 'We're always talking business. I'll be back in a few days.'

She stared at him for a second and came to a sudden decision. She gestured at the Pierce Arrow outside the hangar. 'I'll drive you up,' she said. 'Slowly. We'll stop a couple of days on the way somewhere like Wilmington or Hatteras and rest up. It'll do you good. I've got to go to New York. I haven't been out to my place on Long Island in weeks.'

Courtney glanced at Boyle and Ira caught the hint of a nod from the old man.

'O.K.,' Courtney agreed reluctantly. 'And when I come back we really *will* have a celebration.'

As they left the field, Woolff stared after them, his eyes troubled. 'He didn't leave that dough with me again,' he said. 'I asked him and he said he would.'

They had the engine in at last, a huge black spider attached to the nose of the aeroplane and awaiting all the minor link-ups that would make it a living thing. The nine big-finned cylinders were aluminium and steel, a magnificent construction of machinery whose lightness of weight and extremes of power were to carry them over three thousand six hundred miles of ocean.

They stood beneath it, staring up at it, their feet among the sawdust, shavings and oiled wrappings, awed despite their experience. By the side of the hangar the eight-foot laminated wooden airscrew lay in its crate, its metal tips catching the sun.

The Courtney was looking like an aeroplane at last, a clean red creature with white wings, poised just inside the factory doors. Every man in the place had stopped work to watch the engine being bolted into place, standing around in a small half-circle among the hanging chains of the purchases, eyes on the gleaming black metal.

'Ought to get you there, Ira,' Woolff commented laconically. He had the placid look of a well-fed cat. He was proud of his aeroplane and the arrival that morning of a money draft on a Boston bank had put him at ease at last.

The Wright engineer who'd appeared for the delivery and installation of the engine stepped back from tightening the last bolts. 'Two hundred and twenty horses,' he said. 'Sure, she'll get you there. Whirlwinds have been flying for thousands of hours without failures. All the airlines are installing them, these days, they're so safe, and this one's had a special inspection. Only one thing'—he paused—'you're relying on a cam pump to transfer gas from that big fuselage tank.'

Woolff frowned. 'Sure! Nothing wrong with that, is there? It's a Hughesden. The Boss has an arrangement with Hughesdens for his automobiles.'

The Wright engineer looked doubtful. 'I'd recommend you to get the best there is,' he said.

They glanced at each other quickly and he went on with a gesture. 'It's not my business to design your airplane or run down other people's products,' he said. 'But I'd suggest that the Hughesden's not tough enough for the work it'll have to do. It might run for fifty–sixty hours, which is enough. On the other hand, it might pack up after thirteen, which isn't.'

'They've always worked on Courtney autos,' Woolff pointed out.

The engineer didn't seem impressed. 'Maybe,' he said. 'But their aircraft pumps haven't been properly developed yet. We prefer the Viking internal-gear type.' He shrugged. 'But you're the customers. We can't insist, only advise, but the Viking's more reliable than a cam job and it'll go on as long as the engine's turning.'

He paused. 'There's one other point,' he continued. 'Being what it is, the Hughesden has to be fitted to the floor to work properly. I've seen 'em. That'd mean the pipes would go under your seat where you couldn't get at 'em. I'd always rather have fuel leads where I can see 'em. Especially over the sea.'

He had put up a good argument for the Viking. 'How long would it take to fit one?' Ira asked.

'It could be done as soon as you arrive in New York. We could have it ready for you.'

Ira nodded agreement. 'You'd better,' he said.

Woolff nudged him as the Wright engineer stared into the engine. 'Ira,' he hissed. 'You sure we can afford it?'

Ira's head jerked round. 'I thought we got a bank draft from Boston,' he said.

'Sure, but there are a lot of bills to pay, and the motor's here now. I don't want to ask for any more. It's all "Gimme, gimme, my name's Jimmy".'

Woolff's round face was anxious and Ira nodded. 'O.K.,' he said. 'I'll pay for it myself.'

They discussed fitments and instruments for some time, then a dry waspish voice behind them, as cold as a winter wind, swung them round.

'She sure looks swell.'

Robert E. Lee Nestor, the newspaperman, was watching them with a blank pale face, pointing with the soggy end of his cigar at the Courtney.

Woolff turned on him quickly, his eyes bright with dislike, and gestured at the high square shape of the old Ford Nestor had left in the shadow of the hangar.

'We don't park autos there, Mr Nestor,' he said. 'And put that cigar out! There's a lot of gasoline around.'

Nestor silently dropped the cigar and ground it to extinction with his heel, but he made no attempt to leave. 'Heard there were things happenin',' he said. He indicated the aeroplane. 'Dandy-lookin' ship. Don't know how Courtney manages to afford it.'

Woolff scowled. 'Why shouldn't he manage to afford it?'

Nestor shrugged. 'Hell, I don't know why he shouldn't afford it,' he said. 'Only I heard he was down in town just before he left, trying to negotiate a loan.'

Woolff was staring at him with troubled eyes now. 'You sure?' he asked.

'God's unvarnished and unbuckled truth. The bank manager told me.'

'That manager does a lot of talking for a guy who's supposed to keep his mouth buttoned about his customers' business,' Woolff snapped.

'Sure does,' Nestor agreed amiably, his pale eyes shrewd. 'All the same I heard there were bills outstanding.'

'Regular bird-dog, aren't you?' Woolff growled. 'Well, there aren't. I got a new draft from Boston today. It'll cover everything.'

Nestor nodded, his face as expressionless as a fish's, and

turned to Ira. 'When you-all aimin' to get her off the ground, Captain?' he asked. 'I guess I ought to be here. She looks great. Even Robert E. Lee Nestor'd be willin' to go up in that one.' He turned away towards his car, then he stopped and looked over his shoulder at them.

'Why in hell would a guy as big as Courtney try to negotiate a loan in a hick town bank like we've got here?' he said. 'He tryin' to keep somethin' dark?'

He bent over the starting handle and cranked it, and as the Ford quivered to life he climbed in, and, settling his hat on the back of his head, grasped the steering wheel firmly as though he were trying to wrench it off. Cautiously, a pious follower of the new motoring fad but clearly uncertain of his capabilities as a driver, he let in the clutch and the car moved jerkily on to the road.

Sammy grinned. 'He's so scared of that car, Hal,' he pointed out, 'I bet he drives with the brake on.'

Woolff wasn't listening. He was staring after Nestor with narrowed eyes, his brows down in a heavy frown. ' "Trying to keep something dark," ' he repeated slowly. 'Now what in hell did he mean by that?'

CHAPTER TWO

ALIX ARRIVED the same afternoon, and Sammy, standing just inside the hangar door, turned to where Ira was running his hands over the fabric sides of the fuselage.

'Hold your hat on, boy,' he said enthusiastically. 'Alix is back.'

To their surprise, she was driving a battered, second-hand Chevrolet that swung round the end of the hangar in a wide sweep on to the grass, the front wheels bouncing over the bumps, until it slid to a stop with locked brakes. Woolff opened the door for her, staring in bewilderment at the shabby car.

'Where's the Pierce Arrow?' he asked.

'Sold it,' she said shortly.

'Aw, hell, Alix!' Woolff looked shocked. 'I thought you loved that car like your own child.'

'I was short of dough,' she snapped.

He waited for her to enlarge, but she offered no further

explanation and strode towards the hangar, her short dark hair flying, her eyes frowning.

'Where is it?' she demanded. 'How far have we got?'

Woolff had been gazing at the sorry old car, clearly unable to understand why anyone would want to drive an old Chevrolet instead of the powerful Pierce Arrow, and he came to life with a start and set off after her. But as she turned the corner, she stopped dead and her frown vanished as she stared up at the workmanlike snout of the aeroplane. They had attached the propeller now and secured the bright red aluminium spinner over the bolts.

'My God!' she said. 'You've been quick! Nobody can be as quick as that!'

Woolff beamed with pleasure at the praise. 'I guess we have, Alix,' he said. 'We're way ahead of everyone but the Keystone. We aim to start test flights any day now.'

She didn't appear to hear him and seemed unable to take her eyes off the Courtney, with the single white word DIXIE painted on her fuselage.

As she stood back, her eyes wide with pleasure, Ira and Sammy raised the tail of the machine and swung it round to face her.

'She's just an engine attached to wings,' Ira said.

'She's a dream,' she whispered. 'A dream.'

She moved at last, from one side of the machine to the other in a quick, jerky movement, still fixedly staring up at the propeller.

'What will she do?' she asked.

'Hal says a hundred and thirty. More, perhaps.'

She gazed at them, her black eyes disbelieving, all the anger that had been in her face when she'd arrived completely gone. 'That's a hell of a speed! Nothing can go that fast!'

'I think this one can,' Ira said. 'It's only a guess yet, though. We haven't tested her.'

She didn't seem to believe him and stood gazing at the aeroplane, her expression a mixture of delight and wonder, a smile lifting her mouth, while they all stood in a group round her—Sammy, Ira, Woolff and all the workmen.

'When?' she was saying softly, her eyes still held ecstatically by the sleek red machine. 'When does she have her tests? I've got to know, because I'll provide champagne for every man that had anything to do with her, even the kid who mixed the glue. Real champagne, not something cooked up in a basement. I think we've built a winner here. I'm going to wire Pa. It'll do him good just to see this.'

Courtney himself arrived within twenty-four hours, driving from the station with Boyle in a hired car, and pounding his hand on the horn in an imperious tooting to summon them all from the hangar.

'Where is it?' he demanded. 'Where's this top-drawer, gold-plated, hundred-per-cent Courtney plane Alix says we've built?'

Woolff jerked a hand, grinning. 'In the hangar, Mr Courtney,' he said. 'Right over here.'

As they approached the hangar, Courtney stepping out in front with his huge comical strides, Sammy saw him coming and, with a couple of mechanics, hurriedly began to push the great doors back.

Courtney stopped dead as the plane came into view, his eyes glinting, two bright little spots of colour appearing on his cheeks.

'That her?'

'That's her,' Woolff said.

Courtney's lined face softened and he began to smile. 'She sure looks good,' he said slowly in a low voice.

Ira was just climbing down from the cabin as he moved forward again and halted once more in front of the machine, staring up at the propeller. Alix had joined Woolff and Boyle and they caught him up now and stood just behind him. Courtney was obviously awed by what they had produced.

'Will she do it, Ira?' he asked in a low breathless murmur. 'Will she get across?'

'Ought to,' Ira said. 'Barring accidents.'

Courtney was still eyeing the machine. 'There can't be accidents,' he breathed, almost as though he were praying. 'There can't!'

'I meant weather. No one can guarantee the weather.'

Courtney didn't take his eyes off the plane. 'Sure,' he said. 'The weather! There's got to be a good forecast before we try anything. We'll wait if necessary. There's got to be no mistake with this thing.'

He walked slowly round the aeroplane, nervously tapping the taut fabric of the fuselage as though afraid he might damage it, then he climbed into the cockpit to sit behind the controls.

'When do I see it fly?' he called down through the sliding window at his shoulder.

'One week, Mr Courtney,' Woolff said. 'One week from now.'

Courtney grinned suddenly. 'Rush it, Hal,' he said. 'I have to go to Boston again and I'd like to see her off the ground before I leave.'

'Mr Courtney'—Woolff's tones were firm—'we *can't* rush it. With this thing, you have to move step by step or you'll do something so wrong the whole thing'll fall apart.'

Courtney stared down at him. He seemed to be bursting with impatience. 'Try!' he pleaded. 'Try, Hal! I've got to see her fly! I've just got to!'

Alix glanced at Ira and jerked her head to move a loose lock of hair from her eyes. 'This is going to be one hell of a week,' she said in a low voice.

As they put the finishing touches to the *Dixie*, special tyres arrived from Cleveland and all the instruments were fitted with the exception of the compasses.

'The Pioneer earth inductor's on order,' Woolff explained to Alix. 'Most people use an earth inductor for long trips. Once the needle's adjusted, it warns the pilot if he's straying off course.'

'It'd better be good,' Alix said briskly. 'It's got my two and a half grand riding with it.'

Courtney was in a twitter of excitement, desperate to see the machine fly and constantly putting off his return to Boston.

'I'm losing money every day I stay down here,' he said. 'But I've *got* to see her in the air.'

He was like a child in his excitement, the greying rusty hair wilder than ever, his suit pockets jammed with bundles of papers, his attaché case always crammed with more. He spent the days in the office with Boyle, trying to deal with his business in the north yet never able to put the aeroplane out of his mind, breaking off constantly to watch the work or make suggestions that invariably arrived after they'd already been made by someone else, terrified always that one of the other teams would finish their trials first and be away before they were ready.

'Noel Davis is the only man you've got to fear, Ira,' he announced. 'They say that Pathfinder of his is nearly ready.'

He shoved a newspaper at them, folded at a photograph

of the huge Pathfinder with its three engines and tapered wings.

Sammy stared at it cynically. 'I'd like plenty of air under me if I was in that thing,' he observed. 'I reckon it'll climb like a sick cow on a mountain.'

'They say it's fast,' Courtney insisted. 'Hundred-forty-five miles an hour. I read a report from Pennsylvania on it.' He lit a fresh cigar and gestured with it. 'Byrd's almost ready, too. And that Fokker tri-motor's a good ship. He'd have set off by now if he'd intended going.'

'He's not after the Orteig prize, Pa,' Alix pointed out. 'He says he's not.'

Courtney shrugged. 'Yeah. I read it: "The flight is to be made solely in the interests of aeronautical science and international goodwill." ' He grinned. 'If he got over there first, though, I guess he'd not say "No" to twenty-five grand. Maybe he's hedging his bets in case we whip him. They're saying in New York that Tony Fokker's hopping mad at the way he's delaying, because he wants his machine first across.'

As the petrol lorry drew away, the young Negro on the wing screwed down the cap of the petrol tank, then the big engine crackled to life, smashing the clothes of the mechanics and their labourers flat against their bodies with the propeller's wash. A huge cloud of dust almost obliterated the old De Havilland, and set its wings shuddering as the blast struck them. They all stood by the hangar door, their eyes screwed up against the flying grit, while Woolff sat in the cockpit working the throttles, the Courtney surging and quivering against the chocks like a living thing as the nine cylinders gave out their full power. The exhausts howled metallically, the propeller only a sparkling circle of light, throwing out a hurricane that flattened the grass and sent more clouds of yellow dust whirling across the field.

As the throttle was cut and the circle dissolved into a red-tipped propeller which finally jerked to a stop, Woolff put his head through the cabin window.

'I guess you can take her up, Ira,' he said unemotionally.

The sun had gone behind a small puff of cloud and the hangar suddenly seemed a dark and brooding place. Ira noticed as he stepped forward under the wing that Courtney and the others moved to one side, so they could watch what happened. He stared up at the machine as Woolff climbed down, his plump face moist with sweat in the humid heat of midday.

'You'll like her, Ira,' Woolff said, adjusting his cap.

Ira nodded, aware that this first junction of himself and this brand-new machine could change the whole world and affect his own destiny and the future of the Courtney works. If he were successful in what they were proposing, he could be wealthy and a man of some note, and Courtney aircraft, proved for their endurance by a non-stop flight of three thousand six hundred miles, would be wanted by every airline in America and perhaps the whole world. If he failed . . . He pushed the thought abruptly out of his mind, and stared up at the Courtney, his mind full of unexpected thoughts and emotions.

The war had carried aeroplanes from dubious constructions of string and wire to sound machines that could fly at a hundred miles an hour, and they were now cautiously moving out of this stage into the technological era when manufacturers no longer built by rule of thumb. Many young men—the brave and the skilful as well as the careless and over-enthusiastic—had died to push them this far and there would have to be still more before flying was so normal that men would no longer stop their cars to watch a stunting machine or rush from their houses to watch a frail biplane pass overhead.

In the achievement, however, he and Sammy were going to be achingly alone for a while, beyond all reach of help; and their courage, even though they accepted what they were doing, would be called on to prove itself perhaps in some screeching ten minutes of madness or in a slow draining over the hours, only their confidence in themselves and their machine, only their own strength of character, standing up to the steady ticking away of the long minutes of darkness. It was the thought of this aloneness, rather than the physical danger, that haunted Ira. By the time they'd finished working on her, the machine ought to have as good a chance as any, but after everything was considered it still depended on luck, and it would be then that they would find what they were made of.

Ira had no doubts about his skill or even his nerve. His scarred chin and broken nose were badges of his courage, but this flight he was planning was going to make demands on him he'd never experienced before. He'd flown in combat, he'd flown through storms, had flown aged, sad machines which ought never to have left the ground, and traversed long distances to the last drop of his petrol over vast countries where distant airfields never seemed to grow any nearer. But he'd never flown the distance he was proposing to fly now, a distance at which three or four years back he would have boggled, and he'd never flown non-stop through several hours of darkness when he would have only his instruments to help him. In spite of the time he and Sammy had put in at blind flying, he knew there were airmail pilots in America who had vastly more experience at it than he had.

With luck, however, he knew that with this machine he could achieve a modicum of glory for himself and the men who'd built her. But they must still stick to the tight set of rules built up by airmen over the years to hold their luck together. There could be no letting up on care.

While Woolff held the door open for him, he stepped forward and tapped his hand against the fuselage, listening to the drumming of the taut fabric, then he walked slowly towards the tail, letting his hand slide along skin that was as smooth and silky as a girl's.

Courtney watched him impatiently and gestured with his dead cigar. He was already dressed to go north again and only the imminent first flight of the *Dixie* held him back.

'Ira,' he begged. 'For God's sake, let's see her roll!'

Ira didn't even bother to turn his head and went on fingering the tail surfaces, moving the elevators slowly, checking the split pins and looking for stones, then he passed to the other side of the machine, touching the fin, looking for imperfections or damage, because it was easy enough to harm the fragile surface of an aeroplane.

'For God's sake, Ira . . . !' He heard Courtney's irritated outburst and Alix's sharp reply.

'Shut up, Pa! Leave it to Ira.'

Pausing for a while on the port side, Ira looked towards the curving line of exhausts, black against the red snout of the plane. The Courtney was a beautiful machine, more beautiful than any he'd ever seen so far, the harsh ugly lines of the old biplanes he'd previously flown gone in a sleekness that was moulded for one end only—to carry him a distance of three thousand six hundred miles without failing him, all its imperfections smoothed out to let the air flow freely past, to reduce the drag of friction and to increase and facilitate his passage through the sky. Standing under the port wing-tip, he looked up at it, one hand on the single streamlined strut that passed from the strengthened base of the fuselage, where the undercarriage was married to the framework, to a point just over halfway out on the wing. He studied the aileron, then he moved past the wheel, placing his foot against the tyre to feel its solidity. As he passed in front of the machine, he caught the odour of oil and hot metal.

He stared up at the engine. Only the cylinder heads and exhausts projected from the cowling. The two-bladed wooden propeller had been painted a dull black so that the light on it wouldn't dazzle him as it swung through its circle against the sun, and he studied the gentle symmetry of the blade's twist and stared at the rocker boxes and the way the exhaust manifolds joined the circle of power and flowed backwards, short sharp stabbing metal tubes hugging the fuselage.

Woolff was watching him carefully as he appeared under the starboard wing and stood beside the open door, trying to read the thoughts behind his expression.

'She's O.K., Ira,' he said, almost as though he were afraid Ira might deny it.

Ira nodded and a smile spread across his face. 'Yes, Hal,' he said. 'She's a beauty.'

Woolff's solemn plump face split into a relieved grin, and Ira climbed into the cockpit and wriggled into the seat. Putting his feet on the rudder pedals, he moved his knees slowly once or twice, feeling the pressure of the cables under the soles of his feet and glancing over his shoulder to see the rudder move. Taking the control column between his fingers, he moved it backwards and forwards, watching the elevators rise and fall; then from side to side, his eyes on the ailerons.

Woolff was still standing by the door, his eyes on Ira's face.

'Get Sammy,' Ira said, but before Woolff could turn, Sammy was there alongside them, his keen face and eager eyes belying the ridiculous image the hideous plus-fours gave him.

'Better get in, Sammy,' Ira said.

Sammy grinned and climbed into the second seat, and together they studied the instruments.

'More'n I've ever seen before, Ira,' Sammy observed solemnly, almost as though he were about to worship in some holy place.

Ira's eyes moved over the turn-and-bank indicator that was to supplement their senses in the dark or in cloud where instinct might cause the muscles to make faulty responses.

With the rate of climb and descent clear on the altimeter alongside, they would know, even in the thickest darkness, the altitude and position of the machine in the air and could fly without sight of the earth below or the sky above. There was an air-speed indicator, a tachometer, an oil-pressure gauge and a fuel gauge, luxuries they'd never known on the old machines they'd previously been obliged to fly, and he turned to Sammy and gave him a wide confident smile.

'Let's go, Sammy,' he said.

Woolff grinned and, closing the door, stepped back and joined the others. Ira locked the door from inside and braced himself against the seat, taking a second feel at the rudder pedals and control stick and familiarizing himself once more with the switches. In an emergency he'd need to put his hands on them instinctively. On what happened this morning would depend the reputation of the company and probably himself, Woolff and every single man who'd had a part in the building of the plane.

Woolff was still watching him, his round good-natured face anxious. Behind him, his hair on end, Courtney was chewing at the dead cigar stub, his eyes feverish with excitement, itching for action but having to contain his impatience. Alongside him, Alix watched, her hands deep in the pockets of her coat, the black smoky eyes on Ira's face, and, as he glanced at her, settling himself in the seat, she gave him a nervous unsure smile.

A paragraph about the first flight had appeared in the *Medway Examiner* and the news had obviously got around the town; the perimeter of the field was crowded with children, and along the road were parked groups of cars and trucks, and even a few horse-drawn vehicles. In the tension of the wait, one of the overalled farmers in the parked flivvers along the fringe of the field had grown so excited he had pulled the trigger of a gun and the report had set all heads turning and there had been a lot of laughter and sheepish grinning before they had lost interest and turned again to the small red aeroplane.

At that moment, however, neither the farmers nor the group by the hangar concerned Ira. His attention was entirely on what he was doing, professional, cold and intelligent, absorbed in the details of his task.

'O.K., Hal,' he said, and Woolff nodded and, moving to the propeller, stood with one hand on the blade.

'Switches off?'
'Switches off!'
'Contact?'
'Contact!'

Ira lifted his thumb and Woolff leaned backwards, throwing the weight of his body against the propeller. Immediately, the warm engine caught and roared as Ira moved the throttle forward, jumping to eight hundred and fifty revolutions a minute at once. The pressures and temperatures were normal and the crackling roar filled the hangar. He could see spurts of flame pounding from the exhausts in front of him. He glanced round at the big fuel tank behind him, knowing that, full, it would be heavy enough to crush them both and the hot engine into the ground. He thrust the thought aside. So far no one had come up with an alternative position.

When they took off for Paris they would be nothing more than a huge flying petrol can, surrounded by petrol and breathing petrol fumes. They'd talked for hours about how to get the tank in front of them where it would be safer but, unless they were to fly blind, there was no other place for it except where it was now.

He glanced through the windscreen at the idling propeller. Its tip had been painted red like the plane and he could see a narrow circle of crimson through which the light sparkled. On the cowling, a thin streak of oil that had not been wiped off was now edging backwards under the blast along the trunk of the engine, a black trickle quivering with the throb of the pistons.

Opening the throttle slowly until the rev counter was reading fourteen hundred, Ira felt the machine shuddering with its own power and surging against the chocks. He switched off first one magneto then the other but the engine didn't falter. Every gauge was reading correctly, and he waved away the chocks. Woolff nodded to the mechanics hanging on to the ropes, and the machine rolled from in front of the hangar and across the tarmacadam, lurching slightly as it reached the turf. Glancing at the windsock, Ira saw there was little wind, and as the mechanic on the wing-tip threw his weight backwards, the nose of the machine swung.

For a while, Ira taxied about the field, getting the measure of the controls and opening the throttle in short blasts to feel the reaction of the aeroplane. The fragile machine, nothing more than fabric stretched over steel tubing, had a tendency to waltz in the wind, so that he had to keep jabbing with his feet at the rudder pedals to hold her straight. With the huge main tank behind him full, however, he knew she'd be so heavy it would require the efforts of several men to swing her, and he didn't trouble about her behaviour but turned her swiftly round outside the hangar to face down the field.

As he opened the throttle, the machine seemed to surge forward, the seats thrusting against their backs. The speed built up in seconds and Ira lifted the tail quickly and pulled back on the stick. They felt the plane rise at once, soaring swiftly into the air.

'Hundred yards, Ira,' Sammy crowed. 'No more than a hundred yards before the wheels were off the ground! They've built us a good bus.'

Ira nodded and, glancing at the instruments, put the machine into a climb. The tremendous thrust of the Whirlwind gave them an enormous amount of power, and the aeroplane was lifting rapidly. At three thousand feet, he straightened out, watching the instruments, then climbed, turned, descended in a slow dive, and climbed again. Everything seemed to be working perfectly. Over the hangars, with the word *Medway* painted in bold white letters on the roofs, he saw the line of foreshortened figures on the apron, staring up at him, and the line of cars with their own hired Ford on the end.

Those men below were probably as excited as he was. Though he was in the air, what they'd put together, designed and worked on, was carrying him and Sammy towards the sun.

Over Charleston and staring down at the twin rivers that surrounded the spit of land which pointed like an arrowhead into the Atlantic, he saw ships along the docks and wondered if Ziegler were still there, looking up at him, knowing that the small machine up in the brassy incandescent sky with the sun behind it was what was going to carry his chart workings across the Atlantic. Down there, on that point of land where the oaks shadowed the White Point gardens, heavy guns had started a bitter civil war sixty-six years before, and it seemed incredible that they'd come in sixty-six short years—one lifetime—from the days when the horse was the main method of transportation to machines that were proposing to fly from New York to Paris in one hop. He stared down at Morris and James Islands, at Castle Pinckney and Fort Sumter where it had all started, and at the railway line running almost due north along the east side of the point, alongside the docks and hugging the Cooper River where the oil installations stood.

Pale grey shapes of naval ships edged the land, bright in the sun, and a flying boat lay at anchor on the water, wide-winged and ungainly, not very far from the yacht club with its slender white hulls. Inland, to east and west, he could see swampland, and further inland the gleam of Lake Marion and Lake Moultrie.

He brought his mind back to the job in hand. The aeroplane was so good it was easy to forget why he was there.

'Watch the dials, Sammy,' he shouted. 'The fin pulls us round a little and she's a bit nose-heavy.'

'That'll be balanced with the full tank,' Sammy shouted back, and Ira nodded and pushed across the clipboard and pencil he carried. Sammy took it and jotted down his comments, as Ira moved the control column.

'Slow on the turn,' he shouted. 'But that doesn't matter. We're not going to do much turning. She's all right for long-range flying. Let's see what she'll do.'

He thrust the throttle wide open and the indicator seemed to leap across the dial. They reached a hundred and twenty-five miles an hour in no time, the machine bucking a little in the turbulent air as they flew over the shoreline.

'My God, Ira, she's fast,' Sammy yelled. 'And she'll work up higher than this when we've had another go at her. We ought to get over a hundred and thirty, easy.'

With the bright surfaces of Moultrie and Marion growing larger, Ira turned south again, climbing to four thousand feet, then, throttling back, he held the nose up. Immediately, the machine fell over into a stall and showed a tendency to go into a spin. He pulled her out and climbed again, feeling her stability.

'She's fine, Sammy,' he called out. 'There's nothing wrong with her that can't easily be put right. Let's go down and tell 'em.'

Woolff was lumbering across the grass towards them long before they had swung the machine to a stop and switched off the engine.

'Eight seconds off the ground, Ira,' he said as they jumped down. 'Eight seconds, that's all. What was she like in the air?'

'Fine. She'll have to be watched on take-off, but she's stable and solid. She climbs magnificently.'

'She'll be slower,' Woolff warned, 'with the wing tanks full and a ton of gas right behind your seat.'

Alix Courtney arrived at a run, her eyes alight with excitement. 'She went up like a homesick angel,' she said gaily. 'Ira, for God's sake, take me up and let me fly her!'

Courtney appeared behind her shoulder, smiling like a Cheshire cat. 'She's going to make the name of Courtney famous on both sides of the Atlantic,' he said.

Alix turned indignantly. 'For God's sake, Pa,' she said furiously. 'What about Hal Woolff? And Sammy Shapiro and Ira Penaluna and a few more? What the hell have Courtneys done except big-shot around, snapping their suspenders like a backwoods politician. All we've done is put up a few dollars.'

While they were talking, none of them noticed the hired car that had crept quietly on to the field, and as they turned away from the aeroplane, they saw Boyle walking towards them, a bitter look on his wrinkled walnut face.

Courtney stared at him, his smile gone at once. 'I'm coming, Lave,' he said. 'For God's sake, let me see my plane!'

Boyle gave him an acid smile. 'I've got something I thought you'd like to hear. The *Medway Examiner* just rang the house.'

Courtney scowled. 'What does that fat toad Nestor want now?'

'He thought we'd like to know. Byrd's crashed his plane.'

'*Crashed!*'

Immediately they all crowded round the old man.

'Fokker turned it over, landing,' he said. 'At Teterboro on the sixteenth. He put her down on soft ground, and she was too much weighted forward and turned over. Out of trim, they say. They were all injured except Fokker. Byrd got a broken wrist and they say he was so mad bawling out Fokker he never even noticed till later.'

'*He* won't get away *this* spring,' Woolff observed.

'Up in Boston,' Courtney said, 'they reckon he doesn't *intend* to go this spring anyway.'

Boyle interrupted. 'There's one other thing,' he said, and they turned to stare at him. 'You aren't front runner yet, Felton. Not by a long chalk. Chamberlain and Acosta kept the Columbia Bellanca in the air for two days over Long Island. Two days! Fifty-one hours, eleven minutes and twenty-five seconds to be exact.'

Courtney's face had fallen. '*Fifty-one hours,*' he said harshly.

'That's nearly six hours longer than Drouhin in France last year. It's a new record.'

Boyle passed the sheet of paper across. 'The Columbia Company say now they could be ready for the Atlantic in three days,' he pointed out.

Sammy snorted. 'My God, they'll have to move,' he said. 'That motor'll need a goddam good overhaul after that long. What's the Bellanca look like, Hal?'

Woolff was frowning. 'High-wing mono,' he said. 'Very much like this. Wright Whirlwind power plant.'

'Charlie Levine has control of Columbia,' Courtney said, frowning.

'Who's Levine?' Alix said. 'That salvage dealer?'

'Sure.' Courtney nodded. 'Made a million before he was thirty, out of war surplus. He wants to see his machines flying the airline routes. You've got to push like hell, Hal.'

CHAPTER THREE

THE SAD SWEET SMELL of salt, weed, mud flats and fish hung over the tidelands, and the last shreds of ground mist lay over the fields and swamps all the way from Charleston inland. As Sammy stopped the hired car in front of the hangar, a long line of coloured boys was stretched across the grass of the runway, their feet hidden by the veils of mist, their bent figures followed by a wheelless van apparently floating on the milky vapour as they searched for the stones and chips that might damage Courtney's tyres on take-off.

In spite of the mist, the day was already warm, and as they pushed out the aeroplane the sun lifted over the trees and began to burn the grey veils of moisture off the swamps. The few puff-balls of cloud that had been in the pale morning sky when they'd first appeared at the airfield had gone now and the heavens were a vast flawless blue jewel above their heads.

One of Woolff's men swung the propeller and another leaned against the wing strut to turn the machine into the wind, and Ira lifted the *Dixie* off the field in a steep climb to gain height over the sea. Beyond Fort Sumter and the narrow neck between Morris Island and Sullivan's Island, they picked out the flickering light of a signal lamp and the motor boat that was carrying it.

Ira jabbed a finger towards it and Sammy nodded. The boat was anchored with its bow into wind and, straight ahead of it, a mile away, they could see a fishing smack with a large flag attached to its mast.

'That's our line,' Ira shouted.

They turned above the motor boat and headed north for four miles, then, banking, they dropped to a hundred feet and pushed the throttle wide open. As they passed over the boat, the aeroplane bucking in the unsettled air, they noticed that the airspeed had reached a hundred and twenty-seven miles an hour. Sammy pressed the stop-watch he held as they roared over the fishing vessel.

Throttled back, they climbed up to a thousand feet, Sammy busy over his notebook, then they came down to the sea again for the trip back with the wind behind them. This time their speed jumped up to a solid hundred and thirty-five, and Sammy noted down the relation of airspeed to engine revolutions, glancing at the dials and writing on the pad on his knee. Then, throttling back and setting the throttle at one thousand five hundred and fifty revolutions a minute, which they had decided would be the safest and most economical position, they noted the speed.

'Ninety-five, Ira,' Sammy shouted. 'That's not bad!'

Satisfied, they flew above the shipping for a while, watching the crews on the anchored vessels staring up at them. Then they saw a yacht with a man and a girl on it, waving up at them, and they went down low to give them a better view of the aeroplane, zooming up as they passed just above the mast.

But they forgot the blast from the propeller, which caught the sail and almost blew the boat over, and as they climbed they saw the man had disappeared overboard and was swimming for a neighbouring lighter and the girl was clinging to the mast with both arms and legs, while the little craft rocked in the tornado of the slipstream.

Landing back at Courtney Field, Woolff edged the petrol lorry up to the machine. No one spoke much, all of them a little tense and occupied with their thoughts and calculations. Alix was sitting on the bonnet of the old Chevrolet she'd bought, a cardigan over her shoulders, a cigarette as usual in her mouth, holding the book in which they entered all the results from the data boards. She had flown blind in the De Havilland with Ira whenever Sammy was engaged with Woolff on the Court-ney—both as a passenger and occasionally in control while

Ira watched the results from the other cockpit, but there'd been little conversation between them, and their talk had been only brisk and businesslike, though they'd both enjoyed spinning and rolling at the end of a trip, intoxicated by the lift of the wide transparent wings and the sheer joy of free motion through the sky.

A wind had got up now, ruffling her hair, and Ira stood alongside the Courtney, letting it blow against his cheek to gauge its strength.

'Ought to help a bit,' he said. 'But I'd like to see what she can do without a wind some time. We might have to get off in New York without any help from a breeze.'

The take-offs with a quarter-load and a half-load were not much longer than with unladen take-offs, but as they began to top up the tanks they saw that the run was lengthening all the time.

'She'll be tail-heavy when the main tank's full, Ira,' Woolff advised. 'You might have to be rough to keep the nose down, and you'll have to watch as you climb out, in case of a stall.'

'Once you're up, you can burn off the fuel in the main tank first to balance her better,' Alix said.

On the next take-off, with the loose dust churned into yellow billows behind them, all the weight seemed to go into the undercarriage and the plane shook and shuddered alarmingly as they roared across the ground in a way that was agonizing for a pilot in tune with his machine—like galloping a horse on unyielding stone.

'Four hundred and fifty yards,' Sammy called out, staring at the white posts stuck into the ground. 'She unstuck at four hundred and fifty with three hundred and fifty gallons, but, my God, those bloody shock absorbers are taking some hammering now!'

As they lifted into the air, Ira glanced out of the window at the wheel spinning below him and to his right.

'Make a note to check the tyres, Sammy,' he shouted.

The landing was solid, the plane rattling and protesting, then they heard a bang and Ira was aware of the machine canting to starboard.

'Shock absorber!' Sammy yelled.

Ira moved the stick to port but there was another shuddering jerk that set everything rattling and the machine began to swing a little, the hard pounding of the wheels over the bumpy ground vibrating all the way up their spines.

As they cut the engine, Woolff appeared in his car in a cloud of dust and they dropped to the ground, staring at the shock absorber.

'It's inside,' Sammy said, bending over the wheel.

Ira pulled off his helmet and, tossing it on to the grass, flung himself down by the wheel to examine the shock absorber. While he was still flat on his back, gazing upwards, the old Chevrolet arrived, bumping and swaying over the turf, to swing with rocking springs and shrieking brakes to a stop alongside. Alix stumbled out of it while it still appeared to be moving and she was down on her knees alongside him immediately, kneeling in the dust.

'Ira, for God's sake . . . !'

Ira lifted his head abruptly and stared at her, startled. Her jaw dropped. 'What happened?' she demanded.

Woolff offered her a cigarette. 'Shock absorber went,' he said.

She stared at him and then at Ira. 'I thought—I felt sure—I mean, I saw the wing cant up and I saw Ira fall down, I thought . . .'

Sammy grinned and Woolff's plump face creased in a slow smile. She gazed at them and then at Ira staring up at her, then she reached out and gave him a violent angry push in the chest so that he fell flat on his back again, and scrambled to her feet, brushing the dust and the flecks of grass from her skirt. Her eyes were blazing.

'God damn,' she said furiously.

Ira sat up again, puzzled. 'What was that for?' he demanded.

She seemed to be fighting for words. 'I—I—good grief, I thought you were hurt—and it was only a goddam shock absorber.'

Ira grinned. 'I am hurt.'

She swung round again. 'You *are*?'

'*Now*. That was quite a shove.'

She threw her cigarette at him. She looked confused and embarrassed and Sammy took pity on her, guessing what had been going through her mind.

'Won't hold up much,' he said, rescuing her by changing the subject. 'We averaged a hundred and thirty-one.'

She stared at him for a second then she seemed to get control of herself, but she was still pale, and swallowed awkwardly.

'That's O.K.,' she said, lighting another cigarette. 'That's fine. Fine.'

'And ninety-five with the throttle at fifteen-fifty,' Sammy persisted.

'That's a good speed.' The colour was coming back to her cheeks now and her eyes began to shine. 'You could do the whole trip at a hundred-ten, hundred-twenty.'

'It'd be an economical reading. We'll have plenty of fuel.'

Woolff tapped the cover of the shock absorber with his knuckles as Ira got to his feet. 'We'll have to get something stronger,' he said, frowning. 'There's been no harm done this time but we'd be in a mess if one went just as we topped her right off for the final take-off. We'd have to syphon all the gas out. It'd take hours and you might miss your only opportunity. While we're at it, maybe we ought to have heavier tyres, too. I wouldn't like one to blow. A ground-loop with a ton and a quarter of gas wouldn't be so goddam funny.'

As the mechanics arrived with the truck, they climbed into the cars and headed back towards the hangars. The tests had taken the best part of the day and, as they drove behind the Courtney being towed slowly away, there was a band of yellow low in the sky where the sun had gone. Near the office, they were surprised to see Courtney waiting with Boyle.

'Pa!' Alix frowned. 'What are you doing back here?'

Courtney gave a small tired gesture. 'I wanted to see the plane,' he said, his big voice strangely subdued.

'You came all the way from Boston just to see the plane?' Alix stared. 'What sort of business sense do you call that?'

Courtney brushed the question aside. 'Never mind that,' he said. 'What was the speed like?'

'Fast.' Alix answered shortly, as though she were still angry with him. 'Average of a hundred-thirty-one.'

Courtney nodded. 'Better all come up to the house this evening,' he said. 'We'd better discuss plans. Byrd says he'll be ready in a couple of weeks, after all, and they've only got to fill up the Bellanca for the off.'

The mist came again that night, thin fingers of it reaching out of the swamps and down the long avenue of double oaks all the way to the front porch of *Magnolia*, boring and wandering under the grey veils of Spanish Moss.

Woolff's Sunbeam stood with Ira's hired sedan beneath the high porch alongside the banked azaleas. The frogs were going at it hammer and tongs, honk-honking among the reeds, and the crickets were keeping up their shrill clicking chorus in every patch of grass.

In the big shabby dining room Courtney sat at the head of the long mahogany table, staring down its length at the others, his high stiff collar jabbing at his ears. Alix, her eyes as jetty-black as her hair, was alongside him, and down the table, beyond Boyle, Ira, Sammy and Woolff sat together like conspirators, separated by their profession.

'You were a hundred gallons short of the full load, Hal,' Courtney was saying. 'Why?'

'A landing with a full load might have blown a tyre,' Woolff explained. 'Then we'd probably have ended up with injuries and a damaged ship. As it was, we only lost a shock absorber. We'll have to strengthen 'em.'

Courtney nodded, satisfied. He looked tired, and alongside his hand where it rested near his glass there were two of the purple pills he took from time to time. The puffy eyes in the thin face rested on Woolff for a moment then swung to Ira. Nobody pretended the dinner was a celebration. It was a conference with food.

'How soon can you be in New York?' Courtney demanded.

'We've got to fix the shock absorbers,' Woolff said stubbornly.

Courtney gestured. He looked impatient and Ira noticed that Boyle's eyes never left his face.

'That won't take you long,' he said briskly. 'No more than a coupla days. When, Hal, when?'

Alix stared at him narrow-eyed. 'You're in a terrible hurry, Pa,' she said. 'Why?'

Courtney's eyes swung to her. 'I want to see her on her way to Paris is all,' he said. 'When will it be?'

'She ought to have a proving flight first,' Ira pointed out. 'How long?'

Ira turned a page in the notebook on the table beside him. 'Flying out west just to come back again would be damn silly,' he said, 'because we'd have to cross the mountains twice. But I still think we ought to give her a good test.'

'O.K., Ira!' The words jerked harshly across the table again. 'How long?'

Ira didn't look up. Despite what Byrd said, it was clear his damaged machine wouldn't be ready for another month, while, contrary to expectations after the Bellanca's startlingly successful long-distance flight, it seemed that other factors besides the overhaul of the engine were likely to make an immediate attempt on the Atlantic out of the question.

Little more than a flying test-bed for the Wright engine, the machine had already proved its worth, but while two of the best pilots available, Clarence Chamberlin and Bert Acosta, had been signed up to fly it, it now seemed that Levine, the owner, had also hired a third pilot and the incensed Acosta was talking of backing out, and the Bellanca's chances were suddenly in jeopardy.

Looking down the table, he saw Courtney reach for the two pills on the table alongside his glass and pop them into his mouth. Boyle moved restlessly and gave him a quick nervous look, as though urging him to hurry.

'I thought we might fly to Texas,' Ira said at last. 'Then turn round and fly to New York. That'll put her where we want her and it'll give her a flight of around three thousand miles. It ought to be enough to bring out any defects.'

'Texas?' Courtney rapped out the word explosively. 'Why can't we take her straight up north?'

'We need that long flight.'

'Gee whiz, Ira, time's-a-wasting!'

'Not *that* fast,' Ira said. 'We don't have to break our necks. And I'm not happy about the Hughesden pump.'

Boyle's head jerked up. 'What's wrong with the Hughesden pump?'

'I don't like it,' Ira said. 'The Wright engineer wants the Viking internal-gear type.'

Courtney frowned. 'We've got agreements with Hughesdens,' he pointed out sharply. 'I'd prefer Hughesden instruments and pumps on my plane.'

Alix turned. '*Our* plane, Pa,' she pointed out.

'Oh, goddamit, our plane, then! Look, Ira, is it impossible to use Hughesden equipment?'

'It's not impossible, but I don't want it.'

Courtney sat back in his chair, frowning, and Alix leaned forward, her eyes narrow.

'Pa, what the hell are you up to with Joe Hughesden?'

Courtney flashed a glance at Boyle and gestured irritably. 'I've told you. Nothing. Joe Hughesden's eager to get into the automobile business himself, that's all. He's looking round for a plant. He'd like mine. I guess that's why he's being difficult.'

He turned to Ira. 'Look, Ira, we've got to push this thing.'

'Why?' Alix's question came disconcertingly across the table again.

'For God's sake'—Courtney seemed driven—'because if we're first across it means dough. And we need dough. People always need dough. And we've got a *chance* to be first across. Levine's tying himself in knots trying to find a couple of hero types like everybody else's got. They say he's been after Rickenbacker but *he's* having financial trouble with his auto business and he's got all he can handle. They say he's trying to drop Chamberlin because he's got thin legs and likes to wear plusfours. He wants Acosta and someone else to do the job. He won't manage it. Bellanca himself's behind Chamberlin.' He leaned forward across the table and jabbed the air with his cigar. 'That leaves Davis and the Pathfinder and they haven't even done their load tests yet. *We* could get off first.'

'We'll still fly to New York via San Antonio, Felton,' Ira said mildly.

Courtney's voice rose and he shifted restlessly in his chair. 'You're a hard man to handle, Ira! When, then?'

'As soon as the weather clears.'

Courtney gestured. 'O.K., O.K.,' he said. 'Only, for God's sake, make it soon.'

'As soon as we pick up good weather reports.'

'Lave'—Courtney stared down the table and Boyle lifted his head—'wire New York we're coming. Arrange for a guard. We don't want souvenir hunters doing any damage.'

He turned back to Ira. 'I'll fix gas and oil with Vacuum and Standard. Just make it quick, that's all. We've got the chance of a lifetime.'

Ira watched him in silence. What Courtney said was true enough. With luck they could probably be away even before Nungesser, who was said to be waiting only for the prevailing west-to-east wind to change direction. There was a great advantage in being first at the start line and they had to take a chance somewhere. They weren't conducting a technical experiment as Byrd claimed to be doing. Their machine wasn't even a flying test-bed for its engine as the Bellanca was. They were out simply and solely to be first across the Atlantic, with all the attendant publicity and sales.

He became aware of Alix's eyes on him. 'How about it, Ira?' she asked. 'You *ready* to go?'

He nodded. 'We're ready. We've got all the Rand-MacNally maps we need.'

'You can't beat 'em,' Courtney approved. 'What about the licence?'

'It's through.' Woolff's head jerked up. 'International-experimental. They're painting the number on her tomorrow.'

'It's only fair to point out,' Ira said, 'that if she doesn't behave well, I shan't go for the Atlantic.'

'For Sweet Jesus' sake, Ira!' Courtney exploded. 'What do you want? Angels?'

Ira grinned. 'Don't let it get you down, Felton,' he said. 'I don't expect there to be *much* wrong.'

Alix looked round, the smoky black eyes on his face again. 'How about a passenger?' she suggested. 'Someone who knows the country?'

Ira regarded her gravely. 'The whole point of navigation,' he said, 'is that you don't *have* to know the country.'

She didn't argue, but it immediately became clear that the suggestion had set Courtney's mind racing. He sat bolt upright in his chair.

'Now, see here,' he said excitedly. 'I think you've got a great idea there!'

Alix's head jerked round. 'Forget it,' she said quickly.

Courtney leaned forward eagerly. 'We need publicity now,' he said. 'The ship's built and we've got to start thinking about selling more like it. The press'd go overboard for that. It'd be the nuts, and Alix, you've flown over the whole of the Eastern States on your own, from Mexico to Maine.'

'I said it didn't matter,' Alix said harshly.

'How about this, then?' Courtney offered. 'The boys are flying me back to New York. I'm in a hurry. I'm needed there. I've got to meet a business deadline.'

Alix looked alarmed and her eyes widened. 'Land's sakes, Pa, you know you couldn't take a flight that long! The doctors would throw a blue fit.'

Courtney waved a hand. 'I'll be O.K.,' he said.

'Pa, you're not flying to New York!' Alix's alarm had increased, and she crushed out her cigarette in an ashtray. '*I'll* do it if Ira'll take me.'

Courtney was beaming now. 'O.K.,' he said. 'You go. I'll see that the press are on hand when you arrive. This'll be great—a Courtney arriving in a Courtney plane.'

'You haven't asked Ira yet,' Alix pointed out sharply.

Ira was watching the by-play with interest, and he glanced now at Sammy. They'd discussed the publicity they expected to receive when they arrived in the North because they knew New York was fed on ballyhoo and sensation and the weirdest of publicity stunts. There would inevitably be aeronautical officials to see and perhaps even a local politician or two hoping to make the front pages. There was no real reason why Alix *shouldn't* accompany them.

Sammy caught his eye and grinned. He seemed to have a curious regard for Alix, and she'd always been prepared to swap ideas about aerodynamics, drag co-efficients and thrust and stress factors, whenever he chose to bore her with them.

'There's one snag,' Ira pointed out. 'An experimental licence means we can't carry passengers.'

'Sign her on as an extra crew member,' Courtney suggested.

'It might be a good test,' Woolff said. 'It'd be equivalent to another hundred-fifty pounds of fuel.'

'One-twelve,' Alix snapped and Woolff grinned at her.

She was staring at Ira now, a confused shine in her eyes. The blind flying she'd done with him had been exact and efficient. He knew she wouldn't be merely a passenger and he'd noticed the desperate appeal in her expression.

'All right,' he said. 'We'll start as soon as the fog clears. I'll chart the course tomorrow.'

'Do it tonight, Ira,' Courtney urged. 'Tomorrow the fog might be gone. Sammy—why not contact the Weather Bureau right now? They keep up a twenty-four-hour service for shipping and we might just have a forecast for the morning.'

As the party broke up, Courtney pushed his chair back with a scraping noise across the uneven floor boards. 'How about us all going into Charleston and finding a drink?' he said. 'Lave knows a place where you can get real Scotch. Show the boys around some—the Battery, the old Slave Mart, the Heyward-Washington House and the guns that fired on Fort Sumter.'

Alix frowned. 'I've seen the guns that fired on Fort Sumter,' she retorted. 'And so have the boys. You should be going to bed if you're going back up north tomorrow.'

Courtney looked rebellious. 'I've taken my pills,' he growled.

She gave a bark of laughter.

'If you're on pills, it isn't a night out you want, it's a crutch.'

As they moved into the hall towards the library, Ira stopped to light the enormous cigar Courtney had insisted on giving him, and he heard Alix's voice coming from the dining room, not loud but sibilant, as though she were letting drive in anger at her father.

'You lay off this press business, Pa,' she was saying. 'You're not going to turn this flight into a three-ring circus.'

Courtney chuckled. 'Hell, we need publicity now, Alix,' he said. 'We've finished. We're ready. This is *when* we need it.'

'We can't afford publicity,' Alix snapped. 'We'll get all the publicity we can do with when we get the plane across.'

'Aw, rats, Alix! Publicity's dough, *and we need dough*!'

Ira had lit the cigar now, and was just moving out of the hall, embarrassed by what he'd heard, when Alix's heels clattered across the warped wooden blocks of the floor.

'I don't trust him, Ira,' she said.

He turned. 'Who? Your father? Why not?'

She gave a deep sigh, then she frowned and an uncertain movement of her hand changed into an irritable little gesture.

'He's up to some deal with Joe Hughesden,' she said. 'I don't know what it is but I don't trust Joe Hughesden either. Pa's been dealing with him for a long time now and they never got on. Why should they behave like old buddies now?'

Ira offered her a cigarette and she took it without a word, waiting with nervous fingers for him to light it for her, then she drew deep puffs at it as though she couldn't contain her anger, blowing out the smoke and fanning it away from her face with a savage slapping motion of her hand.

'I expect he knows what he's doing,' Ira said.

She looked up quickly. 'Pa *never* knows what he's doing,' she snapped back. 'He never did. He moves too fast, and when he stops he finds he's done something he didn't intend. I hope to God he hasn't over-extended himself over this damn plane. That two and half thou he promised never turned up.'

Ira looked puzzled. 'Hal paid the bills with it,' he said.

She was silent for a moment, then she moved her head angrily. '*I* sent it,' she said.

Ira drew on his cigarette in silence. 'Would he want you to?'

She frowned. 'He's got nothing to do with it,' she said. 'I'm free, white and twenty-one, and somebody had to.'

Ira studied her for a moment, wondering if he ought to tell her what Nestor had said while she'd been in New York with her father—about Courtney trying to negotiate a loan in Medway. He suddenly wondered, even, if it had been the reason for his urgent and brief visits to the South from Boston.

She was watching him from the shadows, her eyes on his face. 'Did you ever have trouble with *your* father?' she asked.

Ira smiled wryly. 'My mother did. He spent all the house-keeping on aeroplanes.'

She tossed her cigarette aside, half-smoked, and faced him, looking sad and lovely, her eyes bright, the wide passionate mouth managing an uncertain smile.

'Do something for me, will you, Ira?' she said. 'Come with me into Charleston. I feel like some night life after all.'

CHAPTER FOUR

THERE HAD BEEN a drop in temperature and the mist was rolling more thickly than ever out of the swamplands and through the magnolias and live oaks, coming like grey wraiths over the river and filling the fields on either side of the dusty road as they headed for town.

Sammy had offered no objection to driving home alone and Ira suspected he had an assignation somewhere with the girl from the store. Sammy had grown up fast in the last year or two, and there was a devil in him sometimes that made him chase everything that was going, whether it were a girl, money or merely excitement.

Alix drove the old Chevrolet fast and expertly, though she seemed absorbed with her thoughts and took too many risks. Every now and then they saw a cow or a mule among the trees, disembodied and legless among the milky vapour that swirled about it, staring into the headlights as the car bored through the arch of ghostly branches it illuminated with its own lamps.

They crossed the Ashley River and headed down King Street towards the sea. Near the Battery, she stopped the car under the high wall and, without saying a word, got out and stood staring into the mist where they could see the dim lights of shipping through the fog.

The slow groan of a freighter's siren came from beyond the blankness as it edged nervously into the harbour. Behind them the lacy iron balconies of old houses were dimly silhouetted by the glow of lighted windows pushing through the trees and the silent palmetto flags.

As Ira came up alongside her, Alix pushed a cigarette at him and held up her lighter. The glow from a street lamp fell on her face. 'Damn big business,' she said.

'You still on about that?' Ira asked.

She turned on him angrily. 'Sure I'm still on about that,' she said. 'Why is it that when men start making money, they always want more and kill themselves to get it? He's been like this ever since my mother died, as though he has to stop himself thinking that he's alone. Maybe he ought to marry again. I wouldn't mind.'

She paused. 'I was married,' she went on.

'Yes.'

'I divorced him.'

'I heard that, too.'

'Don't you want to hear why?'

'Now's not the time for the disasters and dishonours of the day, Alix.'

She dragged on her cigarette and threw it away only half-smoked. 'You're going to hear 'em all the same,' she said.

She drew a deep breath that was almost a sigh. 'He came from Boston,' she went on. 'He flew aeroplanes. I'd been going around with a boy I'd known at school in New York. We used to go swimming and sailing. He had an old flivver and we used to go to the tea dances and out to Long Island to look at the sea. I guess I thought I couldn't ever be happier. But I grew out of it. It began to seem unreal. You can't live on sugar cake all your life, can you? Then I met my husband. I guess I married him on the rebound.'

She drew another deep breath and moved her hand slowly in a derisive gesture. 'It didn't work out,' she went on. 'Because I was only eighteen. I hated him before six months were up. He said he wanted a home and kids but I never believed him. He liked booze and airplanes and fast cars too much. He wasn't as tough as he pretended to be. I even think he was scared of me a bit. I was always telling him to slow down. One night around Thanksgiving he'd been at his hip flask and he hit the kerb and I was thrown out. I wasn't hurt at all, but he was still in the car when it hit a tree.'

She drew a deep breath and went on in short spare sentences that came out awkwardly—almost as though they hurt. 'He was pretty smashed up. The minister came and begged me to pray for him. Because he was my husband. I couldn't tell him I hated his guts. Because I guess maybe his parents loved him, even if *I* didn't. Yet I felt it was my fault and I tried to do something about it. But I couldn't pray worth a damn. Every time I got started I kept remembering the things he'd called me when he was drunk. In the end I got up and had a cigarette instead. He didn't die. He got over it but we were all washed up. I never lived with him again, and we got a divorce the year afterwards.' She dragged at her cigarette. 'I guess I'm boring you.'

'A bit.'

She managed a twisted smile. 'You never say what you're expected to say, do you?'

'It stops people taking you for granted.'

She managed another smile. 'I won't go on much longer. Only I've got to tell somebody. I've never really laid it on the mat before. Do you mind?'

'Go on, Alix, get it off your chest.'

She sighed in the darkness. 'When it all fell through I went rushing back to the boy from New York. But *he* was married, too, then, and scared stiff of me. He thought his wife would find out. It was all lousy.'

She was silent for a long time. 'I'm sick of men,' she said. 'Most men, anyway. I need someone who's not scared of me, someone who's prepared to offer me a slap across the jaw if necessary. I'm twenty-two now and I've racketed around too long. If I don't do something worthwhile soon, I'll end up jumping out of a window. That's why I wanted to see this plane built. To feel I'd done one worthwhile thing in my life. From now on I'm looking for a man with guts. That's all there is left.'

She stared at Ira, her eyes glittering in the glow of the street lamp. 'You aren't saying very much,' she pointed out. 'Have *you* ever been in love?'

'Yes.'

She seemed surprised. 'You have? When?'

'Not long ago.'

'Why didn't you marry her?'

'She was killed—flying.'

She was silent for a moment, shaken by his words. 'Oh!' She paused, her eyes suddenly concerned. 'I'm sorry. I didn't mean to probe.'

'It's all right. I've got over it.'

'Do you want to talk about it to me?' she asked gently.

'Some time perhaps. Not now.'

'I guess I don't feel like whooping it up, after all,' she said quietly. 'Let's go get a cup of coffee in a diner.'

Her mood was heavy and had never allowed the evening to get off the ground. When they stopped at a roadside restaurant she was still deep in her own thoughts.

On the way back to Medway, however, she stopped the car by the road in a patch of conifers, where they could smell the damp and the pine needles, and they were as alone as if they were in another world, listening to the tick and whisper of the trees and the shufflings of small animals in the darkness.

She smoked a cigarette slowly, not speaking, then, her eyes bright in the glow of the dashboard lights, she threw it out of the car and turned towards Ira. Her face was calm and a little puzzled.

'Are *you* scared of me, Ira?' she asked unexpectedly.

'Why should I be?'

'Lots of men are. We try to be broad-minded about divorce over here but people are still wary of a girl who's been married. They treat you as if you were a fast-buck operator. Cautious. As if you might be infectious.' She looked at him again under her eyebrows and in the semi-darkness it was impossible to tell what she was thinking. 'You're the only man I've met who's never made passes at me,' she pointed out.

Ira grinned. 'It's safer not to.'

'Why?'

'I couldn't be sure of the result. All the same, in the dark and wearing that perfume, I could find my resistance wearing a bit thin.'

She paused, then she moved restlessly alongside him.

'I guess I could make it thinner if I tried.'

'I don't think you'd need to,' he admitted. 'Pity the grass's wet and the mist's on the damp side.'

She laughed—a genuine laugh—and slid along the seat towards him. 'We could put the hood up,' she suggested. 'Or there's a bungalow on the beach. It's locked up. The key's under the porch.'

The fog hung on for the whole of the next day and, though they rang from the airfield at impatient intervals, the story remained the same: Low pressure to the west and south, with heavy cloud over high land; and rain—even ice and sleet—to the north.

The information that Nungesser was about to take off, however, had apparently been too optimistic because, after a report from Paris that he would leave from Le Bourget within a matter of hours, nothing further had been heard of him, though Levine in New York claimed to have got his crew troubles sorted out by making his third pilot, Lloyd Bertaud, the navigator.

'The pilot will be chosen from Clarence Chamberlin and Bert Acosta, both experienced men,' he announced. 'They will appear in flying suits at the last minute and their names will be written on separate slips of paper. One slip will be drawn from a hat and the name on it will decide the pilot.'

It seemed an odd way to choose a pilot for a flight as taxing as one across the Atlantic would be, and could only lead to confusion, lack of preparedness and indifference, and Ira decided privately that perhaps after all they hadn't quite as much to fear from the Bellanca as they'd thought.

They were all a little on edge by this time, nevertheless, because their preparations were complete now and as there was little they could help with at the airfield, the only sensible thing to do was to keep away. Courtney had gone to New York to await their arrival and Woolff was busy strengthening and replacing the shock absorbers and making last-minute checks on the engine, and there was no point in getting in his way.

The bad weather continued to cover the land and the *Medway Examiner* ran a series of wildly improbable stories about their imminent departure which grew more imaginative with every day the bad weather held on.

The final gem arrived one morning while they were still luxuriating in bed, and Sammy sat up with a jerk, spilling coffee and rattling the paper.

'Oh, Jesus!' he said. 'You've been relegated to co-pilot, Ira!'

He threw the paper across and Ira fought to straighten out the sheets.

GIRL TO MAKE NEW YORK FLIGHT. ALIX COURTNEY WILL BE PILOT.

Ira's eyes swept over the words, then he tossed the newspaper aside. The story didn't worry him at all but he'd been disturbed and angry for some time since the drive into Charleston. They had not returned to Medway until the early hours of the morning—Ira at the wheel of the car, Alix bolt upright alongside him, her eyes fixed firmly ahead—passing through the town with the beginning of daylight before the first unwilling mule was on the dusty road to Charleston. Not surprisingly, he'd expected her to show some sign that she was aware he was alive, but he'd seen no sign of her since and when he'd telephoned *Magnolia* she'd put him off with a brief and patently false excuse. After that, the telephone had been answered by one of the old Negroes with the information that she was out.

His eyes brooded on Nestor's headline for a while, then he caught Sammy's gaze on him.

'What the hell are you looking at?' he demanded, and Sammy gestured, his face innocent.

'Nothing,' he said. 'Nothing at all.'

They had barely finished breakfast when Alix arrived unexpectedly, swinging the old Chevrolet round in front of the hotel with a swish of gravel. Her imperious manner was gone and she seemed strangely humble and apologetic. Ira studied her warily.

'I expect you're wondering where I've been,' she said brusquely.

'I thought you'd want to tell me,' Ira replied. 'You seem very hard to get hold of.'

Her eyes flickered away from his, worried and unhappy. 'I didn't want to see you,' she said.

'Why not?'

'I had things to do. I wanted to be on my own for a while.'

She gestured at the headlines in the newspaper on the table, as though trying to brush his questions aside. 'That's none of my doing, Ira,' she said.

'I didn't think it was.'

'It was that damned Nestor. I'd like to hit him over the head with a house brick. He came to the house and asked for a story. I should have held my tongue, I guess.'

She seemed to feel the need to make her protest almost too firmly, as though she felt guilty for her earlier rudeness and was anxious to put it right.

'I told him the truth,' she said. 'That I was just going along as spare crew and that I'd be giving you a spell if you needed one. I don't like publicity of that kind.'

Ira shrugged, uncertain how to deal with her. 'Don't lose any sleep over it,' he advised. 'We'll worry about publicity when we get to the other side.'

Her eyes were still on his face, speculative and troubled at the same time, then she looked up at him, her expression suddenly challenging. 'How about taking me with you, Ira?' she asked.

'We are doing.'

'I mean to Paris.'

Ira grinned. 'For the publicity?'

She frowned and shook her head. 'Because I'm a good pilot and I know what you're aiming at.'

'I've got Sammy,' Ira pointed out gently. 'He's pretty hot stuff, too.'

The velvety-jet eyes were still on his face, steady and appealing. 'I'd like to come, Ira,' she said. 'I've wanted to make the trip ever since we first considered it.'

He shook his head. 'It's no stunt for a woman.'

Her eyes flickered for a moment uncertainly then they lifted again to his, direct and unafraid. 'I've flown blind with you,' she said. 'I can do without sleep as well as you can. I can endure cold.'

'Suppose we have to come down in the sea?'

She flashed him a sudden unexpected frightened look. 'Don't say that, Ira,' she said quickly.

'We might.'

She raised her eyes to his again. 'O.K. I can stand that, too.'

He shook his head. 'No go, Alix,' he said gently. 'It's no job for a woman. We've spent weeks working out weights and balances. We've got it poised on a knife-edge. An extra passenger would have to be counter-balanced with less petrol.'

She studied him for a while, her eyes disappointed, then she nodded, accepting his decision calmly with a little smile that was more wistful than happy. 'I guess so,' she agreed. 'O.K. Forget it. It was always in my mind but you've made your point. I'll just be around to wave you off.'

Sammy had watched the whole interview in silence and as the old Chevrolet moved away, he glanced at Ira.

'Ira, old cock,' he said. 'That girl's got her eye on you.'

Ira said nothing. Sammy was too shrewd a judge of human emotions to be very far wrong.

Sammy grinned at his expression. 'There's no need to start protesting,' he said.

'Who's protesting?'

'I've seen her eyes. When she's talking to me, she's looking over my shoulder at you all the time. When I say something, her head's cocked to hear what *you're* saying at the other side of the room. She shows all the symptoms.' Sammy grinned ruefully. 'I don't know what it is you've got, old lad, but you've got *something*. You've always only had to stand around looking heroic and flashing those baby blue eyes of yours and the dames go down like ninepins. I wish I had it. I always have to work like hell.'

Ira said nothing and Sammy's smile faded. 'There's nothing wrong with her,' he pointed out earnestly.

'Who said there was?'

Sammy seemed to be pleading Alix's case with a surprising vehemence and Ira suspected that, like Woolff, he was more than a little smitten himself. 'She's got more than most dames,' he went on. 'And it's all where it ought to be.' He paused. 'I wouldn't mind handling it myself,' he admitted slowly, 'only I was left at the post weeks ago.'

Ira stood for a moment in silence, his brows down, then he looked up and grinned. 'Let's go through the mail,' he said.

Their mail these days had begun to include requests for signed photographs and offers from various kinds of crackpots who were anxious to put patent navigating instruments, charts or fuel conservation devices at their disposal, and this time there was another letter from China which informed them that the airline they had left behind was not only still managing to function on one old rebuilt De Havilland but was doing so well a second one was being considered. There were also a few offers of marriage, a suggestion that they appear in a movie, and a second letter from Cluff.

'He says he's coming to see us,' Ira said.

'He's one guy I can do without,' Sammy observed. He'd never forgiven Cluff his backsliding in Africa.

'He says he's got some project he wants to talk about.'

'Probably wants to borrow fifty dollars.' Sammy tossed aside the *True Confessions* magazine his girl friend had lent him and reached for his wallet. Fishing inside it among the thick wad of letters he always carried, he produced a photograph, going brown with age and dog-eared with usage.

'See that?' he said.

It was a picture of the two of them with Cluff, whose smiling face stared out at them from the fading print with a strange sort of wistful appeal. He had never been a strong character.

'He borrowed five quid off me when we had that taken,' Sammy said. 'He said he wanted to have a cabinet print done for his family in England. He didn't ever get it done, but I never got my five quid back.'

During the afternoon the weather improved and the day ended in a peaceful sky that changed slowly from yellow to pink, and the last flights of martins were chattering noisily as they swooped above the hotel when Ira was called to the telephone.

It was Alix. She sounded excited.

'Saddle up, Ira,' she said. 'The Weather Bureau just rang! The low-pressure area's moving away and it's clear along the Eastern states.'

'Right!' Ira gestured frantically at Sammy standing near the door, his hair slicked down with brilliantine and wearing a starched collar ready for a date. 'I'll contact 'em myself and ring you back.'

The Weather Bureau confirmed what she'd told him. 'It's moving out into the Atlantic,' they said. 'You'll find it clear towards the Mex border, too.'

'What about further north?'

'Still shut in, but it'll start clearing there, too, within twelve hours. By the time you get up there, it'll be O.K.'

Ira slammed down the receiver and rang *Magnolia* again. Alix answered at once, as though she were waiting alongside the instrument.

'This is it all right,' Ira said. 'We go tomorrow. Take-off time's fixed for four-thirty. Can you be at the field at three-thirty?'

'Sure.'

'I'll ring Hal Woolff. Get an hour or two's sleep.'

She laughed and her voice sounded tremulous with excitement. 'You kidding?'

It was still dark when they arrived at the airfield and there was a mist in the trees along the fringes of the runway, but it would soon disappear when they left the coast and the sun got up. The flight path along the field was still obscure, but Woolff had long since set flares along it to give direction for an early take-off, and a coloured workman was moving along the field lighting them.

'Runway's clear.' Woolff appeared out of the shadows as the hired car came to a stop, his face strained, his manner tense. 'I've had a truck up and down it.'

Even as they climbed out of the car, they heard the roar of an engine and the old Chevrolet drew up alongside. Alix was wearing a fashionable skirt and yellow blouse.

Sammy stared. 'You dressed for flying?' he asked.

She heaved a flying suit and helmet out of the car. 'As much as I need to be,' she announced tartly. 'We don't need fancy doodads. They're going to see that you can travel by airplane without dressing up like a polar bear.'

The men who'd built the *Dixie* were waiting on the concrete apron, some of them with their wives and children.

'Attaboy, Captain!' One of them came forward to shake hands. 'Bring us back a bottle or two from Paris.'

'How about looking up a dame for me, Captain?' another one asked. 'I was a doughboy over there in the war. She might remember me.'

The petrol lorry was just edging away from the aeroplane and Woolff came forward again.

'You've got the fuselage tank three-quarters loaded, Ira,' he said. 'It came in sealed tins and it was all filtered as it went in. Don't forget to get the tail well up because she'll be tail-heavy. You'll probably get some spillage through the vents as you take off, but it's nothing to worry about. And watch that Hughesden pump. If it fails, you'll have to use the hand pump to transfer gas to the wing tank. It'll gravity feed fine from there. O.K.?'

'O.K.' Ira nodded.

'How're you navigatin'? Followin' the railways?'

'No.' Ira shook his head. 'Compass. It'll help us fix how accurate it is, and it'll be good practice. We can check it by the railways during the day and by airfield beacons at night.'

He struggled into his flying suit. Sammy appeared from the darkness. 'All set, Ira,' he said.

There was a grind of gears as the lights of the petrol lorry vanished. Then Woolff reappeared.

'Everything's fixed,' he said. 'Don't forget to make a note of what she uses so we can make an extra check before you leave for Europe. See you in New York.'

They climbed into the wicker seats, with Sammy alongside Ira, and Alix cramped in just behind in the darkness.

'O.K. Switches off.'

'Switches off.'

The engine exploded into life and they sat shivering in the cockpit as it warmed up.

Across the field, they could just see the beginnings of daylight. Trees were appearing through the darkness, faint outlines against the sky, and in the distance the white blur of a frame house. Then Ira lifted his hand and the chocks were jerked away.

The wind was blowing towards the hangar and they were able to swing into position quickly. For a second, Ira sat staring at the instruments, making mental checks, then he glanced at Alix and Sammy, and opened the throttle wide.

CHAPTER FIVE

THE RUMBLE AND CLATTER of the wheels across the bumpy field stopped abruptly as they lifted over the trees. Below them as they climbed towards the east they began at once to see the glow of Charleston, and it was possible to fix the coastline by the way the lights stopped dead at the empty sea. In the grey-blackness, occasional solitary glimmers showed where ships rode at anchor, but they could see the shape of the Bluffs and the curve of the rivers quite clearly from the street lights and the bunched bright bulbs round the shipyards and along the Cooper where the oil installations lay.

The stars were already fading in the sky with the first hint of daylight, and the horizon to the north was growing more distinct. Then ahead of them they saw the orange-red ball of the sun appear out of the pink mists, and the glow was immediately reflected on the dew-wet roofs of half a dozen houses and along a stretch of swamp water.

Alix, sitting behind Sammy, seemed subdued and silent as they turned south-west towards their course. Alongside Ira, Sammy gave directions in matter-of-fact tones, professional and calm for one so volatile, and unemotional as he always was in the air. 'Course two-five-seven, Ira,' he said. 'The wind'll shove us north a bit but we'll get a bit of help from it, too.'

They swung on to course, leaving the sun behind them as they headed over the swamps. Below them they could see steely stretches of water and the feathery tops of the trees, and here and there, where the swamps opened out, a boat and a face turned upwards in the growing light.

Down below were swamp adders and insects, and only a

few paths through the leaning trees and cane brakes towards the scattered patches of cultivated land. It was a lonely area that was difficult to cross, but they were lifting over it now as easily as if they were stepping over a stile.

Flying had introduced a new and simpler element into transport that would one day do away with railways, and they were already on the brink of the new era, about to leave behind the days of stunting and exhibitions as flying became as normal as riding in a train. The end was already on its way for all those who wrested a living from playing up its hazards, because, a few years from now, fliers would be more anxious to show its safety than its dangers.

'Engine sounds O.K.,' Ira said, listening to the steady beat vibrating through the thin skin of the machine.

Navigation was easy. The light was good and it was possible to see for miles. The vastness of the land made it easy at four thousand feet to pick out the landmarks which stood out clearly against the earth, because there was none of the older European chequerboard pattern of small fields. Here there were few hedges, only vast areas of forest showing green among the grey.

They had left the swampy land of South Carolina behind them now and were approaching the border. Two hours and ten minutes over the red earth of Georgia and they could hope to pick up the Chattahoochee at Eufaula. For almost all the distance to San Antonio they would be flying over flat country where, if anything went wrong, they would have no trouble making an emergency landing, because the mountains were a hundred miles to the north and they would see no rising ground until they picked up the Edwards Plateau near the Mexican border. Only when they turned north for New York would they have to cross the high land of Tennessee, Kentucky and Virginia to reach the coastal plain, and that presented no serious obstacle.

They sat in silence for almost an hour, all of them occupied with what they were doing, then Alix leaned forward from the rear seat. 'Statesboro below you, Sammy,' she said quietly. 'We'll be picking up the Oconee River soon.'

Her voice was still subdued but she was reading her map quietly and efficiently, offering only comments that would help Sammy with the navigation.

The sun was rising in the sky now and it was growing warmer in the cabin so that they all had to unfasten their flying suits. It was still behind them at the moment so that the visibility was good, and they climbed to five thousand feet to pick up the Ocmulgee and pass between the town of Americus and Lake Blackshear which Alix identified for them, simply and without unnecessary comment.

'You'll see the Chattahoochee in around forty minutes,' she pointed out. 'Eufaula's on the western bank, on a spit of land. Ought to be right on course.'

The flat land stretched monotonously in front of them, rich and luxuriant and watered by a hundred meandering rivers, green-purple in the sunshine with small scattered towns and villages and clusters of barns where farms lay.

They were approaching the Georgia border now and heading into Alabama. When the rains came, down there the streets of the little towns turned to red mud, grass grew on the sidewalks, and the houses sagged around the narrow shaded squares. It was an area that had never been developed much, a place of few cities, small towns and not many villages, and on a hot day in summer the bony mules hitched to the country carts flicked their tails in the sweltering shade of the oaks, and men's starched collars began to wilt by the middle of the morning. By midday the shutters were closed and the people were hiding in darkened houses that were silent except for the grinding of the noisy summer flies.

It was a long stretch of uninteresting flying, with no variation of course and little to absorb their attention but small towns and airfields with names on the roofs of new wooden hangars that had been built in the recent flying boom, and pointing arrows like aerial signposts marked 'Houston', 'New Orleans' and 'Dallas'. There was little for Ira to do beyond let his eyes flick across the instruments, checking switches, throttle, mixture and stabiliser. Alongside him, Sammy's eyes were moving constantly over the panels with his own, as he wrote down pressures and fuel consumption on a data board or roved over the Rand McNally maps. Behind them, Alix seemed to be sunk in her own thoughts.

The sun had swung to the south and the cabin was growing warm as Sammy directed Ira on to a new south-westerly course and soon afterwards they saw the sea again, breaking into the coastline in vast areas of flooded land that were overgrown with heavy trees. Around midday they saw the vast curving course of the Mississippi and the coastline with its silver-blue inlets like lacy patterns in the grey-green of the shore, and picked out the coastal railway line running from New Orleans and Bâton Rouge towards Houston.

'Nothing wrong with the compass,' Ira commented. 'I've been flying by nothing else for nearly seven hours now.'

To the south of them now was the great swampy delta of the river and the coastline of Louisiana.

'If flying the Atlantic's no worse than this,' Sammy observed, 'the only thing we shall die of is boredom.'

'Don't talk too soon,' Ira said.

They were passing to the north of Houston in the early after-noon when the engine spluttered unexpectedly. Sammy was holding the controls at the time, and he came up out of his comfortable slouch as though he'd been shot. The engine caught again at once and was roaring comfortably enough once more, but they were all listening now with their heads cocked for the next sign of a break.

'I'll take over, Sammy,' Ira said. 'What's the trouble?'

Sammy said nothing for a while, pausing before making any diagnosis. His eyes moved over the instrument panel as Ira adjusted throttle and mixture and checked the ignition. For a while the engine ran smoothly then it began to splutter once more.

'Fuel pressure's falling,' Ira said. 'What tank are we on?'

'Main.' Sammy reached back at once and worked the hand pump for a few strokes. The engine picked up immediately and the fuel-pressure needle moved.

'It's that bloody Hughesden pump!' Sammy snorted. 'We'll have to wire New York from San Antonio. They might have to rush us the new one down.' He turned in his seat, his eyes angry. 'Here, Alix, you take over the navigation in case I have to pump.'

Ira's gaze roved over the instruments. 'Switch off the Hughesden and go on to the wing tanks, Sammy,' he said.

'Right.'

Sammy shifted the petrol cocks and for a while they had no further trouble.

'How much's left in the wing tanks?' Ira asked.

'Not much,' Sammy said. 'When it's used up, we've got to get it up there from the main tank.'

They flew for another hour, then Sammy shifted the petrol cocks again and switched on the fuel pump and they waited to see what would happen. Almost immediately, the engine began to splutter again and Sammy bent, muttering to himself, and checked the drain cock and fuel-feed trap, then he jerked at the hand pump so that the engine picked up once more.

'Pump her steadily for ten minutes,' Ira suggested. 'Let's see how long she'll go before it starts again. How far are we from San Antonio, Alix?'

'Two hours' flying time. Can we make it?'

Ira glanced below them. To the north the ground was beginning to rise a little in blue-green folds, but they were still over flat rolling land. 'If we can keep the engine going,' he said.

'There's nothing to fear from high land between here and San Antonio.'

'O.K.,' Ira decided. 'We'll try and make it. Keep that pump moving, Sammy.'

The sun had passed its zenith now and was shining into the cockpit. Ira shifted uncomfortably in the growing heat, and glanced at Alix, but her face was expressionless and calm as she crouched over the maps.

They were over the middle of a vast flat plain now, with here and there great sheets of rock, as naked as if they'd been laid there at the beginning of time. It was probably the first sign of the rising country across their course, and Ira was watching the ground below all the time now, constantly staring just ahead for a suitable place to put the machine down if they had to. Another great river came up, glinting in the sunshine.

'Brazos,' Alix said. 'We're right on course.'

The engine spluttered again, and Ira moved the mixture control, trying to find a position where it was more successful.

'Could we have got water in the petrol, Sammy?' he asked. 'It was damp enough when we fuelled her.'

'It was all strained, Ira. It's that bloody Hughesden pump, I tell you.' Sammy was silent for a while. 'Maybe we ought to have thought harder about getting that big tank forward.'

'It's too late for that now,' Ira commented. 'We can't take the machine to pieces and build her again. We'll change the pump.'

The engine spluttered again and Sammy bent over the hand pump. Immediately the uneven beat became a steady roar.

'She's being starved of fuel,' Sammy pointed out. 'Every time I work this thing, she picks up.'

'We can make it to San Antonio,' Ira said. 'We can strip the pump down there and see what's wrong. Can you keep it going?'

'I reckon so.'

They continued to head into the lowering sun, the land blank to its farthest horizon. They had left the swamplands well behind them now and were passing over the plainlands of Texas where the new spring grass was just beginning to change from its dusty winter dryness. Another big river came up, and then a line of low hills to break the monotony. The engine was still spluttering fitfully but it never failed to pick up as Sammy pumped.

Alix passed round the sandwiches they'd brought and they all had a drink from the coffee Thermos hung in a bag alongside her.

'How about the fuel consumption?' she asked. 'Won't this throw out the calculations?'

Ira nodded. 'Keep putting down the readings,' he suggested. 'We might be glad of what they'll show us.'

'O.K. You'll see rising ground any time now. San Antonio's the other side of it. It's where the railroad from Dallas and Houston join.'

He nodded, staring ahead. 'I can see the line from Houston. It's right on the nose. Can you keep the pump going, Sammy? I'll not want the engine cutting as we're coming in.'

'You concentrate on getting us down,' Sammy advised. 'I'll concentrate on keeping the engine running.'

Below them, the terrain was changing again and they passed over the steep course of the Colorado and began to see the first spurs of rising ground to their right. Half an hour later, with the ground beginning to take on the characteristic black and white of hard sun and sharp shadows, Ira picked up the glint of metals coming down from the north. Where it converged with the one they were following, he saw a haze hanging over the horizon and knew it was a city.

'I've got San Antonio,' he said.

They swept over the town, picking out the cathedral and the Mission of the Alamo, and the army camps on the outskirts. There were hangars and a group of men staring upwards, and near them a Jenny and a De Havilland with Air Corps markings. At the other side of the hangars there was another group of aeroplanes painted in bright colours, and more figures appearing on the apron as they passed overhead. Ira pushed the stick forward and they began to lose height.

Alix looked up, a pencil in her hand. 'We've averaged around a hundred all the way,' she said. 'We must have been doing a lot more at times.'

Ira nodded, his eyes on the ground. Already he could see groups of people and cars parked near the roadway.

'I'm going in now, Sammy,' he warned. 'Keep that pump going.'

They were a hundred feet off the ground now, then fifty, and as Ira eased the stick back, allowing the machine to settle into a three-point landing, they saw cars starting up and heading out to them across the grass, trailing a scattered group of running figures.

They were surprised to see reporters in the crowd that surrounded the aeroplane. They were round Ira in a moment as he switched off the engine and jumped stiffly to the ground.

'You got Alix Courtney with you, Captain?'

'Yes.'

'We heard from Mr Courtney in New York that you had. She do the piloting?'

'Not this trip. She handled the navigation.'

'She any good at it, Captain?'

'No complaints at all.'

'Why'd you land, Captain? Trouble?'

Ira sought for words that would hedge the truth around with evasions. 'We're on a proving flight,' he pointed out cautiously. 'We're breaking no records.'

'Thought you were going to turn right around and head for New York.'

'We prefer to play safe.'

'Ain't she as good as they say?'

The questions came thick and fast and they were shrewd and sometimes tricky, and as Ira tried to choose his answers carefully, Alix interrupted.

'The ship's fine,' she said enthusiastically. 'She behaved perfectly. There's just one small technical factor that we thought we ought to attend to before making the trip north.'

'How about a picture, Miss Courtney? That's it, in a group, the three of you.'

'How about a smile, Miss Courtney? And, doggone, how about looking at the Captain? As if he meant something to you.'

As they were pushing through the growing crowd to the airfield buildings, the airport manager appeared.

'Thought I'd be on hand in case you needed anything,' he said.

'We need,' Alix admitted. 'Get these newspapermen off our necks and a state trooper to watch the plane.'

'And a room somewhere with a telephone,' Ira joined in.

'You got trouble?'

'We need to contact New York.'

The manager didn't argue. 'I'll fix it,' he said.

'And a corner of a hangar,' Ira added. 'With lights. We have work to do. And what are the weather reports?'

'All clear to the north still. If you can get off right away, you'll be O.K.'

'We can't get off right away,' Alix snapped. 'Hughesdens sold us a bum pump.'

Sammy stretched and tossed his cigarette away with a tired gesture. 'Anybody left for Paris yet?' he asked.

The manager shook his head. 'No. Nothing doing. Davis and Wooster have arrived at Hampton, Virginia, for their final tests, but there's something funny going on there. They say they're worried about the Pathfinder, so I guess you're ahead of everybody but the Bellanca.'

They found a lunch-stand just along the road from the airfield and ate ham and eggs. Alix had recovered her spirits now and was cheerful and smiling. While they were eating, the airfield manager arrived.

'We've fixed an office for you,' he announced. 'We've got two trestle beds in there in case you want to rest. There's a telephone, too, and we've arranged for a corner of the hangar and lights. The boys have volunteered to do anything you need to help. How did she go?'

'Fine. Apart from the pump.'

'Can you fix things? The press's asking.'

A car was outside, waiting to whip them back to the hangar, where they found the Courtney had been wheeled inside and the doors closed. The newspapermen were still waiting and Alix's face was all smiles again at once.

'We'll give you boys a statement as soon as we find out the trouble,' she said.

Inside the hangar, lit with the stark glow of bulbs hanging from the girders in the high empty roof, the mechanics had already stripped off the engine cowling and Sammy climbed up the steps to peer into the still-warm engine. After a while, scowling, he climbed down again and picked up a spanner and a screwdriver, and appeared ten minutes later with the pump in his hand. Without saying a word, he crossed to a bench where a solitary light bulb hung, and bent over it.

'Cam's gone,' he said after a while. 'Sheared off.'

Ira bent over it with him. 'Can you fix it, Sammy?' he asked. 'Or do we need a new pump?'

Sammy peered for a while at the workings of the pump. 'Maybe we can fix it,' he said. 'Spindle's a bit longer than most, but maybe we can file one down.'

The airfield mechanics were standing in a circle round the machine and one of them moved forward at Sammy's words.

'We've got a pump like that in stores,' he said. 'Took it off a French plane three months back.'

'Did *that* one break, too?' Sammy asked bitterly.

The mechanic grinned. 'Yeah. Different dingus, though. How about changing the pieces? Nobody'll know. The one we got don't work and if we change it *you*'ll have a pump that works and *we*'ll still have one that don't.'

'How long will it take?' Ira asked.

Sammy and the mechanic studied the pump for a moment. 'Around two-three hours,' they offered. 'One of us can work on one pump and one on the other.'

'Can we rely on it?'

'As much as you can rely on the one you've got.'

'Any wear on the other cams, Sammy?'

'None I can see.'

Ira was working out mathematical problems in his head. 'How about planning to get off again at daybreak?' he suggested. 'That'll give us a night's sleep.'

'I reckon we can.'

Alix turned away. 'I'll wire New York,' she said.

'Don't promise anything, Alix,' Sammy advised. 'We're only hoping, so far.'

They got down to work immediately, watched by the mechanics who stood in a ring round them, pushing tools forward or adjusting the light.

'That Wright bloke wasn't far wrong,' Sammy commented in a flat contemptuous voice. 'There are better pumps than *this* around. We ought to make sure we get one in New York.'

He placed a screw carefully on the bench and, removing the offending cam, held it out for them to see. 'There she is, Ira.

See how she's sheared off? It gets too much work to do. It's not big enough.'

Alix appeared, squeezing through the door of the hangar. Her face looked gloomy. 'I've got a weather report, Ira,' she said. 'There's an unexpected depression building up in the west and beginning to move east. They don't guarantee anything and we'll have to get off right on the dot to miss it. If we don't, we'll be stuck here for some time.'

Ira considered the problem. 'It's around seventeen hours' flying time to New York, given reasonable conditions,' he said. 'When do they expect it to shut in?'

'We've got twenty-four hours. No more.'

'If we can get off at first light we can just get in before it arrives, providing Sammy can fix the pump and it works. Three hours to repair the pump. Four hours' sleep. How about it, Sammy? Can you manage on four hours' rest?'

They finished the work on the pump and had it re-installed within two hours and three-quarters.

'Gives us an extra quarter of an hour's rest, Ira,' Sammy said.

They were all beginning to feel better as they handed cigarettes round, and it was Sammy who put into words the idea that had been forming in all their minds.

'Ira,' he said. 'How do you feel?'

'*You*'ve been doing all the work.'

'I mean, you reckon you're rested enough to fly the plane?'

Ira grinned, guessing what was in his mind, and Sammy went on eagerly:

'How about getting off straight away?' he suggested. 'I can sit in the rear seat over the pump and Alix can navigate.' He glanced at her with a grin. 'Let her earn her keep. She's not done much up to now.'

Alix gestured at the door of the hangar. 'How about light or the take-off? The sun's almost gone.'

The airfield manager joined in quickly. 'There'll be no taking off tonight,' he said. 'The airfield lights have gone on the bum.'

'They would have,' Sammy snorted.

'Something in the main cable from the town. They're fixing 'em now.'

Alix stared at the sky through the hangar doors. 'We'll have barely enough light to see,' she pointed out.

Ira rowned. 'I think we might fix something,' he said.

He turned to the manager. 'What's it like outside?' he asked. 'Many spectators?'

'Plenty. They've been coming out from town ever since they heard you'd landed. I guess we don't see planes like the Courtney down here much. It's a long way from the Atlantic.'

'Plenty of cars?'

'Plenty.'

'How about getting some lined up along the field?'

The manager stared. 'Come again?'

'To give us a line.'

'You going to take off in the dark?'

'Yes. Think you can fix it? We want headlights along the runway to give us our direction and a few across the end to show how far we can run.'

The manager stared at him. 'I think you're nuts,' he said. 'But, sure, we can do that, I guess.' He smiled ruefully. 'I reckon some of these ghculs'll be only too pleased to have a grandstand view in case you don't make it.'

As he turned away, Sammy rubbed his nose with a grimy finger that left an oily smear. 'If we get off straight away,' he pointed out, 'we can be in New York with a few safe hours to spare ahead of the weather.'

Ira nodded. 'That's what I was thinking,' he said. 'O.K., Alix, let the press know we're off. And pick up the weather again on the way back.'

The mechanics, standing in a group near the aircraft, looked up as Ira approached.

'You goin' to try it, Captain?' one of them asked.

'We're off straight away.'

'In the dark?'

'Why not?'

'You seen the weather report?'

'I'm still going.'

'Sooner you than me, Captain.' The mechanic grinned. 'O.K., we'll get her outside.'

There was considerable excitement as the Courtney was wheeled on to the concrete apron. The crowd had come out to see someone risk his life and they were clearly beginning to think the chances were suddenly good. The wind had got up and was blowing dust across the field from the bare mesas and the sky in the west was coppery in colour, the tops of the hills still pink with the last rays of the sun.

Alix returned. She looked worried. 'It's going to be a squeeze,' she said. 'That low's moving faster than they thought. They reckon it'll be closed in by three in the afternoon.'

Ira nodded, saying nothing, his mind busy. The airfield manager was waiting for them as they reappeared from the hangar.

'I think you're crazy,' he said. 'If you wait they'll fix the lights.'

'We can't wait. We're going.'

The airfield manager shrugged. 'O.K., if you know what you're up to, it's no business of mine. I'm a fine-weather flier myself.'

As they followed the machine, someone raised a thin cheer and torches began to snap on one after another. The newspapermen pounced at once, coming forward in a rush.

'You taking off in the dark, Captain?'

'Yes.'

'Ain't that dangerous?'

'It adds a nice angle to your story.'

As they pushed through the crowd, Ira could see cars along the fence, their headlights shining across the field, and an old jalopy covered with names and slogans—'The Bucket of Trash', 'Waal, Fan Ma Brow'—careered past, packed with youngsters in horizontally striped sweaters determined to get in on the act. Further along, in the distance, he could see more cars moving into position and a group gathering at the far end of the field.

An ambulance roared round the hangar. 'What's the goddam rush?' the driver was demanding. 'Nobody's going to take off in the dark.'

'Sure they are,' a disembodied voice replied from the shadows. 'Over here.'

'Jesus H. Christ!' The ambulance driver's voice sounded awed. 'With *that* forecast?'

Half an hour later, with the sun out of sight behind the rising ground to the west and the field descending swiftly from the purple twilight into the darkness of night, Ira switched on, his head cocked as the engine started with a roar.

'Sounds O.K., Sammy.'

'Nothing wrong with the engine,' Sammy observed shortly, settling into the narrow seat behind Alix. 'All I ask is that the pump holds up.'

Ira glanced at Alix. 'O.K.?'

'O.K.'

'Give it to 'em, Captain,' someone yelled from the concrete. 'Tell them Yankees we got guys down here can still make 'em jump.'

There was another cheer from the crowd, and a series of Rebel yells. Alix was waving through the cabin window to the crowd and Ira saw the flashes of magnesium guns above the press cameras beyond the glass. Ahead of them, the land was already thickening with night and it was only just possible to pick out the silhouettes of the buildings that fringed the airfield. Ahead of them, they could see the hills, their sides boulder-strewn and bare of foliage beyond the few stunted bushes that clung to their sides. Among them lay purple valleys and spurs of rock, and stony black river beds.

He worked the throttle to swing the machine into wind, facing towards the darkening sky. Then he glanced again at Sammy and Alix, and as he thrust the throttle forward to its limit, they began to roll forward into the growing night.

CHAPTER SIX

THE SKY was already blotched with eerie light, ugly as the underside of a frying pan, when, through a gap in the endless cloud prairie below them, they caught a glimpse of Chesapeake Bay.

'Bang on the nose,' Alix shouted, her voice tense with pleasure. 'Right on course!'

They had hit the first cloud around Knoxville and Middlesboro. As they had headed north, the land had disappeared occasionally beneath scrappy puff-balls of haze which eventually became a layer of stratus, and by the time they had reached the Alleghenies and the West Virginian heights the ground was hidden by thick lowering vapour, its rocks and forests vanishing into pale damp mists, the saw-edged summits of the mountains sliding away through the grey opacity to the plains. The Shenandoah Valley, where Stonewall Jackson had rampaged only sixty-five years before, was heavily shrouded with fog, and to avoid the cloud they had swung due east to the winding wooded course of the Potomac and were now passing over the broken inlets of Chesapeake Bay to turn north again with Washington and Baltimore on their left. Swinging east once more, they soon began to pick up the square blocks of Philadelphia and crossed the Delaware into New Jersey.

By this time, the bad weather was rolling thickly in from the west and into Long Island Sound, but their navigation had been exact and through another break in the cloud they identified New Brunswick and almost immediately they were edging over the sliding wisps of grey towards the built-up lands of New York State.

'Wind's increasing,' Ira observed, noting the angle at which they were crabbing along their course. 'We'll just make it.'

The city of New York seemed to come up remarkably quickly, a great sprawl of brick, concrete and steel surrounded by broken inlets. They were all growing a little stiff now and were stupefied by the roar of the engine, but the strange excitement that went with New York managed to reach up to them even in their tiny eyrie of steel tubing and fabric beyond the highest roofs. It was strange to think that below them millions of people were waiting to read of their arrival, itching to see them off across the steep Atlantic stream. Millions of enthusiasts were enjoying the new novelty of broadcasting, listening to the news flashes that came between the bursts of jazz, Rudy Vallee, Beethoven and advertisements for toothpaste, and checking with their newspapers, waiting for the moment when the new contender in the race across the sea would touch down. There was no doubt now that they all knew they were on their way and they were probably even at that moment looking up from the chasm-like streets and listening for the roar of the engine above the sound of the traffic.

There had been no trouble from the pump on this leg of the trip and Sammy had dozed through most of the night. Glancing at Alix, Ira saw that she was looking pale and strained but surprisingly cheerful.

'How's the time?' he asked.

She lifted her head and their eyes met. 'One-thirty. We've averaged over a hundred. We must have put up a record from Texas to New York.'

Ira nodded. 'She'll do,' he agreed.

She gestured ahead of them where the land broke away in a flat-iron-shaped island with, beyond it, a long spear blade pointing east-north-east towards the ocean. Through the broken cloud they could see steely sea, and mist coming in from the west in rolling banks below the puffy grey wisps that slid beneath them on the rising wind.

'Staten Island,' she said quietly. 'Right in front of you. Beyond's Long Island. Curtiss Field's way past the suburbs.'

The Statue of Liberty came up under the wing and they swept along the docks towards Brooklyn Bridge, watching the white bursts of steam as tugs and shipping welcomed them with their sirens. Then a group of wooden hangars appeared out of the mist, with scattered white houses nearby. To one side lay another open space.

'Mitchel Field,' Alix shouted above the engine. She indicated the khaki-coloured aeroplanes in front of the hangars. 'It's Army. That's Curtiss alongside. The one beyond up the slope is Roosevelt. That's where all the activity is. Byrd's outfit's there. He's got a whole set of offices and workshops—probably even a fancy suite as well.'

'Won't help him much when he's out over the Atlantic,' Sammy said.

Through the mist they could see the bright colours of the Jennies and Orioles in front of the peak-roofed wooden hangars, then they realized that a small crowd had gathered, and they could see white faces staring up at them. Rain spattered on the windscreen and began to trickle back, shuddering in the propeller blast. They glanced at each other and began to laugh.

'The nick of time,' Sammy chirruped. 'Couldn't have been nickier.'

The group round the hangars curdled and moved, fragments breaking off as people ran to what they considered would be a better position to see the touch-down. Ira was banking steeply now but, as he levelled off, pulling the throttle back and putting the nose down for the final approach, he jerked upright in his seat and peered forward. Two men had broken from among the spectators and were running across the field into the path the aeroplane would take as it landed.

'For God's sake!' he roared. 'What are those fools up to?'

'Photographers,' Alix shouted. 'I guess Pa told the press as e said he would. They'll be wanting pictures of us landing.'

As Ira worked the throttle and pulled back on the stick to slip over the running figures by a mere few feet, one of them dropped to the wet ground, but as Ira put the wheels down just beyond them, he scrambled up again immediately and raced after the aeroplane, lifting his camera as the machine swung round to head towards the hangars.

Alix was sitting with her face against the windscreen now, waving the newspapermen aside, but they took no notice, and, as the aeroplane came to a stop, one of them lifted his camera again, dodging within inches of the spinning propeller so that Ira had to allow the aircraft to roll to a halt.

'Come on, Captain,' he yelled above the engine. 'Smile, for heaven's sake!'

'I guess we have to go along with them,' Alix said angrily. 'If Pa's arranged it, we can't turn 'em down.'

For sheer safety, Ira switched off the engine and the propeller jerked to a stop. As they climbed down from the plane, they saw more newspapermen had arrived, and they were surrounded at once by yelling men and women, flourishing notebooks and changing photographic plates.

'How about kissing the little lady, Captain?' someone yelled. 'Makes a better picture.'

Alix looked up at Ira, then she reached up and kissed him as the flashlights popped. 'That's for the flight, Ira,' she said, frowning and embarrassed.

An excited face thrust between them. 'What about Chamberlin, Captain?'

'What about him?' Ira said.

'Ain't you heard? Hey, quit shoving!'

The questioner was swept away by the crowd before he could answer and they were almost bowled off their feet, then through the struggling figures they saw a fair-haired, moustached man approaching them.

'My name's Jones,' he said. 'I'm the airfield manager. We've got a hangar ready for you. Follow my car.'

The thickening clouds above the field were sprinkling the grass now and the hangar roofs were beginning to gleam wetly. A few umbrellas went up.

They climbed back into the *Dixie*, then, with a few bored policemen keeping the crowd back to a safe distance, they started the engine again and taxied behind the airfield manager's car through the increasing rain across to the hangar and swung it round.

As he jumped down to the ground again, Ira saw that the crowd had already increased, as though word had got around and people had come running from all over the airfield, ignoring the rain.

146

Someone touched his shoulder and the fair-haired man appeared again. 'You can forget your machine now,' he said. 'I'll move her in.'

He glanced at the *Dixie*. 'She looks good,' he observed. 'And you did well from Texas.'

It was clear that the excitement in New York was much higher than it was anywhere else and, despite the rain, no one seemed to wish to take shelter. The newspapermen surged around them, their clothes wet, fighting to get a good position and shoving to protect their claims. New York was pulling out all the stops, caught up already by the excitement and the glamour. Here was where all the contenders for the Orteig prize were gathering, and tucked away in South Carolina, with only the newspapers to guide them, they had never realized just how much interest had been stirred up.

'The Wright Company said they were sending down a couple of men,' Ira was informed by a breathless official, 'but they didn't know when you were arriving and we got some strange reports from San Antonio.'

A thin-faced spectacled man pushed through the crowd towards their side, pulling irritably at the crowd with both hands.

'I'm Loerner,' he said. 'Fred Loerner. Loerner Publicity. Mr Courtney hired me.'

Alix rounded on him, her eyes angry. 'Why?'

Loerner looked startled. 'Why?' he said. 'Hell, because I guess he thought you'd need me. So we don't get things out of proportion. So we don't get the wrong things printed about you. Publicity's a new conception of business, ma'am. How would anyone know what you were setting out to do unless you told 'em first?'

'Did *you* whip the crowd up?' Alix said.

'Yeah, sure.'

She snorted. 'Then I reckon you aren't earning your money. It's too small.'

Loerner gave her a soured look and then he turned up his collar.

'I do my best, ma'am,' he said coldly. 'And while we're on the subject, how about letting the press get some pictures? These boys have got deadlines, you know.'

They were standing in front of the plane now, surrounded by a growing crowd of men with notebooks and cameras. Sammy had his head down and was wearing the disgusted expression he always wore for what he considered unnecessary demonstrations of emotion.

'O.K., O.K.,' Loerner was shouting. 'Let the Captain through!'

Ira was shoved and jostled to the front and Loerner fought to push the crowds back. The cameramen were down on their knees now on the wet grass, aiming their lenses.

'Come on, Captain! Not so doggone grim. And, say, Mr Shapiro—you look like you ain't expecting much out of this trip.'

Sammy stretched his mouth into a death's-head grimace.

'How about getting Chamberlin over, Mr Loerner?' someone yelled. 'He's right here on the field somewhere. It'd make a picture.'

'Say, how about that, Captain? Any comments about Chamberlin?'

Ira turned to the voice yelling near his ear. 'What happened to Chamberlin?'

'The Bellanca had a crack-up! Haven't you heard?'

'How about putting your arm round Miss Courtney, Captain?'

Ira obliged. Alix fitted neatly under his shoulder.

No one seemed to bother to wait for the answer to any of their questions and after a while Loerner pushed forward and began to drive a way through the crowd. The photographers ran alongside, threading in and out of the excited people, still trying to take pictures.

'Any romance, Mr Loerner?'

Loerner tried to look knowledgeable. 'Not for me to say,' he pointed out.

'No, there isn't,' Alix said under her breath.

'What's all this about the Bellanca crack-up?' Sammy demanded.

Loerner gestured. 'They had a christening ceremony over there. Two kids with a bottle of soda pop. Then Chamberlin took them up with Levine for a treat and a wheel came off. They say he put her down light as a feather. I'm told he did some nice flying.'

'How about the plane?'

'Some damage. Not much. Won't take long to fix. They say he's had the instruments ripped out and replaced, though. I guess he found better ones.'

While they were still struggling towards the hangars they

saw Courtney, swathed in a heavy rubber mackintosh, pushing his way towards them, elbowing through the crowd with Lavery Boyle.

'Ira! Alix! Sam! How did the flight go?'

As they shook hands over the heads of the crowd, Courtney was pushed forward and jostled against them, fighting to keep his feet, and Ira got his mouth close to his ear as they ended up almost chest to chest.

'We've got trouble, Felton,' he said.

Courtney's head turned, his eyes alarmed. 'The ship? What was it? The rain?'

'The Hughesden pump.'

Courtney gave him an anxious look, and his face was long, water trickling down his thin cheeks, as he tagged along behind them through the crowd.

In the distance they could see a hangar with the words, *The America Transoceanic Co. Inc.*

'Byrd's camp,' Loerner said. 'He's said you can use Roosevelt Field. He's got exclusive use of it but he's a fair guy and he says he doesn't want to put anyone to any unnecessary risk. It's the best field and he says anyone trying to get across the Atlantic has the right to the best facilities. He's got a kitchen, mess hall and sleeping quarters over there. *And* an office. He's even got a private line to the New York papers.'

The hangar to which Loerner was leading them was rather different. A wooden sign—*Dixie. Courtney Transatlantic Flight*—hung on the half-open doors, and it was shared by a De Havilland, a Swallow and a Waco.

The rain was coming down heavily as they were jostled into the shrouded darkness. Shaking the water off his hat, Loerner turned round to face the crowd of newspapermen. 'Give us ten minutes, boys,' he yelled. 'That's all. Ten minutes, then we'll give you all you want. Just give 'em chance to get their breath then they'll answer any questions you want to ask.'

The big doors of the hangar were opening now and, turning, they saw the red wings of the *Dixie* over the umbrellas of the crowd, moving towards the hangar.

'It's all taken care of,' Loerner was shouting to the newspapermen. 'We're leaving the doors open so you can see what she looks like.'

The *Dixie* was pushed inside and the tail swung round so that the nose faced outwards, and one of the mechanics stretched a white-painted rope between the half-open doors.

'O.K., boys,' Loerner said. 'You can take all the photographs you want from there. Tomorrow you can look her over, but we've got things to discuss tonight.'

Despite the downpour, the crowd hadn't diminished in the slightest, and Ira, Sammy and Alix were standing in a group with Courtney, still warily watching the struggling. The dripping newspapermen immediately started pushing forward again.

'Hey, Mr Courtney, how about a picture in front of the plane?'

They all stood together in front of the plane again, awkward and embarrassed with all the gaping faces and levelled cameras, trying to talk normally without seeming to be too aware of what was going on. After that the ordeal was repeated in the office with a barrage of questions, and the flashing of camera guns held by soaked, dishevelled men.

'When's the take-off, Captain?'

'As soon as we've checked the engine and got the right weather,' Ira said.

'How about tomorrow?'

'Not a chance. The weather's shut down.'

'How about charts, Captain? What kind you going to use?'

'Same as ships use. No reason why they should object to us using their sea, is there?'

Everybody laughed.

'What happens if you're blown off course?'

'I've got a thousand miles of coastline to aim for. I ought to hit it somewhere.'

'How about a radio?'

'We're not carrying one. Too heavy.'

'Byrd's carrying one, Captain. So's Chamberlin. How about a sextant?'

'Captain Penaluna'—this time it was a woman reporter—'that's a romantic name you've got.'

Ira sighed. It was a familiar line. 'There are plenty funnier in Cornwall where I come from,' he pointed out.

'Captain'—she was almost breathing down his neck now—'is that right you've come here from China and that you were a general in their army?'

Before she could go any deeper into the subject another questioner pushed forward.

'Will Miss Courtney be flying to Paris with you, Captain?'

'No.'

'I guess she'll be the last to say goodbye, though, Captain, eh?'

'Probably not.'

'Hell, don't spoil the story! Why not, Captain?'

Ira grinned. 'It'll more likely be one of the National Aeronautical officials sealing the tanks and fixing the barograph to prove we haven't landed anywhere en route.'

They were determined not to let the romantic angle go.

'You married, Captain?'

'Not yet.'

'Got any plans?'

'Not yet.'

'How about Miss Courtney? You got her down as a possible?'

'No comment,' Alix interrupted, and there was a laugh, and Ira knew that the papers would be full next morning of suggestions of romance.

The newspapermen were pushed out at last and as Loerner shut the door behind him, Alix turned to her father.

'This Loerner,' she snapped. 'He said you hired him.'

Courtney looked uneasy. 'Sure, I did,' he said.

'We can't afford a publicity agent. I told you we couldn't.'

'Rats, Alix, the other outfits have got publicity men! What are we, poor relations or something?'

'If we get across, we'll get all the publicity we need without trying. We didn't need him and you owe me two and a half thou already.'

Courtney looked uncomfortable. 'I'll pay you, Alix,' he said. 'He came and asked. It was hard to put him off. It isn't just what's in the paper. These guys stop the press getting the wrong picture. They look after things.'

She looked tense and angry and it seemed as though a quarrel was brewing up. Boyle stepped forward quickly. 'We've got you and Sammy in at Erwin's Hotel on Fifty-Eighth Street, Ira,' he said. 'I'll be in there, too, because they'll try to picture you coming out of the johnny if they get a chance. Loerner's just round the corner and Alix and Felton won't be far away.'

They all seemed slightly drunk on the excitement, and it seemed to be time to step into the realistic world of fact.

'Never mind the hotel,' Ira said shortly. 'And for the moment let's forget the press. We have things to do. We had to hand-pump fuel all the way to San Antonio.'

There was a long silence so that they could hear the rain on the window and the drips from the great doors into the puddles where the crowd still splashed to get a good view of the *Dixie*.

Courtney leaned across the desk, frowning. 'What the hell's wrong with the Hughesden?' he demanded.

Alix turned on him. 'It doesn't work,' she said bluntly. 'See that your damned Loerner hands *that* out to the press. It might shut Joe Hughesden up.'

Courtney scowled and glanced at Boyle. 'Hughesdens said it was O.K.,' he pointed out.

'Well, it isn't,' Alix retorted.

Courtney turned to Boyle. 'Check that, Lave,' he said. 'I want a run-down on it. I want to know about this pump.' He swung round to Ira. 'I want to see it *work*.'

'And I want a Viking, Felton,' Ira said quietly. 'The Wright engineer advised a Viking and that's good enough for me. The Hughesden's too light.'

Courtney waved his hand airily, as though he were trying not to hear. 'We'll make it work. I'll set up a new one. I'll see we get a guarantee with it, too, this time. A sure-fire guarantee.'

Ira raised his voice angrily. 'I don't want a Hughesden, Felton,' he said. 'We have a Viking on order. The Wright people have it ready.'

Courtney stopped dead, staring at him. In the silence another gust of rain splashed against the window. Courtney opened his mouth, then he changed his mind.

'O.K., O.K.,' he said unwillingly. 'A Viking it is.'

Loerner had reappeared while they were talking and Courtney turned to him as though to avoid facing the problems they were pushing at him. 'Everything fixed?' he asked.

'Sure, Mr Courtney. Do you want the details of the party now?'

Alix whirled. 'Party? What party?'

Courtney looked embarrassed. 'We have to meet some of the people interested in the flight,' he said.

'Why?'

'Listen, Miss Courtney,' Loerner interrupted, 'these people want to know.'

'We can't afford parties,' Alix snapped.

'These are press and magazines, Miss Courtney,' Loerner explained. 'Aeronautical Society representatives. You'll need 'em all before you leave. I fixed it for us all to assemble at

Mr Courtney's hotel. Folks'll be received by Mr Courtney, yourself, and the crew of the airplane.'

'I shan't be there!' The smouldering eyes flashed and Courtney shot her a sidelong glance but pretended not to hear.

Loerner gave a few more details, reading them out so that they sounded like a regimental order. As he turned away, the telephone rang. Boyle answered it. He had been standing silently behind Courtney, old-fashioned, ugly and critical, but rigid with self-honesty. He had been watching Courtney ever since they had arrived, his old yellow eyes on him thoughtfully, like an ancient watchful hound outside a gate.

He spoke a few words into the telephone and looked at Ira. 'It's the Pioneer Instrument Company,' he announced. 'They're sending a man to check the earth-inductor compass.'

Courtney's head jerked round. 'Pioneer?' he snapped. 'Why aren't we using Hughesden instruments?'

'Pa!'—Alix clapped a hand over the mouthpiece of the telephone and glared at him—'the Pioneer's the best earth inductor there is.'

Courtney stared round at the others uneasily. 'I thought we were using Hughesden instruments,' he said.

'If they're as good as the pump they'll have us flying over the North Pole!' Alix snapped.

Trying to ignore the quarrelling, Boyle spoke into the telephone and replaced the receiver, then he turned to Ira, his eyes flickering in Courtney's direction. 'I've contacted the oil companies, Ira,' he said. 'They've promised to put in gas and oil whenever you want it, day or night, and they'll make sure it's checked and filtered. They'll do it O.K. They want to see you get across—especially with *their* fuel. All you have to do is get the aeronautical officials to seal the tanks and instruments.'

As he turned away, Courtney interrupted again, his manner stubborn but uncertain. 'Don't the Hughesden company make a goddam earth inductor?' he demanded noisily.

'It's not like the Pioneer outfit's,' Alix said shortly, as though she'd lost patience with him. 'And it's never been proved. Leave it at that, Pa!'

Courtney was just opening his mouth to argue again when Loerner, who'd been talking at the door to someone outside, turned to them.

'Wright man here about the motor!'

A stocky dark-haired man stepped into the room, his face

wet with the rain. 'Harold Collins,' he said. 'I'm from the Wright Company, Mr Courtney. We have your pump ready to fit.'

Courtney frowned but he said nothing and the Wright official continued. 'Sorry we weren't here when your ship dropped in, but you arrived before we expected. Reports we got from Texas said you'd been held up.'

'Three hours, Mr Collins,' Loerner put in quickly. 'Three hours. That's all.'

Collins turned to Ira. 'Well, either way, you made good time, Captain,' he said. 'I guess you've broken some south-north records today.' He gestured at a fair-haired young man standing just outside in the hangar. 'That's Leon Ortese. He'll work for you or with you. Just as you wish. He'll be here all the time. He's the best you can get.'

He gave a crooked grin. '*We're* in a spot,' he went on. 'Everybody's using Wright engines and we've got to maintain strict neutrality and assign men to every one of the entrants. I guess *one* of you ought to get across, but it's in the interests of our corporation to see you *all* get across. Because, sure as hell, if something does go wrong, *we'll* get the blame, whatever it is.'

CHAPTER SEVEN

IT WAS EXHILARATING to be back in New York. The city was the very heartbeat of a nation that had suddenly found it had an appetite for publicity and sensation, and even crime was operating here on an unprecedented scale since Prohibition had closed all the saloons and bars and started up the vast warring gangs which struggled to control the illicit liquor trade.

Sammy had been looking forward eagerly for days to seeing it again, but by evening the mist had thickened into a heavy rain that kept them indoors, and a wind had sprung up that whipped round the corners of the streets to lift the scattered paper and snatch at the coats of the pedestrians as it howled down the long straight avenues. The depression they'd been racing had slid across the country even faster than they had expected and the wind rose, changing into squalls that rattled the doors and sent the raindrops across the growing puddles in hastening flurries.

According to the weather bureau there was a north-easterly gale blowing in the Atlantic and, according to the ships from whose reports the forecasts were worked out, there were high seas and winds strong enough to force them south before it. A let-up wasn't expected for at least three days, and, following it, there was a whole series of lows coming in with solid headwinds for anyone trying to fly east. Though it would mean that the Bellanca group would be able to patch up their damaged plane, the delay would also enable the Courtney team to fit their new fuel pump and tyres, strip the engine and inspect it for wear and tear and make last-minute checks on airframe and instruments.

The bad weather also enabled Cluff to catch up with them again, because the newspaper stories that Loerner was putting out gave not only their hotel but even the type of shaving soap they used and what they wore in bed, and the telephone rang on the second morning after their arrival. It was Cluff.

'Cluffy! Where the hell are you?'

'Here in New York.'

Sammy, who had been studying with a cynical expression on his thin beaky face pictures in the newspapers of the exhausted competitors in a marathon dancing competition, had sat bolt upright and was now making frantic signs to know what was being said. Ira waved him away.

'New York?' he said into the telephone. 'Why in God's name don't you come over, then?'

Sammy made an agonized face and, clutching his head, flung himself on the bed. 'Not here, for Christ's sake,' he mouthed.

As it happened, Cluff was too far away to oblige.

'I'm not in New York *City*,' he said. 'New York State. Around fifty miles away. Near Newburgh.'

'I thought you were in Canada,' Ira said.

'I was. Congratulations on your engagement, by the way.' Ira's eyebrows shot up. 'What engagement?'

'I heard you were with Courtney Aeronautics and going to marry his daughter.'

'You'd better hear again. It's the first I've heard.'

'*I'm* married,' Cluff went on. 'I married Dulcie Van Der Wee. Do you remember her?'

'Yes, of course.' Ira knew Dulcie well. She was a hard-faced

Johannesburg girl who'd been determined to get away from Africa. He had a feeling that she was capable of eating the easy-going Cluff alive. 'I remember her fine.'

Cluff's voice came again, faint over the crackling wire. 'I'll be coming down to see you,' he said. 'I've got something to ask you.'

Ira's heart sank, remembering that most of Cluff's requests concerned money.

'Oh? What?'

Cluff laughed. 'I'll tell you when I see you.'

They talked a little longer, their conversation chiefly the unsatisfactory trivialities of a long-distance call, then Cluff made his farewell. 'I've got to ring off now,' he said. 'It's costing a fortune and Dulcie's making faces because we haven't got one. I'll be seeing you.'

Ira put the telephone down and turned to Sammy, who sat bolt upright on the bed at once, his eyes fierce.

'What the hell did you tell him to come here for?' he demanded.

Ira grinned. 'He wanted to see *you*,' he said. 'Particularly.'

Sammy pulled a face. 'I don't want to see *him*.'

'He married that Dulcie woman.'

'God help him,' Sammy snorted. 'She was carnivorous. He's determined, I must say. What's he want, for God's sake?'

Ira grinned again. 'Perhaps he's coming to borrow that money you mentioned,' he said.

'He hasn't paid back the last lot he borrowed in South Africa,' Sammy growled. 'You got to hand it to him, though. He's like that bloke who kept asking all the girls if they went to bed with men. He got a lot of slaps across the kisser, but he also got a lot of girls in his bed.'

'So did Cluff,' Ira said.

Sammy nodded thoughtfully. 'Fancy him marrying Dulcie,' he said slowly. 'Remember when she came up from Jo'burg to Moshi to stay with him? Last I saw of 'em both was the night before he left for England. He was as tight as a boiled owl and she was sitting on his bed wondering if it was worth getting in with him.'

Ira laughed. 'You do her an injustice, Sammy,' he said. 'She was trying to sober him up enough to get him to ask her to marry him.'

'Maybe,' Sammy conceded reluctantly. 'He obviously did.'

*   *   *

Because of the continued bad weather, Loerner was able to lay on his reception without difficulty, and Ira and Sammy, sticking out like sore thumbs in their hurriedly bought ready-made suits, were scrutinized by Courtney's colleagues and friends, and a few select magazine and newspaper editors. Woolff had turned up from Medway, strangely naked-looking with a white bald head above his plump red face, and was huddled in a corner with the technical editors of aviation journals, the specifications for the *Dixie* spread out on a table, trying to explain the details in quotable terms.

Though the reception was supposed to be dry, a room had been set aside where good Scotch whisky was being served, and no one said 'No' to good whisky when most people had to drink bootleg gin or drugstore rye. Most of the conversation, in fact, seemed to concern prohibition, the price of illegal drink, where it came from and how poisonous it was.

'I found a place where you can get all the hooch you want. . . .'

'They're smuggling it across from Canada at Detroit. . . .'

'Awful stuff it was—wood alcohol, I guess. . . .'

Sammy was soon more than talkative. 'Sure,' he was boasting, 'we've seen all the sights. The Museum. Grant's Tomb. The Zoo. The boat to the Statue of Liberty and a ride on the Elevated. We did 'em all. The best was the nightclub where we finished up.'

There was a three-piece band, and a girl in misty chiffon with wild red hair was dancing an unskilful Charleston with a man old enough to be her father; and Ira was just growing bored when Alix appeared, despite her professed intention of avoiding the affair, a knockout in a daringly low-cut dress that dragged every eye over to her at once. As he caught sight of her, he was aware again how physically attractive she was.

She was well known around the hangars of the various air-fields he'd visited and he'd heard suggestions that she had no sex appeal, but he'd noticed also that, though the men who flew aeroplanes and worked on their engines were a restless lusty lot, there was never any bad language when she was around, and the observations as she'd walked past, swathed in a thick flying suit and fur collar, had always been low-voiced and admiring. And when she dressed carefully, as she had now, there was no question of a lack of femininity, because she was slim and attractive enough to appeal to any man, her mouth sensitive and soft and her eyes warm. He knew it was only the fact that she never showed helplessness that confused men and put women off, and he watched her now with frank admiration as she approached.

She picked him out unerringly and set course for him immediately, ignoring all Courtney's friends as they moved forward to meet her. Her eyes were bright and she was curiously elated and unexpectedly friendly. He indicated the dress. 'You look a corker in that,' he said. 'What keeps it up?'

'Hope, mostly.'

They danced for a while. In that dress, holding her body against his, it was like clutching someone unclothed.

For a while she was silent, then she began to offer comments on everyone around her in an ear-splitting whisper in her low gruff voice.

'It always gives me a laugh to see this sort of thing,' she observed, gesturing at the crowd, a cynical, completely different person from the dry efficient navigator who had brought them to New York. 'This is the great woolly mastodon. The leading citizens of New York and the private denizens of the newspaper zoo.'

She glanced across the room to where Woolff was now talking to a well-corseted woman with a white-powdered complexion, grey hair and a bosom drawn up to giddy heights under her chin. 'Sob-sister,' she said. 'Probably mad. Poor Hal. He looks as though he's afraid she's going to bite him.'

As the music stopped, her father dragged her away, arguing fiercely in a low voice, and a moment later, as Ira watched them talking to the grey-headed woman with the high bosom, Boyle appeared alongside him.

'Hello, Ira,' he said. He was dressed in a dinner suit that was green with age and with his overlong grey hair and shrewd yellow eyes he looked like some seedy plantation owner in the wrong environment. He sucked at a cigarette for a while and Ira waited for him to speak. He had a considerable respect for Boyle's shrewdness, but the old man was a solitary unfriendly being who had never sought him out much before, and he suspected he had something on his mind.

'These Hughesden instruments,' he said after a while.

Ira turned quickly. 'What about the Hughesden instruments, Mr Boyle?' he said.

Boyle eyed him. Despite the fact that he had never shown much interest in Courtney's transatlantic project, he had a healthy regard for Ira and Sammy. In his time he had lived a life full of financial rewards and devoid of physical risk—something, he had always felt, that put things in the right order—yet, somehow, in Ira and Sammy, whose lives had been full of physical risk but had remained, he suspected, totally empty of financial rewards, he felt curiously he had met someone he ought to envy, and who ought to be able to expect something approaching the truth from him.

He gestured. 'I'm just an old Irishman,' he said slowly, 'and Irishmen are notoriously sentimental about their friends. I've known Felton all his life. I worked with his father before him.'

Ira said nothing and the old man went on awkwardly: 'All the same,' he said, 'I get sentimental about young girls, too. Especially when they look like Alix does tonight. *And* about the young men they dance with—especially when they're brave young men. You're a brave young man, Ira. So's Sammy.'

'What are you trying to tell me, Mr Boyle?' Ira asked.

The old man seemed to writhe inside his clothes. 'My duty's to Felton,' he said, 'but that doesn't stop me having a conscience, too. You ought to know that Felton's got himself into some sort of mess.'

Ira studied the old man for a moment, not very surprised at the announcement. 'What sort of mess?' he asked.

The old man shrugged. 'I don't know yet exactly, because he won't level with me. But he's short of dough and I suspect he's come to some sort of agreement with Joe Hughesden.'

Ira regarded him warily. Clearly, the old man was trying to tell him something without using all the words.

'An agreement that affects the *Dixie*?' he asked.

The old man shrugged again and ran his fingers through his thick hair. 'Could be,' he said. 'I don't know.'

'How much?'

'God knows.'

'Mr Boyle, how about giving me the facts? What's Felton up to?'

'Son'—the old man sighed—'I don't know. I told you once that if he were a good businessman he wouldn't have had me for a lawyer, and maybe that's right. I'm no Clarence Darrow, and I'm too old these days for the way they handle things now. But I've known Felton since he was at college, and pulled a lot of his fat out of the fire because he's never been much noted for his sense of responsibility. He wouldn't have gone off and flown in France in 1917 if he had been. He left a sick wife and a child of twelve when he went. Most of the time he was away *I* looked after 'em because he didn't seem to have thought much about providing for 'em.'

He paused, his lips moving the cigarette about in his mouth, as though what he had to say was difficult and he needed time to choose the right words.

'He lost a fortune in real estate in Florida last year,' he said. 'Did you know that?'

'No, I didn't. Does Alix?'

'I guess so. He's just a plug businessman really. He thought it was sound, but the bottom fell out of it and a hurricane down there last year finished it off. People who sold land at thirty dollars an acre aren't getting their money now and bank clearings have dropped to a quarter of what they were. For God's sake, I only just kept him out of the Harding oil scandals.'

He paused, frowning fiercely. 'He's a damn fool with his money,' he went on. 'But maybe he's not the only one. *Everybody* seems to think this boom's going to last for ever. It won't. We had a slump in 1924 and if people keep on speculating as they are doing, we're going to have another.' He gestured across the room at Courtney. 'He'll be caught,' he prophesied. 'He's a sucker with his money. He falls for anybody's guff.'

A great sigh escaped him. 'But hell, don't we all?' he went on. 'Aren't we all nuts for six-cylinder automobiles, electric ice-boxes, every damn thing they offer—even service-with-a-smile. If they tell us it's good in the ads, we buy it. But this time he's on his own. He's not asked me and, hell, I'm not such a lousy lawyer he can afford to ignore me!'

He paused and gestured with an air of finality. 'That's why I'm warning you, son,' he said. 'I don't know what he's up to and if it were good, I wouldn't worry. But it can't be, or he'd have included *me* in it.'

'Are Hughesdens being difficult about the instruments?' Ira asked.

'I guess they are.'

'How?'

'They want 'em on the *Dixie*.'

Ira paused and drew a deep breath. 'Mr Boyle,' he said, 'if I'm flying this aeroplane, *I'm* saying what we install. It's three thousand six hundred miles and I'm taking no chances.'

The old man stubbed out his cigarette, not meeting his eyes. 'It might be difficult for Felton.'

'That's something Felton'll have to sort out himself!' Ira said. 'It doesn't concern me. It's *his* problem, whether he likes it or not.'

Boyle sighed. 'There are a lot of things coming up that Felton won't like,' he said. 'He won't like to hear, for instance, that Hughesdens might insist. I've talked to 'em and that's how it seemed to me.'

As Alix reappeared at Ira's side, the fragile dress seemed even more revealing than before.

'Made your peace with your father?' Ira asked.

'I didn't know we were at war.' Her voice was clipped and brusque. 'We're spending too much on this jamboree,' she went on. 'I don't like it. And Pa's hitting the bottle. He'll be as stiff as a cigar-store Indian before the night's out.'

'Maybe he's worried,' Ira suggested. 'Boyle just told me it's Hughesdens who are being difficult about those instruments, not him.'

Her brows came down. 'That old crab-apple,' she said in a low voice. 'I guess he's right, though. Pa says they claim they have a right to put 'em on the *Dixie* because they always put 'em on Courtney autos.'

Ira was silent for a moment. 'Alix,' he said after a while. 'How much of the *Dixie* do you own? I mean, how much money have you put in? I think it's more than you said.'

She gave him a curious glance. 'I guess around half now. Why?'

Ira shrugged. 'Nothing, I suppose.'

'You worried about something?'

'I think Boyle is.'

As they talked, Ira saw Courtney begin to head across the floor towards them, trailed by a grinning young man in a dinner jacket whose eyes were firmly fixed on Alix. Alix saw them at the same time and, grabbing Ira's hand, pointedly whirled him round and out of the room towards the balcony. As he vanished through the door, his last glimpse was of Courtney stopping dead in the middle of the floor, his face flushed, and the confident grin sliding from the face of his companion.

There was no one else on the balcony and, because it was cold, she moved closer to him. He put his arm round her, feeling her shiver under his hand through the flimsy dress, and they stared down for a while at the illuminations of New York that lay in square glittering blocks below them, the glow from Broadway lighting the sky. The memory of the clearing in the trees on the Charleston road and the smell of mingled pine needles and perfume was still strong in his mind but he suspected that her interest in him now was chiefly to infuriate her father. Nevertheless he was also young enough not to be indifferent to having alongside him a girl garbed in a staggeringly brief dress and eager to swop kisses behind the curtains.

She glanced behind them and, half-turning, he saw Courtney still standing with the young man in the dinner jacket, both of them obviously disconcerted and uncertain what to do.

'Considering the number of decorations for bravery you can hang on your chest,' she said in a hurried voice, 'you're really surprisingly slow. You weren't so slow that night on the beach.'

Ira grinned. 'I haven't time for a three-alarm whoopee tonight.'

She laughed outright at his description and he gestured. 'You should do that more often,' he pointed out. 'It suits you.'

He saw the young man in the dinner jacket move forward and the flicker of alarm that sprang to her eyes, and he reached out quickly for her.

He didn't have to hold her off and she pushed him away at last with a twisted smile. His collar was under his ear and the scent of her perfume was strong on his suit, and he was aware that she was suddenly looking at him with starry eyes, apparently indifferent to the fact that her hair was awry.

'Can we introduce a small note of sanity into the proceedings?' she asked in an unsteady voice. 'That was quite an encounter.'

He glanced behind him. The young man in the dinner suit had disappeared. 'Who was it?' he said.

She flushed hotly. 'The New York boy I told you about,' she said. 'The one I used to go around with. His wife's in Europe.'

'He seems to have gathered his courage about him. He didn't look very scared of you just then.'

'I didn't want to see him.' She looked up at Ira and gave him a twisted grin. 'Thanks all the same. Intrepid birdmen make a change from businessmen, friends of Pa, and old flames who consider me a pushover because I've been divorced. "Yes, Alix. No, Alix. Oops into bed, Alix." That's all they think of. You weren't serious, were you?'

They were staring at each other with the cautious suspicion

of a couple of hostile bantams, neither of them prepared to give an inch and both on their guard.

'I got the impression *you* weren't,' Ira said.

She gazed at him for a second, her eyes uncertain, then she lit a cigarette and dragged the smoke down in great gulps. 'Doesn't pay to be serious with fliers,' she said shortly. 'It's something I've discovered. They don't think that way. About anything.'

Ira shrugged, aware of the tension between them. 'Some of us do,' he said. 'About some things. Like flying three thousand six hundred miles non-stop. You have to.'

She nodded, her eyes avoiding his. 'Yeah,' she agreed. 'It's a long way.'

Their conversation was still awkward and limping, as though the embrace had made them strangers, and she changed the subject abruptly. 'What happens afterwards?' she asked unexpectedly. 'What will you do after you've made the flight, I mean.'

He shrugged. 'It'll depend on whether we get there first,' he said, 'whether we get there at all, or whether we end up feeding the fishes south of Iceland.'

She turned on him quickly, her face full of anger. 'Don't say that,' she snapped. 'I've told you, don't ever say that.'

She was staring at him now with an agonized expression that was completely at odds with the brusque imperiousness she'd worn all evening. 'You've got to make it,' she went on. 'If you can't, you shouldn't be trying.'

'Fonck ought to have made it,' Ira pointed out mildly, 'but when it came to the point, he didn't. If *we* do, and we're the first, then I don't think we'll need to worry about the future.'

She looked at him strangely, then pulled him from the balcony.

'Pa's got a whole lot of people on his neck,' she said. 'He's just been telling me. Safety devices, Rafts, Parachutes. Radios. They're pressing him hard to install 'em in the *Dixie*.'

'I don't want 'em,' Ira said.

She laughed. 'I don't want you to have 'em,' she said. 'But Pa's done business with some of these people and they're threatening to hold off if he turns 'em down. They're all scared that if you pull it off, they won't be getting a cut of the publicity. They're beginning to realize there's money in this race and they're wanting to get their claws on some of it. You've got a lot to learn about business and a long way to go before you get your wheels off the ground and heading for Paris.'

She gazed at him with a shrewd alert look, then her mood changed again and she gave him a grin that was both youthful and experienced, the knowing grin of a slum urchin who knew the answer to every question in the book.

'That's enough about money for the time being,' she said.

He nodded at her dress. 'Certainly, in that get-up,' he agreed.

She gave him a bright-eyed gay look, new and fresh and young. 'Greed's as straightforward as any other vice,' she said. 'It'll keep. Let's enjoy ourselves. Ever been to Coney Island?'

The visit to Coney Island after the formality of Courtney's party seemed at first like sheer inspired lunacy and, with Alix leading the way, they rode the merry-go-rounds, took in the sideshows, ate popcorn and hot-dogs and had their photograph taken together by a boardwalk photographer. But, just when they seemed easy at last—and for the first time—in each other's company, with all the doubt buried for once, they ran into a large woman with dyed hair and pearls trailing three bored small boys.

'Another flyer, Alix?' she said loudly as Ira was introduced. 'You should be careful. Remember the last one. They're all the same.' She patted Ira's arm condescendingly, beaming at him. 'You can't be trusted, can you? You aviators are too used to taking risks.'

Alix's excited eager look faded immediately and was replaced by the old wary unwillingness, and the evening changed at once. The laughter went out of her abruptly as if it had never been there and she ended the outing by trailing Ira round a selection of drab smoky places where he was inspected through peepholes by blue-jowled men before being allowed to enter. She was suddenly tense and harsh-voiced, and gestured cynically at the noisy crowds standing at the bar drinking concoctions of poisonous liquor while a brassy blonde tap-danced to an orchestra crowded on a dais about as big as a table top.

'The unspeakable knocking back the undrinkable,' she said. 'It's the smart thing these days to get stewed.'

She was suddenly in a dangerous mood and ready for anything. 'Sin's out of date,' she pointed out. 'Freud says so, and anything goes. It's O.K. to get into the back of a car with a boy or drink gin from a hip flask.'

The pleasure had gone from the evening suddenly and her abrasive desire for excitement managed to take away all the joy they had managed to get from each other's company. They parted uncomfortably outside her hotel.

She seemed a little at a loss as she said goodnight. 'It's been a lousy evening,' she admitted brusquely. 'I guess it's my fault. My generation's an unhappy bunch. We've destroyed too many values without producing anything to take their place.' She sighed. 'I guess I must be a brass-bound idealist, because it never works out with me.'

Ira stood on the pavement for a while as she vanished inside the hotel, watching with his brows down, uneasily remembering her bitter philosophizing and aware of an uncomplicated concern for her. He suspected she'd lived so long and unnaturally with some obsession about men, there was no longer much room in her life for kindness and affection and she was now seeking them both with a fierceness that was angry and abnormal.

He was late arriving at the hangar on Curtiss Field the next morning, but Sammy was even later, his face pale, his eyes heavy. He had vanished from Courtney's party early with Woolff and had not appeared at Erwin's Hotel until daylight.

'Jesus, Ira,' he said slowly, holding his head as though he daren't risk leaning too far forward, 'you should have seen the girls we were with. Real eyes and teeth and'—he gestured—'legs right up to here. Wonderful investment, legs—especially with short skirts. Talk about a view.' There was still a smudge of lipstick on his collar, Ira noticed. 'Hal took me to a speakeasy but the police raided the place and a bloke got shot, they said. We had to go like hell through the back door. Then this bloke grabbed me and we found a couple of girls and went back to his place.' He frowned heavily, struggling with his memory. 'I wonder who he was?'

He fought to open the heavy wad of the newspaper, his brows down and looking as though he were having trouble with his eyes. 'They're real arm-breakers, these Yankee rags, aren't they?' he went on. 'And for a country that don't believe in drink they certainly know what to put in coloured water. My head feels like a dog's basket.'

Slowly, as though his hands were weighted, he spread the

newspaper on the desk in front of him and Ira saw his expression change and a flicker of a grin appear on his face.

'Listen to this, Ira,' he said. 'In the gossip column. "Everybody loves a lover and rumour says there's talk of a romance between Alix Courtney, divorcée daughter of Felton K. Courtney, and the man her father is financing for his transatlantic flight, Englishman Ira A. Penaluna. . . ." ' He looked up at Ira suspiciously. 'Ira, it isn't true, is it?' He seemed suddenly indignant that he hadn't been told.

Ira lifted his eyes from the maintenance sheet he was studying. 'Save your breath, Sammy,' he said. 'It's only newspaper talk.'

Sammy stared at him for a moment longer, his face thoughtful, then he bent over the paper again.

' ". . . 'China' Penaluna, as he is known"—Lor', since when?—"is the famous Captain Penaluna who made his name in France by shooting down 45 German planes. In 1919, in Russia, he was responsible for destroying five Bolshevik machines, and in China, as a general, he is credited with collecting another three for his bag. . . ." '

'Sounds as though I ring 'em up on a cash register,' Ira commented.

Sammy had just rolled back in his chair, hooting with contemptuous laughter, when the telephone rang. Courtney's voice came over the wire, cautious and hesitant. Like Sammy he seemed to be suffering from the previous night's entertainment.

'Ira,' he began, 'I've been doing a lot of thinking. You'll remember there were a lot of my business friends at the party last night.'

Ira's eyes met Sammy's across the desk. 'I met a few,' he agreed, wondering what was coming.

'They raised an interesting point, Ira. If anything happened to you on this flight, it'd get a hell of a lot of publicity. It might even look like a lack of preparedness and that'd take a lot of living down.'

'Who by, Felton?' Remembering Boyle's words, Ira couldn't resist the sarcasm. 'You, in your office? Or me, floating about face-down in the Atlantic?'

Courtney appeared not to have noticed. 'People who put money into business expect results, not failure, Ira,' he said. 'When we have success, it has to be seen as success, and when we have failure, that has to be seen as success, too. I've learned to back both sides of the coin. If you succeed, all well and good, but if you fail, I want to make sure you'll be safe.'

Ira drew a deep breath. 'Felton,' he said. 'What the hell are you getting at?'

Courtney paused and Ira guessed he was transferring his cigar from one side of his mouth to the other.

'What safety devices are you carrying, Ira?' he asked.

'Very lights, smoke bombs and a twelve-pound two-man raft developed by Byrd.'

There was another long pause, then Courtney's voice came again. 'You figure that's enough, Ira?'

'We talked it over carefully. That's as much extra weight as we can carry.'

'It still isn't much. You ought to have more than that.'

'We pared it down to the limit.' Ira was beginning to grow suspicious now. 'The whole enterprise rests on how light we can keep the aeroplane.'

Courtney wasn't finished. 'You thought about a radio, Ira?' he asked.

'No.'

'Why not?'

'They're too heavy. And, Felton, I don't want radios. It's petrol I want.'

'Fred Loerner came up with a newspaper story about a guy who's invented a lightweight one. Couldn't we get you one?'

'I'd like to see it first.'

'Ira'—Courtney sounded worried—'we've been offered dough to use parachutes and life rafts and a few other things.'

'Like radio?' Ira said.

'Well, yes, I guess so.'

Ira drew a deep breath. 'Listen, Felton, we worked out all this long since. You know we did. We know just what we can carry. With anything extra and a full load of petrol, we'd never get off. My answer's simple. It's "no".'

'Ira. . . .'

Ira was beginning to grow angry. 'We knew in Medway what we wanted, Felton,' he said. 'And that's as much as we want. All these other things will make her too heavy. Either we risk our lives with too little or we risk them with too much. Take your pick. Insist, and we'll be taking your aeroplane off through the wall of the hangar at the end of the field and that'll be that.'

There was a long silence at the other end of the telephone

then Courtney's voice came again, dubious and worried. 'O.K., Ira,' he said unwillingly, 'I guess you're the boss.'

Putting down the telephone Ira picked up the file in which they kept all the progress and maintenance sheets and slammed it to the desk in a fury. No one in the office said anything, then Sammy began to light a cigarette.

'Big Chief Penaluna has spoken,' he said dryly.

They were still staring at each other when the telephone rang again. His eyes on Ira, Sammy picked it up, listening for a while, then he held it out. 'For you, Ira,' he said.

It was Loerner. 'Hello there, Captain,' he said. 'I've got some news for you. I thought it might interest you. I've just been in the agency offices with the story of last night's shindig. They were all hoppin' around like fleas on a mad dog. They'd just got a wire in from Virginia.'

Ira was in no mood to listen to Loerner. 'What is it?' he snapped. 'Civil War broken out again?'

'No, Captain.' Loerner sounded hurt at his tones. 'And it's nothin' to laugh at, either.' He paused. 'Or maybe it is at that. For you, anyway.'

'Come on, Fred.' Ira was growing irritated. 'What have you got?'

Loerner paused. 'Hold on to your hat, Captain,' he said. 'You're probably front runner now. The Pathfinder crashed at Hampton. Davis and Wooster were both killed.'

CHAPTER EIGHT

THERE SEEMED to be a great deal of confusion about the first stories of the disaster. Although every newspaper in New York plastered the crash across its front pages, they all appeared to carry a different account of how it had happened.

It seemed at first that Davis and Wooster had been killed immediately, then that they'd been burned to death, but then it seemed that the vast tri-motored Pathfinder hadn't caught fire at all and they'd been suffocated by fumes leaking from a split petrol tank into their cabin. As each new livid account was devoured for details and the newspapermen crowded up, wanting their comments, the air of uneasiness in the Courtney hangar that Courtney's demands had started spread and grew deeper.

'Makes you think,' Woolff said soberly. 'It might have been us.'

'Not in the Courtney,' Ira said firmly. 'We're not flying a giant with three motors.'

'All the same'—Sammy's face was grave—'it shows there's more to this business of getting across the Atlantic than just flying.'

Ira laughed. 'Particularly on mornings like this with everybody having the heeby-jeebies,' he said.

Sammy looked at Woolff and his mouth twisted in a wry smile. 'It's a hell of a long way, all the same,' he pointed out.

'We just flew two thousand nine hundred miles,' Ira said.

'With a stop after the first one thousand two hundred,' Sammy reminded him. 'To fix a sprung pump.'

Ira didn't reply. He knew the way Sammy and Woolff were thinking. A change was coming to flying. Everyone who knew the first thing about it was aware of it, because the new inventions that were appearing were removing the blind spots and proving that aeroplanes were no longer too hazardous for daily use. But it wasn't hard, nevertheless, to believe that perhaps the strides they were taking were sometimes too big for them, that they were perhaps trying to run before they could walk, that the change that was coming was coming too soon.

'Suppose the pump goes one thousand two hundred miles over the Atlantic?' Sammy persisted. 'There'll be no San Antonio field *there* to put down on, no bunch of grease-monkeys to produce a dud pump and take the bits out for us to use.'

Ira gestured impatiently. 'Suppose the wings fall off?' he said. 'Suppose the Wright Brothers had thought about wings falling off or pumps going? They'd never have got off the ground. Blériot wouldn't have got across the Channel. Alcock and Brown wouldn't have made it to Ireland. In this kind of flying, Sammy, you've got to take a risk somewhere. You can't expect guarantees.'

While Sammy was eyeing him, still not entirely convinced, Alix appeared, driving a hired car. As she edged it into the group of newspapermen outside the hangar, they pushed forward immediately and began to fire questions about Davis and Wooster at her. Her face was pale and set, but as she opened her mouth to answer Ira took her arm and whisked her towards the hangar, brusquely shoving the newsmen aside.

'Not here,' he said shortly to her from the side of his mouth.

'Everybody's just waiting to see us all getting the wind up. Let's get inside before we pull the cork out.'

She swung round as Sammy slammed the door behind them and stood with his back to it, watching them with sombre eyes. She seemed a little lost and out of her depth.

She made a nervous movement with her hand, the harsh excitable Alix of the night before lost again in one of the bewildering changes of personality that made up her character. 'Ira,' she said. 'Are we doing what's right? Trying to fly to France, I mean.'

Ira smiled. 'Plenty of other people seem to be thinking of doing it, too,' he reminded her.

She glanced at Sammy and Woolff by the door then she turned to Ira again. She had obviously been thinking the same thoughts that had occurred to them. 'But are we *advanced* enough to be doing it?' she said. 'Or are we trying it ten years too soon? We're not away yet from the wooden-hangar-cow-pasture-landing idea of flying. It's only two years since they court-martialled Billy Mitchell for believing in airplanes. We don't know much about instruments, and we don't know a damn thing about ocean-crossing.'

She was watching him with a tormented expression, as though for the first time she'd really stopped to consider the odds. 'Fonck's crew,' she said. 'Davis and Wooster. The way those guys flying the mail go in. Every other week there's one lost. For heaven's sake, Ira, I've never sat down and thought about it until now! It's like the casualty list for a battle!'

'Perhaps their luck was out,' Ira said.

'Suppose *yours* is out?'

Ira's eyes were sombre. The thought had occurred to him, too. For this project they were attempting, they were going to need all the good fortune they could muster. With the best aeroplane and the best motor in the world, with all the best preparations and the best organization, a little bad luck could still kill them. Head winds. Bad weather. A faulty spindle in a fuel pump. A speck of dirt or condensation in the petrol feed line. A sharp stone the wrong way up on the runway on take-off. There were a thousand things that had to fall neatly into line.

They were all a little like sailors on uncharted seas, all of them on a course that had never been traversed before, and though their knowledge was increasing with every test they made, they were still feeling their way—if not exactly in the dark, certainly not yet out of the shadows. None of them really knew what they could expect of their machines and, callous as it seemed, even the deaths of two men might add something to the accumulated knowledge of those still alive. They all accepted that neither Noel Davis nor Wooster would have begrudged them that.

He became aware that Alix was still watching him, her eyes burning with intensity. Over her shoulder he could see Sammy waiting, too, his back still against the door, his thin face peaked, and Woolff, his big cap sideways on his head as usual, his eyes troubled.

'Good luck's largely a matter of hard work and preparation,' he pointed out. 'There's nothing wrong with the aeroplane, and with the Viking pump instead of the Hughesden, there's nothing to stop the Whirlwind turning for its nine thousand hours. It's time we stopped worrying about luck and started thinking about infallibility, because *that's* what'll get us across the Atlantic, not mascots and crossed fingers and prayers.'

When the first shock had gone and realism had set in, Davis's death seemed to provide a good opportunity to study what might conceivably go wrong with their own aeroplane and Ira demanded that Loerner dig up every report on the crash he could lay his hands on.

Loerner looked puzzled at the request. 'Will it help any?' he asked.

Ira nodded. 'If they did something wrong,' he said, 'knowing what it was might stop *us* doing it, too.'

The dull weather persisted and, since it was clear there was to be no flying, they spent the day installing the new fuel pump and compass, and fitting a carburettor heater and the special thirty-by-eight tyres with strengthened walls which had arrived from Cleveland.

The late papers were still printing stories of the Hampton crash but the reports were unreliable and they were unable to get the facts straight until the following day when they gathered in the office and Loerner pushed typewritten sheets across the desk at them one after another.

It appeared now that a mixture of all the stories they'd heard made up the truth. There'd been discussion about the Pathfinder's chances for some time because, on his earlier flights in Pennsylvania, Davis had seemed to be a little dubious about his machine and had insisted on more complete tests, and the rumour that had been going the rounds that all was not well with it now seemed to be true. Although the Pathfinder was fast, when delivered from the factory it had been found to be over half a ton heavier than expected and every calculation that had been made about fuel had been thrown out.

When the final load tests had begun, full tanks had brought its weight up to almost a ton more than its engines had ever hoisted into the air before and, balanced on a pinpoint as the calculations were, it had been necessary to make a last check that the machine could lift the necessary weight before flying to New York for the trip to Europe.

As they had begun their run, however, the Pathfinder, like Fonck's machine, had moved far too slowly. It had taken the whole length of the field to gather sufficient speed and, even as it had lifted into the air, it was clear that its climb was not steep enough, and that the trees at the end of the runway, which it had cleared with ease on earlier unloaded flights, were going to be in the way. Davis had banked the machine to the right to avoid them but, poised only just above stalling as the over-loaded machine was, the turn had brought the speed down just too low and the nose had dropped. Davis had had to make a quick decision to set the machine down, but the land ahead of him had been marshy and the watchers had seen a huge splash as the big biplane had disappeared from sight.

They had started running at once, but they were too far away and, though the aeroplane was far from a total wreck, the nose was buried deep in water and soft wet soil and the big tanks behind the crew had moved and crushed the cockpit. Trapped and breathing fumes from spilt petrol, Davis and Wooster had died of suffocation and drowning.

Ira listened grave-faced as Loerner gave him the facts.

'This makes you front-runner,' the publicity man ended soberly. 'Chamberlin's not decided yet whether he's taking a radio or not and there's talk of more trouble between him and Levine.'

Ira frowned. 'There's still Byrd,' he reminded. 'He's got his arm out of plaster now.'

Loerner gestured. 'Byrd!' he snorted. 'They're saying in the newspaper offices that he doesn't want to go until he's seen it can be done.'

'Perhaps one or two newspapermen would like the job instead,' Ira growled. 'As four men have been killed so far in this little circus, maybe he's just being sensible.'

All the same, the situation *had* changed radically, he knew, and he studied the little red monoplane with worried eyes.

'What's eating you, Ira?' Sammy asked.

Ira rubbed his nose. That morning he had walked the length of the runway on Roosevelt Field, noting the dips and hollows and the rough patches that might damage an overloaded under-carriage, and he had discovered that the winds across Long Island had a strange habit of changing direction. Mostly they blew from the south-west during the daytime, so that a take-off would be over the hangars and blocks of houses, but if they could be ready before daylight and get off before the night-time wind changed, they would have a clear lift over fields and a golf course, with only a set of telephone wires to worry about.

He turned to Sammy and grinned. 'Maybe I ought to have done what my father did,' he said. 'And started building my own planes. It'd have been safer and I might have been wealthy now.'

Sammy jeered. 'You'd miss the excitement.'

Ira shrugged. He had a feeling that the excitement of aviation was probably already gone, just as the joy of seafaring had gone with the passing of the sailing ships. Intuition and instinct—the knowledge of where inspiration began and impulse left off—which had been as important to the first of the men who had braved the air as it had been to ships' captains like his own grandfather, with their sense of wind and weather, were being slowly thrust aside by invention and by small bright numbered dials and quivering needles. The mystique was already fading because the day was approaching when the sky between continents would be as familiar to man as the route marks along the highways, when instruments would be more important than instinct, and pilots would be merely men who could understand the banks of coloured switches.

He drew a deep breath. 'I'm getting sentimental, Sammy,' he grinned. 'Perhaps it's a sign of age.'

Since the party, Courtney had not been near the hangar. Several times they had rung his apartment without success, and now, with a dozen small technical queries cropping up, they were informed he was in Washington and had left no forwarding address.

Woolff became indignant. 'I'd have said his place was right here on the field,' he pointed out.

Alix glanced at Ira. 'He asked me last night if I'd like a bigger share in the Courtney,' she said slowly.

Ira looked at her quickly. 'And would you?'

She said nothing for a moment, then she raised her eyes to meet his. 'I said I would.'

Woolff looked worried. 'Can you raise the dough?' he asked.

'I can sell the bungalow at Medway.'

'Will you?'

She paused before answering. 'I guess maybe it would be a good idea if I did,' she said.

Courtney's continued absence and the need for money that had obviously prompted his offer to Alix was in the minds of all of them as they arranged for coffee and settled down to thrash out the problems implicit in the scribbles, in notebooks and on old envelopes and scraps of paper. Most of them were trivial in themselves but were surprisingly important when fitted into the whole.

'Instrument board lights, Ira,' Woolff said, striking a line through a note he'd made. 'Suppose we have a circuit failure? Nothing big but enough to stop you seeing your instruments.'

'How about a torch?'

'I'll get a couple at the five-and-dime.'

'I guess we can still afford something better than that,' Alix said. 'I'll buy 'em.'

'O.K.' Woolff glanced down at his notes again. 'That miniature radio Loerner came up with.' He grinned. 'I looked into it. The guy's a crank.'

'I thought he might be,' Ira said.

Woolff shrugged. 'So do we carry a radio?' he asked. 'Byrd's got one. He's even got a waterproof one as well in case they ditch, and a kite to carry the aerial, and an automatic sending device in case they're all knocked unconscious.'

'He's also got a distiller in case they run out of water,' Ira pointed out. 'And three weeks' rations in case they're in the sea that long. Let's concentrate on the possibilities of flying, not ditching. But since we're on the subject, how about getting a rope net put over the rubber raft? If we *do* have to go in, it'll be like trying to scramble aboard an eel.'

'O.K.' Woolff's pencil moved across his notebook, then he

looked up. 'How about getting the *Dixie* from Curtiss Field to Roosevelt Field for the take-off?'

'Fly it,' Alix said at once.

Woolff looked dubious. 'It'd waste a lot of time,' he said. 'We'd have to wait for daylight and we couldn't risk flying her with the tanks full. We'd have to fill her up after she arrived. It'd delay us.'

'What's the alternative?' Ira asked. 'We can't taxi her across. There's a bank in the way and, loaded, she'd burn the engine out, anyway.'

Woolff rubbed his nose. 'It's only a little bank,' he said. 'We could make it if we were careful. We could maybe arrange a tow and manhandle her up the bank. It'd save waiting for daylight.'

Ira nodded. 'Sounds sense,' he said. 'Let's look into that, Hal.'

'O.K.' Woolff made another tick on his pad. 'When do we check the compasses, by the way? The Pioneer man, Goldsborough, says he's ready any time.'

'Let's make it this afternoon. We'll check the carburettor heater at the same time.'

As Woolff sat back, Sammy looked up. 'Mail,' he said, stubbing out his cigarette. 'There was a bloke here yesterday offering a thousand dollars for us to carry a bag of letters to Paris. Stamped "First Atlantic Flight" or something. He says they'll be worth a fortune in a year or two's time.'

'Providing we make it,' Ira pointed out dryly. 'How much do they weigh?'

'He said around a pound.'

'Seems reasonable. Who gets the money?'

'You do,' Alix said. 'I checked with Lave Boyle. Newspapers and book publishers'll be falling over themselves for the story, too, and there'll be prizes from oil companies and fees for goodwill tours and personal appearances. You could make two hundred and fifty thousand dollars with luck.'

Ira chuckled. 'Let's make it two hundred and fifty-one and then we can take over some of the money *you've* invested. Tell him we'll take a limited number, Sammy.'

Sammy nodded and glanced down at his notebook. 'Another bloke,' he said. 'Yesterday. Rang to see if we'd be photographed in front of a cigarette advert. To advertise the cigarette. They're willing to pay a lot of money.'

'Do we smoke 'em?'

'No. But he said it didn't matter.'

'How about Byrd's offer of his runway?' Woolff asked. 'He said that we could have the same facilities as the Bellanca people.'

'I'll go and see him and thank him. We might be glad of it.'

'Fine,' Woolff nodded. 'How about his ramp? He says they're having one to give 'em a flying start.'

Ira grinned. 'Sounds about as safe as detachable under-carriages. Let's leave it.' He pushed at his notebook, frowning. 'I still wish we could have had the fuel tank forward of the pilot's seat,' he said slowly.

'You couldn't,' Sammy pointed out. 'How would you see?'

'This Ryan they're building in San Diego's supposed to have its tank forward,' Ira said. 'Chamberlin heard they were going to fly it with a periscope.'

Sammy gave a derisive snort. 'You can't fly an aeroplane with no forward view!'

'No,' Ira said thoughtfully. 'Not unless you've thought of a way of doing it first.'

The discussion finished, they set about deciding their final route. They removed all the superfluous paper from the charts and glued them together in a long sheet so that they could simply unroll them as they progressed across the Atlantic from west to east. Their efforts to draw a weather chart proved more difficult, however, because the information they were able to collect about the North Atlantic was erratic and none too reliable.

Later in the day, Loerner arrived with a flood of mail, and Ira and Sammy began to compete with each other over the offers of marriage.

'One here,' Sammy said, grinning, 'that says if I won't have her, will you?'

Loerner also brought half a dozen showgirls with him and posed them in front of the Courtney. His stunts always seemed to lean far more heavily on girls than aviation.

'Can they fly?' Sammy asked, staring at them with interest.

'Hell, no!' Loerner gave him a pitying look. 'But you've got to have girls! Everybody has girls! Who wants to look at a guy with spats and a fedora just because he's an official of the Aero-nautical Society. You have to be a live-wire in this game. People want legs. We need ballyhoo. Everybody else's got ballyhoo. It can make a football player into a national figure. It lifted

Babe Ruth to the level of the president. We don't need *less* girls. We need *more*—together with a band and maybe some bathing beauties in one-piece suits.'

None of the girls he produced knew anything about aeroplanes, however, and most of them couldn't have cared less. Only one of them, by the name of Mae Minter, showed enough interest to want to look inside the engine and watched while Sammy struggled to get a screwdriver round an awkward corner.

'Try a nail file,' she suggested, digging into her handbag. 'My Pa was a mechanic. He often used one.'

When the suggestion worked, Sammy pocketed the file and promptly made a date with her.

'She's bright, Ira,' he said. 'Reads books.' He grinned. 'I once read a book myself.' He looked sideways at Ira. 'She's got a friend,' he said. 'How about it? There'll be flying tomorrow.'

Unfortunately the friend wasn't in the same class as Mae Minter for intelligence, and when she claimed to know a restaurant where they wouldn't be recognized she turned out to be over-optimistic, too. As they emerged on to the wet streets a flash-gun popped at once.

'Romance, Captain?' the photographer yelled. 'What happened to Alix Courtney?'

Their pictures were in the tabloids the following morning, cut down and rearranged in a more cosy grouping and, somewhat surprisingly, it brought Alix Courtney down to the field in a hurry. They were bending over the desk in the office when she appeared, going through the demands for autographs and photographs, and the offers of advice, business propositions, religious tracts and bibles.

She threw the paper on to the desk, her face white, and Ira stared down at his own face with that of Sammy and the two showgirls outside the restaurant.

'If we've got to have publicity,' she said harshly, 'we might as well have *good* publicity.'

Ira looked up at her, saying nothing, and her face reddened and twisted bitterly.

'I'll go if I embarrass you,' she snapped.

He got to his feet quickly and, pushing her into a chair, thrust a cigarette at her. The anger died out of her face abruptly, to be replaced by a desperate appeal that made her look like a schoolgirl suddenly.

'Did you enjoy your night out?' she asked in a low voice, her eyes not meeting his.

'No,' Ira said.

Sammy looked indignant, but before he could protest, Ira went on. 'It just happened,' he said. 'It wasn't planned. The photographers did the rest.'

She gave a shrug, changing step quickly. 'Damn newspapermen,' she said. 'Give 'em a chance, they'll louse everything up.'

She fiddled clumsily with her cigarette. 'It didn't matter,' she went on, a shade unconvincingly. 'I didn't come down here because of that.'

'No?'

'No. I thought you'd like to hear I've got a buyer for your story.' She paused, then she continued in a brittle, unsteady voice, her arrogance melting to unhappiness: 'Loerner wanted to sell to one of the respectable dailies Lave Boyle favoured. I went to the tabloids. They'll pay you six thousand, which is a hell of a lot more than Loerner was offered. I got Lave to fix a contract for you.'

'Win *or* lose?' Ira asked with a smile.

She gave him a quick, scared look. 'Win *or* lose,' she agreed. 'So long as I survive.'

She stared at him, her face expressionless, then she closed her eyes exhaustedly. 'So long as you survive,' she said, rising and pushing the chair back abruptly. 'And that's really all that matters.'

Sammy gazed after her as the door closed, then he looked at Ira. 'You know, old lad,' he said thoughtfully, 'she'd eat out of your hand if you wanted her to.'

Ira shrugged, already only too well aware of the dangerous currents of emotion that ran so violently through Alix Courtney, and Sammy went on hotly.

'You think being the owner makes her different?' he demanded.

'Not different. Just more complicated.'

Ira glanced through the window to where Alix was stalking in her long stride across the hangar floor. As she pushed through a group of mechanics standing in the doorway, a man in an overcoat and hat spoke to her, but she brushed past him as though she hadn't even seen him.

'She's got it bad,' Sammy pointed out. 'She's in love. It's pretty simple.'

Ira shook his head. 'She's as simple as Lucrezia Borgia,' he said. 'Come off it, Sammy. You make her sound as frail as a pressed rose. She knows flying and she's as tough as Old Nick's nag nails.'

Sammy snorted. 'Women are never *that* tough,' he said shortly.

He turned back to his work and there was an awkward silence in the office for a while, then the door opened and the man they'd seen in the hangar stood in the entrance, smiling at them. It was a moment or two before Ira's frown vanished.

'Cluff!' he said.

Sammy looked up, his eyes smouldering. His glance was clearly intended to turn the newcomer into Lot's wife there and then. He'd always insisted Ira had taken the wrong partner in Africa and he'd never forgiven Cluff for the indifference that had ruined their first venture into business and the insistence on his share of what was left that had almost beggared them.

Cluff stepped into the office, his expression embarrassed, and Ira noticed that his too-good-looking features had thickened a little, as though he'd been drinking a lot. He had a double chin now and his blond hair had suddenly begun to thin, and somehow there was a look about him of a man who had not found life easy. He'd never been a very determined or resourceful man and the old machines and tenuous finances with which they'd tried to run their airline in Africa had persuaded him that hanging on by the skin of the teeth wasn't much of a life.

'Hello, Ira,' he said. 'They told me I'd find you here.'

Sammy had risen to his feet now, his face unrelenting, and Cluff pushed the conversation along awkwardly.

'I never thought when I walked out on you,' he said, 'that I was walking out on two chaps who were going to be famous.'

'We've a long way to go before that,' Ira pointed out. 'Three thousand six hundred miles to be exact.'

Sammy's eyes, still hostile, were on Cluff. 'What the hell are you doing here?' he said.

Cluff turned to Sammy, whose expression indicated that he expected the meeting to affect his pocket, and his mouth twisted in an embarrassed grin. 'There was nothing much in England so when I married Dulcie we went to Canada. There wasn't much in Canada either, though, so I went back to flying. Up in the north. But it was too bloody cold. If you didn't drain the oil within five minutes of landing, nothing on God's green earth would get you off before spring. Ira, I want to ask you a favour.'

Knowing Cluff's nature, Ira half-expected it to be a request for a loan.

'When I saw your name in the paper,' Cluff went on, 'I thought it couldn't possibly be you because the last I saw of you, you were wondering how to pay the bills.' He paused, glancing at him. 'Look, let's go and find a hotdog stand. Somewhere we can talk.'

They drove unwillingly to the airfield diner and Ira noticed that Cluff allowed them to pay for the coffee without argument.

'O.K.,' he said. 'What's the mystery?'

Cluff grinned. 'Ira, *I'm* going to have a shot at the Atlantic, too.'

Sammy's sudden movement slopped coffee to the table, and he began to dab it up with a rag from his pocket.

'*You* are?' Ira said.

'You think I could?'

It didn't require a second's thought for Ira to doubt it. Cluff had never had the patience to plan anything well. Nevertheless, married, he might have changed, and Ira answered cautiously.

'Maybe you could,' he said. 'If you worked at it hard enough.'

Cluff gestured. 'Dulcie's in it with me. And I've got a Canadian engineer called Pelletan. We've all put every cent we've got into it.'

Sammy had hardly spoken until now, and as he stuffed his rag away, he studied Cluff for a long time, his eyes contemplative.

'You know what you're doing, I suppose?' he asked.

'Sure,' Cluff grinned. 'It's make or break, this time, Sammy.'

'What you got?'

Cluff gave an embarrassed smile. 'Well, she was a Bréguet but I'd call her more of a Pelletan-Cluff now. She had no engine so we made modifications and rebuilt her to save money. We got a second-hand Hispano-Suiza motor.'

'You'd be better with a new one,' Sammy grunted.

'It's not done many hours,' Cluff shrugged. 'And we couldn't afford a new one. It took nine thousand dollars to build her—everything we could scrape up.'

'When are you planning to take off?' Ira asked.

Cluff made a self-deprecatory gesture. 'That's what I want

to see you about, Ira. We've got nothing arranged for weather reports.'

'Why don't you see the Bureau here? They're helpful.'

'We're too far away.'

'How in God's name have you managed to keep it from the press?'

Cluff grinned. 'Most of the preparations were done in Canada. Up in the wilds. The press aren't quite the same there as they are here. When they did enquire, we put 'em off with a story that we were developing a mail plane.'

'And now?'

'Pelletan's got an uncle here, farming. He's got a bit of money.'

'Well, that's something. You need money.'

Cluff grinned. 'Unfortunately,' he said, 'he's no millionaire and we've gone as far as we can go.'

Ira studied him warily. 'Are you in need of money?'

Cluff grinned. 'Always,' he said. 'But you needn't look like a frightened stag. I don't want it from you. We've got enough, even if we've none to spare. We've done all we have to do. We're proposing to start at Newburgh, fly down here and pass over New York, and then on out to the Atlantic. That way it keeps it quieter. We flew her down from Toronto in one hop.'

'How far?' Sammy asked.

Cluff moved uncomfortably inside his clothes. 'Nothing really,' he said. 'Nothing like that trip you did from San Antonio. It's only three hundred and eighty miles or there-abouts.'

'Didn't you check?'

'We haven't got around to worrying about that yet. We're not ready. We need another week or two.'

Something in the way Cluff was talking worried Ira. 'Cluffy,' he said. 'Do you realize what you're taking on?'

'Yes, of course.'

'I wonder if you do. You're proposing to fly three thousand six hundred miles in a machine that's only done three hundred and eighty so far.'

'No!' Cluff gestured. 'We flew her from Quebec to Winnipeg, and Winnipeg to Toronto. Two legs—six hundred and fifty and five hundred and fifty. She gave us no trouble.'

'It's still not much,' Sammy said.

'It's make or break,' Cluff said again, and they sensed there was a touch of desperation behind his words.

'What can she lift?' Sammy asked. 'What fuel load?'

'Ton and a half. We worked it out.'

'I hope you did. It's a fine point of balance.'

Cluff smiled, a sad lonely smile. 'I *think* we did,' he said. He gestured with his coffee cup. 'I never thought I'd see you over here. I couldn't believe my eyes when I read your names. But I knew there couldn't be two people with a name as potty as Ira Abel Penaluna.'

Ira stared at him. 'Look, you haven't come out with it yet,' he said. 'What's it all about? Why did you come and see *me*?'

Cluff gestured. 'Well, there's no need to spread it across the face of the newspapers,' he said. 'But I know you and Sammy are pretty hot stuff as a team. I wondered if you'd come out and give my bus a try for me.'

Ira put his cup down. 'It's out of the question, Cluffy,' he said firmly. 'You must know that. I'm under contract to the Courtneys. I can't go around testing the opposition's machines for 'em.'

Cluff smiled. He seemed to smile a lot these days, as though he'd got used to smiling to get the things he needed.

'Of course,' he said. 'I see that. I didn't really expect you could. But there's nothing to stop you coming out and looking at it, is there? I mean, I know you've had a look at Byrd's plane and Byrd's had a look at yours. There's no harm in giving it the once-over, is there?'

CHAPTER NINE

THE CLOUD, wind and rain that continued to blanket the western fringes of the Atlantic left the hangar damp with a dampness that seemed to get into the bones. The gales brought on by the low-pressure area had finally cleared the coastline but they had left behind a fitful sunshine and layers of heavy low stratus that sprinkled the city with rain and took the light out of the day. Once they had checked and re-checked every nut and bolt, every screw, every wire and locking washer, every grease point, every cylinder and rocker arm, every valve spring, every instrument, there was no more they could do but put on an appearance of working whenever the press appeared, and the waiting for the weather to improve became intolerable.

Courtney had still not been to the hangar and the publicity antics that Loerner expected of them became a tedious bore. They had already shaken hands for the cameras with all kinds of celebrities from the designer of the engine they were to use, to Byrd and Chamberlin and Acosta, and the legendary Tony Fokker, a pink-faced smiling Dutchman like an overgrown schoolboy with his dimpled chin. René Fonck, back in America again for another try with the brand-new Sikorsky, appeared outside the hangar, small, dumpy, overcoated and spatted, a very different man from the slender young killer Ira had met nine years before during the war. He was older than Ira and now approaching the stage in life when a man ceased to have the lean and hungry look of youth, and he obviously didn't enjoy the reputation that his crash the previous autumn had hung around his name.

'This is more dangerous than war,' he said, jerking his hand at the gaping sightseers who'd turned up to stare. 'I think they come to see us die.'

He was probably not far wrong, because death wasn't far from anybody's mind since Davis's crash, and the newspapers seemed to hang on every test take-off and landing as though it were to be the last. Even the unknown contender in faraway San Diego came in for his share of morbid expectancy.

Captain Charles A. Lindbergh, former airmail pilot, narrowly escaped disaster when the plane he is grooming for a transatlantic flight almost collided with a Curtiss Hawk fighter from North Island. . . .

'Any comments, Captain?' A pressman pounced on them as soon as they put their noses out of the hangar.

'Well, he certainly got off the ground with his periscope,' Ira grinned.

They allowed a few of the more responsible newspapermen into the aeroplane, Sammy explaining the workings of the big Wright Whirlwind while Ira described the instruments they were proposing to use, their fuel consumption, their cruising speed, and the difficulties they'd had in overcoming the problem of lifting their vast load of petrol.

'What about measuring drift, Captain?'

'Smoke bombs,' Ira explained. 'They ignite on contact with water.'

'How about navigation lights?'

'I don't think we'll need them over the Atlantic. There won't be much traffic.'

'Any special visual aids?'

'Only Mark I eyeballs.'

'You'd better get going soon, Captain,' one of the newsmen said, 'or you'll be too late. This guy in San Diego sounds pretty hot stuff and Nungesser's repaired the damage he got from that hangar fire he had. There's a story around that he's on his way any hour.'

They were still clambering in and out of the machine when Courtney arrived at last with Boyle. He looked ten years older, and surprisingly grey-faced. He walked round the aeroplane and sat in the cockpit for the pressmen to take photographs, all the time with a forced smile on his lips and a cigar clamped between his teeth. When the pressmen had gone, he motioned with his head to the office and it was only then that Ira noticed that with him there was a stout middle-aged man in rimless pince-nez who clutched a brief-case to his chest.

Courtney pulled out a chair and sat down with a slow heavy movement, staring sombrely at Ira for a long moment.

'This is Joe Hughesden, Ira,' he said at last. 'Hughesden Instruments. He wants to talk to you about that pump.'

Ira's brows came down over his eyes. 'Has the pump design been altered, Felton?' he asked.

'No need.' The man with the pince-nez gestured. 'Hughesden pumps are the finest in the world.'

'My information's different,' Ira pointed out. 'I think you can save your breath, Mr Hughesden.'

Hughesden held up one finger. 'Listen to me, young man . . .' he began in an arid professional voice.

Ira interrupted him sharply. 'Mr Hughesden, can you fly an aeroplane?'

Hughesden looked startled. 'No,' he said.

'Then I'm not interested.'

Hughesden frowned. 'Young man, this is business, not flying. My lawyer will be coming to talk to you.'

'*He* can save his breath, too, Mr Hughesden. I'm not in the habit of using an interpreter when I'm talking English.'

Hughesden turned to Courtney. 'Felton, see here. . . .'

Courtney made a weary gesture with his hand. 'Hell, Joe, you can see what Ira thinks!'

'He hasn't even listened to me!'

'Mr Hughesden,' Ira said. 'We had a Hughesden pump on the *Dixie* when we left Medway. By the grace of God, we got to San Antonio instead of coming down in the middle of the desert somewhere. I don't take chances like that twice. The Wright engineers advise me to use a Viking. I'm using a Viking.'

Hughesden stared at him, scowling. 'You may eat your words before long, young man,' he said, then he turned, scowled at Courtney and vanished from the hangar.

Ira stared after him, aware of Courtney alongside him searching for words of explanation.

'Ira . . .' he managed, then he stopped, slammed on his hat and set off after Hughesden. He looked defeated. Boyle gave Ira a sharp questioning look then he, too, reached for his hat and followed.

Sammy grinned. 'Well that sent *him* off with a fine old flea in his ear,' he commented.

Ira shrugged. 'I'm not so sure, Sammy,' he said. 'He didn't strike me as the sort of man to have people talking to him like I did.' He frowned. 'What did he mean by that bit about my "eating my words"? And what the hell is Courtney up to?'

'You think he *is* up to something?'

'I'm damn sure he is! He wouldn't have produced Hughesden otherwise. It might pay us to get Alix to make a few enquiries.'

As it happened, it proved unnecessary. The following morning, they were busy by the plane, checking their lists and going over their final arrangements for departure, when Alix Courtney's hired car arrived, swinging round the hangar and coming to a stop with a screech of brakes and a scattering of gravel. Her brows were down and her mouth was tight. Woolff carefully put down the spanner he'd been using and turned to meet her as she climbed from the driving seat, but she ignored his greeting, slamming the car door behind her angrily and heading straight past him, as though he didn't exist.

Stopping in front of Ira, she lit a cigarette with shaking fingers and jerked a hand at the Courtney. 'Put that third seat back in her,' she snapped. 'I'm flying with you.'

For a long time, they stood staring at each other, then Hal Woolff came up behind her and touched her arm.

'Alix, for God's sake . . . !'

She wrenched her arm away from him, her face pale with fury, her eyes like a black explosion.

'I said, put that third seat back, Hal,' she insisted, her voice full of shrill metallic urgency. 'I'm flying to Europe with her.'

For a moment, Ira studied her face without saying a word

then he jerked his head at Woolff. 'Close the doors, Hal,' he said quietly. 'There'll be no press visits today. We aren't on view.'

Woolff stared at him for a second, then at Alix Courtney. Sammy touched his arm.

'O.K., Ira,' he said as they turned away.

Without another word, Ira took hold of Alix's arm and began to lead her towards the office, aware of the warmth of her flesh between his fingers, and the surprising fragility of her. She glanced up at him, her black eyes raging, and tried to snatch her arm away, but he refused to release her and she found herself almost running alongside him.

'Where's your knout?' she said, her words bitten off short by fury.

Ira ignored her, and pushing open the office door, almost threw her into the chair. Then, seeing the agony in her eyes, he relented enough to offer his cigarette packet and jerk his lighter out. Angry, she looked younger than ever and with an incandescent loveliness that made his heart thump suddenly in his chest. For a while, as she dragged at the smoke, furious and wretched, he said nothing, waiting until the hangar doors rumbled together.

'Now,' he said, turning to face her. 'What the hell's all this about?'

For a long time she didn't answer, dragging at her cigarette as though her life depended on it, then the words tumbled out in an angry torrent. 'I'm going with you,' she said. 'I've made up my mind and I'm going, and nobody, not even you, is going to stop me.'

Ira rounded on her, angrily. 'I've already told you once why you can't!' he snapped.

Standing by the Courtney in the hangar, Sammy and Woolff watched the scene through the windows of the office, Sammy's face blank and unemotional as he saw Alix screw her cigarette to fragments in the ashtray and stand up, her face close to Ira's, her cheeks pale, her eyes blazing. Then, suddenly, she turned away and threw herself into the chair again, the fury fading from her face. He could see the glisten of tears on her eyelashes.

'Ira,' she was saying. 'He's sold out to Hughesdens!'

It was a moment or two before what she was trying to tell him penetrated Ira's anger.

'Sold out to Hughesdens?' he said. 'What the hell do you mean, sold out to Hughesdens?'

'That's what it was all about!' She turned away to fish another cigarette from a packet in her pocket. 'That's what all the mystery was about over those instruments,' she choked. 'He's sold out. I'm not staying here a day longer than I need. I'm coming as a passenger.'

Ira looked up. 'Not if I say you're not!' he pointed out.

'A lot of my dough's in that plane'—she sat up furiously, her anger returning—'and it tells me that *you* can't say I can't.'

Ira held on to his temper. 'Alix, listen,' he said. 'We've spent two months working on that machine, working out load charts, testing every scrap of equipment so she'll take off with a loaded weight of two and a half tons.'

'I only weigh a hundred and twelve pounds. It won't make any difference.'

'It might make all the difference in the world!'

'You've got a safety margin!'

Ira gestured, slicing the air with the flat of his hand. 'I didn't plan to take you with me,' he said. 'And I don't intend to. And, for God's sake, who's *is* the bloody plane now?—ours or Hughesdens'?'

The question seemed to halt her fury. 'It's still ours,' she said in a shaky voice.

Ira stared at her, puzzled. 'Then what the hell difference does it make?' he said. 'Why *shouldn't* he sell out? Perhaps he wants to take it easy. You're always telling him to.'

She spoke slowly and carefully, as though he were too stupid to catch the import of her remarks. 'He's sold out his auto business,' she said. 'Everything he possessed in Boston. Not because he wants to take it easy. Not to please me. Because the old fool got himself in a mess.' She almost choked. 'He sold *my* stock, too. I hadn't much but it was enough. I hadn't got it tied up tight enough, though, and Joe Hughesden grabbed that, too. Pa's been overplaying his hand for years—ever since 1924. He brought out a new brake system and he thought he was going to make a killing. But the other companies said it was dangerous.'

'Was it?'

'No, it wasn't. But what they said stopped him selling. He ought to have got out then. I asked him to. But, instead, he put up prices to meet costs until he was selling his sedans for nearly three thousand dollars. It was too much, Ira. Nobody wanted them and he must have started borrowing. I guess he went on borrowing until nobody would lend him any more. He even tried in Medway. Medway, for heaven's sake! A piddling little place like that. And *they* turned him down, too!'

Ira had suddenly become cold and quiet. 'When did you find this out?' he said.

'Lave Boyle just told me,' she said, her voice breaking. 'He's been trying to put it off ever since he found out last night.'

Ira frowned. 'That's what he must have meant when he said Hughesdens might insist. Alix, where's your father now?'

'He's in Boston with Joe Hughesden. He's trying to raise money to save the property in Medway. He ought never to have built the *Dixie*, Lave said.'

'What about the aeroplane, Alix?'

She looked up at him and gulped back a sob. 'He didn't sell the aeroplane,' she said. 'I told you he didn't.'

Ira gestured angrily. 'I know that,' he said, 'but, for God's sake, when a man goes down, all his creditors start chasing him. The bills all come in at once. I know about it. It happened to me. I didn't have a thing left when they'd finished. If they don't get paid they might try to grab the *Dixie*. How much of it's still his?'

Her face had fallen and she had grown pale. 'Not much, I guess, now.'

Ira leaned over the desk, resting his weight on his hands. 'Alix,' he said, 'he's got to turn it over to you. And Lave Boyle's got to make sure any agreements you make are tied up so tight they can't be undone. You've been financing this plane for a long time, haven't you?' She lifted her head, her eyes moist. '*You* raised that two and a half he first offered when we decided to rebuild. You sold the Pierce Arrow, didn't you?'

She nodded miserably, all the fire gone from her.

'When he offered you that bigger share, did you take him up?'

'Yes. I sold the bungalow at Medway.'

'Could you raise the rest of the money to buy him out?'

She looked desperate. 'Ira, there's nothing left. I even sold some jewellery. It came to more than I could raise in cash.'

'What about his debts?'

She made a quick movement of her head. 'He's up to his ears. You're right about the bills. If they come in too fast I might not be able to meet them. We've got all the expenses of this hangar and the mechanics' wages.'

Ira straightened up. 'I'll help,' he said. 'I've got a little. So's Sammy. So's Hal. We can do without salaries. But, Alix, you've got to get hold of Boyle, and you've got to move fast. We've got to stop anyone else getting their hands on the *Dixie*.'

She looked at him with an agonized appeal in her eyes. 'I'd rather go with you, Ira,' she said. 'I'm serious. I've never asked favours of anybody where flying's concerned. I can do my share. I'm not afraid. I wasn't just a fare-paying passenger on the trip to San Antonio and up here.'

He took both her hands in his. 'No, Alix, you weren't,' he agreed earnestly. 'But we weren't fully loaded then either. When we take off from here it'll be slopping out of the vents. And you're going to have plenty to do in the next few days, anyway. You've got to find your father and Boyle and get them to turn the *Dixie* over to you completely because, by God, if he doesn't and we make it across the Atlantic, it won't be *you* who'll get whatever comes of it, it'll be Hughesdens or somebody else.'

She seemed to pull herself together with a jerk and managed a stiff smile. 'O.K., Ira,' she said. 'I'll do that. Then I guess I'll get a boat to Europe and meet you when you arrive.' She had recovered her self-possession at last and as she wrenched open the door she jerked her head with a sharp familiar motion to remove a lock of black hair from her eyes. It was the same movement that a half-tamed cornered mare would give as it prepared to bolt.

'Why in God's name didn't he tell us?' she said bitterly. 'Why didn't he give us a chance to organize something? As sure as God made little green apples with worms in them, I'll never forgive him for the way he handled this.'

The door slammed so hard behind her one of the panes fell to the concrete hangar floor with a tinkle of glass.

As she passed the Courtney, she paused for a moment, staring up at it, then her shoulders squared and she vanished from sight. They heard the roar of the hired car's engine starting up, then Ira jumped for the door and yelled across the hangar: 'Sammy!'

CHAPTER TEN

. . . Felton K. Courtney, owner and part-designer of Dixie, *transatlantic mount of Captain Ira A. Penaluna, has announced that he has unloaded all his interest in the Courtney Automobile Works at Boston, Massachusetts. With them, it is expected that the Courtney Aeronautical factory at Medway, South Carolina, goes too.*

Mr Courtney's daughter has stated that the Courtney transatlantic machine has been acquired by herself, Captain Penaluna, Harold Woolff, co-designer, and Sam Shapiro, co-pilot, but despite Miss Courtney's statement it now seems inevitable that its chances are very slender and that a take-off is most unlikely. Miss Courtney's name has recently been romantically linked to Captain Penaluna's. . . .

Sammy lay in bed, staring critically at the comment, then he threw the newspaper across to Ira. 'How's it feel to be in business again?' he asked. 'I'm looking forward to making my first million.' He grinned. 'Lave Boyle certainly got a move on.'

Ira was staring at the newspaper himself. His face gazed out at him with Courtney's and Alix's from among the glaring headlines on speakeasy raids, exposed love-nests and the doings of film stars, and as Sammy spoke he looked up. 'They don't give us much of a chance,' he said. 'They've written us off already.' His eyes brooded on the newspaper for a while then he crushed it into a ball.

'. . . romantically linked to Captain Penaluna's,' he snorted. 'They don't leave it alone, do they? I expect it was that creepy bastard Loerner.'

Sammy shrugged. 'Don't know what you're complaining about,' he said blandly.

Ira tossed the newspaper aside. 'I came over here to fly an aeroplane,' he said. 'Not to get hitched.'

Sammy pulled a face. 'Things don't always work out the way you expect,' he said.

He had hardly finished speaking when the telephone rang. It was Alix. She sounded in low spirits, as though she'd been crushed by the news of her father's disaster and hadn't recovered.

'Ira, I've seen Lave. It's all fixed.'

'It's in the paper.'

'It is?' She seemed surprised. 'He says he's fixed it so tight nobody will ever unfix it again.'

'Thank God for that!'

'How are we for money?'

'Hal says all the bills are paid. What did you end up with?'

'I ended up with a mortgage on the house on Long Island. It was the only thing I'd got left.' Her voice wavered uncertainly and she sounded as though she were trying to stop herself crying. 'Ira, do you think we pushed him into this when we insisted on going ahead with the *Dixie*?'

Ira paused. The thought had occurred to him, too. 'No, Alix,' he said slowly after a while. 'I don't. Five thousand dollars wouldn't have made much difference. Not to selling up the Boston factory.'

'It might have just made the difference between safety and disaster.' Her voice fell almost to a whisper. 'There's one other thing, Ira,' she went on. 'Lave says Hughesdens are still insisting. About the instruments, I mean.'

Ira's brows came down. 'They can't insist! The machine's *yours* now. How *can* they insist?'

'I don't know.' Her voice shook once more. 'I just hope to God the weather clears and you get away.'

The machine was as ready as it could be and the most they could do was check and re-check everything. The Wright engineers were standing by in case of a break in the weather and they had contacted the petrol and oil companies and the aeronautical association officials who would have to seal the tanks and instruments and fix the barograph in the cabin. Unfortunately, the weather still stubbornly refused to change and the Weather Bureau firmly refused to accept any responsibility.

'Not a chance,' they insisted. 'There's fog around Newfoundland and no sign of clearing over the Atlantic.'

Ira left the airfield early. After the first flurry of interest by the press over Courtney's statement they'd been left severely alone. They'd already been forgotten by a public that sought only success. No one believed that the machine had been salvaged from the ruin of the Courtney businesses. Courtney had crashed and it was already clear that everyone thought that their Atlantic machine had crashed, too. Ira was still angry when he got to the hotel and the fact that Sammy, certain of not being called for the flight, had arranged to meet Mae Minter, didn't help his ease of mind as he found himself alone to brood on his thoughts. During the early evening, he worked over his charts again, re-checking winds and headings, with a flask of strong coffee sent up from the restaurant by his side, and he was just sitting back, staring at the coast of Ireland, trying for the hundredth time to familiarise it, when the telephone rang. It was the hall porter.

'Captain'—he sounded excited—'you heard? Nungesser's off! He made it!'

Ira sat bolt upright. 'In *this* weather?'

The porter's voice rose. 'Seems it's O.K. in France,' he said. 'It was on the radio. They broke into a fight programme. He's passed Ireland and he's due here tomorrow.'

Ira turned in his chair to stare at the window. 'God help him,' he said soberly. 'How about getting a late paper for me?'

'I've got one, Captain. It's got something about him. I'll send it up. Hey, wait a minute'—the porter seemed to be laughing—'Mr Shapiro's just come in and he's got one in his hand. I guess he's heard the news too. He's just headin' for the elevator and, gee whiz—is—he—movin'—fast!'

Sammy was making double-quick time. Ira had hardly put the telephone down when the door burst open and he came running in.

'Ira,' he yelled. 'Nungesser's off!'

'I just heard from the hall porter.'

'You did?' For a moment, Sammy seemed disappointed, then he thrust out the newspaper he was carrying, the sheets crackling and falling apart as he tried to hold it with one hand and point to the smudged type with the other. 'Look! "Nungesser Over The Atlantic, *White Bird* Due In New York Tomorrow".'

Paris. May 8—As the sun rose above the horizon this morning, Captains Charles Nungesser and François Coli started their heavily overloaded Levasseur biplane, the White Bird, *rolling over the ground at Le Bourget aerodrome for the start of their transatlantic flight westward to New York. . . .*

Once, near Nancy on a visit to the French, Ira had been challenged by Nungesser to a mock dog-fight. He'd been older than Ira and already with his reputation made, but there had been no result because they'd been so evenly matched. Neither of them had been able to manœuvre his machine into a killing position, and they'd finally had to drop to earth with empty tanks.

'Monsieur Penaluna'—Nungesser's pronunciation of Ira's awkward name had sent the English visitors into fits of laughter—'I think we had better go to the bar and see if we can't drink each other under the table, because we shall never reach a decision this way.'

Ira drew a deep breath that was heavy with nostalgia. Now, with Coli, Nungesser was attempting something which had never been done before and it was impossible not to be impressed by his cold courage. Even to Ira, who was proposing to do it himself, the idea of flying through the anonymity of darkness, cutting themselves off deliberately from any hope of help, was chilling. Whatever prizes were at stake, they were still offering themselves as sacrifices to the future of a new form of transport which, despite the beliefs of the men involved in it, refused to budge from the realms of week-end sport. Nungesser's faith in it was implicit in the fact that he was not only flying against the prevailing wind, a decision which had necessitated carrying extra fuel and had therefore increased his risk on take-off, but that he was also chancing, at the end of his flight, a forced landing on the inhospitable iron-bound coast of Labrador instead of in Europe where he would nowhere have been far from rescue.

Sammy's thoughts were obviously following a similar path. 'It'd be nice if we could go out to meet 'em as they come in,' he said sombrely.

His words brought Ira to earth with a bump. 'We probably couldn't afford the petrol until we've got our affairs straightened out,' he said.

Sammy looked at him shrewdly. 'How much did you put into it, Ira?' he asked.

Ira gave him an embarrassed grin. 'All I've got,' he said.

Sammy stared. '*All you've got?* Why? Because, if you hadn't, Alix would have gone bust, too?'

Ira nodded. 'I suppose so,' he agreed. 'How about you? How much did you risk?'

Sammy laughed. 'All *I've* got,' he said. 'For the same reason.'

They grinned at each other. 'Talking about girls,' Ira said, 'I thought you had a date.'

Sammy chuckled. 'I did,' he admitted. 'But this is bigger than a date. It's all right,' he explained. 'Mae understands.'

Ira gestured. 'You ought to marry that girl, Sammy,' he advised. 'You're one of God's chosen few. And now, if we've got any bathtub gin left, how about having a drink to Nungesser?'

The first thing they did on waking the following morning was to telephone the Weather Bureau. 'Not yet,' they were told.

'Nungesser's off,' Ira pointed out sharply.

'He's taking a chance, Captain,' the voice at the other end of the line said patiently. 'We've promised to let you know. There's a high-pressure area moving up O.K., but it's slow.'

Slamming down the telephone, Ira went for the newspaper and his heart leapt as he saw the headlines. Nungesser was already across the Atlantic, it seemed. A destroyer had sighted his great white machine off Cape Race, Newfoundland, heading towards New York.

Sammy switched on the radio and they caught the announcer in excited mid-sentence '. . . believed to have passed Nova Scotia already and to be heading for Portland, Maine. Crowds are already beginning to gather at the Battery for a good view of the French fliers when they put down in New York harbour. . . .'

Sammy stared at Ira, his eyes alight. 'By God, Ira,' he said. 'I'm glad *somebody* did it, even if it wasn't us!'

No work was done anywhere that day, as the whole of New York waited for the arrival of the Frenchmen. Blond, good-looking, fantastically brave in the finest French tradition, Nungesser's headlong spirit appealed to the American nation. He had been the darling of Paris society when he'd been invited to the States by the Aero Club of America, and he'd taken advantage of the visit to get himself engaged to a New York heiress before he'd left for home. The fact that the marriage had ended in divorce had never caused any cooling-off of affection.

The two aviators—Coli, with a patch over a destroyed eye, Nungesser with his scars and the platinum plates his wounds had necessitated in jaw, knee and foot—had a stature that was heroic. Not only the French nation's hopes rode with them in their big white biplane, but also the hopes of the Americans who were generously unpartisan about the result.

On every street corner, men and women were studying the headlines, and all over Curtiss Field, officials, pilots, mechanics, petrol-truck drivers and chauffeurs were crowding round radios to listen to the news flashes. The weather had not come up to expectations and the high-pressure area that had been expected to help Nungesser had not yet materialized. In the end, fighting the sleet and the head winds all the way with the Frenchmen, Ira borrowed a radio which Woolff set up in the office in the hangar, trailing a wire through the window and over a nail outside to make an aerial, and they all stopped work every time a programme was interrupted for an announcement.

First the white machine was reported at Portland, and then over Boston, and Woolff grinned.

'They're making good time,' he said.

During the morning, with Sammy out trying to find the latest newspaper, Boyle arrived with a shaken Courtney, bringing a folder of papers to sign. Courtney looked exhausted and grey-faced and, as he hooked forward a chair with one foot and sat down, Ira had the strange impression that it was a different man inside Courtney's skin, doing all the things Courtney did, looking like Courtney, but still someone else, someone who was curiously flat and diminished and like an old photograph of himself.

'I'm glad it's over, Ira.' His booming voice sounded oddly cracked. 'I'm only sorry it took so long because it looks as though it's probably too late now. Nungesser's almost here and you're landed with a plane that's broken no records. Just a plane.'

Ira shrugged. 'She's a good one,' he said.

Courtney moved his shoulders wearily. 'I didn't expect this, Ira, when I brought you over here,' he said. 'God knows I never expected this. I thought the *Dixie* would pull me out of trouble, but it came up on me too fast.'

'Forget it, Felton,' Ira said.

Courtney seemed in the mood to unburden himself. He appeared to feel weighed down with guilt and needing to explain. 'They were pushing me, Ira,' he said. 'I'd got myself in a hopeless mess. Hughesdens have cleared all my business debts and squared me away with enough to live on, but I guess the field and the house at Medway'll have to go.' He looked at Hal. 'It's a lousy way to tell a guy he's out of a job.'

Woolff managed a smile. 'I don't need a job, Mr Courtney,' he said. 'Not now. I own part of an aeroplane. A good one, too. We've only to get her across and we're all in the money. Even if we're not first.' He looked puzzled and worried for a moment, then went on quickly: 'Hughesdens can't *really* insist on us using their damn pump, can they?'

Courtney went red and slammed his hand down on the desk. 'No, by God, they can't!' he said. 'Sure as hell they can't! I let 'em try in the hope they'd hold off a while longer but when you said "No", they pulled the plug on me. But there's no contract that I ever signed with them that allows them to put their damned instruments on the *Dixie*. None at all!' He gestured angrily. 'I wish to God I'd never gone in for this stupid competition,' he said bitterly. 'I might have raised the dough to square Hughesdens and the bank then.'

Boyle's heavy head lifted. 'Forget it, Felton,' he growled in his old cracked voice. 'Stop kidding yourself. The house and the airfield and everything you have down at Medway wouldn't have settled *your* debts. The house's a white elephant and the airfield consists of a strip of land that no one wants—not even for building—a few sheds that are falling apart, and a few planers, sanders and sewing machines. A few thousand dollars altogether.'

'The *Dixie* would have saved us,' Courtney insisted.

Boyle wasn't impressed. 'Until she's flown the Atlantic,' he said, 'the *Dixie*'s nothing but a few steel tubes and a roll of canvas fitted to some other guy's motor. Twenty thousand dollars' worth. You needed more than that, Felton.'

Courtney stared at him and, as he rose to his feet angrily, his chair fell over backwards. Woolff moved forward to pick it up but Courtney brushed blindly past him so that the chair went down again and Woolff staggered. As he vanished, Woolff shook his head.

'He sure isn't the man he used to be,' he said.

Boyle shrugged. 'I wonder if he ever was,' he said slowly. 'He could build cars but he sure as hell couldn't carry corn. When he made any dough he always spent it instead of putting it back in the outfit.'

'He'll come back,' Woolff said loyally.

Boyle shook his head. 'Not him,' he said. 'He's in the tumbril. He's finished. He's tired. He's worn out. There's nothing left. He's been carrying too much for too long. That's why, when it fell apart, it fell apart quickly.' He shrugged. 'At least they didn't get the *Dixie*. There's no chance of that now.'

'And no chance of Hughesdens insisting on our using their instruments?' Ira asked.

Boyle was pulling papers from his attaché case and he looked up slowly. 'I didn't say that,' he said.

'You mean they *can*?' Woolff asked.

Boyle tossed the papers to the desk. 'I don't know whether they can,' he said. 'Felton says they can't—you heard him—but they're talking mighty damn big! They think they'd make big profits if you pulled this thing off.'

Ira turned away angrily. 'With a Hughesden pump, we might not pull it off,' he said.

Boyle grinned. 'There's one thing,' he said.

'What's that?'

'If the weather breaks and you go, they sure as hell can't bring you back.'

'Mr Boyle!' Ira smiled. 'A lot of the point's gone out of that now. The *Dixie* would be just another plane that made it. I wouldn't be the *first*. Nungesser's across already.'

The old man looked up, then he bent over his paper again quickly. 'You'd still make a profit,' he said shortly. 'Even if not a big one. Now let's get down to signing these papers. Where's Shapiro? He jumps about like a flea on a dog's back.'

Even as he spoke, they saw Sammy running across the hangar, flourishing a newspaper.

'Nungesser's been seen!' he was shouting. 'Over the mainland! Over Portland and heading for Boston! It's definite! They'll be here this afternoon!'

It was a feat worth getting excited about and Ira's anger evaporated at once. There was no feeling of envy or frustration in him, no feeling of disappointment that they'd been beaten, only the same high sense of elation that was felt everywhere on Curtiss Field.

'I'm glad they've done it,' he said sincerely. 'If only to shove out the noses of all those people who said it *couldn't* be done.'

He turned to the charts of the Atlantic, measuring distances with the span of his hand and working out speeds and times in his head, then he paused and frowned. He looked round at Sammy, suddenly concerned, and saw Boyle's tired eyes on him, dubious and sceptical.

'Sammy,' he said slowly. 'It seems early. I wonder if these reports are genuine.'

'They must be,' Sammy said enthusiastically, tossing the newspaper at him. 'It's there in print, isn't it?'

Ira tossed the newspaper back at him. 'Sammy, they say I'm "romantically linked" with Alix.'

Sammy's expression changed. 'You think it might not be true?'

Ira gazed at the sky through the window. 'The Weather Bureau says there are head winds and fog round Newfoundland,' he pointed out. 'And their high's vanished.' He shrugged, putting the uneasy thoughts from his mind. 'Perhaps it's just that Nungesser's faster than anybody thought,' he ended.

Sammy grinned again, his doubt dispersed. 'Clarence Chamberlin says he's going out to escort 'em in,' he said. 'He says the city's preparing the biggest welcome there's ever been.'

*　　　*　　　*

As the day wore on, the headlines grew more excited. Nungesser had been seen over Maine and Newburgh and was finally said to have appeared low over Boston, just to the north of New York.

Down at the Battery and along the piers down the Hudson and East Rivers, the crowds were gathering. Fire-float crews were standing by and the coastguard cutters by the Staten Island Ferry were manned to pick up the two airmen and tow their machine to safety when they landed. But as evening approached, no further reports came in. Nungesser had not yet reached Rhode Island or Connecticut, and now, it seemed, the report that he'd been seen over Boston had turned out to be false.

No one felt like going home. The news of the arrival of the *White Bird* would inevitably reach the airport first and everyone hung about the hangars long after the estimated time of arrival.

'Head winds,' Sammy said in a flat voice. 'They'll have been delayed.'

But there was a strange gap in time. If Nungesser and Coli had passed Newfoundland early in the morning, they'd already completed the worst of their journey and there ought to have been confirmed reports of their appearance somewhere over the American continent. The *New York Times* was suddenly running sober stories that seemed to refute all the earlier sightings, because no one, it seemed now, had ever clearly seen the Frenchmen after they'd left Ireland and if they had, in fact, crossed the Atlantic, they would inevitably have made for the safety of the land and should have been over Maine by the early afternoon.

In the early evening they drove from Long Island over the Queensboro Bridge and down to the Battery through the deep lanes of the Forties, already lined with taxis found for the night spots. Round the J. P. Morgan building, the Stock Exchange and the government offices there were big cars, small cars, new cars and old cars, even one or two horsed carriages, and Battery Park was thick with people lining the water's edge. Faces were growing anxious in the gloom.

Ira stared at the sky in the growing darkness, then he cocked his head and tried to listen for the drone of an engine over the noise of the traffic and the anxious voices all round him. He didn't expect to hear it. He had waited in the past on too many aerodromes for too many missing aeroplanes to return.

'Come on, Sammy,' he said, turning away at last. 'I don't like wakes.'

Part 3: The Flight

CHAPTER ONE

NUNGESSER WAS LOST. The newsboys were shouting 'Extra' on the corners and the newspapers were printing headlines which one minute said he'd been picked up and the next said he hadn't. The Navy was still scouring the silent northern waters for the great white-painted biplane, but there was already something of a funeral oration about the stories the press were carrying now.

The two airmen had said goodbye to their relatives and friends in the earliest light of the day and, as the first grey glow gave them their route, they had climbed from an open touring car into the *White Bird* in front of thousands of Parisians who had been making their way all night to Le Bourget to see them off. As the motors had started, they had posed for photographs in their heavy flying kit, but as they had climbed into their seats all that could be seen of them had been the tops of their heads in the open cockpit.

There had been silence and tears as the *White Bird* had begun its run. News had not long been in, that a compatriot, St Romain, was missing with two companions while trying to fly the South Atlantic from the bulge of Africa, and Nungesser's attempt had seemed to most of the crowd like self-immolation. His machine weighed almost five and a half tons and its speed was surprisingly low. The crowd had gasped as Nungesser had made his first attempt to lift it into the air.

The wheels had risen only a few feet before the heavy aeroplane had banged down again on to its bulging tyres, but after another three hundred yards, three-quarters of a mile from their starting point, Nungesser had at last managed to get it off the ground and it had disappeared from the sight of the crowd towards the west, climbing slowly, agonizingly slowly, up to three hundred feet. Five hours later, its detachable undercarriage discarded, it had been firmly sighted off southern Ireland, thundering out into the Atlantic against an increasing head wind.

The following day's reports, which said it had been seen over Newfoundland, had sparked off celebrations in France, and as French newspapers had described its landing in New York and had even quoted Nungesser's greetings to the New World, impromptu parades had filled the streets of Paris. Then, however, as the hours had trudged well beyond the time limit, the *New York Times* had found that the reports were false. The plane had in fact never been seen again after it crossed the coast of Ireland. Somewhere over the gloomy Atlantic, where the depression had deepened and the head winds had begun to lift the tops off the grey waves, Nungesser and Coli had vanished into the mists and the rain.

'Six dead!' Fred Loerner's voice as he brought the finality of the news to them was shocked and worried, and beginning to be a little sceptical. 'Captain, is it worth it?'

Ira said nothing and Loerner went on: 'Hundreds of thousands of dollars' worth of highly complicated machinery destroyed already,' he persisted. 'Hell, the leader writers are asking if it oughtn't all to be called off and I'm not surprised. Some guy in France—some general—is comparing you all with gladiators.'

Ira managed a twisted smile. 'Perhaps he's not far wrong,' he commented.

'They're saying'—Loerner gestured despairingly—'they're saying that all that's required's a good engine and a lot of luck and that anyone with sufficient skill and enough financial backing ought to succeed some time.' He frowned. 'I reckon even success'll have its drawbacks,' he ended. 'It'll only encourage a whole lot of others without any skill and without any backing. I reckon it's time somebody called a halt!'

The arguments seemed indisputable and, remembering Cluff's inexpert preparations, Ira could almost agree. Yet it wasn't as simple as Loerner made it, he knew. Technology couldn't stand still. It rested as much on the courage of fliers like Nungesser and Coli as it did on the graphs and the columns of figures worked out by the designers who sat crouched with their set-squares over their tilted desks. There had to be a challenge, there had to be a risk to life, or nothing would ever move forward, and without such men as Nungesser there would never be any point in the figures or the graphs. Unless men were prepared to risk their lives to prove them right or wrong the whole thing came to a standstill and there could be no hesitant step forward towards the next goal. Knowledge that was worth anything had always been paid for with blood, and Nungesser's death gave all the other crews not only a reprieve, but, like Davis's, probably also a little more knowledge.

The competition was still far from over, but they were all feeling depressed, nevertheless. Sammy's face had worn a stunned expression as they had left the Battery and headed back towards the hired car.

The afternoon newspapers were full of the deepest depression. Nungesser's disappearance seemed to have cast a blight over the whole aviation scene. After a whole night of searching, nothing had been picked up in the dark northern waters that gave any hint of what had happened to him.

Even relations between America and France seemed to be suffering as a result of the disaster, and the American ambassador in Paris was said to be seeking to delay the departure of any further machines because he believed that the arrival of American-built aeroplanes in France just then, with the fate of Nungesser and Coli still in doubt, might be misinterpreted. It was being claimed there by the disappointed French that the American Weather Bureau had refused to provide the reports Nungesser needed of the western shores of the Atlantic; had even given him misleading information to prevent him beating the crews now poised in New York.

Anti-American feeling had been strong for some time in Europe. The whole of the Continent was still in debt to the United States and, like all receivers of doles, no one thought very highly of the donors. The war-loan dispute had been going on far too long, and the apparent triumph of Nungesser and Coli had seemed to indicate that the arrogant and wealthy Americans didn't have an option on success. The gloom that had followed the first transports of joy was deeper because of the false success. The rumours that now swept Paris were only a symbol of it and the American press was being roundly damned for its wild inaccuracy and the irresponsible reports of the first false sightings.

Woolff seemed as numbed by Nungesser's disappearance as if he'd been a personal friend.

'Chamberlin was waiting to fly out,' he said heavily. 'But nothing happened.'

'Perhaps they're down somewhere between Newfoundland and Nova Scotia or Nova Scotia and Maine.' Ira was not without feeling, but flying was a profession where the deaths of friends had to be faced without alarm and he was already occupied with the next step. 'They're supposed to be able to float.'

'Yeah,' Woolff nodded. 'I guess we'll find out in tomorrow's papers.'

Everywhere on the airfield radios were blaring. No one seemed to have the courage to turn them off in case the programme should be interrupted by the flash message that would announce that Nungesser was safe. It was almost as though by switching off they would be cutting off the last hope of rescue. There was a desire everywhere to see the Frenchmen saved.

The public desperately wanted *someone* to succeed, yet each fatality, headlined and pictured to the extreme, only served to whet its appetite for more, because there was something of the twilight heroes of legend about these young men who were flying off into the stormy skies against the vast resources of the tempestuous ocean that lay athwart their route. And even as the newspapers held their mourning rites, a new contender had appeared in the west, as prepared as Nungesser and Coli had been to offer himself to the advance of aviation. The young airmail pilot testing his machine in San Diego was reported to have left for the East Coast to join the race, a young, untried, unknown man with an unknown aeroplane who was proposing to make the journey to Paris alone.

'Hell, Ira, he can't be any good! There's no money behind him!'

It was a fallacious argument but it appeared to suit Woolff's low spirits. Even the news that Bert Acosta—finally sick of Levine's manœuvrings—had thrown the Bellanca camp into a panic by withdrawing from the crew on the lame excuse that he weighed more than Bertaud, didn't help to jerk him out of his misery, and he railed on about the youngster from San Diego as though he had a personal dislike for him. 'He must be nuts, trying it alone! Who's going to do his navigation?'

'Who is he anyway?' Sammy said, and his indignant question echoed the thoughts of the whole continent. No one had heard of the young pilot until a week or two before and the newspapers still continued to spell his name in a variety of ways. No one seemed to know anything about him, except that he existed, that he had superintended the building of his plane in San Diego, and that he had some means of piloting it with a periscope from a closed cabin so far back he had no forward view.

It was known that he was too young to have served in the war and that his career couldn't match that of any of those famous names who had been and were still involved in the competition, and that a lot of his life had been spent barnstorming, parachute-jumping and performing hair-raising feats on the wings of planes for the excitement of gala crowds in the Middle West.

It didn't seem exactly the background for a long-distance pilot and he didn't seem a very serious contender, but even in his loneliness there was a curious purposefulness, as though he'd weighed up the risks and was prepared to take them. He had taught himself to fly, it seemed, on an old Jenny, was a pilot in the National Guard with a useful background of army discipline, care and training, and he had carried mail through hundreds of hours of night flying—a factor which couldn't be ignored because night flying was something on which none of them was very experienced.

'Me,' Acosta admitted. 'I'm strictly a fair-weather pilot and nothing else.'

Behind the mourning for Nungesser and Coli, and the concern with whether the Bellanca would sort out its legal problems and the Courtney its financial difficulties, there was a vast new interest stirring, a new upheaval of excitement that seemed to surpass even the ballyhoo and publicity stunting that had gone on already. With the disappearance of Nungesser and the emergence of the young man from San Diego, the contest really *had* become a little like a gladiatorial contest. As one contestant was removed from the scene by death and others still had trouble buckling on their armour, the crowds were getting ready to cheer a new champion.

A new and exciting hero had appeared—though he was still competing for space in the newspapers with the loss of Coli and the heroic Nungesser—and the whole of New York was suddenly poised waiting for his arrival.

Ira was sitting with his feet on the desk, smoking and trying to persuade himself he was relaxed and indifferent, when Alix appeared. She had not been near them since her father's financial collapse, but now, just as she had been when Davis and Wooster were killed at Hampton, she was in need of reassurance once more.

Her arrival at the hangar had gone almost unnoticed. The press, concerned with the imminent arrival of a new and possibly more exciting competitor, had soon lost interest in the Courtney. Financial troubles usually meant an abrupt disappearance and a quick sale and no one really seemed to believe any more that the Courtney was still in the race.

Ira lowered his feet as she appeared. Though the press seemed to regard their failure as highly likely, failure in itself didn't make news, but to Ira the very possibility meant a great deal more. They had all of them—Alix, himself, Sammy and Woolff—invested far more than they could really afford and if they went down they would lose far more than their reputations. Every penny they had was aboard the Courtney and if she failed to get off the ground they would be left only with the clothes they stood up in.

Alix appeared to be carrying the load for the lot of them, just at that moment. She looked thin and tired, as though she'd spent several sleepless nights worrying over it, but as she saw Ira's eyes on her, she lifted her head with a hint of the old imperiousness and tried to face his gaze without hesitation.

'I thought there might be something I could do,' she offered in brisk no-nonsense tones that hid a great deal of uncertainty.

There was nothing that hadn't been done a dozen times already but Ira found a list of figures for her to check. They had all been checked before by himself and Sammy and Woolff but he pretended they needed going over yet again for safety, because he knew that above all else she needed something to occupy her mind, full as it was of Nungesser's fate.

She finished within a few minutes, and because he was unable to find anything else for her they sat talking uncomfortably, their conversation full of awkward little pauses.

She was taut-faced and tense, working round every subject imaginable except that of Nungesser and Coli, trying to discuss their own prospects while still trying to avoid the possibility of failure, even merely sitting still and staring blank-eyed at Woolff's graphs and curves and the lists they'd made to make sure that nothing was forgotten.

Ira watched her warily, because she appeared not to want comfort, yet he knew her presence in the hangar was only because she needed to be among them.

While she waited, sitting silently, her brows down, her face

204

pale, Cluff rang again, uneasily asking if Ira had heard anything about Nungesser that he, up in Newburgh, had missed.

'There's nothing,' Ira said shortly. 'Nothing's been announced officially, but I don't think there'll be anything now.'

Cluff's voice sounded dubious, as though he didn't wish to believe what Ira was saying. 'Surely *someone*'ll find them, Ira,' he said.

'Not now, Cluffy,' Ira replied. 'You know as well as I do that they won't.'

As Cluff rang off, he turned to find Alix's eyes on him. She was lighting a cigarette with nervous hands.

'They're saying your chances of survival are nil,' she said abruptly. 'They're saying that nothing justifies the waste of money and loss of life, because in the end nothing'll be gained from it.'

'Who're saying?' Ira asked.

She moved her shoulders in a shrug. 'People,' she said. 'In the restaurants. On the Elevated. On street corners.'

'Let's listen to the experts, shall we?' Ira suggested, brushing the thought of failure aside. There was no room for doubt. If any of them doubted, none of them would ever leave for Europe.

She looked up at him, her eyes large and tormented. 'Ira . . .' she began. He turned to face her. 'Ira . . .' she said again, then she seemed to lose her courage and was unable to say whatever it was had been in her mind.

She screwed out her cigarette unsmoked and rose to her feet. 'I'm going,' she said. 'I've got things to do.'

She had removed her coat and hat and she now pulled them on again without speaking and moved to the door. Outside the office, in the hangar, she stopped again and glanced at the *Dixie*. She looked at Ira and managed an uncertain smile, then, turning her back on him, walked off across the hangar to where she had parked her car.

Ira stared after her in silence, wishing suddenly that Sammy were there, or Woolff. But Sammy was out on the airfield somewhere, probing the secrets of the other crews, and Woolff was arguing in one of the workshops with the Wright man, Ortese, about fuel pumps. He was still nervously concerned that Hughesdens would foist their pump on them, and was trying to reassure himself that, if they did, they could make it work.

The hired car drew away, the small figure of Alix hunched

behind the wheel, and Ira turned back to his desk. He had just drawn the folder on the *Dixie* towards him when a newsboy put his head round the door and tossed across the late paper they always bought.

'Have to hurry, Captain,' he said. 'The back runner's coming up—fast!'

Ira opened the pages. Among the wild stories that contrived to make national heroes out of gangsters, football players and film actors, there was a startling new story reaching into the headlines from the mourning follow-ups for Nungesser and Coli.

FLYIN' FOOL REACHES ST LOUIS. 1,550 MILES IN 14 HOURS 25 MINUTES.

'Good God!' Ira jerked the paper open in front of him on the desk.

He pushed his chair back and leaned over the sheets, his eyes following every detail of the story. In his own quiet way, without a crew, unhampered by the disputes that had plagued the Bellanca and were now hovering over the Courtney, and backed by a set of businessmen who provided only money and no advice to a man who knew his job better than they did, this new pilot from the west seemed to be moving more steadily towards his goal than anybody else. He had crossed the country from San Diego to St Louis in record time—farther than any pilot alone in a plane had ever flown non-stop before, and faster than anyone had ever travelled from west to eat.

He had taken off in the late afternoon with his tanks only half-full and had landed at St Louis with sufficient fuel still left to indicate that his machine's range was well beyond the three thousand six hundred miles which separated Paris from New York by the great circle route. He had left St Louis again that morning, and was expected in New York at any time.

As he finished the story, Ira sat back, his eyes sober and thoughtful, then he leaned forward once more and started again at the beginning. He had just spread the paper carefully in front of him a second time when the door slamming open thrust aside his thoughts, and the sheets slid with a soft rustle to the floor as he turned.

It was Sammy. 'It's that chap with the Ryan!' he burst out. 'He's here!'

'Already?' Ira suddenly became aware of people running past the window and heard the urgent, anxious *snap-ahah, snap-ahah* of someone trying to start a car. As the engine caught and revved up and the car began to grind away past the door, he pushed back his chair with a scraping sound.

'Hang on, Sammy,' he said. 'I'm coming!'

Sammy vanished again, disappearing as abruptly as he had come, then reappeared once more like a demon king.

'What's it look like?' Ira demanded, reaching for his jacket.

Sammy grinned. 'Not much different from the Bellanca or us,' he said. 'Looks a tidy little flivver. Single-engined. He's coming in now.'

They ran from the hangar, following the crowds heading for the field. Threading among the running people were motor cars, their horns roaring, and beyond the hangars Ira saw Byrd's big tri-motored Fokker, newly repaired and tested, droning away in the distance.

The little silver-painted plane was banking steeply when Ira first saw it, hanging in the air, it seemed, as it turned for its final approach, and they saw men with notebooks heading out on to the field. A lorry roared past with news cameras on tripods in the back. The excitement was twice as intense as when the Courtney had arrived.

'Tell those guys to keep outa the way,' someone yelled. 'They'll get hit! Give the guy a chance to get in!'

They stood at the edge of the apron, staring at the sky, watching with hundreds of other people. The silver plane was making its final approach now, like the Courtney a small inexpensive-looking machine with a single wing. Struts ran from the base of the fuselage where the undercarriage joined it, and it looked neat, with clean lines, and followed the conventional high-winged design that was being followed by all aircraft manufacturers, but they noticed that the absence of a windscreen enabled the nose to sweep back smoothly to give a tidy streamlined effect.

'Looks smart,' Sammy said admiringly.

Ira nodded. 'Looks fast,' he said. There was no getting over that dash across country.

The silver plane came in at an angle to the wind and settled neatly, passing in front of them as it came to a stop. Photographers, newspapermen, airfield mechanics and clerks all began to run and the machine was immediately surrounded by yelling people. As they watched, a tall-fairheaded figure who looked no more than a boy appeared, shouting at the crowds to keep clear of the propeller. Above his head they could see the name of the plane painted on the nose beyond the heavy square-looking shock absorbers and behind the exhausts of the Wright engine . . . in plain lettering, as simple and unassuming as the man himself seemed to be, *Spirit of St Louis*, four short words neatly lined up on the dimpled surface of the metal where the shark nose flowed back from the aluminium to join the square fuselage . . . *Spirit of St Louis*.

CHAPTER TWO

SUDDENLY the whole set-up was different. There was a dedication about the newcomer, a professionalism despite his youth, a quiet determination that persuaded older men to do his bidding, a knowledge of what he wanted, that provided a far more serious competition than any of them had ever dreamed existed from the stories they'd heard of him. And to the general public, sickened by the tabloids' diet of smut, sport and sudden death, tired of Byrd's caution, the Courtney's failure and the battling in the Bellanca camp, there was nothing about him to stop them taking him to their hearts; even, in fact, a gleeful feeling that, despite his lonely one-man set-up he was challenging not only the elements but the powerful financial organizations that backed Byrd and the Bellanca. His backers sensibly made no demands on him and left him to do his job, and his was the only project not hampered by outside interference, and had no crew members to enter into disputes.

Even the fact that he was proposing to brave the darkness of the Atlantic alone gave him an extra appeal. There would be no one to help him, no one to support him with encouragement, and his quiet determination caught the public's fancy in a feeling that he was martyring himself, a feeling that he was doubling the risks by facing alone what Nungesser and Coli had faced together and failed to conquer. There was an aura of heroism about him that was missing in the other camps simply because he *was* alone and had never been involved in argument.

Hal Woolff summed it up neatly, making an unexpected switch of sympathy towards the newcomer as his transparent honesty reached out to him. 'The country needs somebody like this kid,' he said. 'There's been *too much* big business, too much prohibition that doesn't prohibit and too many goddam hoodlums taking up the news killing each other.'

Clad in army breeches and thick stockings, the newcomer worked quietly over his engine with the Wright representatives who had been assigned to him, checked his instruments with the Pioneer officials, read the weather reports and double-checked his charts, and because he was so quiet, because he was so indifferent to the publicity he had attracted, he was unable to throw off the crowds. Always there were people outside his hangar, many of them girls who came simply to stare, and the press immediately deserted the other camps to follow him about, constantly calling him 'Lucky' and 'The Flyin' Fool'—though there was something about this young barnstormer-turned-airmail pilot that seemed to indicate that neither description fitted. He had worked out the risks and balanced them with his chances, and suddenly, to Ira, it seemed that of all his opponents this was the one he needed to watch most.

The Bellanca's litigious disputes and the Courtney's financial problems aside, since everyone was ready and the weather forecasts were poor again, the chances now were that every plane on Curtiss Field would be taking off together, and everyone became secretive overnight about his plans. Suddenly there were four aeroplanes poised for the start, and the prospects of a race appealed to the public. With the publicity that had been given to the attempt by the newspapers, they were looking forward to the kind of competition the sports pages loved to stir up.

But with the rain falling steadily once more and the great square blocks of steel, brick and concrete that made up New York shrouded in mist, things had come to a standstill and there was no longer any reason to refuse Cluff's insistent demands over the telephone for them to go and see his machine. Remembering his defection in Africa without a great deal of gratitude, Ira had half-hoped to avoid the duty, but Cluff's persistence wore him down.

'We're ready, Ira,' he said excitedly. 'And there's a local high in northern New York State, so we might even manage to show you her paces.'

He sounded boyish in his eagerness and, as always, unconcerned with whether it suited anyone but himself.

'She looks tremendous,' he went on. 'You'll like her. If we haven't got as good a chance as the rest of you, I'll eat my hat. When are you coming?'

Sammy made an irritable gesture with his hands. 'For God's

sake, Ira,' he said. 'Let's go and get it over and done with or he'll never leave us alone. With this weather there'll be no take-off for twenty-four hours. It'll be a waste of time, anyway. Everything that Cluff ever did was.'

Arranging with Woolff to telephone Cluff's number if there were any sign of a change in the weather, they drove north towards Haverstraw that night, to reach Newburgh before daylight the next morning. Roaring along the line of the Hudson through small clusters of white houses where lights were just beginning to come on among the trees, they could see the Catskills on their left, beyond the high maples, blue-purple against the growing light. An old farmer in braces wearing a felt hat with a brim like a frilly pie crust, his trousers seat hanging loose round his skinny rump, stopped the mud-caked Ford he was driving to give them directions.

'The Pelletan place?' he said. 'Ain't that the place where they got that airplane?' He jerked a stringy arm. 'Sure, I know it. Up the road a piece. White gates. Name's on the shingle outside. And, say, you tell them avviaytors to keep that machine of theirs quiet. This used to be a peaceful neighbourhood and folks don't get no quiet around these parts any more.'

The Pelletan farm was set in the middle of a huge stretch of woodland a long way from the main road, and, as they drove through the trees in the growing daylight, it wasn't hard to see how Cluff had managed to avoid publicity.

As the road swept round in a huge curve in front of a large red-painted wooden farmhouse and they came to a stop, a girl appeared in the doorway. She was obviously several months pregnant.

'Ira Penaluna! I bet you don't remember me!'

At first Ira didn't. Dulcie Cluff had lost the hard-bitten look he recalled, and marriage seemed to suit her. Her harsh blonde hair had changed to brown and her lean features had filled out. Her expression was softer too, and her eyes were gentle. She looked as though their assessment of her had been wrong and she enjoyed being married to Cluff.

Ira grinned. 'The last time I saw you, Dulcie, you were trying to decide to go to England with Cluffy. It seems you did.'

She nodded and held out her hand to Sammy. 'Hello, Sammy.' she said. 'You've changed.'

'I'm a bit older,' Sammy said.

She vanished into the house, and as she returned, wearing a

red and black Canadian lumberman's coat, there was a crackling metallic roar from among the trees behind the building. As they turned their heads, it grew to a howl then subsided to a drone and finally died again. Ira glanced at the girl and before she caught his look on her he thought he detected uncertainty and apprehension behind her eyes as she cocked her head to listen.

Then she saw him watching her and the expression changed again abruptly. She turned away. 'That's her,' she said. 'I'll show you where to go. They've got her in a big barn at the top of the meadow.'

'What's she like?' Ira asked. 'Good?'

She paused, then she turned, her eyes shining, though he was still certain that deep down behind them he saw fear and anxiety.

'She seems enormous,' she said enthusiastically. 'We haven't registered her yet because we weren't sure how she'd turn out, but she'll do it all right.' She pulled the jacket round her and climbed awkwardly into the car.

'I'd never go back to South Africa,' she said, trying to overcome the hesitation in the conversation. 'I didn't know there what life could be like.' She looked at Ira shyly. 'Perhaps that's being married. It makes you grow up. *I've* grown up. And you don't have to be blind to see we're starting a family. George says I look like a Salvation Army big drummer.'

'Do you mind him flying?' Ira asked.

For a fraction of a second she hesitated, then she shook her head firmly, so that he realized she had pushed all selfish thoughts of security to the back of her mind as she had immersed herself in Cluff's ambitions. 'No,' she said. 'If he has to fly, I mustn't stop him. He has high hopes, too. They bought the machine in Canada and prepared her themselves. Pierre Pelletan's splendid. He thinks he's got a future as a designer.'

Ira glanced at her quickly, sensing a mood of over-confidence in Cluff and his partner. A lot of people imagined themselves designers, he thought wryly. Even he or Sammy could have designed a sound aeroplane, but it wouldn't be the aeroplane for the Atlantic crossing, and no converted machine like Cluff's was likely to be, either.

Somehow, behind Dulcie Cluff's chatter, he sensed that she felt the same, and he drove silently for a while, his mind busy as the car bounced in the ruts, then the voice alongside him broke into his thoughts as she gave him directions. Following the road until it became a mere muddy track through the trees, they stopped eventually at the top of a long slope towards the river. In the growing daylight, they could see a few lights in the valley and the pale streamer of smoke where a train sped northwards towards Montreal.

They turned among the trees and saw the vast barn with the black and yellow shape of a big biplane outside. It looked strangely clumsy and, with years of experience behind him, Ira knew at once that it lacked the necessary quality for a long-distance high-speed flight.

Almost before the thought had taken root in his mind, however, Cluff came forward to meet them, followed by a small smiling man with black curling hair.

'Thanks for coming, Ira,' he said. 'Hello, Sammy. Sorry to hear about Courtneys going bust.'

Sammy's eyes flashed. 'We're not as bust as all that,' he said stoutly.

Cluff glanced at Ira. 'I read that you were out of the race,' he went on. 'The newspapers said so.'

'The newspapers say some funny things,' Ira pointed out. 'We're still in.'

Cluff stared at him for a moment then he turned to Sammy, smiling, puzzled.

'If Ira says we're in,' Sammy said, 'then we're in.'

Cluff gave a short laugh. 'Well, I reckon we might be right on your tail. I'm glad you came.'

Sammy nodded again, not hostile but giving away nothing in the shape of friendship.

'This is Pierre Pelletan.' Cluff indicated the dark young man behind him then jerked a hand towards an older man coming out of the barn. 'And this is his uncle. He's been a great help. You must stay for a meal. Dulcie's a great cook. If I'd known, I'd have grabbed her earlier.' He gestured proudly at the black and yellow machine. 'You'll be wanting to look over her,' he said. 'She's magnificent, isn't she?'

They walked slowly round the plane, Ira touching the elevators and rudder thoughtfully, noticing that the strange awkwardness came not from the Bréguet design but from the different tail surface they'd added. An open cabin where it had clearly been originally enclosed gave it a stripped-down look, but though the machine outwardly had an immense look of power, it looked clumsy, too, and there was something about it that seemed to indicate it would be slow on the controls.

Cluff was waiting eagerly for their opinion, running his hand lovingly over the enlarged ailerons they'd fitted.

'We bought her in Quebec,' he said. 'She'll do around a hundred.'

Sammy's eyes were narrow and Ira could tell from his manner that his thoughts were the same as his own. At the tail, he stopped, staring at the wheeled platform that supported it.

'That's to give us a faster start,' Cluff pointed out. 'I heard Byrd was going to use a ramp. I thought this might be a better idea with the runway we've got.'

Sammy stared silently down the slope. The machine was poised at the top, the chocks beneath the wheels, and Cluff, aware of the disapproval in his manner, went on eagerly.

'Fonck used the idea,' he said.

'And it came adrift,' Sammy pointed out with brutal frankness.

Cluff shrugged and Ira noticed that his eyes seemed old and lonely.

'You ought to make it stronger,' Sammy went on remorselessly and Cluff frowned. 'And you ought to have heavier tyres.'

'We decided they were heavy enough,' Cluff said.

'What's her weight?'

'Just over two ton.'

'And fully loaded?'

'About six.'

'What's the engine give?'

'Around six-fifty.'

'Don't you know?'

'Yes.' Cluff seemed to hesitate and somehow they had a feeling that the estimate was largely guesswork. 'Six-fifty.'

'It's as well to be certain.'

'I'm certain,' Cluff said more firmly. 'I know.'

'You ought to,' Sammy said bluntly. 'It pays.'

Cluff shrugged. 'It makes no difference,' he pointed out. 'We've got everything ready and we can't afford to start chopping and changing now.' He gestured at the machine. 'I suppose we couldn't persuade you, Ira'—he paused—'I mean, tell us what you think of the feel of it.'

Ira shook his head. 'I'm under contract, Cluffy. It just isn't ethical.'

He climbed into the machine, however, and past the vast petrol tank into the open cockpit.

'It had a housed cockpit originally,' Cluff called up to him. 'But when Davis and Wooster were killed, we took the top off and fixed a cowling to keep the wind out. It'll be cold, I suppose, but it'll help to keep us awake.'

The big machine reminded Ira curiously of Noel Davis's machine and, remembering what had happened to that, he sought for words to dissuade Cluff without appearing to resent his competition.

'We've got a nice runway,' Dulcie Cluff pointed out enthusiastically.

'It doesn't look very long,' Ira said.

'It's three-quarters of a mile.'

'You might be glad of that missing quarter.'

Cluff shrugged. 'There isn't another one available and the slope's equivalent to another five hundred feet.'

Ira stared down into the valley with narrowed eyes. 'It's not very smooth either, Cluffy,' he said. He jerked a hand at a dirt road that ran across its centre from one meadow to another. 'What's that?'

'It's a cow path to the barns. We took down a fence and made two fields into one.'

'Looks a bit rough.'

'We had a roller over it.'

'It still looks rough,' Sammy said. 'And it crosses at an angle. One wheel'll hit it before the other. You might find a shock absorber'll go.'

Cluff suddenly seemed faintly annoyed with their comments, as though he felt they were being unhelpful, and Ira tried to change the subject.

'How does she climb?' he asked. 'You're going downhill into a valley. You'll have to climb out of it at the other side.'

'We can do it,' Cluff said firmly.

'What revs can you get?'

'Eighteen hundred. She's flown nearly two thousand miles on it.'

Cluff sounded defensive now and Ira spoke earnestly. 'Cluffy,' he said. 'Any machine ought to be able to stay up once it's off the ground, so long as the pilot stays awake. It's getting her off fully loaded. We've worked on this problem for weeks. Have you? Or have you just guessed at it?'

'A bit of both,' Cluff admitted with a smile. 'We've always got her off before.'

'Fully loaded?'

Cluff hesitated. 'Well, no. I suppose not.'

Ira climbed behind the controls, watched from below by Pelletan and Cluff. Dulcie Cluff stood behind them, large and awkward, clutching the lumberman's jacket round her as though she were cold. The suggestion of apprehension that he'd seen in her eyes had returned.

The cockpit was a shabby botched-up job, vastly different from the stripped-down but still well-finished cabin of the Courtney. Silently, he worked the stick and watched the ailerons move up and down. Looking back, he noticed it was impossible to see the tail.

'Oughtn't you to devise some scheme for watching your rear end?' he asked. 'Once you're away, you'll have no idea what's happening to that extra undercart.'

'It's just not possible,' Cluff said.

'Couldn't you fix a mirror or something? You've got to know when to cut the throttle if something goes wrong.'

They had clearly hurried the modification without enough thought either for design or for preparation, but Cluff was looking sulky now and was running his hand through his pale blond hair as though he thought Ira was being merely obstructive. He had clearly expected praise and their doubts were irritating him.

'I think we can do it,' he said.

'How much petrol are you planning to carry?'

'We can get four hundred gallons in the tanks.'

'It's barely enough, Cluffy—even in still air.'

Cluff gestured angrily. 'We've got a dozen cans in a rack in the cabin as well. We can top up after we've been flying and dump 'em. It'll make it four-fifty.'

Sammy was frowning heavily. 'It might be enough,' he said slowly. 'Can you lift 'em off the ground? What's the wing-loading work out at?'

Cluff didn't seem too sure and was obviously becoming restless. He had been eager to show off his toy, and he was desperately seeking their approval. He ignored the question and turned to Ira.

'Think she'll do it, Ira?' he asked.

For a moment, Ira moved the stick about between his knees and worked his feet on the rudder pedals. He decided the time had come to be honest.

'No,' he said.

He saw Cluff's face fall and Pelletan begin to frown. Dulcie

215

Cluff, whose expression had been growing more and more anxious as they'd talked, glanced nervously at her husband.

'Not even with this runway?' Cluff said.

'Not even with this runway,' Ira said firmly. 'I don't think your tyres are heavy enough. I don't think your engine's new enough to develop the revs you want and you've had no works expert on it. And'—he jerked his hand forward—'I'd rather take a heavy plane off along a flat runway that ends in a flat field than down a hill into a dip. There are big trees down there, Cluffy, and you've got to gain a lot of height quickly. In any case'—his voice fell—'I doubt if you'll get that far with a load on. I think your undercart'll go on the rough ground.'

Cluff looked stubborn. '*I* think we'll make it.'

Ira shrugged. 'O.K.,' he said. 'I'm not a designer. I only fly the planes, but I know what they're trying to put into their machines and I don't think you've done it. Ask Sammy here.'

Cluff turned but Sammy's sombre face precluded the need to ask the question.

Dulcie Cluff's face had gone pale. 'Don't do it, George,' she said quickly.

'Oh, for Christ's sake,' Cluff snapped. 'We're all right!'

She stared at her husband, her face beautiful in its concern for him. She was still clutching the ugly jacket about her, awkward, clumsy, her expression begging him to reconsider. Then she glanced at Ira, a suddenly bitter glance as though she lay at his door all Cluff's ambitions, as though she felt it was because of what he was attempting in New York that Cluff's uncertain temperament was being directed into channels where it didn't belong. Her eyes rested on his face for a second, then swung back to Cluff's, tragic in their intensity of despair.

'No, please, George!'

'Why not?' Pelletan looked angrily at Ira and spoke harshly, the question coming abruptly and rudely. 'Why do you say we can't fly her?'

Ira shrugged. 'I'd suggest doing a bit more thinking first,' he said. 'Not only about aeroplanes, but about organization. Get some curves worked out and decide what you're setting out to do. Get some expert advice.'

'That's why I got *you* up here,' Cluff said bitterly.

'O.K.,' Sammy interrupted. 'And that's what you got. You heard what Ira said. *That*'s advice. And it's bloody good advice to my mind! Don't try it.'

'For Christ's sake'—for some time as he had listened to their comments, Cluff had been building up a head of steam and now it burst out in an infuriated frustrated rage—'we flew the bloody thing from Quebec to Winnipeg and from Winnipeg to Toronto, and Toronto to here! We came up that bloody slope right in front of you.'

'What was it like?' Ira interrupted. 'Bumpy?'

Cluff glanced at Pelletan. 'It stopped us,' he said shortly.

'I can see a dozen folds in it on the way down.' Ira glanced into the valley again. 'If it makes you bounce before you're ready, it'll be curtains. Look, Cluffy, I'll try to get Hal Woolff up to look at her. He might as a favour to me.'

Cluff gestured angrily. 'Let me take you up and show you what she can do.'

'No.'

Cluff turned away, his face sullen. 'Well, stay here then and let me show you how she gets up off the ground.'

Ira glanced at Sammy. 'No harm in that,' he said. 'I'll watch and then I'll think again.'

'O.K.' Cluff was reaching inside the plane now for a helmet. 'We'll show you.' He gestured at Pelletan who gave them a quick confident grin and produced his own helmet.

'She's half-full now,' Cluff went on. 'That's more than she's ever had to lift before. If she gets up all right with *that* load, we'll try her again at three-quarters before we try the full load.'

Dulcie Cluff's face was tragic now. 'Why not leave it for today, George?' she suggested. 'Think about it. Sleep on it. Perhaps tomorrow you'll come up with a solution.'

Cluff gestured angrily at Ira. 'Tomorrow,' he said, 'he'll be back in New York with his wealthy friends. We'll do it now while she's warm.' He glanced at Ira and went on with a trace of bitterness in his voice: 'Does your contract allow you to swing the prop for us?'

Ira nodded silently and Cluff climbed into the cabin of the aeroplane. Settling himself into the pilot's seat as Pelletan locked the door behind them, he held up his thumb.

'O.K. Contact.'

Sammy gave him a cold contemptuous look and, linking hands with Ira, they put their strength into the pull. The big engine burst into a crackling roar and the few blackened maple leaves that remained in the folds of ground from the previous autumn whirled back into the barn with the scraps

217

of chaff and grass clippings. Moving to one side, Ira and Sammy took up a position alongside Dulcie Cluff, who held her clenched fists to her mouth, watching, her eyes suddenly empty.

Pelletan's uncle stood behind her, his heavy gnarled hands hanging by his sides, his eyes on the plane, his face devoid of expression.

For a while, Cluff let the engine tick over, then he lifted his thumb again and Sammy and Ira jerked the chocks away. As the throttle was opened the big machine began to roll forward, lumbering clumsily over the brow of the hill towards the valley, then, as it reached the slope, speed began to build up quickly.

'Not much head wind, Ira,' Sammy commented flatly. 'He won't get much help.'

The old farmer who had directed them from the main road had appeared on the track alongside the field now, slogging up the hill in the muddy old Model-T. Seeing the big plane begin to move, he drew his car to a stop and they saw him stand on the seat to watch as the metallic howl of the engine filled the valley and rebounded from the trees.

The machine was gathering speed more quickly now and as it crossed the cow path to the next meadow, they saw the wings swing abruptly as the starboard wheel dug into the softer earth. As Cluff wrenched the machine straight again, a small cry escaped his wife but she didn't move and, glancing at her, Ira saw she still had her fists against her mouth, her eyes wide and large.

Cluff tried to haul the machine on to its course again, but it began to swing once more and at the next fold of land it swerved even more wildly and, as it shot over the curving ground, they saw the wheels leave the grass. Nobody spoke as the wheels slammed back on to the brow of the next fold with a spattering of muddy earth, then, quite clearly, they saw one of the struts of the rear undercarriage slowly buckle. Immediately the whole framework began to break loose and drag behind the plane, the struts flailing the ground and throwing up clods of earth, one of the wheels detaching itself and bouncing high into the air.

'For God's sake,' Sammy breathed. 'Close the bloody throttles!'

In his seat up at the front, however, Cluff had no means of seeing what was happening behind him and the heavy plane

218

slammed onwards, bouncing and swinging, the struts of the ruined undercarriage tearing the tailplane to shreds.

It was obvious now that Cluff would never get the machine off the ground and they saw fragments of wood fly into the air from the damaged elevators. Then the rudder, which he was using to correct the yaw, seemed to become jammed by part of the damaged undercarriage, and the machine swung suddenly to starboard again and began to career wildly across the slope in a wide arc that grew tighter and more dangerous with every yard.

A thick groaning sound escaped the old man behind them. Dulcie Cluff's hands opened and covered her face, and a thin wailing sound came from her throat, hoarse and terrified like a frightened animal's cry.

Neither Sammy nor Ira spoke as they watched the plane with narrowed eyes and taut faces. Cluff had obviously realized at last that something was wrong and they saw the broken auxiliary gear finally fall away as he pulled the release lever. But he was already far too late and the wreckage bounced up under the tail surface, hammering at the ground in a loud whacking sound that they could hear even at the top of the slope. Even while the howl of the engine died as Cluff slammed back the throttle, the machine was swooping wildly for the next fold in the ground, hitting it at a sharp angle. As the wheels lifted and touched again, Ira saw the starboard shock absorber go and started to run. A wing-tip touched and crumpled, then—as though Cluff had jerked the stick hard over to lift the weight off the damaged side—the machine swerved to port. But the collapsed undercarriage slammed down again at once, dragging the machine back to starboard, until it was almost facing uphill again, and the rattling swaying juggernaut swung wildly towards the fence, mud and clods of earth flying into the air in its wake.

The old man watching from the muddy Ford dropped back into his seat abruptly and let in the gears to pound up the hill out of the way as the Bréguet smashed through the fence exactly where he had been watching. They saw split rails flying up into the air, piercing the wings and fuselage, then the whole machine began to disintegrate into flying fragments of wood, steel and fabric.

The trees jerked wildly and they saw the brushwood waving as the huge plane, completely out of control now, smashed through it.

A long yellow wing rose into the air—quite slowly, it seemed—like the agonized pennon of an exotic dying bird, then at last it came to a stop, its tail high in the air, and the leaves began to flutter down on top of it, and Ira and Sammy were pounding across the field as fast as they could go.

The Bréguet had ploughed its way through fifty yards of brush and had ended up with its wings torn off and scattered about in fragments of wood and fabric, and they had to fight their way through the smashed shrubs and splintered trees. Stumbling over the twisted metal of an engine cowling and past the broken fragments of the rear undercarriage, they stopped among the flattened brushwood, fighting for breath and wondering how to get at the two men inside the wreck. The cockpit was ruined but Ira could see Pelletan trying to fight his way out. Plunging into the tangled splinters of timber and torn fabric to wrench wood and metal aside, Ira was trying to drag him clear when he heard the thud of the petrol tank going up. He was sprayed with burning petrol that half-blinded him as he heaved at the screaming Pelletan, then with a jerk the Canadian came free and they fell clear of the flames. As he looked round for Cluff, smelling his own singed hair, he saw Sammy trying to fight his way into the cockpit, one arm across his face. His jacket was already alight and Ira scrambled to his feet and leapt after him.

'Sammy, you bloody fool!'

Diving into the black smoke again, he felt the heat shrivel his skin, and, grabbing Sammy, he swung his slight frame round with all his force and flung him clear. Throwing himself after him, Ira fell across him, beating out the flames on his jacket and hair and arms.

Pelletan was rolling in the grass now as though he were in a fit, his face black with burns. There was thick blood on the blistered flesh and his mouth was a pink hole soundlessly screaming with pain. The farmer with the Model-T came across the grass at a lumbering run to where Ira was just scrambling to his knees and helped him to drag Sammy away from the searing heat.

'The other guy didn't get out,' he was yelling hoarsely. 'Danged things, they're always killing folk and smashing barns down!' He was making little plunging runs at the flames then stopping and stumbling away from the heat, his eyes shut, yelling all the time in a distraught hoarse voice, tears running down his gaunt face.

Ira climbed slowly to his feet, his face hard, aware that he'd lost his eyebrows and some of the hair at the front of his head. The cockpit had collapsed under the flames now and was nothing but a bright glow like the open door of a furnace, which scorched his face and forced him back from the smoke. There was no sign of Cluff.

The farmer was still hopping about on the edge of the blaze, scared and horrified. 'He's burning to death!' he yelled. 'How do we get him out?'

Ira dragged him back. 'We don't,' he said shortly. 'We can't. Save your breath and go and get help. It's about time someone around here started behaving with a bit of intelligence.'

The old man gaped at him, his mouth open, then abruptly he swung round and began to shamble off across the grass to where his car stood, his hat falling off unnoticed, his knees lifting, his arms pumping.

Ira stared after him for a second, then he swung round to Pelletan who had flopped back in the grass now and had rolled over on to his face, heaving himself about on his elbows like a blackened seal, his legs broken and useless, and Ira saw that his clothes were burned clean away and that the flesh of his back was wrinkled and ugly in a livid scar.

Sickened with rage, knowing Pelletan wouldn't live, Ira lifted Sammy gently to his feet, his jacket burned and looking strangely bare without eyebrows or eyelashes. His face was a vivid pink and he was staring down at his hands. He lifted his eyes, his expression shocked, then gazed down at his hands again, and Ira saw they were raw with burns. For a moment, overwhelmed with anger, he was unable to speak, then as he looked up, he saw the older Pelletan lumbering heavily towards them down the slope, his mouth working as though he were trying to shout something and couldn't. Behind him, still where they'd left her, where she'd been when the machine had begun its roll forward, Dulcie Cluff stood as though petrified, her hands to her mouth, her whole clumsy frame hunched up and shaking with terrible tears.

It was late when Ira returned to Erwin's Hotel. Boyle was waiting in the apartment, smoking a cigarette. He looked angry.

'Ira,' he said, jumping to his feet. 'I've been waiting for you. Where the hell have you been?'

Ira dragged his jacket off and flung it into a chair. 'Getting myself into something I shouldn't,' he said heavily.

Boyle gestured. 'Ira, I've been going through all Courtney's contracts ever since the war. Hughesdens have nothing on us. Nothing.'

Ira said nothing and the old man continued eagerly: 'The only contract over instruments was one he signed for them to supply gear for his automobiles. I guess we just decide they're bluffing and go as soon as we can.'

He thrust a late paper forward as Ira began to search for cigarettes. 'And the sooner the better,' he ended. 'Have you seen this? There's a report in now about a new guy in the race, a guy called Cluff. Some hick reporter in Newburgh's filed a story about a converted Bréguet.'

Ira lifted an expressionless face to the old man's. 'You needn't worry about Cluff,' he said slowly.

Boyle stopped dead. 'You know about him?' he asked.

'Yes, I know about him.' Ira took the cigarette Boyle was holding out. 'He's dead. I was there when he killed himself.'

Boyle's jaw dropped. 'Killed himself?'

Ira nodded. 'Burned to death. And while we're at it, we've got to get a replacement for Sammy. He's in hospital and likely to be out of action for some time.'

CHAPTER THREE

'NOBLE though its conception, this competition will inevitably drag behind its trail-blazers a whole host of under-financed, under-prepared imitators, of which, unhappily, this was the first.'

The county coroner's comment on Cluff's death was well justified by the events, and though Ira and Sammy had come out of it well—'These two young aviators did all they could to dissuade the dead men from flying and, having failed, did everything in their power to save their lives when they crashed'—it had been a high price to pay. The bereaved accusing stares directed at Ira by Dulcie Cluff showed quite clearly that she felt it should have been he who had died, and even the stiff naval condolences of Byrd—'We need people like Sam Shapiro to stop these people killing themselves'—didn't help much.

The newspaper stories had been vivid and left nothing to the imagination. With the foot-deep headlines in glaring black, it seemed that their one intention was to show how dangerous flying was, with photographs of the wreckage and tear-jerking interviews with the widow under the sombre staring words.

Ira insisted on going himself to fetch Sammy from the hospital at Newburgh where he'd left him.

Sammy was brooding and silent, his face patched with bright scorched skin. Mae Minter was with him, and had been ever since Ira had telephoned her. As they settled him in the big car Ira had hired, she was talking of removing him from Erwin's Hotel to her own apartment so she could look after him. Sammy didn't raise any objections and even seemed to think it had sorted out a lot of problems. He regarded his hands with a wry defeated smile, his eyes lifting to Mae's pretty, anxious face, his expression surprisingly gentle and sad.

'You don't have to offer sympathy,' he said gruffly to her. 'Gifts of money are O.K., of course, or you could mention me in your will.'

'Shut up, Sammy,' she said brusquely, and through her concern Ira sensed she was relieved that he was out of the race.

Sammy didn't argue, watching her for a moment before he spoke again. His voice came harshly. 'I ought to have had more sense than to go in like that,' he said. 'Cluffy never had a chance and it'd have been me, too, if Ira hadn't yanked me out.'

As he watched Sammy hug his bandaged hands to his chest while Mae stuck a cigarette between his cracked lips and lit it for him, Ira began to feel vaguely responsible for his injuries. Though neither Alix nor Hal Woolff had uttered a word of blame, he'd known all along that Cluff's attempt would be under-financed and under-prepared and knew he ought not to have wasted time on it. Only the pull of old friendship had taken him to Newburgh.

Sammy seemed surprisingly calm, however, despite the pain and the disappointment. For all his youth, he was very much a citizen of a harsh modern world that demanded toughness and cynicism and a ready acceptance of hard blows.

'Well, it's put *me* out of the running,' he said. 'Who'll be taking my place?'

Ira shrugged. 'Everybody we've tried is either under contract, not keen, or just plain scared.'

'Bert Acosta was free.'

'Not any more. He's negotiating with Byrd.'

'What about Alix?'

Ira turned and stared at him long enough for the car to wander across the road. He wrenched it back to the right and put the brakes on. Sammy was staring at him with a bland expression on his face and Mae was gazing from one to the other of them, bewildered.

'What gives?' she demanded.

'What are you getting at, Sammy?' Ira demanded slowly.

Sammy managed a painful smile. 'She's good,' he said. 'She knows her navigation, she's flown blind and she'd like to go. What more do you want?'

The apartment seemed big and lonely without Sammy, and for a long time that evening Ira brooded on what he'd said.

There was little about the Courtney that, with his own background of engineering, he didn't understand, and to do without Sammy simply meant that he was doing without someone who could only confirm his own fears if anything went wrong in mid-Atlantic. Alix Courtney not only knew how to fly and how to navigate but she also knew how to use instruments—something that plenty of experienced pilots admitted they knew nothing about—and, in spite of her quick temper, she had a ferociously exuberent vitality at times and was not the sort to panic in a crisis.

The idea of a woman attempting an Atlantic flight seemed a little startling at first, and he knew that plenty of people would be shocked by the idea. But plenty of women were flying now and some of them were already talking about attempts on long-distance records. In England, he knew, there were already two who were proposing to finance attempts on the Atlantic, while in America there were others who only needed the finance to set off themselves. Piloting an aeroplane over long distances required not strength but skill, intelligence, courage and determination, all of which Alix possessed in abundance. The more he thought about Sammy's idea, the more it made sense, and whatever the coroner at Newburgh had said, they couldn't abandon their attempt merely because of Cluff's foolishness and the disaster it had brought on Sammy.

He was still turning over the suggestion in his mind when the doorbell rang. It was Boyle.

'Ira!' He sounded excited as he stepped inside the apartment and shook the rain off his coat. 'I've found a guy who might be willing to take Sammy's place.'

Despite himself, despite his doubts and his wary cynicisms, the old man had been caught up in the events surrounding the Orteig competition, and his enthusiasm was growing daily.

'He's an airmail pilot with plenty of flying hours,' he said. 'We've got to get hold of Alix so we can work something out. Felton's in Washington trying to raise some dough to get started again. In any case'—Boyle shrugged—'it's nothing to do with him now. Alix's the major stockholder.'

Ira paused, Sammy's words still ringing in his head. 'What do you want me to do?' he asked. 'Go and find her for you?'

Boyle nodded. 'Her telephone isn't working,' he said. 'There's a line down out Long Island way somewhere. And we've got to come up with something soon. The lobby's full of newspapermen wanting to know what's happening now that Sammy's out.'

'Have you told 'em anything, Mr Boyle?'

'No.'

Ira lit a cigarette thoughtfully. 'Go and tell 'em,' he suggested.

'Tell 'em what? We've fixed nothing.'

Ira smiled. 'Tell 'em Sammy's not out of the running yet,' he said.

Boyle's jaw dropped. 'They'll swallow *that*,' he snorted.

'I'm sure.' Ira grinned. 'But at least it'll keep 'em busy thinking, and give me a chance to slip out without being followed. I have a feeling that this is something that'll be best done without newspapermen around.'

As Ira left the hotel, the streets were damp and there was a never-ending stream of cars along Fifth Avenue, steel-and-glass monsters that seemed to advance, glowing with light and roaring like herded cattle, out of the distance down the glittering canyon towards him, swinging round the corners and past the traffic policemen, orderly, modern and terrifying in their numbers. The din was appalling, and the stink of engines, exhaust smoke and hot oil nauseating; the human beings, driven to the sidewalks by the machinery, seemed to flow in pale uncertain tides beneath the electric signs that jittered nervously above them.

There was a mist coming in off the Atlantic, however, and the new developments in Queens, just across the East River, looked stark and ugly in the damp. The motor road alongside the railway was empty of traffic and the red pumps of the new petrol stations came out of the mist like huddled sentries in front of the large signs, 'WE FIX FLATS'.

The Long Island house was a low frame structure inside a white fence and surrounded by lilacs. It was small and built on the fashionable north shore between two huge empty holiday homes that probably cost a fortune to rent, and as Ira stopped the car, it was blanketed by the swirling grey fingers coming off the Sound.

He left the car some distance away and walked through the mist. As he reached the porch and was about to press the bell, the door opened and an elderly coloured woman in hat and coat, just about to step out, cannoned into him.

She gave him a scared wide-eyed look in the gloom and promptly began to back away. 'She ain't in,' she announced at once in a loud voice, then beyond her across the hall Ira saw a slender figure against the light.

'Who is it, Abbie?'

'Captain Thing. Dat guy with the name.'

The dark figure appeared in the hall and gestured from the shadows. 'O.K., Abbie, I'll handle it. You'd better get on home.'

The old woman stared at Ira suspiciously then she edged round him, muttering under her breath, as though his strange-sounding name was a talisman she were afraid of. As she slammed the door behind her, Ira turned to face the shadows along the hall and Alix switched the light on. She was wearing a thick skirt and the familiar green jersey, and carried a coat over her arm. The smoky black eyes regarded him steadily.

'Hello, Ira,' she said in a whisper. 'How's Sammy?' She came forward and lifted a hand to touch his forehead and singed eyebrows. 'I guess you were both fools to go up there, but I guess what you did was brave, too.'

She stared at her feet for a moment before she lifted her eyes to his. 'What happens now?' she asked. 'Who's taking Sammy's place?'

'That's what I've come to talk about.'

She looked tired and strained, as though her father's affairs had exhausted her. She moved her head wearily as they went into the living room. 'I guess I don't really mind who you get, Ira,' she said slowly. 'So long as he's sound.'

She stared at him for a moment, the black eyes unfathomable. 'I was just going out.' She gestured with the coat she was carrying. 'How about coming with me? I like walking in the mist. We can talk out there.'

As she turned and began to dig into a closet for a coat, he looked round the room. It was comfortable but shabby, with pictures of horses and cars and aeroplanes on the walls, and low lights and an old radio playing classical music softly in a corner. There were also a few family photographs over the fireplace, one of Alix, one of Courtney and one of a dark-haired, dark-eyed woman he took to be her mother, Courtney's dead wife. Then, unexpectedly, he saw his own face staring dimly out at him with Alix's from a small frame by the window and he recognized the picture they'd had taken together on their visit to Coney Island.

She caught his eye on it and her face looked defiant.

'I thought I threw that away,' he said slowly.

'I rescued it,' she pointed out quietly. 'It was a good picture. I liked it. It was a great night till that damned woman loused it up. She made the whole evening seem rotten.'

They were silent for a moment then she held out a man's ulster she'd unearthed.

'Your father's?' Ira asked as he put it on.

'No.' She looked at him with hard, unhappy eyes. 'It belonged to my husband.'

She seemed to be waiting for him to make some comment but he remained silent as he held the door open for her. She glanced at him as they began to push through the mist between the houses towards the sea. Dim yellow lights shone through the dampness and there was a raw ocean smell coming from the Sound.

'His name was Herb Elliot,' she said.

'You don't have to explain to me,' Ira said quickly.

'I guess I do,' she insisted.

'Alix, I don't want to know about him. He doesn't make any difference. It's none of my business.'

'Like hell it isn't,' she said angrily, but she made no attempt to explain.

They stopped by the beach, smelling the sea and the damp loneliness of the night. She was silent for a long time, then she hunched her shoulders, thrusting her hands into her pockets and nodding towards the waves. 'When I stare out there,' she said, 'I keep thinking how far it is to France and what it'll be like in the darkness.'

'Think you could face it?' Ira asked casually.

For a moment she said nothing, standing motionless with her back to him, then she turned slowly to face him. 'What did you say?' she asked.

He grinned. 'I said, do you think you could face it?'

'Face what, for God's sake?'

'That distance and that darkness you were talking about.'

She was only a disembodied shape in the mist and her face a mere grey blur in the shadows, but he knew her expression was one of bewilderment, anger and irritation.

'What are you getting at?' she demanded.

'I thought I'd made it clear.'

'I don't like people teasing me,' she snapped. 'Not even you.'

'I'm not teasing you. I'm asking you to take Sammy's place.'

For a long time she didn't speak; when she did, her voice was soft and uncertain. 'You mean that, Ira?'

'I've thought it all out. You're as good a navigator as Sammy. You're probably as good a pilot. You're as good on instruments and you know the plane. The only thing you can't match him in is engines and I don't suppose, even if you could, it would help us much in the middle of the Atlantic.'

She was silent for a long time. 'You don't *have* to take me,' she said.

'No,' Ira said. 'I don't and it so happens Lave Boyle's found another pilot. I'd rather have *you*.'

'Why?' Her voice was still wary. 'Because I've got the qualifications? Because I know the ship?'

He shrugged. 'That's some of the reason,' he admitted. 'But not all of it. I know I could rely on you. But I don't think that's all of it, either.'

Again she was silent, then she seemed at last to absorb what he was saying and turned completely round to face him.

'Ira. . . .' She lit a cigarette quickly and he could see the wonderment and delight and excitement in her face in the glow of the match.

'Ira. . . .' She tried again, as though she couldn't trust herself to speak, then she snatched the cigarette from her mouth and tossed it away in a long curving arc and flung her arms round him, her cheek against his so that he could smell the faint scent of the perfume she used. ' . . . Oh God, Ira, what the hell did I do before you arrived?'

*   *   *

Back at the house, she moved about excitedly, hardly able to contain herself. She wrenched off her coat, shaking the drops of moisture from the fur collar, then she pulled the ulster from his shoulders and tossed it down by the door. Turning towards the kitchen, she bumped into chairs in her haste and inability to contain her eagerness.

'Open the bourbon,' she said, 'and I'll show you how to make a mint julep.' She was bewildered and ecstatic at the same time and she lit a cigarette, then snatched it from her lips and tossed it into the fireplace.

'No,' she announced. 'I'll cut 'em down. I've got to go into training.'

Almost immediately she lit another, caught his eye and laughed as she crushed it out. 'Maybe in time I'll get 'em down to a million a day,' she said. 'I'll try, anyway, Ira. I'll try.'

She pushed him into the kitchen and dragged out a stool. 'Stay for supper,' she begged. 'I guess I'm no cook but I can manage a steak.'

They discussed their plans while she busied herself at the stove, her cheeks flushed, her eyes bright, not quite in control of her voice, throwing questions at him and answering them herself in the same breath, then they sat over the steak and eggs, with a pad of paper between them, first one and then the other writing as they talked of all the things she'd have to do.

'Forty hours is a long time,' Ira pointed out. 'A lot of people will say it's no trip for a woman.'

'I'm not scared,' she said quietly.

Afterwards they huddled in front of a fire of driftwood that spluttered and crackled and threw out sparks on to the hearth, maps across their knees, and discussed plans for a long time with the radio playing softly in the shadows. Then, as they laid the sheets aside, her hand touched his and she took it and held it without embarrassment, and for a while they talked in fits and starts, until it dawned on Ira that it was long past midnight. As he stirred, she turned towards him, uncertain in her drowsiness, one hand to her forehead, brushing the hair from her eyes. The rain was beating gently at the windows now.

He rose to his feet. The fire was dead in the hearth alongside them and the radio had long since stopped. She rose with him, standing in front of him while he jerked his tie straight. Beyond the window, the rain dripped from the eaves.

'Alix. . . .'

Drowsily, as though the action were instinctive, she lifted her arms and put them round his neck. For a moment, she clung to him like that, then she snapped to wakefulness and her head lifted and her arms dropped. She stared at him for a second in embarrassment then she frowned and turned away abruptly.

'You need a button sewing on,' she said sharply, touching his jacket.

He nodded. 'I caught it on something on the *Dixie*,' he said. 'Sammy's often said I look a bit like a rag-picker's mate. He's rather a snappy dresser himself.'

'I'll do it for you.'

She found a needle and thread and he watched her as she sewed, sitting on the floor in front of the dead fire, aware of the quick swell of tenderness in her eyes when she looked up at him as their hands touched, and the glow of her white skin; knowing well that behind that tense and prickly pride of hers there was an unexplored warmth and happiness.

She bit the thread off and sat winding the cotton in and out of her fingers for a moment uncertainly, then she put it down and looked up at him frankly.

'Don't go yet, Ira,' she said. 'I get scared when I'm alone. Sometimes I feel I've got lost in the darkness and I'm never going to get back to the light.'

She was sitting very straight on the floor beside him now, her head down, the black hair falling forward over her face, and he suddenly found he wanted to grip her shoulders tightly, to feel her flesh and bones through the thick fabric of that shapeless jersey.

She turned to look up at him and he saw there was a faint grateful smile on her lips. 'You've done me more honour tonight than I've ever been done before,' she said slowly.

He didn't answer and she lifted her head and gazed at him anxiously with wide poignant eyes, suddenly looking like a little girl, well washed and ready for a party.

Then he saw she was trembling, her whole body shaking, and, as he leaned forward with a sympathetic movement, she shook her head. 'No! Leave me alone,' she said quickly. 'It's all right. It's nothing. I'll get over it. You help, Ira. By God, you don't know how much you help!'

She was still trembling and behind her eyes there was also a suggestion of doubt. The trembling stopped at last and she lifted her face to his, staring straight into his eyes. 'I'm in love with you, Ira,' she said unexpectedly. 'I have been for some time. I tried not to be. I didn't want to be. I was in love with a flier once before and I always swore I never would be again. But it didn't work out that way. There was nothing I could do about it.'

She spoke quietly, in matter-of-fact tones, her voice steady, her eyes fixed on his, her face as pale and smooth as marble. For a long time, Ira didn't reply, conscious of the undercurrents of emotion flowing between them. She was still staring at him, her eyes burning themselves out in her head, a sudden trace of fear in her expression.

'Aren't you going to say something?' she demanded.

He put out his hand and her thin fingers curled round it fiercely. 'Sometimes when I was on my own,' she said, 'I used to hold my breath and think of you, because I felt so—so homesick.'

As they rose to their feet, she was trembling again, staring at him with eyes that were dangerously bright now and challenging.

'This is an age when morals don't seem to matter much,' she said slowly. 'After the war, they handed people like me this lousy world, all knocked to pieces and coming apart at the seams, and wondered why we didn't get excited about it. Because of that, I used to take a pretty easy-going attitude to things and I thought it was the right way to live. But it isn't, Ira. I know it isn't, so that's why I'm saying what I am. I told you I'm in love with you. I am.'

She turned away from him and he became aware of the emptiness of the house, the weight of darkness spilling thickly out of the corners to the centre of the room. There wasn't a sound about them beyond the drip on the leaves outside, steady like the soft beating of a heart.

She was standing with her arms at her sides, her back to him, and he took a step forward and standing behind her, folded his arms over her bosom. She lifted her hands and laid them over his and they stood like that for a long time and he felt her draw a deep shuddering breath. Then she moved in the circle of his arms and turned to face him, surprisingly still and quiet. As she lifted her head in one of the bewildering changes of mood that made up her character, he saw she was smiling mischievously at him.

'My father always used to say that I'd have to be careful with men because they'd only want me because I had money.

231

Makes sense, I guess. People do have an objective attitude towards sex these days.'

Ira smiled. 'Nobody's objective about that,' he said.

She flashed him a grateful look that contained the hint of a smile, as though she appreciated that he was helping her. 'Do *you* want me, Ira?' she asked. 'I have no money now.'

He grinned. 'You don't need money,' he said. 'You're quite a dish without it.'

She gave an unexpected gurgle of laughter, all her uncertainty gone. 'Hand on heart?'

'Cross my throat. You'd stir a bishop.'

She took his hand and led him from the room. Eventually, she faced him again, her arms slack, her shoulders hunched, staring at him with an appeal in her eyes in the subdued light. Then she stepped out of her shoes and it came as a shock to him to see how small she was, standing before him. As he moved towards her, she sat down on the bed, close to the edge, her feet and knees close together, and looked up at him, her face pale and expressionless.

When she reached up for him, they fell back together, and he banged his forehead on the bedpost, and as he swore, they burst into unexpected noisy laughter. Then, suddenly, abruptly, they stopped, staring at each other, and in one movement, almost as though they were both actuated by the same emotion, the smiles died and they reached out, their mouths seeking each other, their hands desperate in their urgency.

CHAPTER FOUR

THE WATERY SUN penetrating the mist that persisted over Long Island had an impermanent look about it, as though it hung indecisively in the sky, glowing uncertainly through the opaque whiteness that lay over the land. Behind the house, the hollows were filled with little purplish swirls and the grass was heavily beaded with dew that left dark marks as the first workmen heading for the truck farms trailed their feet through it.

As the light caught his face, Ira stirred, dragging at the sheet that was twisted round his shoulders, and as he opened his eyes the first thing he saw was Alix, sitting on the edge of the bed, with a blanket wrapped round her, barely covering her, one slim naked arm outside it, staring down at him. She looked bewildered.

He smiled. 'What's wrong?' he asked.

She gave a sad puzzled movement of her shoulder. 'I was just looking at you.'

'What was I doing?'

'Nothing. Just sleeping. I've never looked at a man sleeping before.'

'Never?'

'Not just looked.' She paused. 'I guess I've seen it before but I've never *looked*.'

She paused and the corners of her mouth lifted uncertainly.

'Last night . . .' she began.

'What about last night?'

She gave a little shiver and managed another small smile. 'Fine training for flying the Atlantic,' she said with a shaky laugh.

He pulled her to him gently and for a moment he felt her shivering, then she released the blanket and slipped down into his arms again. For a moment, she lay with her forehead against his, then she buried her face in his neck and he felt her shudder. After a while she lifted her head again and this time the smile was sure, bold and unabashed, belonging to the old confident Alix.

'The female when properly constituted,' she said, 'always sobs out her troubles on the staunch male shirt-front.' She drew a deep luxurious breath. 'I guess I'm a properly constituted female. I sure as hell feel like a properly constituted female.'

Ever since their arrival in New York, the first thing Ira had done every morning on waking was to stare out of the window at the sky. He and Sammy had done this every single day at Erwin's Hotel before telephoning the Weather Bureau for a forecast.

Now as he turned over, he smelt coffee and saw Alix standing in the doorway. She threw the *New York Times* at him.

'Sky's bright,' she said shortly.

'It is?' He sat up abruptly, and began to turn the sheets of the newspaper quickly, crumpling it in his hand as he looked for the weather report.

233

Alix had disappeared again and she returned with a cup of coffee which she pushed at him. 'Radio says it might be showing signs of improving,' she said.

She helped him spread the newspaper on the bed. Sensing the excitement hanging over what had long since become known as the New York–Paris Derby, the *Times* had taken to printing regular forecasts compiled from seagoing ships, and for the first time in a week the prospects suddenly looked healthy.

'The lows are dispersing,' Alix said.

Ira grinned up at her. 'You may be flying sooner than you expect.'

He grabbed for the telephone, then he remembered that it was out of order. Slamming it down, he threw Alix a cigarette and, forgetting his coffee, he dragged on his clothes and hurried outside through the clearing mist to find a telephone at a garage. The report from the Weather Bureau sounded more promising than anything they'd had for days.

'It *may* be clearing,' he was told. 'Reports suggest that a high-pressure area might be building up over the Atlantic. We don't know when, but we suggest you might start preparing.'

Alix was waiting on the porch for him, holding out his coffee, when he returned at a run.

'What do they say?' she asked eagerly.

He grinned. 'That it's time we got down to the field,' he said.

When they reached the hangar, the light was being picked up by the hangar roofs and the wet tonneaux and hoods of automobiles parked alongside the airfield buildings, giving the morning an unearthly glow, a diffused light that didn't seem to come from above at all, but from behind the sheds and houses, even from among the parked vehicles and from behind the dim moving figures of workmen.

Woolff was standing by the Courtney, looking exhausted, his cap more drunken than ever. 'I was here at five-thirty,' he said. 'I thought I'd better be. I woke early and it looked good enough to check with the Bureau. They thought there might be some good weather starting any time.' He had hardly finished speaking when the telephone rang. It was Sammy, telephoning from Mae Minter's.

'Ira, have you seen the forecast?'

Ira grinned. 'Why do you think we're down here *this* early?'

'Are you going?'

'If the weather turns up, yes. All we have to do is inform the

234

airfield manager and the police and get hold of the petrol and oil people.'

'I'm coming down.'

Sammy appeared in a cab soon afterwards, giving Ira a curious look as he climbed awkwardly to the ground. 'You've got a look like a cat that's been at the cream,' he observed.

Following Ira into the hangar, he gestured at the old Chevrolet standing outside and the pair of slender overalled legs hanging out of the cabin of the Courtney. 'I wondered if you'd put my idea to Alix,' he said. 'Looks like you did.'

'Yes,' Ira nodded. 'I did.'

'And?'

'She will.'

Sammy chuckled softly. 'It musta taken you some time to persuade her,' he said. 'Mae rang the Bureau for the forecast last night and we telephoned Erwin's three times to warn you. They said you hadn't got back. So I rang this morning. You still hadn't got back.'

Sammy's first meeting with Alix was awkward and they were both a little uncertain with each other, then he grabbed her impulsively with his bandaged hands and pulled her towards him to kiss her. 'I'm glad it's you who's going, Alix,' he said. 'I can't think of anybody better!'

She seemed startled by the gesture, then she flicked a glance at Ira, her eyes shining with pleasure, and she put her arms round Sammy and kissed him back wholeheartedly. 'And I can't think of anybody whose place I hate taking more,' she said.

Sammy gave her a shy look. 'Think nothing of it,' he said. 'It's all part of the service.' He grinned and, a little embarrassed by the unexpected show of emotion, he turned away. 'I'd better get somethin' done,' he muttered gruffly.

But although he'd arrived to offer himself for anything they wanted from him, his hands were too clumsy in the big bandages, and in the end, after fidgeting in restless frustration for a couple of hours in the office with performance and maintenance sheets, he set off for the Ryan hangar. 'P'r'aps I'll find out how he flies without a forward view,' he said.

Since the reporters had long since given them up and their interest lay at the moment in the Ryan hangar, they remained untroubled, and Alix stayed unnoticed at the hangar all day, studying the lists of figures and the charts they'd prepared,

235

sharing a meal of hot-dogs and coffee with them, interested and excited and absorbed.

During the afternoon, Boyle's car appeared. 'Ira,' he said. 'Where the hell did you get to last night? I waited for you.'

Ira grinned and glanced at Alix. 'I got held up,' he said. Boyle gave them a suspicious look, his yellow eyes boring into them, then he gestured with his thumb over his shoulder. 'I've got that pilot outside,' he pointed out.

Ira grinned again. 'We don't need him now,' he said.

Boyle looked startled. 'We don't?'

'Alix is going in Sammy's place.'

'Alix?' Boyle's jaw dropped. 'But I told you, we've got a pilot.'

'Send him away again,' Alix suggested.

Boyle looked defeated. 'I can't, Alix! He's out there now in the hangar looking at the plane. You'll have to see him.'

The man he ushered in was small and withered with a deeply wrinkled face. He looked a little like Boyle himself.

'Ed Blower,' Boyle said. 'He's been working on the Chicago-Detroit mail run.'

Blower gestured with his thumb. 'Nice ship you've got out there, son,' he said condescendingly to Ira, in a dry rasping voice like the rustle of dead leaves.

Ira studied him dubiously for a while. 'How old are you, Mr Blower?' he asked.

'Forty-nine.' Blower grinned. 'I got to fly DH4s in France, but I guess I altered my age a bit.'

'You flown long distances before?'

'It's four hours Chicago to Detroit. Going by way of Fort Wayne.'

'I mean like the San Antonio–New York flight.'

Blower shrugged. 'I fly, son. I don't migrate.'

'How about instruments?'

'Son, birds don't fly in fog. Neither do I. When the fog comes rollin' in, I get down—quick.'

Alix stared at Boyle. 'You can't get down over the Atlantic, Lave,' she said quietly.

While they were still arguing, Courtney arrived. He stopped in the doorway, his eyes pouchy and tired, his face haggard with strain. He glanced at Blower.

'Who's this?' he demanded.

'Ed Blower, Felton,' Boyle answered. He glanced at Alix. 'I guess I hired him to take Sammy's place.'

Courtney spoke to Blower for a while, then he gestured to Boyle.

'Ask him to wait outside a minute, Lave.'

Blower disappeared and Boyle gave Courtney a curious stare. 'Did you raise any dough, Felton?' he asked.

Courtney shrugged. 'Never mind the dough now,' he said. He gestured with his head at the door. 'That guy's no good,' he said. 'I'm no expert these days, but you don't have to be a Billy Mitchell to see he hasn't got the sort of experience *we* need.'

Boyle glanced at Alix and she opened her mouth to speak, but Courtney drew a deep breath that seemed to come from his boots, heavy and slow, as if it were painful.

'So what do we do about Sammy Shapiro?' he asked, staring at Ira as though it was his fault that their chances had been affected by Sammy's injuries.

Alix dug out a cigarette with quick nervous fingers. 'I'm going instead, Pa,' she said.

Courtney's jaw dropped. '*You* are?'

'Sure! Why not?'

Courtney gestured angrily. 'For God's sake,' he said. 'A girl!'

'What's wrong with a girl?'

'Alix, you're crazy! *You* can't go off on this tomfool trip!'

Alix's eyes flashed. 'It wasn't so goddam tomfool when Sammy was doing it, Pa!'

Courtney gestured again, the movement strangely weary under her briskness, his eyes as numb and expressionless as oysters.

'There are plenty of other pilots around—men—who'll do the job.'

'Where? *We* haven't found any. Only that old bum outside.'

Courtney looked a little desperate now. 'Maybe if Ira ran through things with him . . .'

Alix sliced the air with the flat of her hand in a derisive gesture. 'He's no damn good,' she said. 'You know he's no good. You said so. He probably can't navigate without beacons.'

'He doesn't have to. That's what Ira's for. We just want him along to spell him when he's tired. Ira can tell him what to do.'

'He can tell *me* what to do!'

'You haven't the experience.'

'Pa, you know damn well I've got the experience! More than Ed Blower, for all his talk. He's well named.'

Courtney turned to Ira with a small condescending smile. 'You know Alix, Ira,' he said, running a hand through his untidy hair. 'She was always one for excitement.'

'Don't apologize for me, Pa!' The words exploded across the room in a harsh shout. 'I can do the job! I'm *doing* the job!'

Courtney's objections seemed to crumple before her anger. As though he were too tired to argue, he waved his hand exhaustedly. 'O.K.,' he said. 'O.K.' He paused and went on slowly. 'You could always fly,' he admitted. 'I taught you myself. I guess it just makes a difference with a thing like this when it's one of your own family who's taking the risk.'

'You don't object?' Alix's anger had dissipated abruptly and she was watching him with anxious eyes now.

Courtney shrugged. 'How the hell *can* I object? It seems to be settled. I guess we'd better tell Fred Loerner about it and let him get it out to the press.'

'No!' Alix's eyes were hot. 'There's been enough ballyhoo around Curtiss Field just lately and they've written us off anyway. Let's leave it as it is until we're certain.'

Courtney eyed her. 'They'll want to know who's taking Sammy's place,' he said.

'Let 'em want!'

'They won't let you alone.'

'We'll tell 'em Sammy's not as badly hurt as we thought and that he's still flying.'

'They'll never believe you.'

'They'll survive.'

While they had been speaking, Courtney's face had been going grey, and Boyle, who had been watching him closely for some time, pushed a chair forward quickly. Courtney sat down abruptly and clicked his fingers, his eyes swinging to Boyle so slowly they seemed to creak in their sockets.

Boyle turned to Woolff. 'Water,' he snapped. 'Quick!'

As Woolff disappeared, Courtney fished in his pocket with stumbling fingers and extracted a box, and as Woolff returned with the water, he dug out a couple of purple pills and swallowed them. For a while, he sat in silence, all their eyes on him, his hand waving Alix away as she fussed round him.

Boyle stared at him, his eyes compassionate. 'Felton,' he said quietly. 'Did you get the dough you were after?'

Courtney stared at him, then he shook his head slowly.

'You didn't?'

'No. They don't believe I can do it.'

The old man glanced quickly at Alix, a fixed look of desperation in his eyes, as though all his own efforts to take some of the weight off Courtney's shoulders were all brought to nothing by Courtney's stubborn insistence on trying to raise funds. He fumbled hurriedly with a cigarette. 'Felton, for God's sake, why don't you stop?' he said at last. 'You'll be all right. Sit back. Get better. You can worry about money later.'

'Later's no good. I can try in Pittsburgh. I've got friends in Pittsburgh.'

Alix stepped forward. 'Pa, you'll kill yourself!'

Courtney said nothing, then he picked up his hat without a word and slowly, laboriously, rose to his feet.

They watched him stalk through the hangar, suddenly an old man. Alix's eyes were scared. 'For God's sake,' she said in a whisper to Boyle. 'How sick is he? He's on the ropes!'

Boyle took off his spectacles and polished them. 'He's pretty sick, Alix,' he said.

'Is he still trying to pull things together?'

Boyle shrugged. 'He's been trying to raise money in Washington.'

'Again?' She looked startled. 'So he can lose it all again?'

Boyle shrugged. 'When a man's once had money, Alix, he'll never stop trying.'

'Do you think he'll manage it?'

He paused, then he shook his head. 'You heard what he said. He's got nothing new to offer.'

She gave him a frightened look. 'Is it my fault, Lave?' she asked. 'All this illness, I mean.'

The old man turned angrily. 'Your fault? How the hell could it be *your* fault?'

She shook her head, as though trying to rid herself of a feeling of guilt. 'I've wondered again and again if we drove him into spending too much,' she said. 'Over the *Dixie*, I mean. We persuaded him.'

Boyle snorted. 'If he'd had the sort of cash he ought to have had,' he observed, '*ten Dixies* wouldn't have made any difference. And in any case, he didn't find the dough— *you* did.'

She nodded, a little reassured, but still not quite certain. 'Is it because I'm flying with Ira, then?' she asked.

The old man stared at her for a while, thinking, then he

239

shook his head firmly. 'This has been coming a long time, Alix,' he said. 'The doctors have been warning him for two years. If it hadn't happened today, something else—Joe Hughesden or some damned lawyer—would have done it tomorrow.' He put his hand on her shoulder. 'He always tried to do too much, Alix. He used to be the driving force behind Courtneys. He was never a great businessman but he could certainly keep things humming. If he wasn't there, we always started losing money. He wore himself out keeping things going.' He sighed and reached for the battered old velour he wore. 'But not for a long time,' he ended. 'He ought not to be worrying more than necessary. I've done a bit of checking around. He's worse than he thinks.' He glanced to where Courtney was approaching the hangar door, his stride bent-kneed, his head sunk on his neck. 'He's an old man, Alix.' He gave another sigh and clapped his hat on his head. 'I've got to go,' he said. 'Bear it in mind.'

As he opened the door he almost bumped into Sammy, who gestured with a bandaged fist towards Courtney. 'What's up with Felton?' he said.

Boyle ignored him and he watched silently as the old man hurried after Courtney across the hangar. There was silence for a while and Sammy said nothing as he saw Courtney climb heavily into a cab, helped by Boyle. His eyes were hard and he was struggling with his bandaged hands to open a packet of cigarettes. Woolff pushed one of his between his lips and lit it, and Sammy drew a long satisfied puff and blew it out.

'I thought he was sick some time ago,' he said.

'Dry up, Sammy,' Ira said, and Sammy glanced quickly at Alix. She had dropped into the chair her father had vacated and there were tears in her eyes.

'The old fool,' she said. 'The poor old fool!'

Late in the evening, long after Sammy had been picked up by Mae Minter, the telephone rang. It was the Weather Bureau. 'There's just a chance, Captain,' they said, 'that you'll be able to get away at first light tomorrow.'

'You sure?' Ira said.

'Sure we're sure. It might not come to anything, but it might pay you to be ready.'

As they rang off, Ira telephoned Mae Minter's apartment and got hold of Sammy.

'Sammy,' he said. 'Better get down here if you're interested. We're probably off any time. We need to talk.'

When Sammy's cab arrived, Ira and Hal Woolff and Alix were already in the office.

'We might as well check our plans now,' Ira pointed out. 'If they don't work for tonight, they'll work another night. Sammy, you'll be contacting the Wright men. They promised to come whenever we wanted them. Get 'em down to the field, together with the officials. Hal, you'll be doing the final inspection and digging out that mechanic with the truck you've got lined up, to tow the *Dixie* over to Roosevelt. Sammy can handle any other arrangements. Just make sure the barograph's installed and the tanks are sealed. Alix, how about your kit?'

'It's here.'

'O.K. You can arrange for police to control the crowds and for petrol and oil. I'll be at the Weather Bureau for a last check over the charts.'

They talked for a while about their plans, going over them several times with meticulous care so that nothing should be forgotten. As they left the hangar to get some sleep, Sammy stopped and looked at the sky.

'Heard anything about the Ryan outfit?' he asked. 'I bet *they've* not missed the weather. Everybody was clammed up all of a sudden when I was over there this morning.' He gestured. 'He let me have a look round, though. His plane's "blind" all right and he's got the tank smack in front of him with the instrument panel fitted to the back. But he can see ahead with his periscope and upwards through a skylight in the cabin roof. He takes off and lands by sticking his head out of the side window. He reckons he won't need much else, the route he's flying.'

Ira looked thoughtful. 'Many crowds over there?'

'Thousands. Mostly madwomen trying to get near enough to touch him.'

Hal Woolff pushed his cap to the back of his head.

'There was a reporter from one of the tabloids around *here* this afternoon,' he said. 'He wanted to know who was flying with you, Ira. I told him Sammy. He didn't believe me. He didn't even believe we'd go. They don't believe anybody at the moment. Levine's still talking about records but he's dropped Bertaud now and Bertaud's not going to let 'em take off without him. He's taking out an injunction.'

Sammy grinned. 'That's a handy thing to have on your back just as the weather shows signs of clearing,' he said.

Woolff chuckled. 'They're in real trouble,' he agreed. 'This guy thought Levine was talking through a hole in his head. He thought *I* was, too, I guess, when I told him about you.'

While they were still laughing in the opening of the hangar doors, a small brown sedan drew up nearby and a stout man in a navy blue coat with a velvet collar climbed out and crossed to them, carrying a folded paper. He glanced curiously at Alix, and they assumed he was a reporter.

'You Alexandra Sabra Beaumarchais Courtney?' he demanded. He gestured at the aeroplane behind them in the hangar. 'Owner of that ship, with Ira Abel Penaluna, Samuel Amos Shapiro and Harold Kenneth Woolff?'

She nodded. 'Yes. That's right. What's all this?'

The man in the blue coat glanced towards the brown sedan. Two other men had climbed out of it now and were standing alongside it, watching them. He turned again to Alix and slapped the folded paper into her hand. As her fingers closed on it instinctively, he indicated the other two men.

'The required two witnesses,' he said. 'I represent the Hughesden Instrument Company Incorporated. That's an injunction. You'll not be flying without Hughesden instruments.'

CHAPTER FIVE

CLOUDS still covered the sky but they were higher now and seemed thinner, so that the light seemed to have grown brighter. The depression which had been hanging about off the coast of North America on and off for so long was at last showing the first hesitant signs of dispersing. It looked as though the Weather Bureau would be right in the end. The greyness persisted, however, and the lights that hung among the girders above the red *Dixie* seemed dim and weak in the cold gloom of the hangar.

Ira stood in front of the machine, staring at the name painted on the side and the black smooth cylinder heads of the Wright engine, his hands deep in his pockets, his eyes baffled and angry, his heavy brows down. The newspapers had picked up the story of the injunction from Hughesdens, and the telephone conversations with Lavery Boyle had been acrimonious and had got them precisely nowhere.

Hugging his bandaged hands, a cigarette hanging from his lips, Sammy eyed him with a faint trace of irritation on his face, as though his cynical insistence on realism was wearing a little thin before Ira's stubbornness, because there were seals on the hangar doors now to prevent them wheeling the machine out and there was a lawyer's official outside, a thick-set man with a grey velour hat and a dead cigar in his mouth.

'Ira,' Sammy said for the tenth time. 'You've got no alternative. You've *got* to have the Hughesden instruments.'

Ira gave a restless movement of his shoulders as he shrugged off Sammy's nagging. 'The Atlantic's cold and wet, Sammy,' he said pointedly. 'I don't want the Hughesden pump. Not if I can help it.'

They were all feeling depressed as they gathered in the office and Woolff produced a bottle of whisky wrapped in brown paper and thinly disguised to look like a pair of shoes. Pouring several solid measures, he splashed in water from the tap and handed the glasses round.

'The whole lousy set-up makes me want to vomit,' he said bitterly. 'If we'd only had our twenty-four hours of good weather yesterday, we could have gotten her out on the field. And if we had, not even Joe Hughesden nor any of his minions down to the smallest snot-nosed office boy could have sweet-talked us out of going. And that's God's blessed and unflyblown truth!'

His plump features quivered with indignation and his normally mild eyes blazed as he worked himself up into a destructive fury. Sammy smiled faintly.

'Take it easy, Hal,' he advised. 'The steam's coming out of your ears.'

Woolff refused to be calmed. His plump face was drawn with worry and he gestured angrily. 'They think we won't make it,' he said. 'This on top of the sell-out finished us as far as the papers are concerned. They think we're done for.' He stared at the window. 'We'll miss our chance,' he went on. 'The weather'll break and we'll miss our chance.'

'Let's not get in a muck sweat, Hal,' Ira advised. 'Alix and Lave Boyle are up in Boston now and they ought to sort it out for when the weather changes. Hughesdens haven't got a leg to stand on and we've still time. The Bellanca crowd are still fighting with each other. Levine's trying to say now that Bert Acosta's still going but the Byrd outfit says he's signed on with *them*.'

'There's nothing holding up the Ryan,' Sammy pointed out in flat tones.

Woolff swept his hand down in a flat derisory gesture. '*He* doesn't count,' he said. 'He can't do it—not on his own!'

As they talked, the telephone rang. It was Boyle. The old man sounded as though he was seething with fury.

'I'm ringing from Boston,' he said. 'We've had three lawyers, including me, in the office here in this goddam talk-fest. They're quoting that contract that gives them the right to install their pumps and compasses.'

Ira exploded. 'We don't want a bloody Hughesden pump!'

Boyle sounded distraught. 'You might *have* to have one,' he announced. 'The contract says—and I've seen it—that Hughesden instruments are to be fitted to all Courtney vehicles.'

'An aeroplane's not a vehicle.'

'The contract doesn't differentiate and for the purposes of the law, they're claiming it is. They say it travels on wheels over the ground and therefore it's a vehicle. By the time we've managed to unclaim it, it'll probably be too late. They're after all the publicity they can get because they know there'll be sales if you get across, and they want to be able to say you did it with their equipment.'

'Using *their* equipment,' Ira snapped, 'we probably shan't. Can't you call 'em off?'

'I'm doing all I can.' The old man sounded weary. 'I shan't stop, I promise.'

Suddenly, Ira wondered how Alix was. Of them all, she was probably suffering most. 'Is Alix there?' he asked.

'No. She's already left for New York. She's gone to Long Island.'

'Is she coming down here?'

'I guess so. She was wondering if she couldn't raise some more dough on that house of hers to fight Hughesdens. Law costs money. It isn't worth much but it'll fetch a bit and she's determined to put everything she's got into this project.'

'Mr. Boyle, there isn't a project as long as Hughesdens' man's on the door of the hangar. Won't they accept a settlement?'

'What do we pay 'em with? Felton's trying to drum up some

244

dough again. He went to Pittsburgh as he said he would. Some old wartime buddy he knows.'

'We could probably raise a bit more between us.'

'Ira'—the old man seemed weary of arguing—'you're wasting your time. So's Felton. All the dough in King Solomon's Mines won't buy 'em off. It's not dough they're after. It's publicity. They say they have a contract to install their instruments on Courtney vehicles *and they're going to install 'em!*'

Ira exploded. 'This is crazy!' he snorted. 'We're not a Courtney vehicle now, in any case.'

'You were when the plane was built!' Boyle sounded terse and angry. 'You can't get round that, and the contract was signed by Felton and Joe Hughesden. I've seen it. In 1922. Nobody thought of flying the Atlantic then.'

As Ira put the telephone down, they heard a car come to a halt outside the door with squeaking brakes, and Alix appeared. There were a dozen reporters waiting, but she dodged them and slid quickly through the door, which was promptly slammed behind her by Woolff.

'I've put the house on Long Island up for sale,' she announced. 'It'll probably raise a few thousand dollars after we've paid off the mortgage.'

'Alix, forget it,' Sammy said quickly. 'We'll raise the money somehow. We don't need the house.'

'What's the good of a house,' she said shortly, 'without an income to keep it up?'

She leaned against the door and lifted her eyes tiredly. 'They wouldn't remove the injunction,' she said. 'They're after blood.'

'We heard,' Ira said. 'Boyle rang.'

She stared at him for a moment, as though what he had said hadn't sunk in. 'They won't do a thing to help,' she went on. 'They've got us over a barrel and they're aiming to keep us there. They dressed it up a bit, of course, telling us that it wasn't Joe Hughesden's wishes, but that they had to look after the investments of all the little people who'd got their money in Hughesdens.' She gave an explosive laugh that was harsh and mirthless. 'Little people! Anybody'd think they'd got elves putting their dough in these days. The only thing that's little bout Hughesdens is Joe Hughesden's mind.'

'What about your Pa, Alix?' Woolff asked.

She looked at him unhappily and shook her head. 'He wired. He'll get nothing. We can forget Pa, Hal. Lave's right. He's a sick man and I'm not going to be the one who knocks the props from under him.' She pulled off her hat wearily and tossed it on to the desk. 'We've got no choice. We've got to accept the Hughesden instruments.'

Ira frowned. 'It's not quite as simple as that,' he pointed out. 'The Wright engineers don't think much of the Hughesden pump either, and if we refuse to use a Viking as they recommend, they say they can't be held responsible.'

Her eyes flickered miserably. 'They're washing their hands of us?'

Ira sighed. 'Not quite. But while they were prepared to offer what was in effect a guarantee with their engine before, they're not prepared to now. That's what it amounts to.'

She looked at Sammy and Woolff. 'O.K.,' she said. 'Do we accept the Hughesden pump and compasses, or don't we?'

'You said it yourself, old love,' Sammy pointed out. 'We haven't much option. The weather's picking up all the time. We've got to make up our minds now or we might miss it.'

She looked at Ira and he shrugged. 'I'm afraid Sammy's right,' he said.

'Okay.' She straightened and jerked up her head. 'Let's go ahead. I'll ring Lave Boyle and tell him to let Hughesdens know we agree. They've had men here on the field waiting to do the job for days.'

Woolff sighed and turned away. Half an hour later, sick at heart, he was dismantling the fuel pump while Ira was unscrewing the compasses.

Time was important suddenly. The weather over the Atlantic seemed to be improving rapidly, despite the layer of cloud along the coast, and at once everyone began to keep his own counsel, and the rumours of take-off multiplied as they tried to rush the final preparations for the Courtney.

Since they'd entered the competition with the expressed intent of getting to Paris first, it was pointless to consider anything else, and, since a risk had arisen, then the risk had to be taken. The Hughesden pump was hurriedly reinstalled by the Hughesden engineers and fuel leads were ripped out and replaced as they struggled to fit the Hughesden earth inductor and liquid compasses, and one other which Sammy insisted they take for luck, one so small, he called it the Chicks' Own.

246

'Only weighs a few ounces,' he insisted. 'And you never know, it might be the best of the lot.'

The last screw was finally tightened, the last adjustment made, and the last reading corrected, but as they began to wait edgily for the weather again, the high layer of cloud began to sprinkle New York with rain again. Despite their continued optimism, the Weather Bureau remained adamant in their refusal to give a clear go-ahead because there were so many things that had to be exactly right—so many conditions that had to be fulfilled to make a take-off worth while. There had to be no fog on either side of the Atlantic so that they could check their compasses at the beginning of the flight and find Le Bourget at the end. The wind had to be favourable and there had to be no chance of low-pressure areas across their course for at least thirty-six hours. It was impossible for the Bureau to give them all these conditions at once, of course, and they would have to settle for whatever suitable permutation came up first. And since it was difficult to pick up enough information from the empty areas of the Far North, they knew as well as the Bureau that the high-pressure systems had to be big and with a chance of being prolonged before they dare risk going.

They spent the evening swinging the new compasses and re-examining the wiring while Woolff and Sammy checked the fuel pump. Then Ira took the machine up for a final test, but though they could find nothing wrong, all of them in their hearts were aware of a deep uncertainty. There seemed to be an air of unreality about it all now. The newspapers were still insisting that if they went, Sammy was to be the co-pilot, but they obviously didn't believe their own stories, and neither did anyone else.

They were all weary and it was dark when Ira and Alix dropped Sammy off in the increasing rain at Mae's apartment, and as they headed for Long Island and the drab building lots and construction sites slipped behind them, they were both deep in thought. As they let themselves into the little house near the beach, the telephone rang, harsh and abrupt in the darkness, breaking the silence with its peremptory summons. Alix whirled to stare at it.

'Leave it, Ira,' she whispered, almost as though her voice might be heard. 'It'll be the newspapers.'

He shook his head. 'It might be the Weather Bureau.'

Her eyes held his as he picked up the instrument.

'Alix?'

Silently he handed the telephone over and he heard Boyle continue. 'Say, Alix, who's that? What's going on there?'

'Never mind what's going on here, Lave,' she snapped. 'What do you want?'

'Alix'—Boyle sounded in a panic—'I guess you'd better come. It's your father.'

'What's wrong with my father?'

'He collapsed.' Boyle's voice sounded high and frightened and a little out of control. 'He just got back from Pittsburgh, and the elevator man found him. He was scared, and, hell, now that I've seen him, so am I! The doctor says it's his heart. I guess you ought to come over here.'

Alix paused, her eyes on Ira's, then she nodded. 'I'll come, Lave,' she said quietly.

'Make it quick, Alix!'

She turned to face Ira as she put the instrument down. Silently, he reached for her coat and held it up.

'You heard?'

He nodded. 'Come on, Alix. Let's go.'

When they arrived, shaking the rain from their clothes, Boyle was standing by Courtney's desk going through papers, an ashtray alongside him full of stubbed-out cigarettes. The room was stale with smoke.

'My God,' he said as they appeared. 'This is one hell of a time to have him sick. The whole world's falling down round our ears. It's a good job you took over the *Dixie*. They're dunning us well and truly now. The airfield and the house'll have to go.'

'We expected that.' Alix shrugged, her voice unemotional. 'What's my father say?'

Boyle looked at her, his wrinkled old face grey and tired. 'Alix, your father's saying nothing,' he said in a flat voice. 'Go take a look.'

Courtney was in his bed, propped up on pillows, his face collapsed and ancient, the eagle nose paper-thin and transparent-looking, the untidy russet-grey hair suddenly wispy.

'Father!'

There was a nurse standing by the bed. She shook her head. 'He's under sedation,' she said. 'He can't hear you, Miss Courtney.'

'Nothing?'

'Nothing.'

'What's the doctor say?'

The nurse shrugged. 'He says he ought to pull through eventually, but it's affected his left side.'

'A stroke?'

'I'm afraid so.'

'Permanent?'

'Maybe not, but he'll have to take it easy from now on. It's going to be a long business. He's been overdoing things for too long. The doctor's due back any time. You'll be able to talk to him.'

After a searching look at her father, Alix turned away. Her eyes fell on Ira's and she allowed herself to be led from the room. Boyle was still leafing through papers.

'What happened?' Alix asked.

'I guess he pushed himself too hard. The doctor said he's got to give up everything. He's got to take a long rest. Maybe he's got to go on resting for the remainder of his life.'

'What caused it?'

Boyle gestured. 'He was still conscious when I arrived. He said Joe Hughesden came. He rang him and asked him over.'

Her eyes glittered. '*That old bastard!*'

'They had a fight of some sort.'

'About the contract?'

'He said so.'

'Is that what brought this on?'

'I guess so. Felton hoped to talk him out of it but Joe Hughesden wants his pound of flesh. It happened just after he left.'

Alix looked at the worried old man, her face compassionate. 'I guess you need a drink, Lave,' she said, crossing to the table where the decanters stood. 'Maybe we all do.'

She mixed them all drinks, then she went into her father's room again, and they talked desultorily until she reappeared.

'I'm wasting my time in there,' she said. 'I'll be better off out here, making sure everything's taken care of.'

She seemed a different person suddenly, at that moment surprisingly like Courtney himself had always been, and Ira realized she'd lived so long in her father's shadow, she'd almost lost her own identity as she'd blundered her way towards a discovery of herself.

'Lave'—she was swinging round to the old man at the desk now—'what about his affairs? What's left?'

Boyle hesitated.

'Come on, Lave. Let's have it.'

Boyle gave her a twisted smile. 'Well, Hughesdens saw him all right. . . .'

'Never mind what Hughesdens did. We're finished, aren't we? What Hughesdens gave him's gone on debts. Come on, Lave, level with me. You know what he always said, "God made the earth in six days. You've got six minutes to say all you want."'

The old man gave her a sick smile. 'I don't need that long, Alix,' he said. 'Ten seconds'll do. There's *nothing* left.'

Alix crushed out her cigarette. 'Can you get someone to look after him, Lave?' she asked.

Boyle nodded. 'Sure. My daughter's a widow. She'll move in. I'll telephone her right now.'

'Then I guess if we get a chance, the best thing we can do is go. If we succeed, we might lick Joe Hughesden yet and it'd be the best thing in the world for Pa if we did.'

It was early morning and the rain had eased a little when they left Courtney's apartment, and as they turned the car towards Queens the decision to telephone the Weather Bureau was a last-minute suggestion on Alix's part. She was tired, but strangely the strain had vanished from her face and she was coldly calm.

They stopped at an all-night diner and she vanished to use the telephone. The pavements were still greasy with rain and the tops of the skyscrapers were still out of sight in the clouds. As she returned, Alix looked excited.

'It's clearing,' she announced. 'They were right. It's the high they've been waiting for but they didn't expect it to appear tonight.'

Ira's face lit up. 'You sure, Alix?'

'It's still a risk, but that's what they think. The low-pressure area over Newfoundland's moved north and they say this high they're expecting'll be colossal. The storms over France are diminishing to local proportions.'

'What about over the sea?'

'There's still some bad weather to the north—maybe even electrical storms—and they're not prepared to say what it'll do, but the general outlook's improving all the time.'

Ira grinned and she went on.

'There's one other thing,' she said.

'Go on.'

'The Ryan crowd's got it, too. They were on their way to the theatre but they think they've cancelled and intend to take off in the morning.'

'How about Chamberlin and Byrd?'

'They've heard nothing from them.'

'Let's check with their hotel.'

They went back to the telephone on the counter of the diner and it was obvious that what she'd been told was right. Lindbergh had not gone to the theatre, though it had been his intention originally, and he was now in his room with a guard on the door to make sure he got some sleep.

'How about Chamberlin?' Ira asked.

'We've no idea.' The desk clerk was not very interested. 'No special arrangements far as I can tell. Didn't Bertaud take out an injunction? Isn't he still tied up with that?'

Ira glanced at Alix as he put down the receiver. 'Lindbergh's going to have a go,' he said. 'He's trying to get some sleep. He's got to fly forty hours without a break. What about it?'

She frowned. 'I hate leaving Pa, in spite of what I said, now it comes to the point,' she admitted wretchedly. 'How long would we be away?'

'Two days for the flying. A week or so back by sea.'

'Should we go, Ira?'

He stared at her, then he nodded. 'Yes,' he said. 'This time we should.'

She gazed at him, begging him to make her mind up for her, then she nodded. 'O.K.' she agreed. 'We go.'

He didn't waste any time arguing her decision. She had been quite right. There was nothing they could do for Courtney, and success might be the best cure of all for him. 'I think we might be able to leave them all at the post,' he said. 'If Lindbergh's getting sleep now, he can't be away before full daylight. But *we* can sleep as we fly because there are two of us. We might get an hour or two's start on him. Get a cab to Mae's and get hold of Sammy. Ring Hal from there and get him to the airfield.'

'How about the Wright men?'

'They'll come. Sammy and Hal will organize things. Someone'll have to arrange for the police to control the crowds if Lindbergh's outfit hasn't done it already. I'm going to have a long hard personal look at that weather map.'

*　　　*　　　*

When Ira arrived at the Weather Bureau there was on doubt that the weather was clearing.

The low-pressure area over Newfoundland was edging back and, though it was stubborn, a vast high was thrusting north in its place. The wind was also dropping and the weather was expected to remain fair all the way along the American coast from Massachusetts and New Hampshire to Nova Scotia, with only light north-westerly breezes. Over Nova Scotia the winds were westerly and there was no fog so far, and it was reported clear, too, at St. John's, Newfoundland, where a steady wind from the west was blowing. Out in the Atlantic, the high-pressure area was beginning to shoulder away the days of fog and rain that had prevailed for so long. If it continued, conditions would be good as far as Europe, though local storms still persisted over France.

'How about wind? Any better higher up?'

'We've got no data but we think it'll be from the west.'

When Ira reached Curtiss Field it was still raining and there were a few scattered groups of onlookers about. But the hangar was empty and Sammy was crouched over the telephone in an office that suddenly looked bare, with the charts and flying equipment gone. Mae Minter was sitting opposite him and she gave Ira a nervous smile as he entered.

'*New York Times*,' Sammy said as he replaced the receiver. 'They've heard from somewhere that we're off. They keep telephoning weather reports. It seems all right. Chatham reports it clear with no wind and it's much the same all the way to Maine.'

'What about Nova Scotia and Newfoundland?'

'Light winds over Nova Scotia and a twenty-mile-an-hour westerly off the coast of Newfoundland.'

'Sounds O.K. Anything for the rest of the way?'

'They're a bit worried about that low to the north and the storms off Europe.'

'We'll chance it. Where's the *Dixie*?'

'On the way to Roosevelt Field. Hal dug out that mechanic with the truck. You can take off the minute it's light.' Sammy grinned. 'That bloke'll make a bit of money tonight. He's offered a tow to Lindbergh, too.'

'How about the Bellanca and Byrd?'

Sammy chuckled. 'Ira, we're ahead of everybody. We've got our machine over at Roosevelt already and Lindbergh's still not arrived. There's no sign of anyone at the Bellanca hangars and they say Byrd's still got more tests to fly.'

While they were talking, Alix appeared. She looked pale and tense.

'This is it, Alix,' Ira said as they went out to the car together. 'How do you feel?'

'Damned scared.' She nodded and repeated the phrase, almost as though she were saying it to herself like a litany. 'Yes. Damned scared, Ira.'

He touched her hand and looked at Sammy. 'Everything else fixed, Sammy?'

'Everything. Police are already there. Lindbergh's people phoned them. Same goes for the press. Petrol and oil will be going in already. Hal Woolff's taking care of it.'

'Fine. Jump in, Sammy. Let's go.'

CHAPTER SIX

THE RAIN SLID DOWN through the beams of the headlights, straight and silvery and shining, dissolving in the puddles on the sidewalks and along the gutters. Mist hung in the air and the sound of falling water and the hiss of tyres were surprisingly loud over the hired car's engine. Suddenly, Ira realized he'd never noticed rain before, but now, with his thoughts on the coming take-off from an over-wet field, he found he was dwelling uncomfortably on Cluff's crash. Nothing could have brought home so clearly to him just what could happen to them in an overloaded plane, if their calculations were wrong or his judgment were not accurate, because it had happened also to Davis and to Fonck. He glanced at Alix but she was concentrating on driving and her face was pale and tense.

The word that someone was leaving had already spread and cars and taxis were heading for Roosevelt Field in a solid stream. A gate loomed up, then a group of people, dripping with rain and shivering under umbrellas. They moved forward to get a clear look at them through the streaming side screens, their faces white in the mist, then a Nassau County policeman started to force them back and the inevitable camera flashes went off.

'Lot of people here,' Ira observed as a thin cheer went up, and one of the reporters grinned.

'I guess you're not the star, Captain,' he said. 'Nobody thought you'd go. They're waiting for the Ryan. He's got solo billing. You still taking Sam Shapiro?'

Ira evaded the question. 'We go as soon as the tank's full,' he said. 'We're all ready.'

'What about the weather?'

'It's clearing. Have you heard anything of the other crews?'

The reporter shook the rain off his hat and glanced upwards at the streaming sky. 'I guess they don't feel they'll be leaving in *this* stuff.'

Ira could see water dripping from the hoods of cars and the hats of people waiting in the darkness, and red flares were blazing near the hangar and torches flashed in the hands of officials through the mist.

Hal Woolff appeared. 'She's almost ready, Ira,' he said. He indicated the sealed drums of petrol and the red five-gallon cans which were being passed up to the Wright engineer, Ortese, kneeling on the wing to pour them into the tanks through a big funnel lined with a chamois leather cloth.

'I've fixed coffee and rolls and cold sausage,' he went on. 'It should keep you going for two days. All the maps and charts are aboard.'

'How much longer, Hal?' Alix asked.

'Minutes, Alix. We're almost finished.'

Sammy was standing on one side in the roped-off square, watching, a lost expression on his face. Mae Minter was with him, pale and tense and a little out of place among the overalls in her fashionable clothes. Every now and then she moved closer to him and clutched his arm nervously, as though the fact that two people—neither of them much older than herself—were about to risk their lives in the darkness over the Atlantic was worrying her, so that she had to keep moving restlessly, like a child watching high-wire performers at a circus.

Loerner appeared, followed by a man wearing a parson's collar. Some of the financial troubles that had beset the Courtney had reached his ears and he looked gloomy, as if he were beginning to feel his fees were suddenly unlikely to be paid. 'For God's sake,' he said. 'Nobody told me! It was the hotel that got me up. Why didn't you let me know?'

'Forgot,' Ira said shortly. 'There's a lot to do.'

'I saw Sammy,' Loerner went on accusingly. 'He's still got his hands bandaged. You *still* saying he's flying with you?'

'If we change, you'll be the first to know, Fred.'

Loerner gave him a suspicious glance and dabbed at his wet face. He managed a wintry smile at Ira. 'I've heard that the French are waiting to welcome you,' he said. 'Because you're English, I guess. That Nungesser business didn't do us Yanks a lot of good over there.' He stared round him, still with the clergyman treading on his heels. 'Say, shouldn't somebody inform Mr Courtney?' he demanded.

'I should forget my father,' Alix said. 'He's got enough on his hands at the moment.'

'Boyle then?'

'Boyle'll turn up. Stop worrying.'

'Hey, Mr Loerner,' one of the reporters interrupted, 'what's the Reverend for? Is he the new co-pilot?'

To their relief, Loerner turned away, brisk and efficient and now occupied elsewhere. 'This is the Reverend Westcott Bone,' he said. 'Wedderburn Lutheran Church. He'll be saying a short prayer just before the airplane leaves.'

'The hell he will!' Alix snorted to his back. 'Whose idea was that?'

Loerner turned and gave her his thin smile. 'Mine,' he said. 'I felt a prayer was the right thing to have as you took off.'

She gave him a contemptuous look. 'You confine your activities to keeping the crowd back,' she said, 'and leave our souls out of it. It'd be a damn sight more use.'

Woolff gestured over Loerner's head, pointing behind him. 'Byrd's here, Ira. He wants to wish you luck.'

The naval man's handsome face appeared out of the shadows. 'Best of luck,' he said.

As they shook hands, the camera guns flashed and the thick magnesium smoke set the crowd coughing. 'What about the Navy?' someone called out, and Byrd gave a twisted smile.

'They're beginning to think I'm the world's prize boob,' he said. 'But I'm after knowledge, not records.'

'Fokker's supposed to be coming down, too, Ira,' Woolff pointed out as Byrd left. 'And Grover Whalen and Chamberlin and Orteig's son.'

Ira glanced at his watch. 'They'll have to hurry,' he said. 'I can't wait.'

Sammy had left Mae now and was talking with Collins, the Wright official, by the engine. Alix moved away a little, alone in her isolation, watched curiously by the whispering crowds who shifted and curdled as the police and the few pressmen moved among them. No one bothered her and she seemed lost in a morass of her own thoughts.

'Barograph's fixed,' Woolff said. 'They'll seal the tanks just as soon as we're ready. We've got four hundred gallons in, so far. She'll have four-seventy-five when we've finished.'

Ira nodded. 'That's a hundred and seventy-five more than she's ever had before,' he said. 'What'll she weigh?'

'Five thousand three hundred.'

Ira smiled. 'Let's hope the Whirlwind's built to lift it.'

'The engine's in perfect shape. It ought to deliver more than it was built for.' Woolff looked at him. 'How do you feel?'

'As though I'm being prepared for execution.'

Woolff nodded at Alix. 'How about . . . ?'

Ira smiled, but he realized it was a little stiff. 'She'll be all right. How's the ground?'

Woolff's face grew sober. 'Soft, Ira,' he said.

Ira glanced at the sky and felt the rain on his face. 'It'll be softer still by the time Lindbergh gets here,' he pointed out.

'The wind's right, though,' Woolff said. 'But it's due to change.' He gestured at a dark spiral of smoke beyond the field drifting lazily towards them. 'Lindbergh'll probably have to take off the other way.'

He looked at the dark sky. 'It doesn't look so goddam promising, Ira,' he said uneasily.

Ira nodded without speaking and Woolff went on nervously: 'Nobody's pushing you, Ira.'

Ira managed a wintry smile. 'I know,' he said. 'The decision'll be mine.'

'*I*'m not asking you to risk your neck just to break a record or win a prize,' Woolff said earnestly. 'I can do without both. You don't have to worry about me, Ira, if you think the weather's too bad.'

Ira slapped his shoulder and said nothing, and as he moved away Woolff stared after him, his eyes anxious.

Collins reappeared. 'Almost ready, Captain,' he said. 'I've checked structure and controls and the tyres are up to pressure and axles greased and the bearings are oiled.'

Ira stared at the bulging rubber. 'They'll need to be,' he said. Surrounded by mist, cut off by the damp particles that hung in the air, and achingly alone with his decision to go or not to go, he began to walk along the runway, feeling the wet

256

clayey ground with his toe and watching how the water oozed up round his boot. He noticed the eyes of the watching people rest on him, distant, speculative and wondering. They knew the chances as well as he did and many of them had been there when Fonck had crashed in flames.

He noticed Hal Woolff alongside him again, gesturing ahead at the runway.

'Police have cleared it,' he said. 'And it's marked halfway along. You'll know how far you've got to go.'

'I'll make up my mind there,' Ira decided. 'If we seem too slow, I'll close the throttle. If we seem O.K., I'll chance it.'

He glanced back. Not far from where they stood was the little dip in the ground marked with a bent propeller where two men from Fonck's Sikorsky had died eight months before. The ground was still bare and blackened where the great machine had burned.

Ira drew a deep breath, knowing just what Fonck had been faced with. It wasn't easy for a pilot to decide whether his machine had passed the point when safety had gone and a take-off had to be abandoned. With an overloaded machine, the margin was terribly slight.

Silently, he dug at the turf again with his boot, aware that the rain had stopped at last, then he looked up at Woolff. 'I wish it were all concrete, Hal,' he said. 'A nice stretch of new road would be useful down here. If there'd been one handy, I'd have used it.'

Woolff nodded and Ira stared along the field. He had walked its length many times and knew every dip and hollow. At the far end there were only telephone wires and then open country where people were already waiting on the golf course to see him pass overhead.

Probably thinking they were in the best position to see the crash, he thought wryly. The spectators weren't all aviation enthusiasts and the attitude of many of them to aeroplanes was only that they fulfilled their appetite for death-defying bravado. It would be all the same whether they succeeded or whether they failed. The excitement would be of the all-or-nothing sort. ENGINE FAILS. PLANE PLOUGHS INTO CROWD. It didn't matter what the headlines said or what the reasons were. It wasn't hard to believe that the crowds weren't all there just for a take-off.

Sammy appeared. His face was strangely solemn. 'She's ready, Ira. They've sealed the tanks.'

'O.K.' Ira turned, making his decision, his features set. 'Let's go.'

A man was standing by the plane, smiling, and Ira recognized him as the official who'd arrived to seal the instruments and the tanks and fix the barograph. He held out his hand. 'Everything's ready,' he said. 'I'd better wish you good luck.'

Woolff's mouth twitched in an uncertain smile. 'Watch that tail-heaviness, Ira,' he advised in a flurry of nervous and unnecessary last-minute advice. 'Keep the nose down till you're well clear and watch for a stall as you lift off. She'll be awkward till you've burned off some of that main-tank gas. We've got somebody following in a roadster with a fire extinguisher, just in case.'

Ira nodded, hardly hearing, then Alix appeared out of the mist. She looked tired and he knew that she must be.

'Ready?' he asked quietly.

She nodded.

'Get into your gear, Alix,' he said. 'And keep out of the way till the last minute. You don't want any interviews with the press.'

She nodded and pushed through the crowd to where she had parked her car. Ira touched Sammy's arm.

'Sammy,' he said. 'Disappear! We don't want anybody suspecting a switch. They'll tear her apart if they do and she's got as much as she can handle at the moment.'

Sammy didn't argue and vanished abruptly.

From where he was standing with his parson, Loerner had been watching the little episode. As Sammy vanished, his eyes grew narrow with suspicion and he slipped under the wing and appeared alongside Ira.

'What the hell are you guys up to?' he demanded. 'Sam Shapiro'll never fly with his hands bandaged like that.' He stared at Ira for a second, then he swore. 'By God, you'd got this thing planned!' he said indignantly. 'Alix Courtney's going in his place!'

Ira grinned. 'You've got it, Fred!' he said. 'First go!'

Loerner looked round, as though he were desperate to get his hands on a telephone. 'For sweet Jesus' sake!' he said. 'This is the story of the year, and now you tell me!'

'Hold it, Fred!' Ira grabbed his arm. 'Nobody's passing it on to anybody yet. Alix needs newspapermen bothering her just now like you need a dose of the smallpox. Leave her alone.

258

Half an hour from now, we'll be away, and then you can tell who the hell you like.'

Loerner's mouth opened and shut for a while and Ira grinned. 'Why don't you just relax, Fred,' he suggested, 'and enjoy the spectacle? Your fees are safe and if you wait around, you might even see the Ryan following us.'

Loerner stared at him, baffled, and Ira gestured.

'Fred, say nothing and you can have your sky-pilot say his prayer.'

Loerner scowled, then he shrugged. 'I guess you're right,' he said. 'There isn't a goddam thing any of us can do now, not even if the sainted aunt of the Apostle Paul's going.' He extended his hand and managed a grin. 'Except wish you the best, I guess.'

Ira shook hands. 'Right, now let's get on with the business before the wind changes. We don't want to have to transfer the plane to the other end of the field.'

Watched by the crowds—some of them straight from the nightclubs and still in evening dress—he walked slowly round the *Dixie*, just as he had when she'd first been rolled out for his inspection at Medway. He moved the rudder and the elevators, checking the hinges, then he walked along the starboard side of the machine, running his hand along the fuselage, his eyes flickering over the wing surfaces, along the ailerons and round the wingtips, then he moved to the front of the machine, his eyes on the bulging tyres and the newly greased axles, round to the other side, and to the pilot's cockpit.

Woolff was waiting for his nod of approval.

'O.K., Hal,' he said. 'Get Alix, then start her up.'

Alix appeared wearing her bulky flying suit buttoned to the neck, her hair tucked out of sight inside a white helmet. Heavy goggles and a scarf hid her face but Ira could see she was nervous.

The last goodbyes were said, and the camera guns flashed once more as Ira shook hands with celebrities. A reporter pushed forward. 'How about Mr Courtney, Mr Loerner?' he asked. 'Is he coming down to see the take-off?'

Loerner gestured. 'Miss Courtney's making the decisions today,' he said. 'The *Dixie* belongs to a consortium she heads and *she'll* be seeing it off.'

Ira smiled. 'You're doing all right, Fred,' he said. 'You can wheel on your parson.'

As he spoke, the engine started with a crackling roar and

little jets of flame and puffs of blue smoke jerked from the exhaust stubs. Woolff, sitting in the cockpit, glanced down from the window at Collins who was standing in front of the machine, staring up at the engine. Ortese was gazing at the quivering wings, then he walked slowly down the length of the machine to study the tail.

Struggling into his flying suit, Ira was aware of the curious looks of the crowd. They were clearly of the impression that he no longer belonged among them.

Sammy appeared wearing Hal Woolff's overcoat and a voluminous cap pulled low down over his eyes. In the poor light, with the milling crowd, nobody looked twice at him.

As the cameras were lowered for the last time, Boyle's stooping figure pushed through the newspapermen. He stood by the cockpit and began to shout above the engine.

'The hotel woke me, Ira,' he said. 'They'd heard and they thought I ought to know.'

'How's my father?' Alix demanded.

'He hasn't changed, but he'll be O.K.'

As they turned towards the plane, Loerner's parson stepped forward, his spectacles on the end of his nose, dandruff like cigarette ash all over his collar.

'We should be glad to have the company of the Lord with us on this trip,' he shouted above the engine.

Sammy glanced under the brim of his cap at Ira, his expression sharp. Sammy had a dislike of all forms of religion and was cynical about the Almighty.

'May the wings of His angels support you'—the droning voice rose over the pounding of the cylinders—'May their guidance direct you. May His great love wait over you and His great compassion protect you.'

As the prayer came to an end, they climbed thankfully into the machine and Woolff leaned into the cabin to push a harness belt across to Alix. Behind him, looking like a strange sort of bodyguard in the long coat and cap, his bandaged hands thrust deep into his pockets, Sammy grinned up at her.

'I reckon you can get to Paris without any help of that kind,' he said. 'Them wings he was talking about would be a bloody sight better flapping about underneath to lift her off when the time comes.'

Ira had climbed into the other seat now and Sammy went round to him. 'This is it, Sammy,' Ira said.

'Look out for Isaac!'

Ira grinned. 'Wish you were coming too, Sammy.'

'Aw'—Sammy took his hand from his pocket and nudged him with the back of his bandages—'you'll be well looked after.'

Alix gave him a thin tense smile, and as he stepped back into the crowd, Ira saw a reporter move forward, look closely at him, then turn angrily to Loerner. Sammy grinned at him, impulsively took off his vast cap, and waved at Ira. Loerner gave him a resentful look and occupied himself with the sudden flurry of argument among the reporters. One of them moved forward, as though he were intending to try to question Alix even as she sat in the cockpit, but Loerner pulled him back and Ira slammed the door hurriedly and locked it.

Alix gave him a bleak smile, as though she couldn't trust herself to speak, clearly nervous but holding herself well in check.

Strapping himself in, Ira put one hand on hers. She looked up at him for a moment, then she turned away and began to pick up the maps.

Sitting in the cabin, amid the acrid fumes of petrol, Ira took out his log book and filled it in briefly. It wasn't his habit normally to enter details before a flight but this time it might help to indicate who he was if anything happened to them and it was found.

Date—20.5.27.
Type aircraft—Courtney-Wright.
Marking—N2 209.
Journey—New York–Paris.
Pilot—Self.

He left the time spaces empty, then after staring at it for a second he thrust it into his overalls and sat back, looking at the rev counter. Frowning, he moved the throttle forward and felt the plane surging against the chocks, and listened to the drumming roar of the engine.

'She's not giving full revs,' he shouted down to Collins who was standing by the cabin. Sammy moved forward from the crowd to join them and held up his thumb.

'She will, Ira,' he said. 'Soon as you get above the weather. Lindbergh's'll be the same, I bet.'

Ira frowned. 'It's not when I'm up I want the revs,' he said. 'It's *now*.'

Collins looked anxious from behind Sammy. 'Can't do anything about it, Captain,' he said. 'Wait for the weather to change, you'll see a difference.'

Ira nodded, making his mind up. He had to go now. If he waited for the weather to improve and the revolutions to increase, the start he'd gained over the others would be lost.

Loerner approached the side of the machine. 'They say Lindbergh's arrived at Curtiss,' he said. 'He'll be here any time.'

'O.K.,' Ira nodded, and opened the throttle wider, his gaze fixed on the round dial of the tachometer. The needle moved up, paused and stopped, still short of maximum revolutions.

'It'll catch up,' Sammy yelled.

Ira nodded again, not speaking. No matter what Sammy said, or Hal Woolff or Collins, the decision was still his. He had to decide whether it was safe to launch this overweighted machine into the air and risk his own life and that of his passenger.

He pulled the throttle back, listening to the idling engine, and his eyes met Alix's. She was sitting in her seat, her safety belt fastened, holding the roll of maps and charts they'd made up.

She gave him a questioning look, but he didn't say anything, sitting motionless, surrounded by the sharp smell of dope, warm oil and hot metal, almost as though he were communing with himself. The runway was soft and he could see huge puddles glinting in the early light. The rain on the grass would act as a brake for the wheels and, with an engine delivering less power than they expected, they were taking off with more weight aboard than they'd ever lifted before. It was a decision that rested more on instinct than on what he knew from the performance curves the machine would do. Despite all the figures and the tests they'd made, everything was thrown away when the weather didn't measure up and they were back once more to instinct—seat-of-the-pants flying, by guess and by God, call it what they would—the subtle alchemy of sheer experience. He turned and glanced at her.

'Everything stowed?' he asked.

'Everything stowed, Ira. Earth inductor on course.'

He paused. 'I'd have been happier with the Viking pump,' he said, 'and our old compass. You might as well get that on record in the log just in case.'

Woolff had joined Sammy and Collins alongside the machine. He seemed to guess what Ira was worrying about. 'It's a new pump,' he yelled. 'It was built specially for us. I told 'em about the cams and the spindles and they strengthened 'em.'

'They said they'd had one like it working for sixty-five hours without trouble,' Sammy added.

'I hope we can trust 'em.' Ira said. He paused, still concerned with the shortage of revs.

'Let's listen to the engine again.' He gestured to Collins and Woolff and revved the engine, staring narrow-eyed through the circle of light where the propeller revolved. The sound of the engine was smooth and powerful, and he cut the throttle.

'You won't get better,' Collins yelled up to him. Behind him, Woolff gave him a nervous smile. He seemed more worried than Ira. Ortese nodded.

'She sounds perfect,' he said.

'Sammy?'

'Ira, you'll never have a better engine under you.'

Ira grinned and buckled his safety belt. 'That's what I thought.'

Ahead of him, he could see the first streaks of day showing in the east, a low bar of light along the horizon. Houses were taking shape around him in the distance now, and the low outline of the tree-fringed hill by the golf course. Somewhere out there, unseen still, were the telegraph wires he had to clear. He could see the poles now, faint sticks against the first light of the sky.

Sammy waved and pointed. 'Lindbergh,' he said.

Ira glanced in the direction he was pointing and saw headlights moving towards them down the field, and the faint outlines of an aeroplane's wings.

'They've still to fuel up,' Sammy shouted. 'It'll be eight o'clock before he gets off.'

Ira glanced across the cabin at Alix. She was not wearing gloves and he could see her knuckles were white and the map of New York and Long Island was creased where she gripped it.

She caught his eye on her and her mouth jerked in a small smile, and Ira signalled to the men standing beside the plane and pulled down his goggles.

'Let's go,' he shouted, and they stepped back to where Loerner was waiting with Boyle and the parson and the small group of newspapermen.

Sammy took up his position alongside Mae and Ira saw her grab for his bandaged hand nervously. Sammy turned his head towards her, startled, as though surprised that she should be at all doubtful about the outcome, then he waved at Ira.

'Keep 'em flying, Ira,' he yelled in a high cracked voice.

Ira waved back and he saw the chocks jerked away from the wheels, then, crouching forward in his seat, as though he were urging the machine forward, he grasped the control column and thrust the throttle wide open.

For a moment, it seemed as though the thunderous roar of the engine were merely an illusion and that the circle of light where the propeller revolved were not part of the machine. For a while there appeared to be no sign of movement forward, then, glancing down at the wheel alongside him, Ira saw the tyre was moving slowly over the grass, the water oozing out of the ground under its weight.

It seemed strange and unreal, as did Loerner struggling beyond the wing-tip with an arguing reporter. As the plane edged forward, Loerner gave the reporter a shove, snatched off his hat, and his blank suspicious face broke into a wide grin as he began to wave it hysterically. Alongside him, the reporter stared indignantly at him for a second, then he, too, snatched off his hat and began to wave.

Woolff and the Wright engineers and a couple of officials had laid their weight behind the struts and began to push, their clothes blown flat against their bodies by the propeller blast, their skin plastered by the muddy water that was blown into their faces, and, lifting his gaze, Ira saw Sammy staring enviously at him as he slipped slowly out of sight. Beside him, Boyle watched. He had been waving his battered hat but he was grasping it now in both hands, twisting it with apprehension, leaning towards his right as though he might urge the heavy machine forward with his own will; and, as though on a screen and detached, Ira saw the crowd cheer and the reporters lift their pencils and make a note on their newspapers of the time of departure.

The wheel alongside began to move faster, though it was still desperately sluggish, anchored to the ground by the soft earth and the rain. His eyes flickering over the dials, Ira wondered suddenly if the engine were failing him at the last moment, then he realized the crowd had slid away behind him at last and that the machine was beginning to pick up speed. Woolff was running alongside the wing-tip now, and Ira could see him shouting, urging the machine forward, then, as the speed increased, he, too, fell away behind, panting.

Pushing the stick forward, trying to get the tail up, well aware that with that enormous tank in the fuselage behind him the machine was tail-heavy to a dangerous degree, Ira could see that the sky was already fractionally lighter ahead of him and the band of light on the horizon broader. Feeling the stick quivering in his hand, he was aware of Alix leaning forward, too, as though she also were trying to urge her weight to the nose to ease the load on the tail.

'Tail's up, Ira.'

The machine still felt sluggish, sullen and even unstable as the weight of the petrol shifted. Unless they could get up sufficient speed, unless it accepted its burden, they were in danger of stalling on take-off, held down by their own tremendous weight. The sound of the engine sounded thin and insufficient and, with none of the feeling of urgency in the aircraft that it had given before, it was as though Ira were trying to lift off the ground something that was dragging anchors across the turf.

He glanced quickly down alongside him and saw the spinning tyre and the shuddering landing gear. This was where Fonck had failed. If he once allowed the *Dixie* to change course, all the tremendous weight would be thrown across the axis of the wheels, and the undercarriage would collapse. A wing-tip would touch as they slewed round, and the result would be a fiery death like Cluff's.

He thrust the thought from his mind and concentrated on what he was doing. Beside him, he was aware of Alix sitting rigidly, her thoughts the same as his, her mind as aware as his of the dangers.

He eased back on the stick now, trying to raise the nose from the ground, trying to judge the exact spot where the machine would lift, and he felt the controls grow more taut and knew that the speed had built up sufficiently for the wings to bite at the air. With the load they were carrying, all the accepted positions for the tachometer needle were pointless. It depended entirely on his own skill and whether he had enough experience to judge when and how to lift the *Dixie* from the ground.

They were approaching the halfway mark now and the speed was approaching sixty-five miles an hour and he could feel the wings finally beginning to support the weight of the machine. But the runway seemed as though it would never be long enough. The halfway mark blurred past in a flash of white and, as the machine lurched a little on a patch of uneven ground, Ira's heart thumped heavily in his chest as he waited for the dangerous swing that might collapse the strained undercarriage or burst the overweighted tyres.

The grass was a green blur now and there was a surging power in the engine at last, a feel that told him that the machine was beginning to ride on the air instead of the wheels. His eyes were glued to the runway now and he could no longer take them away to glance at the instruments. From this point on, it was the sense of his hands and 'the seat of his pants'—the feeling an experienced pilot had for his machine, the sure knowledge that he was safe—that would tell him when to make the final decision.

The machine bounced and everything rattled and creaked as it came down heavily. If he didn't get off now, it would be almost too late, because they were beyond the point when they could still stop in the length of the runway. If he left it too late, the plane would smash over the perimeter of the field, ploughing ahead still at full speed with all its tremendous weight to give it a momentum that could only result in disaster because behind them were one and a half tons of fuel poised to crash down on the hot engine and explode into flames.

The wheels were off the ground at last and the rumbling beneath them ceased abruptly, but the sluggish machine settled again, canted over at a dangerous angle, and he saw spray shoot over the wing as the wheels brushed the surface of a puddle. Then they were lifting again, the end of the field rushing towards them, and he could see the narrow sticks of the telegraph poles growing swiftly larger. The machine bounced again, lurched, one wing low, dipped and straightened as he corrected with the stick, and he sensed, rather than saw, Alix's fingers tense on the edge of the chart.

They were climbing now, still lopsided, but climbing, poised in the rush of air past the surface of the wings. It was now when they were most vulnerable. He had to lift them over the telephone wires, yet he dared not try too soon or too quickly or they would lose forward movement and stall. The machine had only just reached flying speed and was still labouring and now was the moment when he had to exercise the greatest care.

There was no longer any stopping, though. He could only

go on now, trying to hold the machine up, careful not to climb an inch too much, praying they'd have acquired sufficient of those precious feet in height before they reached the wires.

A tractor flashed below him to his right, then the wires were immediately ahead of him, looping in long arcs across his path. His heart thumping, he saw them slide beneath them, with a matter of a dozen feet to spare, and saw pale uplifted faces watching them from the fringes of the golf course. The hill lay just ahead and he turned to the right slightly to avoid it, putting on only the shallowest bank in the knowledge that too much would cause them to lose speed and slide off the turn into the ground.

He hardly dared use the controls, so fine was the point on which they were balanced, but the machine was beginning to climb faster now and the trees on the hill slid away behind them so that his chest heaved in what he felt was the first breath he'd drawn since he'd opened the throttle.

They were a bare two hundred feet from the ground still, by no means sufficient for safety, especially with that tremendous weight of fuel behind them, then he saw Alix glance at him and realized that, except for the tightening of her fingers on the maps, she had hardly moved since they'd started their run.

He looked cautiously at the tachometer. It was still reading short but the revs hadn't fallen any further, and levelling off slightly he eased the throttle back gently. Trimming the aircraft a little with the stabilizer, he felt it become easier under his hand and for the first time he realized how tightly he was gripping the stick.

He throttled back again, sensing that the machine was safe at last, that they were riding on the air with taut controls.

'Sixty-three degrees, Ira,' Alix called out above the roar of the engine, and he moved the stick to bank cautiously on to course.

'Sixty-three,' he repeated. 'On course.'

He turned his head towards her at last and his stiff face slowly relaxed in a smile. She was watching him with large eyes that were scared and proud at the same time.

'I wouldn't like to do that again in a hurry,' he said.

CHAPTER SEVEN

You never your life your own can make
Unless you're willing that life to stake.

THE OLD JINGLE his father had been fond of quoting to his mother when she had complained about the risks he took in the fragile machines he'd built with their always dubious motors, came back to Ira now as the *Dixie* laboured upwards above the estates and truck farms of Long Island. Though in the end his father had paid with his life for his desire to master the air, there must have been moments like this one, Ira knew—as one of his frail constructions had lifted off the ground—when he'd felt like a god, moments no earthbound creature could ever know or understand. Sitting alone in a fragile machine of metal, wood and fabric, supported by the pull of a single uncertain propeller, he had been a man in command of his own destiny, staking all he possessed, even to the final sacrifice, in the belief that it *had* to be staked for the sake of knowledge and truth and all the things that made a life worth living—just as his son and his passenger were doing now, fourteen years later.

They too were alone now, achingly alone with their own poor courage, beyond the reach of any help if anything went wrong, beyond help and alone from the moment Ira had opened the throttle at the end of Roosevelt Field.

There had been better aviators than he was, Ira knew, but a lot of them were dead because their luck had run out when they hadn't expected it to. Men had been lost in combat or in peace-time cross-country flying simply because fortune had turned its back on them. Harry Hawker, who'd tried to fly the Atlantic in 1919, had known all there was to know about aircraft. He'd designed them himself, had built them and test-flown them, but he'd had to ditch his plane, nevertheless, because some trivial obstruction had caused his radiator to boil. His luck hadn't been entirely out on that day, however, and he'd been rescued, only for it to vanish two years later when his machine had blown up in the air. John Alcock, who'd been first across the neck of the North Atlantic, had not lasted more than six months after his flight before he'd hit a tree trying to land in fog. Aviation had never been a profession for people who feared death.

*   *   *

The map alongside him rattled and he saw Alix glance at him. She had hardly spoken since they'd climbed into the machine, but the tension had gone from her now and he saw she was relaxed, sufficiently a pilot to know that the first worst hazard had passed. The engine had done all they'd asked of it and the *Dixie* had proved that all Hal Woolff's calculations had been right. She was no longer just a question mark, a guess despite all the figures.

Danger wasn't behind them, however, and wouldn't be for another thirty-six hours—longer if weather or luck were against them—but they had to face their obstacles in stages, and the first stage was safely in the shadows. The second obstacle was getting themselves on course, because without a correct beginning they would be wrong all the way and, since a great part of their flight would be in darkness, they had to be accurate. From now on, they could only put their faith in the knowledge of other men that was written into the testimony of their maps and charts. They could not afford to doubt the printed sheets they held in their hands because without them they were blind. With those sheets they held the earth spread before them, all its routes and turnings clear before their eyes.

Almost as though she sensed his thoughts, he saw Alix was looking for landmarks below to check against the map, watching for the bays and buildings and the curves of land that corresponded to the symbols under the ink line they'd drawn across the paper.

Now that they'd cleared the field and were nearing the sea, they had run into mist again—the grey haze off the Atlantic moving down from the north, which had just cleared sufficiently over Long Island to allow them to become airborne. They were still flying low because it was possible at that altitude to pick up their landmarks through the murk. Ahead of them they could see the broken shoreline and beyond it the steely grey of Long Island Sound with its little indentations, villages and farms and the groups of big holiday homes.

'Looks better ahead,' Alix observed. 'Mist's thinner and the clouds are higher, too.'

They were suddenly at ease together after the days and weeks of strain, and Ira settled himself in his seat, watching the dashboard, while Alix watched the ground. Oil pressure, oil temperature, fuel pressure—all normal. Tachometer building up a little as it should. Speed 103. Compass reading 63.

Altitude 500 feet. He moved the rudder a little to bring the machine's nose on to course.

'Let's work round the tanks,' he said above the engine. 'We don't want fuel slopping through the vents if we hit bumpy weather. Put her on to nose tank first.'

Alix's hand moved to the cocks and Ira nodded. 'Centre, nose, right wing, left wing, main,' he said. 'Let's work round them for a while, then we'll go on to main and get rid of the nose heaviness, and then back on to rotation. Note 'em in the log.'

They were flying over the mouth of the Nissequogue River now, under a layer of grey stratus, and, ahead of them, about two miles away, distinct through the clearing haze, Crane Neck Point stuck out into Long Island Sound in a narrow curve of land marked by circling sea birds.

'You'll see New Haven on your left,' Alix said.

Now that they were away from the land and above the haze, the light was that full crystal light that only aviators knew and the cabin was flooded with a glow.

'Aeroplane on your left.' Alix tapped his arm and pointed and, glancing across the cabin, Ira saw a Jenny approach, looking like an insect at first, sidling towards them, then growing larger as it turned in front and took up a position alongside. A man was standing in the rear cockpit, a camera levelled at them. The pilot waved and Alix lifted her hand. It would make a good picture: The *Dixie*'s farewell to New York.

'I bet they were disappointed we didn't do a Fonck,' she commented.

Outrun by the more powerful *Dixie*, the Jenny soon fell behind, and as they left the land behind them the machine lurched in the rougher air above the junction of land and water, and Ira glanced quickly at the wings. They were lifting far more weight than they ought and were moving enough to worry him.

'Let's hope we don't get much of this,' he said.

They had reached a height of a thousand feet now, and as they left the shore behind them the turbulence subsided and the *Dixie* rode easily on the air again as they began to head across Long Island Sound. In the distance in the increasing light through a patch of clearing haze, they could already see the faint shadow of the Connecticut coastline.

In their thick flying suits, there was surprisingly little room in the cockpit, and their elbows and shoulders constantly brushed against each other. Knowing how quickly the constant friction could become an irritation, Ira signed to Alix to relax.

'Take a rest,' he advised. 'I can watch the chart.'

For the first time, the old imperiousness returned. 'I'm O.K.,' she said sharply. 'I don't need a rest.'

But she handed him the maps, nevertheless, and slid down in her seat, her eyes on the instruments and the notes she was making in the log. Below them the sea looked smooth as silk, with no indication of waves—empty, lonely and cold—and he saw her frown as she stared down at it, and knew that her mind was filled with the same niggling thoughts that kept forcing their way through the confidence they felt in their machine.

The Connecticut shore was blue with haze and Ira dropped the nose a little to lose height so as to pick up their landmarks more easily. It would give them their first indication of how the compass was working.

The blue, grey and lavender mottling of the land slid forward to meet them, passing under the nose. Beyond, they could see the trees in their spring green, a misty green that came from young, incompletely opened leaves. A few boats and a solitary ship driving along the coast, drawing its snail-trail of foam across the water behind it, showed them where New Haven lay on their left, tucked inside the inlet of the Quinnipiac.

'Earth inductor's reading a couple of degrees easterly,' Ira commented. 'Unless there's a breeze from the north we don't know about. We'll have to watch that. We should pass Providence on our right. Let's see how we hit them.'

As they passed over the coastline, the turbulence hit them again, but it didn't seem as bad as on the coast of Long Island. Ahead, the layer of grey stratus was still very low and to avoid it they descended even further. With a compass that was a degree or two off-true, it was important to be able to follow the course they'd intended, and, watching the clouds, noticing how they clung to the high land and nestled against the hills, he prayed that there would not have to be any detours at this stage in the flight.

'Fisher's Island below on your right, Ira,' Alix said, looking down. 'We're still heading slightly east of our course.'

Ahead of them through the mist lay Rhode Island and the scattered islets of Narragansett Bay, and Ira frowned, knowing they should have been further to the west at this stage. But the sky was much clearer now and the layer of grey stratus had changed to strato-cumulus, while further ahead they could see gaps between the patches of greyish cotton wool.

Adjusting the course, Ira saw that the cloud base was lifting rapidly now and a glance at the dials showed that there was nothing wrong with the engine. It was irritating to find a fault in the compass so early in the journey but it was nothing to grow alarmed about. If they had no worse to contend with they had no need to worry, and already they'd burned off around a hundred pounds of their excess weight.

Alix glanced at the dial readings and marked them off on the log, working out fuel consumption and the state of the tanks.

'How's she flying?' she asked.

'I'm not having to hold the nose down so much. Another hour or two and she'll be nicely balanced.'

They could see the vast holiday houses of Newport now, and the railway line curving north to the smoke pall of Providence and beyond, then turning east again to the coast at Boston. Between Pawtucket and Taunton they flew over small fields between stone walls that were full of cows and sheep scattered like beads on grass that was the new livid green of spring.

'So many villages here, it's hard to pick 'em out,' Ira said.

'That's Attleboro.' Alix jerked a hand to her left. 'Right ahead's Norton. Easton just beyond.'

'How's the wind?'

She peered down at the rising columns hanging listlessly in the air. 'None worth speaking of.'

'I think the weather's clearing, too,' Ira said. 'They said it would along the coast.'

They had been flying for two hours and a quarter now, and apart from the trivial problem of the compass, things were going better than they could have expected.

'Come on to sixty-nine degrees,' Alix said. 'Hold it for an hour.'

The great curving arm of Cape Cod was almost behind them now, and they could see the smoke haze of Boston mingling with the clouds. They were heading over Massachusetts Bay into the Gulf of Maine and aiming for Nova Scotia where Nungesser and Coli were first believed to have been lost. The land was behind them now and the grey sweep of the Atlantic lay ahead, vast, mysterious, endless, wet and cold. Ira had always somehow regarded it as dark, but there it was below them, bright with the day's light. From now on, for two hours, there would be no landmarks to set against their charts, no means of checking their compass, only the rolling grey waters of the North Atlantic. They were depending now entirely on the number of times to the minute the cylinders would fire, and the number of times the propeller would revolve, depending on the fragile wings that kept them aloft and the sluggish compass needle that was to hold them on course.

Considering what they proposed to do, regarding it unemotionally in the cold light of day, Ira found his worries rested entirely on the Hughesden petrol pump. It had already been said that success would prove little because so much depended on luck—and certainly with engines and aeroplanes developed almost to the point of certainty, luck was the only really doubtful element about the flight. And to Ira luck meant one small spindle supporting the cam by which the Hughesden pump operated. As far as the actual flying was concerned he was remarkably at ease. Although he'd never attempted such a flight before, he'd often found his way above cloud by compass, and tracked across the empty lands of Russia, Africa and China. He'd never been obliged to follow railway lines ('Flying by Bradshaw', they'd called it in the Flying Corps) and had never had to descend to read the names on railway stations, which was how some pilots made their way around. He'd decided early in his career that with the range and power of aeroplanes constantly developing, it was no good navigating by that sixth sense that experienced men were supposed to possess. He'd never believed much in it because it invariably turned out to be sheer luck, and inspired hunches often turned out to be guesswork that would have been thoughtless impulse if they'd been wrong.

Ahead of them now were two hundred and fifty miles of water, and, while a seat-of-the-pants flier might conceivably make his landfall in Nova Scotia, it would require more than luck and a sixth sense to carry him accurately over the two thousand miles from Newfoundland to his next landfall in Ireland. The smallest error, the slightest fault that showed in the short leg to Nova Scotia would be multiplied ten times by the time they reached Ireland.

He glanced down at the sea. An indication of the lack of

wind was the absence of white caps on the waves or the shot-silk marks across the surface where it brushed the water. From above it looked like a steely sheet, and descending to seek the denser air below, they flew for some time over a restless surface that looked cold and a cheerless grey-green in colour, neither warm with friendliness nor brooding with animosity—just existing.

'She's riding better,' Ira observed, adjusting the stabilizer again.

There were a few fishing vessels below them now, scattered across the surface of the sea, and sunshine sparkled on the water ahead of them so that he became aware of the warmth of it on his hands through the glass of the windscreen. The gaps between the clouds were increasing now, vast areas of brilliant blue surrounded by ivory towers of cumulus, rising one on another, tower on tower, keep on keep, then, beyond them, the vast plain of the open sky.

Alix was sitting silently alongside him, and he glanced at her, wondering what was going through her mind as she busied herself with charts, courses and fuel consumption. Throttling back a little further, he adjusted the mixture so that the speed dropped a fraction, because it was less of a strain now to keep the tail up with almost three hundred and fifty pounds of fuel from the tank behind them already used.

He glanced down at the sea again and noticed from the movement of the waves that a breeze had sprung up, blowing them south and slightly east. It wasn't what they wanted, because it only accentuated the fault they'd found in the compass, and they discussed the drift for a while and decided to adjust the earth inductor to it, in the hope of being better able to work out the error.

The rising sun on the windows at the side of the cockpit was making it uncomfortably hot now and Ira noticed that Alix had unfastened her flying suit. She passed him a cold sausage without speaking, and as he munched it he gestured at the controls. The look she flashed at him showed gratitude for having something to do, and for the trust he placed in her.

'Stick close to the course,' he advised. 'Then we can work out what the compass's doing when we strike Nova Scotia.'

She nodded, still not speaking, and for an hour he sat comfortably alongside her, marking down instrument readings, his eyes drifting over the dials. It was pleasant to relax a little, moving his legs as much as he could to get rid of the

274

cramp, and his mind drifted back to the powered box-kites in which he'd first taken to the air—his father's biplanes, Cody's towering two-decker, the early Henri Farmans where he'd sat out in front at the mercy of the weather, judging his angle by the elevator set like a tea-tray before him and working out his speed by the noise of the wind in the birdcage of wires about him.

What he was sitting in now was a man-made comet by comparison. Able to fly for hours at a mile and a half a minute, sleek and streamlined, its drag elements reduced only to a couple of struts and an undercarriage, and able to cross the vast width of the Atlantic in only thirty-six hours, it was years ahead of its time.

'Land, Ira.'

Alix's voice jerked him back to the present and he sat up and stared ahead. A vast purple-grey shadow stretched into the distance on their left and he could see hills piercing the horizon.

'Nova Scotia.'

Alix nodded calmly. 'We're still edging to starboard all the time. I think that's Wedgeport on your left.'

Ahead of them the vast land mass that made up the eastern-most tip of Canada stretched, patched with green and barren, between the areas of pine, and he realized they were moving up the eastern coast when he'd expected to strike it seventy-five miles to the west so as to fly the length of the Bay of Fundy and over the easternmost point of Prince Edward Island into Cabot Strait and the mouth of the St. Lawrence.

If they continued to follow the course the Hughesden earth inductor suggested, they'd miss St. John's on the tip of New-foundland by as much as forty or fifty miles.

CHAPTER EIGHT

'FIVE DEGREES,' Ira said. 'I reckon it's five degrees off true.'

'Not much,' Alix commented.

No, Ira thought. It wasn't much, but it was enough. They had around thirty changes of course between their present position and Paris, and the error was sufficient to throw them a long way out at the end of a two-thousand-mile leg. With the

275

wind from the north, it could have them trying to identify the tip of Ireland somewhere well down in the Bay of Biscay with their petrol low.

'Let's forget the earth inductor,' he suggested, 'and use the liquid compass. Let's allow for the error and see how we strike Newfoundland.'

The ground beneath them now was dotted with trees, ugly boulders and small still patches of water. There seemed to be remarkably little land cultivation and few settlements, as though the bare sparse countryside had defied all efforts to make anything of it.

Alix was studying the water and the shadows of the clouds. 'There's a wind here,' she pointed out. 'Thirty miles an hour, I guess.'

The bare hills on their left rose into a range of peaked mountains, and Ira indicated that she should climb.

'Watch the tail-heaviness,' he advised above the roar of the engine. 'The weight's not burned off yet.'

She opened the throttle and the *Dixie*'s nose lifted and for a while Ira watched for the signs that their overload had unbalanced the plane in its new attitude. She carefully adjusted the stabilizer, however, and there was only a little turbulence now that didn't seem to worry her.

'Halifax,' she said, and looking down he saw the fortified eminence and the long harbour, with its double entrances on either side of McNab's Island, and the narrow channel to Bedford Basin. Railway lines curved into a terminus from the west and down to the docks between low wooden houses.

Alix gestured towards the harbour. 'Six hours to Halifax is O.K.,' she said.

In spite of their northerly position, it was warm in the cabin now, and Ira opened the ventilator. The cold current of air seemed to wake them both up, and he glanced at the dials, noticing that the oil pressure had risen slightly.

Halifax was behind them now and they were flying along the broken coastline, a mass of small bays and inlets and small settlements of wooden houses, but the land itself looked rugged and rocky, and uninvitingly hard to work.

Over the land, as though the air were matching its mood to the harsh soil below, clouds were building up, great squadrons of cumulus, the first outriders quite close to them like the vedettes for a mighty army that was bearing down on them, dark and ugly and blotting out the whole of the northern horizon with its regiments. Below them the land was blurred by the angled shapes of squalls.

'Rain,' Alix commented.

'Let's hope that's all it is.'

The machine was already lurching a little in the turbulent air; and the lakes below, which earlier had been still, were now ruffled and they could see the feathers of movement across the water where the gusting wind struck them. The calmer waters along the shore were delusive because they were in the lee of the craggy land mass, but further out they could see white horses, as though the wind were strong and fierce.

With the wind on their port side, they knew that the worsening weather was directly ahead of them and, crabbing into the squalls at a broad angle to compensate for drift, they could now see the solid mass of the storm athwart their route.

'Are we turning south away from it, Ira?' Alix broke the silence that had settled on them as their thoughts became occupied with the weather and the increasing gustiness.

Ira shook his head. 'Not yet,' he said. 'Let's keep to the course if we can. It can only blow us away from the coast a little, and it might not be much.'

The turbulence was increasing steadily by this time, tossing the machine about violently with the uncomfortable lurching motion, jarring the wings' roots as the spars shuddered and shook in the buffeting. They fastened their safety belts again, aware that in spite of the amount of fuel they'd used, they were still heavily overloaded for such a small plane. Taking over the controls again, Ira moved the throttle back and let the speed drop. It was like driving a ship into the teeth of a storm. As the buffeting increased, they had to reduce forward way to reduce the shaking.

Below them the hills and lakes were blurred by the rain now, and the clouds about them were increasing, crowding in on them, purple-grey and ugly, the rain hammering at the glass in front of their faces as though the avenging army behind the vedettes were hurrying to protect the silences of these northern skies from the interlopers from the south.

The wind had increased tremendously by this time and, try as he might, Ira could not keep from his mind the question: Had they misjudged the weather? Would it become worse and should they have waited a day longer? They were crabbing across a wind that was gusting up to fifty miles an hour now, zigzagging a little to dodge the columns of rain that smashed deafeningly against the windscreen, blinding them as effectively as if it had drawn a blind in front of them. The cabin was lit up by the glare of lightning and Ira moved the stick to turn them away from the storm. Visibility returned as the squall died abruptly, though flurries of rain still struck the windscreen, jerked, shuddered, moved against all the laws of gravity upwards as the wind drove them before it. Writhing lines of water shivered over the engine cowling and back to the windscreen, trickling along the surfaces, cowering and recovering behind the cylinder heads where there was some protection from the propeller's blast. Alix began to knock it off her flying suit as it forced its way through the door.

'Up periscope,' Ira said laconically. 'Down to ten fathoms.'

Below them the roads and rocks and roofs were reflecting the lurid light that streamed down from the sky, and the few ribbons of smoke from the scattered huddles of buildings were shredded by the storm. They had descended again to avoid the clouds and, pouring the machine down the contours of the ground, as they swept up and through a narrow saddle between the hills they could see the trees on either side of them bending under the press of the wind.

As they reached the jagged edge of the cold front, the waves across the little lakes below leapt under the buffeting of the wind, whose direction veered rapidly, and swung back again each time they hit a fresh squall.

Then gradually, as they pressed further along the coast, the wind steadied and began to blow from the north and west, still carrying them south, but helping them along their route.

As the last of the rain blew from the engine cowling, Alix peered at the instruments.

'We can do with less of that,' she observed.

Ira nodded, letting her have the controls again now that the buffeting had ceased. Patches of clear sky had begun to reappear, and there was no point in not taking rest. Before they'd finished, they'd both be fighting fatigue.

They were flying now over deep forests, black shadows on the grey-green of the earth, and patches of swamp and trees that were full of life. From time to time, they saw huge clouds of water birds over the lakes, their wings beating against the wind, and Ira remembered how he'd once seen them rising from the calm backwaters of the Yangtze in China. From below they would look like vast islands of reeds at first, then there would be a fluttering and a stirring along the edges, a restlessness as though the reeds were disturbed from beneath, until they finally burst into the air with a clatter of wings and the slapping of webbed feet on the water, to circle in a black cloud, filling the heavens with the throbbing sound of their cries as they darkened the sky with their numbers.

The storm has fallen away to the north now, a retreating army defeated in battle, and patches of cumulus, great dragging covered waggons of white and purple, lofted upwards almost beyond sight. On the ground, now as they pressed further north, with the sun obscured by a high layer of thin grey-yellow cloud, they could see flecks of white against the walls, the last of the winter snow, still clinging to the exposed places where the bite of the wind riveted them to the earth away from the sun. To the north-west there was a woolly patch of fog reaching out into their path, and, checking the magnetos instinctively, Ira glanced about him, looking for landmarks against which they could check their course.

Small fishing settlements passed beneath their port wing, huddling under the rocks and sheltered by the trees, the ships lying in rows along the docks. Inland they could see small farms and even the neat rows of orchards.

'Chedabucto Bay coming up,' Alix said, reading his thoughts. 'Sydney ahead on your left.'

Ira nodded and turned his attention to the fog again, but it proved to be nothing more than a long wide island of haze, clinging to the coast. Beyond it, they could see the sun glancing obliquely through the clouds to strike the sea in patches of unexpected colour and, as they cleared Chedabucto Bay, the light was reflected by the roofs of Sydney, wedged in among the narrow northern inlets at the very tip of the land, the last fragment they would see for some time until they struck Newfoundland. Picking out the chain of hills stretching from east to west to Cape Chignecto and—beyond the steely strip of Lake Ainslie—the steep turrets of Ingonish surrounded by patches of cloud, Ira made a quick calculation.

'Five degrees,' he said. 'Is the liquid compass out, too, Alix? Is that what you make it?'

She was silent for a while as she made small hurried calculations. 'That's it exactly,' she said.

Fortunately, the air about them was devoid of clouds and squalls, and they checked their position without difficulty. The ground was quilted here and there with snow now, though its streams and lakes reflected the blue clearness of the sky against the darkness of the earth.

Already they had slipped off course, and as Ira gave a new reading they angled back towards the route they sought. So far, they'd been fortunate enough to have had clear weather to make their checks, but during the night ahead of them or if they ran into fog or heavy cloud they'd have no knowledge of how much their compasses varied. They were having trouble in no other direction, however, and the engine beat out its song without hesitation. They readjusted the earth inductor confidently.

'Tanks, Alix?'

'Right-wing tank. We've got rid of a lot of that overload from the rear tank now. How's she flying?'

'Fine. Tail heaviness's gone. Let's keep working round them now.'

As Ira lifted his eyes to stare ahead again, the coast slid away to the left below. Before them was another two hundred miles of ocean before they would pick up their next landfall in Newfoundland, which they'd planned to strike at Placentia Bay so as to cut across the narrow neck of land to Harbour Grace to make their final check at St. John's. When they left St. John's they would already have flown almost half of the way to Ireland and would still have farther to fly than Alcock and Brown. Despite the storms, however, it was probably the easier half, though from that point on there would be no landmarks on the restless plains of the sea, and the emptiness of the night would spread no pathways ahead of them.

In these northern waters, too, there would be no ships to whom they might fly in case of trouble, because they were too far off the shipping routes. But they'd left the clouds behind them now over the land, and apart from a few high streaks of cirrus the sky was clear ahead of them.

Alix took the controls again, settling into her seat and peering over the engine cowling where the last threads of water from the squalls they'd passed through jerked and shuddered behind the projections. Her face was calm, and it was clear no thoughts of danger or apprehension were running through her mind. Her dark eyes were forthright and unemotional, and Ira knew she'd never panic whatever happened; and in the last extremity, there'd be no complaints, no accusations, no acrimonious blame. She had the right temperament for ventures of this sort, and her behaviour was beyond reproach.

The sky was quite clear now except for scraps of high cirrus, and the sun was bright enough for them to see on the underside of the wing the shadow of the registration letters painted on the upper surface. The engine note was deep and safe, all the dials reading exactly as they ought, and Alix shifted in her seat, moving on the cushion, one hand on the control column, the other hovering over the throttle, the mixture control, the switches, constantly checking that all was well and functioning as it should.

'Keep this course, Alix,' Ira said. 'We should see Placentia Bay in two hours' time. You'll have high land on your left and only a narrow strip between you and the Atlantic.'

'O.K.' She nodded and Ira sank back in his seat. Turning his head, he saw her eyes on him briefly and her mouth lifted in a smile.

The sea looked colder now, paler in colour than they'd previously seen it, as though the wind were stirring sand from the vast depths below the turbulent surface. Now that they were over the sea again, with nothing against which they could check their course—no item of interest to impinge against a drowsy mind to jar it into wakefulness—tiredness flooded across him. The previous day had been longer and more arduous than either of them would have wished, but there had been no foreseeing it and, in the emergency of Courtney's collapse, no way of avoiding it. On their trip from San Antonio to New York, they had been less taxed by events, despite the faulty pump, and had known at this period in their flight that half their journey was behind them so that their wits had been alert for the crossing of the Appalachians, and they had been wide awake for signs of the storm they'd been racing.

This time, however, they had started tired and they couldn't feel that they'd reached the hump and were nearing home. They had another twenty-five hours—more than a whole day—before they could know their journey was ending, another journey as long as the one they'd already flown before they could feel they'd completed even half the route. And two hours from now there would be nothing ahead of them, no mountains, no rivers, no landmarks to jog their minds to work, only an unending stretch of ocean to dull their wits.

When he glanced again at Alix, her head had fallen forward a little but her expression was alert and relaxed and the lines that had already begun to form on her face were smoothed away. There was a great deal of fine spirit in her, he thought, and a great deal of courage, up to now probably all wrongly applied and driven by her father's failed ambitions into all the wrong channels.

The sun had passed its zenith now and was sinking behind the aircraft. Ahead, the colour of the heavens was deeper, because it was from that eastern sky that the night would rise to meet them. Ira moved in his seat, feeling no great need to be on the alert. Alix could fly a course accurately, and if he fell asleep she would wake him in an emergency.

He turned his head and she smiled. 'Eight hundred and fifty miles flown, Alix,' he said.

'It'll do,' she said. 'I think the wind's coming round behind and there's ice below.'

She jerked her head forward and Ira sat up as fragments of dazzling white caught his eyes. A great field of frozen water lay below them, tumbled and broken, the pieces—as big as tennis courts and ten feet thick—forced on end by the pressure.

She was staring down with narrowed eyes. 'Wasn't it somewhere here the *Titanic* hit?' she asked.

'Further south. It breaks off the northern ice field in the spring and drifts towards the sun.'

The light was coming up at them from below now, striking the roof of the cabin to give a double brilliance to the day.

'Byrd flew over this sort of thing to the Pole last year,' Ira said.

She made a movement with her shoulder. 'Didn't help him much today.' She gestured at the ice. 'If it was smoother, you could land on it, do an overhaul and take off again.'

'Suppose you didn't make it? I wouldn't fancy spending a night down there.'

They talked idly for a while, watching the twisted moon-surface of the broken white field passing below them, the sun glinting on the angles of the up-ended floes as though on the facets of a diamond. Every now and again as the ice flung the sun directly back at them, there was a flash of gold that was dazzling and unexpected, and here and there the water showed in black angular streaks zigzagging to the north. Along them wisps of fog clung low over the water, following the line of the gaps in thin patches of mist.

Alix's eyes were roving over the instruments and her hand hovered over the throttle. 'How about bringing it back a bit,

Ira?' she suggested. 'We're making good progress and it'll conserve fuel.'

'O.K.'

As the tachometer needle fell back a fraction, she looked at him curiously.

'You *ever* been lost, Ira? Completely lost, I mean.'

'Not half. Once in 1919 in Russia. I ran out of fuel. A farmer with a cart towed me back. I was scared as hell. Bolshevik cavalry was around.'

'What was it like being in the middle of a revolution?'

'It's worse when it's someone else's revolution.'

They were merely talking for the sake of talking, letting their thoughts drift idly as the conversation drove away the listlessness that came from the drone of the engine and the long hours of sitting still. The sun was lower now and as it fell the lassitude of evening came on them strongly. They'd done a good day's work already, and they'd had no sleep the night before, and the prospect of staying awake listening to the pounding of the exhausts was a daunting one because it would be only too easy to fall asleep after dark when there wasn't even a horizon to look at.

Could that have happened to Nungesser and Coli? Had they reached this very area when sleeplessness had caused their eyelids to drop so that they'd recovered consciousness to find the horizon already spinning up to them, alert too late to save themselves? Or had dulled senses carried them into the craggy cliffs of Newfoundland, to smash into the granite rocks at the end of their flight, in some lonely spot where their machine had fallen back into the sea unseen so that they'd apparently disappeared into the darkness? Or had they been more successful than anyone knew and would they still turn up, somewhere in Canada, their landfall overflown in the night?

Ira jerked himself back to common sense, knowing such a thing was impossible. Such beliefs were simply hope persisting beyond reason, as it always did.

The beat of the engine was beginning to numb their senses now and the routine checks they made were a welcome break in the monotony. After eleven hours of flying it was easy to relax.

Ira was peering intently at the charts, however, and a worried look appeared on Alix's face as he sat up and began to stare ahead.

'Alix'—his voice was concerned—'we ought to have hit Placentia Bay by now. I reckon Hughesden aircraft compasses are about as well developed as Hughesden pumps.'

He gestured forward.

'Should be right ahead and below us,' he said.

He glanced at the clock, frowning. They ought to have been well down the neck of the bay now and heading for the strip of land that separated it from the north coast of Newfoundland.

He sat forward in his seat, peering towards the north-west Instinct alone told him their course.

'Alix,' he said. 'Turn north-east.'

She swung the machine to port, both of them staring ahead now, uneasiness gnawing at their stomachs.

'I've been on course all the time,' Alix said after a while, her eyes anxious.

'I know that. Don't worry.'

'There!' Her quick eyes caught a shadow ahead of them and she opened the throttle at once. So far, in spite of the small things that had gone wrong, neither of them had worried much, but now they suddenly awakened to the fact that they might easily have gone on ploughing over the North Atlantic, into the empty ocean south of Greenland, further and further towards ice and snow and oblivion.

'There, Ira!' Alix's hand jerked. 'That must be St John's!'

They were able to pick out a small city, set in a deep crevice in the iron cliffs, a huddle of flat-roofed buildings circling the edge of an inlet. Ragged mountains surrounded it, the entrance to the harbour a bottleneck between the peaks. It was filled with fishing boats, their thin masts moving gently on the swell that edged round the entrance from the sea, and they saw men moving along the wharves with ropes and tackles and barrows.

'We must have been forty miles to the south of our course,' Ira said. 'That damned Hughesden's getting worse.'

They flew along the rugged coastline for a time, their eyes on the mountains. A few of them carried snow on their eastern and northern sides where the sun couldn't reach, and the splashes of white made the craggy slopes look ugly and threatening.

'Wind's freshened again from the west,' Alix said. 'Look at the smoke.'

Thin fragmentary ribbons streamed towards the Atlantic,

and the *Dixie*'s wings rocked as she was caught by the gusts coming through the mountains.

Fortunately, they had found their landmark in time, and their engine was still sound, and if they flew their course, even with a margin for error, they could hardly miss Europe. Nevertheless, it was a sobering thought that, after eleven and a half hours of flying, their compass was proved wholly uncertain at a time when there was nothing ahead of them but two thousand miles of the Atlantic's steep stream.

'Better take a look around, Alix,' Ira suggested. 'This is the last view of land.'

Ahead of them was only the unknown. Only Alcock and Brown and the American flying boats heading for the Azores had successfully gone before them.

'Keep checking with Sammy's Chicks' Own, Alix,' Ira suggested. 'We can probably get an idea then how much the compass is out.'

He felt her move restlessly in the seat alongside him, and glancing at her he saw her brows were drawn down.

'When we get back,' she said, 'I'll go see that Hughesden lawyer and sock him on the nose. I didn't like him much, anyway.'

CHAPTER NINE

THE HORIZON was already taking on the rich blue of evening, the colour coming up out of the east like a slowly rising curtain, and with approaching darkness came an edge of worry to pervade their senses.

Alix leaned forward and moved the magneto switches one after the other. If the rev counter needle had flickered back to its stop as a magneto failed to respond, there were still fields in Newfoundland within reach where they might safely have set down their machine while it was still daylight. They were still in a position to turn on their course and reach safety if trouble arose, but soon they would reach a point when it would become safer to go on and, with night upon them, that point would be arriving in the hours of darkness when their calculations might be affected by fatigue. In a very short time, even the barren landing fields of Newfoundland would be denied to them, too, by the darkness that would obscure the folds of the land, and there would be only the lights of St John's beyond the purple glare of the exhaust to give them direction, and nothing to help them to earth but their skill and their luck.

Rested, Ira took over the control column as darkness fell. Below them the sea was growing fainter and the land had fallen far away behind. The wind was blowing strongly from the north-west now, carrying them southward towards the shipping routes and away from the shortest crossing, and they would have to watch this all the time to compensate for drift, particularly with the earth inductor giving wrong readings. During the night, it would be largely guesswork, because they would no longer be able to gauge the strength of the wind by the feathery streaks they could see on the surface of the water.

He glanced down at the map across his knees, just able to make it out in the last of the light. Errors of course were the chief hazard of long-distance flying, as trivial faults multiplied with every additional mile and each change of course. An error of a mile after ten miles became ten after a hundred and four hundred after four thousand. An error now could throw them out as much as five hundred miles by their journey's end.

Night flying over charted country was a lonely business at any time, but to fly in unbroken darkness without the guidance of beams or the knowledge that somewhere ahead was a well-lit landmark was a daunting prospect even to the most experienced. And over an ocean as big as the Atlantic, with the knowledge that they would see no more landmarks for at least sixteen hours, Ira found his mind full of the dead weight of irrelevant hopes, with, behind them, a realistic prayer for just a little luck. In spite of the knowledge of flight, they hadn't really conquered the air, and men as skilled as he was who had laid their plans no less carefully, whose machines were just as well designed, had disappeared into the darkness over oceans, vanishing into oblivion as if they had flown into a cloud and never reappeared. Without luck, he could drift off the face of the earth as surely as St Romain fifteen days before over the South Atlantic, or Nungesser on the very route he was following now.

He glanced again at the map but it was growing too dark now to see anything more than the outlines, and in the shadowy sea below them there was nothing now by which

286

they could fix their position; and, since they had vanished east into the growing darkness, nothing by which anyone else could fix it, either.

Someone at St John's would have seen them as they had passed overhead and radioed a message to New York that they had been seen heading out into the Atlantic. If trouble occurred later, such a message would fix their course and help a search, and it would set at ease the minds of Sammy and Hal Woolff and the Wright engineers. When a pilot disappeared over the horizon his ground crew always shared his apprehensions and the nervous strain that came with the first hint of trouble. No self-respecting mechanic lived without anxiety and no excuse about bad weather or errors of judgment gave solace to him as he tortured himself about wiring, fuel, and valves, and the possibility of having overlooked some small but vital adjustment that might cause the death of his pilot.

Nevertheless, those down below who had seen them pass overhead had had no knowledge of the wind in the upper air, no information about drift or faulty compasses, and this fact made them painfully alone with their problems, cut off from the rest of the world by the few hundred feet of altitude and the few miles that separated them from civilisation.

They began to see more white objects like sails below them and realized they were the conically shaped tips of icebergs linked together by wisps of woolly white. Patched with the broken fragments of floes that had become detached from the northern icefield, the sea was obscured by streaks of thickening mist which ran into each other to form a broken bank of fog.

'All O.K. so far,' Alix said, reading out the instruments. 'Compass course 87. Altitude 1000 feet. Revs 1700. Temperatures and pressures fine.'

'How do the compasses compare?'

'There's a hell of a gap. I think the liquid compass is wandering too, now.'

Ira was silent for a while before replying, curiously grateful for her presence and the steadiness of her voice.

'We've still got Sammy's Chicks' Own,' he said. 'We can always fall back on that.'

Despite their small anxieties, they had started the night with things so much in their favour, the first faint suggestion that something was wrong appeared quite unexpectedly.

It came six hours later, soon after midnight, with the stars bright and frosty above them. The day had slipped away suddenly, disappearing into the mists that hugged the American coastline, and they were flying by the stars instead of the compass card.

They'd been flying in darkness now long enough to feel confident and poised in time, a minute point of life hung in space above the night. Overhead, they had only short glimpses of the sky, and although they had climbed higher to get a better view of the stars, the patchy cloud persisted in a blurred unevenness that obscured the view. The wind had changed, however, just before darkness, and though they couldn't tell exactly, to judge by the fuel consumption, it was now right on their tail and helping them along their way.

Ira glanced at the illuminated dots of the compass card. So long as he could still see the stars, the unreliable dead eye of the compass wasn't much of a problem, but even while his mind dwelt on the subject, the stars disappeared again as a patch of cloud obscured them, and his eyes flickered to the ball of the turn-and-bank indicator and the altimeter needle. He was glad now he'd spent those hours over Charleston with nothing to help him but his instruments, because his senses were crying out that the instruments were wrong. It was easy in dark or cloud to feel you were flying one wing low or in a nose-down position because the senses seemed to lose their anchorage when there was no horizon, and pilots who had tried to correct a plane's position by them had found themselves sliding off on one wing to smash into the ground before they could recover.

After eighteen and a half hours of the sonorous beat of the engine, however, it was hard, with nothing to do but watch the needles, to stop the eyelids from drooping, but they'd climbed up to six thousand feet in an attempt to escape the cloud and their view of the stars suddenly grew clearer again and they were able to lift their eyes from the instruments once more. Ira would have preferred to have been even higher but they were still heavily loaded and the machine laboured when he tried to lift her further. He glanced at the dials on the dashboard. All the readings were normal enough, and as he flipped the magneto switches he hardly got a response from the needle.

With the end of daylight the cabin had grown cold again and they'd fastened up their flying suits. Clouds lay on either side and ahead of them now, masses of weirdly shaped cumulus, shadowy bulging curves too high to climb over and too widespread to make it worth trying to fly round them.

Ira studied the cloud mass warily, despite the exaltation the majesty of it produced in him, seeing soft foggy valleys and sharp black chasms and caverns, towers and arches as clear-cut as icebergs, festooned with splendid garlands of mist, all swirling and moving in the currents of the upper air. His experience told him their sides were full of danger and his instincts indicated that the only way to deal with them, short of turning back, was to go down to sea level. But that was too dangerous in the dark and a detour would use too much fuel, and he decided it was perhaps wiser to try to work his way through. The hammerheads of cloud towered probably to twenty-five thousand feet but there were plenty of breaks and the valleys were wide between the misty bulwarks.

He glanced upwards, assessing the height, and had begun to pick his way through the clefts and gorges with the purple exhaust glowing against the mist and the stars clear and sharp above his head when there was a white flash of lightning behind them that seemed to light up every swiftly moving valley and tower and showed up the fan-shaped spread of the anvil heads above the route along which he was trying to pick his way. The lightning came again—and again—until the clouds seemed a living wall of light, then they hit the first of the air pockets.

The first jolting was not severe but they heard the fittings rattle and he saw that the plane—the wings, even the air about them—was touched with the greenish incandescence of St Elmo's fire, so that they seemed to trail a tail like a comet. The next blow was harder, shaking them in their seats, then the jolts began to come like the blows of a giant fist to press them against safety belts and plummet them downwards so that the altimeter unwound crazily and the airspeed increased to a shrieking hundred and eighty, before hurtling them upwards again through the churning walls of mist, draining the blood from their brains and making their arms leaden. Working the throttle, Ira saw that the lightning had turned purple, as vivid as the exhaust flashes in front of them, and the machine began to shake and swing and shudder as disturbed air among the boiling cloud chasms caught it.

Unexpectedly, from among the maelstrom of swiftly moving cloud, rain and hail crashed noisily against the windscreen, bringing them both bolt upright in their seats at once. They couldn't even see the blue-blackness of the night now, only those jumping, jerking, shuddering streams of water that quivered in the slipstream across the glass. The plane was shaking violently, shuddering and swinging with an exhaustingly violent motion that put a strain on their muscles and nerves, and as the crash of the storm grew heavier and louder, they realized they were running into hail.

The engine sounded ragged and Ira worked the throttle until its beat smoothed, then the hail hit them again with a crash like a giant wave and the instruments seemed to go mad once more.

There was a terrific flash nearby that seemed to toss the machine about as though it were a leaf, and water began to drive its way into the cabin in a spray.

The compass needle was swinging wildly now, moving backwards and forwards in weird long sweeps as it was affected by the storm, and Ira's anxiety increased because, now that they could no longer check their position against a map, they had to rely entirely on the dial of a clock and that uncertainly swinging needle. They seemed to go on fighting the storm for what seemed hours, the aeroplane one minute sinking terrifyingly towards the surface of the sea as though the engine had cut and she were in a nose dive, the next rising like a lift between the shafts of cloud. Then it was swinging from side to side as though it were a pendulum until they felt sick and shaken with the motion, their bodies aching with the violence, their minds numb with the noise of the storm and the protesting cries of the overstrained machine.

Neither of them spoke as Ira fought against the controls. With the size of the storm area, there had been no sense in trying to fly round it and they simply had to hang on and fight their way through it. The rain continued to clatter against the windscreen and Ira could feel it soaking through the leg of his flying suit and spattering on his face in little flurries of fine mist.

There were times when he felt the windscreen would give way with the force of the squalls, but the little machine fought back, driving steadily into the teeth of the storm so that his confidence began to return.

The buffeting grew less at last and he felt that perhaps they had passed through the centre of the storm. Then abruptly, just as the strain seemed to lift, the dashboard lights went out and they were in terrifying total darkness without even the instruments to correct the directions of his senses.

For one horrifying fraction of a second, it was like the end of life itself, before his mind absorbed the absence of light and his instincts reacted to the emergency.

'Torch, Alix!'

A light flashed on almost as he shouted, and he saw her glancing at him nervously as he drew a deep relieved breath.

'Rain must have short-circuited 'em,' he said shortly. 'Thank God we thought of torches. What's the time?'

'Ten-forty-five. New York time.'

'I reckon we've got another three to four hours of darkness. Perhaps it'll sort itself out when the rain stops.'

Even as Ira replied, the violence seemed to go out of the storm, though it was some time before the buffeting ceased. They began to take stock of their position, searching the aircraft for signs of damage.

'Any icing your side, Alix?'

She flashed the beam of the torch through the window and he saw the faint glisten along the leading edge of the wing, like a snail trail in the darkness.

'Nothing to worry about,' she said.

He nodded, reassured. There wasn't enough to clog the venturi tube, but they would have to remain alert for it, because in the cloud it could form swiftly, loading the wings and jamming the controls or lining the rim of the carburettor airscoop.

They checked the fuel lead trap for dirt and water, draining off a spoonful of petrol to free the lead of impurities, but it was an instinctive safety precaution only, because the Whirlwind was still firing steadily and safely, the metallic beat drumming through the framework of the machine.

The rain continued fitfully for some time, rattling against the glass, the water running backwards, sideways and upwards in its narrow thread-like streams, small rivers on a miniature map, blurring the vision even of the night, but there was no violence in the wind now and the controls were no longer stiff and harsh to the touch.

'We'll go down a bit, I think,' Ira said. 'We might get out of it altogether.'

He put the stick forward and levelled off, but the squalls persisted and he stared ahead through the scattered streaks of water on the windscreen, wondering if they should swing south. Though a turn would increase the distance they had to fly, it might take them out of the area of the storm. They seemed to be out of danger now, however, and it was probably unwise to increase the distance unnecessarily. He decided to hold his course.

Alix turned her head. 'We must be pushing a hundred and twenty,' she said. Despite the storm, she sounded calm.

He eyed the compass, wishing it would settle down, then he gestured across the cabin. 'You'll have to give me readings on the Chicks' Own,' he said. 'Is it working?'

'Better than the others. It doesn't hold but it's not crazy.'

For some time they flew in silence, a thousand worries nagging at them despite their smallness. While they knew how compasses generally behaved in relation to the poles, how they were affected by turns and speeds and the position of the aircraft, there was little they could do once the sensitised steel of an individual instrument no longer reached for the true magnetic north. Under such circumstances, from being an aid to navigation, a compass became only a hindrance, a twisted signpost, a sun coming up in the wrong quarter of the globe, a North Star moving out of its accustomed sphere, and they couldn't tell from it whether they were flying in the direction they wanted or had wandered off course or even turned round and were heading back the way they had come.

The rain had stopped completely and Ira peered into the blackness, wondering just how wrong their course might be, his eyes searching for the sky and a sight of the stars. Ahead of him the blue glow of the exhausts made a barrier of light between them and the night, and made reading the instruments more difficult.

The beam of the torch moved and the chart rattled alongside him as Alix studied it. He glanced at the clock. In New York by this time the next day's newspapers would be almost on the streets, and the late sub-editors would be watching the agency messages to find out if anything could go into the late-news columns. DIXIE OVER NEWFOUNDLAND. They'd already have a reference to their last sighting, and everyone would be wondering now if they'd been seen over the Atlantic. By tomorrow evening, they'd be waiting for reports of a sighting from Europe and by this time tomorrow night, the late-news men would be working on reports that they'd arrived.

Or that they'd *not* arrived.

He realized he'd been flying by the senses for some time now for though soft calls of course kept coming from Alix, instinct told him it wasn't safe to put too much trust in the readings from the compasses. He was well aware that it was wrong to fly by the senses rather than by the instruments, but the Hughesden earth inductor was wildly wrong and the liquid compass was still uncertain.

He suddenly noticed that the turn indicator showed that he was flying left wing low and he realized his eyelids were drooping and that the soft calls from the other side of the cabin had ceased. His mind had become separate from his body and fatigue was making him detached and probably not aware of small things that might be wrong. He had just come to the lethargic decision to wake Alix when the first hint that something was wrong brought him bolt upright in his seat, aware that the engine had missed a beat. The hesitation had been so faint he'd hardly noticed it but it had immediately sounded an alarm in his mind and he was awake at once.

'Alix! Hear that?'

'Yes!' Alix's voice was clipped and brisk and she was as awake as he was.

'Did I hear something or was I half asleep?'

'You heard something.'

A flash of rage seared his spirit, mingling with the apprehension that could not be held back, then, knowing that anger couldn't help them in their present situation, he forced himself to be calm and to listen with his head cocked for the slightest pause in the beat of the engine.

They were both alert now, on edge, every sense quivering to catch whatever it was that had brought them to wakefulness. It had been almost too fragile to discern, a fragmentarily different note in the throb of the engine, a pause, something that didn't fit into the steady roar to which they'd been listening now for not far short of a whole day.

He glanced at the instruments. The fuel pressure seemed normal but the engine was beginning to run raggedly, spluttering and jerking as though trying to wrench itself from its bearings. He moved the mixture control but the coughing continued and, coldly, he went through all the normal procedures before making a diagnosis, checking altitude, mixture, ignition and carburation.

'Might be condensation,' he suggested. 'Or a spot of rainwater. It was wet enough when she was filled up. Try draining the trap.'

293

She leaned forward, checking the reservoir in the fuel lead that separated water from fuel, but even as she did so, the break in the engine note came again with a heart-stopping unexpectedness almost as though the *Dixie* had halted momentarily in its easy flight. This time it was a distinct hesitation, as though the pistons had stopped to catch their breath, and this time, as his eyes flickered over the instruments, he saw that the fuel pressure had fallen.

'Crank that wobble pump, Alix,' he said quickly. 'It's the Hughesden!'

Her fury burst out of her in an impassioned cry. 'That God-damned Hughesden!'

As he heard the squeak and hiss of the pump by his seat, Ira glanced downwards towards the blackness beneath him. There was nothing to be seen below but he knew that down there the waves were unrolling with the sluggishness of great depth, black, unfathomable and uncontrollable. If they had to ditch now, it would be God help them in the dark.

'I think it's cleared.' Alix interrupted his thoughts. 'Shall I keep on pumping?'

'No. Give it a rest. It might have cleared itself.'

Even as he spoke, however, the hesitation came again.

'Pump, Alix,' Ira said quickly. 'Where are we?'

The charts rattled as she gave him their position. 'Nineteen hours out, and seventeen-fifty miles to go.'

Ira nodded. They were committed now to continuing because they'd reached a point almost as near to Europe as to America, a point where, with the wind blowing strongly from the west, it was safer to carry on rather than traverse the area of the storm and cloud again on a return course.

'Not much choice, is there?' he said.

'We ought to be able to make it.'

'So long as it grows no worse. If the spindle shears like it did on the way to San Antonio we'll be flying without a pump.'

'Can't we use the hand-pump?'

'For twelve-fifteen hours?' Ira kept his words calm because there was a sudden edge of alarm in her voice.

'How about gas?'

'No problem, so long as it gets to the motor. What tank are we on?'

'Main.'

'Keep her on that. If the pump packs up altogether, we'll go on to wing tanks.'

294

'O.K.' Her voice was calm again now.

'And let's have something to eat,' Ira suggested. 'It looks as though things might grow interesting from here on, so let's start with full stomachs.'

She began to pass cold sausages and rolls, and the tin cup of coffee. The coffee was almost cold now, but it was refreshing and they felt better for it. Just as Ira was finishing it, they caught the third hesitation from the engine, this time a much longer one. Carefully, he set the cup on the floorboards by his feet, moving without panic, his mind clear with the clarity of experience.

'Pump, Alix,' he said, and as the hiss and squeak of the pump started, they heard the engine catch again.

'Keep it going,' Ira said. 'Let's give it a few minutes this time.'

For a while, they sat listening to the roar of the engine, and as she stopped pumping, the steady note continued for a time, then, quite unexpectedly and with a horrifying emptiness after the hours of sound, it stopped dead without warning.

The silence was tremendous and terrifying, particularly in the darkness, and it seemed that the ears would never adjust to it It was a silence of death, doubt and non-existence, and it stunned them so that they could feel neither fear nor hope. Suddenly, there was nothing. Ira shouted at once:

'Pump, Alix!'

He forced himself to keep calm, his hands moving quickly and surely over switches to check they'd not been knocked off accidentally, his eyes flickering over the dials. The law that said that for safety he should direct the nose of the plane downwards instead of clawing for altitude seemed insane just at that moment, but though his heart rejected the idea, his mind told him coldly that the teachings of ten thousand instructors, many of them long since screwed down in Valhalla, were dead right.

The nose of the machine was down now and they could hear the rush of air past them as they dived. Somewhere in the darkness, he heard the rattle as the coffee cup rolled, and he was aware of Alix groping for the cocks to the petrol tanks. The beam of the torch on the dashboard had not wavered.

'Right-wing tank,' she announced calmly, her voice loud in the silence. 'Pump off.'

Ira checked the switches and the throttle again and thrust the stick further forward.

'Hold tight,' he said. 'This is going to be steep. What's the altitude?'

'Five thousand five hundred.'

'Let's hope the engine starts.'

They were dropping steeply now and they could hear the whine of the wind rushing past. It was a horrifying experience with the sea hidden by the darkness and only the unsteady beam of the torch to illuminate the instruments.

His eyes flickering occasionally to the turn-and-bank indicator, Ira watched the altimeter unwind, his mind busy as it grappled with the problems of the emergency. He felt aware of nightmare imaginings as his mind raced ahead to the question of how long he dared keep up the emergency dive to restart the motor. Some time soon, whether the engine fired or not, he'd have to pull out and if by then there was still no sign of life they could only begin to consider the best way to put the machine down in the sea in the darkness.

The altimeter needle was still moving backwards, a thousand feet or more, until it was reading only four thousand, and he worked his feet on the rudder, fish-tailing the machine, aware that he was holding his breath and that his heart was thudding in his chest.

'Three thousand eight hundred. Three thousand seven. Three thousand six . . .'

Alix was calling off the altitude in a loud steady voice, as Ira, his heart cold despite his calm, stared with narrow eyes at the turn-and-bank indicator. Then, with a bang, the engine caught. Ira's heart seemed to stop, as though his mind refused to believe what it heard, and as he eased the stick back gently the altimeter needle began to slow down.

'Three thousand five. Three thousand four. . . .' The readings were coming more slowly now, but not slowly enough, because the machine was still heavy with the petrol it was carrying and he couldn't risk wrenching off the fragile wings by pulling it out of the dive too quickly.

'Three thousand.' Alix paused as the needle steadied and began to move the other way. 'You've got her.'

Ira drew a deep breath and he felt her move uneasily in her seat alongside him. If the engine had been silent for another minute, their lives would probably have ended in a splintering crash, the sloshing sound of sea water and the blackness of oblivion.

'I'm going up again,' he announced. 'Let's have plenty of

height in case that happens again. I'll get as high as I can. It'll use petrol but we can't risk being too low.'

He had been on the point of saying that, whatever happened, they mustn't risk ditching in the dark, but he changed his mind abruptly and decided not to. There was no point in voicing his fears—not yet, especially with the engine beating strongly again now.

'How are the gravity tanks, Alix?'

She looked at the readings in the log book. 'Hundred and sixty gallons. Most of what we've burned has come from the main tank.'

'Let's keep her on gravity as long as we can. We'll go on to main tank and hand pump as late as possible.'

Ira glanced at the chart, his mind working out little sums. They were burning roughly nine gallons to each hundred miles they flew, and with what they still had in the wing tanks, they would still have several hundred miles to go—several hours of pumping—when they were forced on to the main tank.

It was a long time, but if he leaned the mixture and cut the revs there was still a chance they could do it.

CHAPTER TEN

THE MOON was edging up behind the mass of cloud now, illuminating the curves and peaks of mist, touching the edges with silver and throwing night-black shadows into the valleys so that they looked like vast pits leading to death itself. There were islands and continents below them and about them, and enormous towering mountain ranges as the silver glow drove through the screen of cumulus. Above, thin cirrus-like layers picked it up on their undersides, then the moon itself emerged, pale, cold and disinterested, a celestial witness to the struggles of the tiny winged machine threading between the clouds towards the east, a minute speck in the vast complications of the heavens, a mere insect dwarfed by space and the tremendous towering cloud formations.

They were waiting now for daylight, saying nothing, trying not to say anything, aware that nothing they said could help, aware that it was wiser to save their breath for the effort they knew they would have to make before long.

At least, daylight would give meaning to their efforts. With daylight they would see what they were doing, and be able to orientate themselves above the heaving sea.

Already they had switched from the nose tank to the right-wing tank and from the right-wing tank to the left-wing tank. Any moment now they would have to switch to the centre tank, and after that they could expect little more than an hour's grace before they were trying to maintain height with only a small hand pump between them and failure.

'Centre tank,' Alix said, moving in her seat and reaching forward to adjust the cocks. 'Gives us an hour.'

Her voice was quite calm and Ira nodded.

'Let's run it as fine as we can,' he said. 'But let's change before she stops. We can't risk having the engine cut again.'

She leaned forward to look at the charts and he saw there were smears of blood across the paper. She caught him looking at it and held up her hand. In the light of the torch, he saw there were deep gashes on her finger-ends.

'The petrol cocks are sharp,' she said. 'It'll be worth remembering when we build the next machine for the airlines.'

She gave him a compass bearing, and as he repeated it he found himself wondering how much he could rely on it. Even Sammy's Chicks' Own was a Hughesden, and if it were as unreliable as the others, there was no knowing where they'd hit the European coast.

The sky was brightening a little now, however, with the first hint of morning twilight. It was close to the longest day of the year so that they had the full advantage of the short hours of darkness, but there was still no sign of the sea below, nothing but a vast stretch of grey woolliness like the back of an old sheep that they knew was low-lying fog, clinging to the ocean, no gaps in the endless grey prairie anywhere. It was hard to believe there was another world beneath them.

Ira's hand moved over the stabilizer. As the petrol in the wing tanks burned away, the machine was becoming tail-heavy again, as it had been when they'd set cff. It had been his intention to burn off enough from the fuselage tank to balance the machine but that plan had had to be shelved now and with every mile they flew the machine was growing progressively more tail-heavy.

Below them there was still no break in the fog, and Alix seemed to sense the thoughts that were racing through his head. She put her finger on the map.

'There,' she said. 'That's where we should be—if the compass is reading anything like true.'

They appeared to be on course, but Ira had an uneasy suspicion that they'd been led astray during the hours of darkness, though he had no proof beyond an experienced pilot's feelings that something was wrong.

'Last night,' Alix said, 'I thought of suing the Hughesden Company over what's happened, but then I thought again. I guess there'll be no suing done. If we succeed, we'll succeed in spite of them. If we fail'—she paused for a moment as though she didn't wish to consider the possibility—'then we'll offer no excuses.'

They took a sight with the drift indicator, trying to work out the wind velocity and balancing it against the petrol left in the tanks.

'I think the wind's been almost on our tail most of the night,' Ira said. 'We're probably further along than we think.'

It was a comforting thought and they sat in silence for a long time, watching the clock, stupefied by the roar of the engine which had been pounding at their senses for almost a whole day now, then Alix shifted restlessly, her hand reaching forward.

'This is it, Ira,' she said. 'We've got to go on to the main tank and use the hand pump. Do you want me to hold off any longer?'

Ira shook his head. 'No,' he said. 'Let's go on to it now. It pumps a pint a stroke. That's eight strokes to the gallon. The wing tanks hold a hundred and fifty gallons or around one thousand two hundred strokes. We're burning roughly nine gallons—seventy-two strokes—an hour, over a stroke a minute. I'll take first spell. You fly her because we'll have to pump pretty steadily from now on.'

As he gripped the pump handle, he began to wonder for the first time if they would have been wiser to carry the heavy radio that Courtney had wanted, then he thrust the thought aside. Under the circumstances and knowing all they had, they were right to refuse it, and it was no good whining now when they felt they might need it. With the extra weight, they might never have cleared the telephone wires at the end of the runway, might never have been able to edge round the tree-fringed Long Island hill. Their point of balance between success and disaster at that moment had been such that only a few extra pounds might have proved fatal.

299

For a long time, he pumped with his left hand while Alix handled the controls, the engine beating strongly and certainly, then, as his muscles grew tired, she took over with her right hand while he handled the controls.

As they exchanged jobs, he saw she was looking at him with a warm expression, almost as though she were in his debt and glad to be sharing the danger and the work, as though she'd learned things about herself she'd never known before and might never have known but for this.

He reached out his left hand and laid it on hers for a second, and her eyes lifted towards his, quite unafraid.

'How about the pump?' she asked. 'Is it likely to seize up?'

He shook his head. 'They've been used for refuelling for hours at a stretch.'

The fog over the water was breaking up a little now, and with the glow of the rising sun in their faces they descended towards it. The wisps seemed to snatch at the wings as they passed through it, then they saw the waves beneath them at last. The spray indicated the wind was still behind them but there were a lot of white caps, as though the waves were steep, and Ira found himself unable to avoid calculating how best to drop the machine among them if he had to. It was a bitter thought after flying so far.

For a long time, neither of them spoke, then as the pumping slowed and Ira's eyes swept over the dashboard again, his hand hovering over the throttle, he suddenly noticed the smell of petrol had increased. For a while he made no comment, hoping it was imagination. With the vast tanks they carried and the amount of spillage through the vents that there'd been, the whole machine had stunk of fumes from the start, but it seemed now to be growing more powerful. He glanced at Alix, wondering if she'd noticed it, too, but she said nothing and continued to pump steadily. Then he decided the smell was increasing all the time and he saw that she kept turning to look back at the tank behind them.

'You've noticed it, too?' he said.

She nodded. 'What is it, Ira? A leak?'

He moved his shoulders uncertainly. 'Might be. Maybe those Hughesden fitters weren't as good as they claimed. If it's only a small one, we've nothing to worry about. We can always punch a hole in the floor to let it out. If it's a big one, we'll have to face it when we come to it.'

'Will it get worse?'

'Vibration won't help. I'm just praying it isn't in the lead from the main tank through the pump. If it is, we can't transfer.'

They were both glancing about the cabin now, studying the fuel pipes leading to the wing tanks.

'It must be somewhere out of sight,' Alix pointed out.

'It would be!'

'That lousy contract!' she said bitterly. 'I don't know what to say.'

'Not your fault.'

'Maybe it wasn't but I still feel guilty. As long as I live I shall feel responsible if we fail.'

The sun had appeared now, shining into their faces and glinting on the water, and they could see spray whipped off the crests in rainbow wisps that gave them the drift. Alix watching it with strained eyes.

The thought of failure had kept occurring to Ira, too, during the night, but he had constantly thrust it out of his mind. Now that she'd spoken of it, however, it seemed easier to face and he made a decision with which he'd been toying for some time. It was easy to ignore their problems but it was pointless taking unnecessary risks which could in the end prove nothing.

'I'm turning south,' he said abruptly. 'I'm sorry, Alix, but with this leak I don't see any alternative. If anything happens we've got to be where we've got a chance of being picked up. I think we're still north of the shipping routes. I'll fly south-west for a while and see what happens.'

She didn't reply, depressed by the thought of failure. The day was brilliant and there was so much hope about it, it was hard to accept that the chances of success were beginning to slip further through their fingers all the time.

Clouds still lay in front of them and to each side, particularly to the north, and the sun was sprinkling diamond points of light across the water towards them. But their speed had dropped as Ira leaned the mixture to make the most of what fuel they had left. He decided that as they drew nearer to the coast of Europe they were running out of the area of strong westerly winds and were now hardly being helped at all.

Patches of cloud shadow looked like islands ahead of them and Alix glanced at him and jerked a hand forward. Ira shook his head.

'Cloud,' he said shortly.

'For a minute I thought . . .'

'So did I. But it isn't.'

She had seemed overjoyed for a second. 'I thought we'd made it,' she said slowly.

They were both growing increasingly aware of stiffness and cramp by this time. They'd been wedged into the narrow cockpit, hardly able to move, for nearly thirty hours. It was hot, too, with the sun streaming towards them, and the flying suits they'd worn against the chill of the night were suddenly too heavy.

They studied their calculations for a moment, trying to work out their position, but without a landmark or a true reading on the compass they were unable to judge how far from success they were or how near. They had been driving eastwards at high speed during the night, with the wind on their tail, and Ira found himself wishfully thinking that perhaps they were nearer to land than they had imagined. If they could only make a landfall they could hardly be said to have failed, even though they couldn't qualify for the prize they sought. Whatever happened now, theirs would not be a humiliating failure, and there was still a hope that they might even succeed. If the wind had been blowing strongly all night—and by the look of the waves, it might well have been—they might have averaged even a hundred and thirty miles an hour at times.

The brilliance of the sun on the sea was making them squint and he realized he was watching the water now for signs of life, for the first signs of Europe. The smell of petrol was growing stronger and he was satisfied to accept that their chances of reaching Paris were dwindling all the time, but he forced himself back to the problem of navigation, all thought of drowsiness gone and alert now as he would ever be. He had a feeling that they were near the tip of Ireland, probably en route for Cornwall, or probing the peninsula of Brittany. Their deliberate deviations from course had been small.

His eyes narrowed abruptly as he saw movement below that did not belong to the sea and he squinted down into the glare that the sun was bouncing up. There were birds below them, not one but several. Though he couldn't make out what they were, they were the first sign of life they'd seen and he prayed that it was a hint of approaching land.

'Look, Alix! Birds! Probably land-based birds!'

Even as he spoke, the engine began to splutter again—for the first time since the terrifying stoppage during the night.

'Keep the pump going, Alix,' he said quickly.

'It *is* going. It's been going all the time. It's never stopped.' The words came in gasps and his eyes flickered across the needles. The smell of petrol was suddenly becoming overpowering.

'I'll pump,' he said. 'Take the controls.'

As they changed jobs, he worked the pump furiously for a while and the engine picked up again. Clearly it was being starved of fuel and what he had suspected was obviously true. The wing tanks were being emptied faster than they were managing to fill them.

As he worked, he managed to lift the floorboards with his right hand. There seemed to be several inches of fuel beneath his feet and he reached into his pocket for a screwdriver and jabbed it downwards through the plywood floor. He waited for the petrol to drain away, but it didn't appear to diminish and he realized then that with every movement of the pump he heard a strong hissing sound over the engine that told him that the faster he pumped, the faster he was causing it to leak.

'It's in the line to the wing tanks,' he said. 'We're pumping it away.'

He looked at Alix, his heart heavy. With every stroke, they were wasting fuel.

'We've got to consider putting her down if we see a ship, Alix,' he said bluntly.

It was a hard thing to say, after all they had endured, and he saw the spasm of misery cross her face. Then she got control of herself again and nodded. 'You're the boss,' she said.

'Keep on course,' he said. 'I'll try not to waste too much petrol. I daren't stop pumping to find the leak, but I'll try.'

Unfastening his seat belt and half-turning in his seat, he traced the fuel flow from the pump to the wing, but the leak appeared to be underneath his seat somewhere and he brought up his hand with fingers moist with the precious liquid.

As he looked at it, he remembered what the Wright engineer had said when they'd first discussed using a Viking pump. 'I'd always rather have fuel leads where I can see 'em,' he'd announced. 'Especially over the sea.'

The words seemed to have a cryptic quality now and Ira peered forward, praying that somewhere ahead, among the islands the cloud shadows formed, he would see something that was real.

Ahead of them now a layer of stratus lay, flat and heavy

across their path. Could it be Ireland? Cloud often formed along the coast where the air temperature changed, and his eyes narrowed as he stared. Could he detect something beneath it, something that was darker and more solid than the ephemeral islands they'd seen constantly since daylight that were nothing more than shadows?

He was aware of a terrible desolation as he stared across the empty miles of the sea. They were now beyond the sight and beyond the awareness of human beings, and if they had to put down here, alone, in the sea, they were probably also beyond help. Fear crowded in at the knowledge of the enormous emptiness. There had been many times before when he'd been in danger, but none of them seemed now as terrifying as this awful aloneness.

Then he realized that Alix's hand was on his arm and she was pointing, 'Ira!' Her voice was high and thin with excitement. 'Ships!'

His eyes swung in the direction she pointed, and he was aware of an immediate lifting of the spirits. Heading out towards them was a small vessel, and beyond it another and still another.

The ships were beneath them now, trawlers of some sort, small vessels with a funnel set towards the stern. Then beyond them, almost unbelievably clear as it emerged into the sunshine from a patch of shadow, they saw the black and white lines of a passenger liner, heading east, its quarter towards them.

Their eyes met and through the strain he saw that Alix was smiling. He was just trying to make up his mind whether to take a chance and head for the land that must now be near when the engine began to bark, shaking the whole machine as it spluttered and coughed, and he made up his mind at once.

'Make for the big ship, Alix,' he said. 'They'll have wireless and they're heading for Europe.'

As the nose turned, the engine spluttered again. Ira pumped more quickly and even as the hiss of escaping fuel increased, the engine caught again. The leak was obviously growing worse and they had no option now but to play for safety.

He drew a deep breath. 'I'll take her,' he said. 'Keep pumping as long as the engine fires.'

He adjusted the stabilizer to combat the increasing tail heaviness, the engine firing in fits and starts. The awareness of failure that lay heavily on his heart as he fought to keep the

Dixie's nose up was relieved only by the knowledge that it hadn't come from any lack of effort on their part. They need not reproach themselves, because the attempt had probably been doomed from the start by the twisted litigation of the Hughesden Company. Even against the odds, they'd come within an ace of succeeding and he was conscious that his bitterness was tempered with a certain amount of pride.

'Get the Very pistol out, Alix,' he said. 'And when you fire it, make sure they see it.'

They were losing height rapidly now as the engine poppled and spluttered and they lost speed; and with the increasing tail-heaviness, he had to keep the stick well forward to avoid stalling. By this time there was no sign of the fishing vessels that had indicated that land was not far away, but the big ship was just ahead of them now and they were directly in front of its port bow.

Alix was struggling to open the window, and suddenly, while he was still keeping his eye on the ship, she snatched at his arm.

'Ira!' Her voice cracked with excitement. 'Look! Look!'

In their efforts to keep the ship in sight, they had taken their gaze off the horizon and as his eyes followed her pointing finger, he saw a purple-grey shadow beyond the port wing-tip just emerging from the bank of scrappy cloud.

Alix's eyes met his, excited and moist with tears of happiness. 'It is, it is,' she was shouting. 'This time it is!'

He stared in the direction of her finger, hardly able to believe his eyes, but there was no mistaking the clean line of a coast jutting out towards them and the veil of cloud hugging the shoreline.

He stared at the ship below them, faced with a decision that was as agonizing as any he'd ever had to make. Below them, there was safety. To port of them was their goal, though in trying to reach it they could easily fail and die in doing so. He glanced at the altimeter. The needle hung uncertainly at four thousand feet.

'I'm going for the land,' he said abruptly and, giving him a quick smile, she slotted the Very pistol back into its rack.

'Pump, Alix,' he said, putting the machine in a bank to port. 'Give it all you've got. Never mind how much we waste. There ought to be enough left to carry us that far.'

With the pump squeaking and hissing behind him, he held the turn until the nose of the machine pointed towards the land, keeping the bank shallow so as not to lose any precious height. As he straightened out, the engine faltered and picked up again, then they were heading towards safety, with the Whirlwind putting out full power whenever it wasn't starved of fuel.

Ira's hands were sweating as he stared towards the distant coastline. The distance between them and safety seemed to have grown no less and from their height and the visibility he guessed they were sixty to seventy miles away. He knew instinctively from the feel of the aircraft under his hands that it would take all his skill to hold it in the air that long.

The engine jerked, coughed and faltered again and his heart died within him, then, as he worked the throttle he heard the pump's thump and squeak increase in tempo as Alix bent over it, and he caught the hiss of escaping fuel growing louder. But the sick and halting engine picked up again, firing spasmodically, and his eyes flickered instinctively across the pressure and temperature gauges. The temperatures were building up, he noticed, and the pressures were falling and they were barely holding altitude as power came and went.

The engine vibrated, cut and caught again, and he tried to claw upwards for a little more height, then it spluttered and stopped and he had to drop the nose again to a gliding angle, only to pull the stick back once more as it caught again.

The minutes dragged by, each one slow-moving and agonizing, his heart stopping each time the engine cut, his breathing halted until it caught again. They were still flying but they were moving forward now at a crippled speed that was barely enough to keep them airborne.

'How's it going?' he called over his shoulder, hardly daring to take his eyes off the horizon as the aeroplane trembled on the point of stalling.

'Keep her flying,' Alix panted. 'I'm O.K. How far now?'

'It looks just the same, but it can't be.'

He glanced round. The sea was empty again now. The big ship was miles off their starboard wing, heading east towards safety, its look-outs with their eyes on other points by this time. If they came down now, they'd never be seen. Their chance of rescue was gone, and he began to study the sea below for a sign of scattered fishing boats from the harbours that lay just ahead of them.

There was no sign of life, however, nothing beyond the scattered gulls low over the surface of the water, and he stared ahead again, certain in his mind that the land was nearer but unable to recognize the fact.

Alix glanced up. 'How far, Ira?' she asked again.

He didn't bother to reply, his attention absorbed in the fight to retain height. Below them the sea was rough and he knew it would be dangerous to put the *Dixie* down in it. He turned his eyes to the land again. It was undoubtedly nearer now, and the outlines were clearer, the mountains sharper and the line of cloud merely scattered groups of puff-balls. He could see the outline of hills now, then he caught sight of a small fishing boat beneath them, heading out to sea. Here was another chance of safety if he chose to take it, but he deliberately ignored it, holding the nose of the machine up, stretching out the last yard of flight and the last spoonful of petrol.

The stink in the cabin now was appalling, and glancing down he could see petrol sloshing round his feet, and as he glanced over his shoulder towards Alix, he saw her shoulders jerk and realized she was quietly gagging behind him, her stomach revolted by the fumes.

She lifted streaming eyes in a sweating weary face. 'Keep her flying,' she choked. 'Isn't there anything we can throw out to lessen the weight?'

He managed a twisted smile. 'We threw it all out before we took off,' he reminded her.

The machine was staggering closer and closer to the land still, houses on the shore plain now along a boulder-strewn coast, and he snatched at the map, trying to identify their landfall. He hadn't time to dwell on it, however, as the engine spluttered and demanded his attention. Then he saw more fishing vessels, hugging the coastline, and a strip of sea shining metallically just behind the hills, and realized that what lay ahead of them was not the mainland but a large island just off the coast.

'It's probably Dursey,' he said, staring at the land and comparing it with the map across his knees. 'The mountains and the bay correspond. But the town there doesn't fit.'

Alix managed a tired smile. 'Whatever it is,' she said, 'it's Europe.'

The *Dixie* was only floating forward now, its height varying constantly as power came and went, but the land was only close ahead of them by this time, with barren islands to the north and green slopes lying against the side of low corrugated hills. Ira searched the map again. They weren't high enough now, however, to see the outline of the mainland clearly and the mountain tips were actually higher than they were, old, bleak and barren, while below them the water grew closer and closer to their wheels in a narrow circled bay, dotted with rocky islets.

He was holding the machine in a fine point of balance in a speed just above stalling, but they were still losing height. Alix, twisted stiffly in her seat to pump, was beating her clenched left fist softly against her knee, and he realized her mouth was moving as she prayed silently for them to reach the land just ahead, willing them almost every inch of the way.

'We'll do it,' she panted. 'Just!'

He jerked his head forward at a brown sail on the ruffled surface of the water. 'There's a fishing boat down there,' he said. 'If we ditch now, they can fetch us out.'

The hills ahead looked the colour of bilberry juice and he could see a huddle of houses round a makeshift pier jutting out over a collection of loose boulders, then they slipped over one of the tiny islands, a mass of tangled thorn trees, mountain ash, hazel bushes, ferns and briars, and a few loose-stone walls that looked as though they were falling down with neglect.

The large island had grown close enough now for them to feel certain of success and he was still trying to identify their landfall when the engine spluttered again. Alix's head ducked down at once and the pump's squeak increased in tempo and the smell of petrol grew stronger, but just as Ira was beginning to look for a suitable field into which to put the machine down, the engine spluttered and finally died.

He had grown so used to it picking up again after each faltering cough, it came as a shock to realize that at last it wasn't going to. This time it had finally halted, and after windmilling for a few turns the propeller jerked and stopped in its circle, and all they could hear was the soft rustling of the air past the skin of their fragile machine. The silence after the roar filled their ears with menace, and the shock took away their breath as if they'd been plunged into an icy pool.

He had managed to claw upwards again with the last burst of power but with the drag of the motionless propeller, their speed had dropped again and he had to put the nose down to a steeper angle to avoid stalling, the engine silent with the silence of death.

There was no time now to consider where they might put the machine down, only to go through the motions of putting her down safely, and Ira decided to chance landing her with the wind behind him. As his eyes roved ahead, flying by feel, he noticed instinctively the painted surface of the motionless propeller was worn right through in places so that he could see the laminations of the wood. The inside of the blades and the whole front of the machine looked as though they'd been struck by a cloud of hurled stones, and it was only then that he realized how violent had been the storm they'd passed through during the night.

His ears still seeming to hear the metallic roar of the dead engine, he was aware that Alix had pulled herself upright in her seat and was sitting rigidly alongside him, her face white with strain and exhaustion, her lips pale to the point of disappearance, her fists so tightly clenched her knuckles shone white. He sensed her watching him as he struggled, and he knew that her expression was a mixture of anger and deep disappointment.

'Finish,' he heard her say.

They were only just above the water now, stretching their glide out to the last inch until it was impossible to hold the plane off any longer.

'Hold tight,' he said abruptly. 'We're going in. We'll not make the shore.'

They were among a fresh group of islets now, mere humps in the water, when the wheels whipped the top off a wave, and he eased back on the stick, trying to force the last few feet of flight from the aeroplane, then, as another wave came towards them, he wrenched back the stick, heaving the nose up. They heard a slap like a clap of giant hands as the nose dipped, then the wheels, digging into the waves, acted as a brake, and they were slammed heavily against the dashboard and water spurted in at them through the doors.

Half-dazed from a blow on the temple, Ira flung himself at the door. The weight of the sea held it shut, and as he burst it open a great gout of water hit him in the face and blinded him. He fell into the sea, and as he came to the surface he saw the machine floating above him, its tail lifting gently, the elevators sagging, the rudder flapping idly as it moved, and he reached out a hand to cling to it for support.

There was no sign of Alix and for a moment he thought she'd been trapped inside the cabin. He was just on the point of diving down when her head appeared, her hair plastered across her face, and through its black strands he saw blood on her forehead. Her eyes were wild and afraid and she was gasping with a hoarse croaking sound as she fought for breath.

Beyond her he saw a fishing boat with a brown sail lurching towards them, its bows plunging into the waves. Thankfully he started to work his way towards her round the half-submerged starboard wing with its lifting aileron, but he was hampered by his heavy clothing and there was nothing to grip hold of and the water kept hitting him in the face and shocking him with its saltiness.

The *Dixie* was floating with its tail and port wing in the air, swinging gently and, with that great expanse of fabric catching the wind, still moving steadily through the water towards the east like a ship under sail.

Fighting his way round was difficult but he reached Alix at last as she hung on to the port strut with one tense white hand, fighting to keep a grip against the waves that snatched at the heavy flying suit and threatened to sweep her away. One arm hooked round the strut, he tried to push her towards the wing, but her arms were numb from the cold water, and as she fought to climb on to it she gave him a desperate look and shook her head, her eyes frantic.

'Hang on,' he spluttered. 'Just hang on!'

He fought his way to the wing, dragging himself face down across it, but it was slippery and its movement was violent enough to make it difficult, and the water was breathtakingly cold, deadening his senses so that his fingers were numb as he grabbed for Alix's collar and heaved her up to lie across the edge of the wing. 'Let me go, Ira,' she whispered. 'It doesn't matter. I don't mind. Save yourself.'

He brushed the hair from his eyes and spat sea water. 'Don't talk nonsense.'

She seemed to have lost her courage and he realized she was dazed. Then he saw that the blood was welling up under her hair, and realized she must have struck her forehead much harder than he'd thought against the windscreen when they'd hit the sea.

'It doesn't matter, Ira'—she was shaking her head angrily now, her voice pleading—'let me go!'

She tried to push his hands away, but, his fingers twisted into her collar, he hung on to her while she fought to free herself. A feebly swinging hand hit him across the face and her finger caught agonizingly under his eyelid, but he slowly inched her higher and higher until she lay face downwards across the wing, her feet still in the water, lying like a fish in a basket, gasping and exhausted and staring at the cold sea in front of her face.

Then he became aware that they were lying close to the windward side of one of the humps of rock that stuck out of the water. As he watched, the sluggish swinging movement of the aeroplane stopped with a soft jar. The tail began to move round towards the east at once like a pendulum as the breeze flowed past the fin, turning them into wind like a boat at anchor, and it dawned on him then that they had been set against some underwater projection of rock that had probably caught the submerged undercarriage.

He gave a half-hysterical laugh, and inching Alix higher on the wing he held her head up so she could see.

'We made it,' he yelled in her ear. 'Alix, we made it! We've actually reached land!'

CHAPTER ELEVEN

FOR A LONG TIME neither of them moved, the water slapping at their faces, cold and wet, and, now that the first excitement had died, despairingly aware of failure.

The *Dixie* showed no sign of sinking. Air was trapped in the tail and the empty tanks were keeping her afloat, the magnificent Wright Whirlwind under the surface of the sea, one wing half out of the water, the great white word, *Dixie*, like a banner on the red side of the fuselage.

Neither of them spoke, both occupied with the same bitter thoughts. But for Courtney's failure and the Hughesden Company's vengeful insistence on their rights, they would easily have succeeded because Hal Woolff's aeroplane was as good as he'd said it would be and, except when it was starved of fuel, the Wright engine had shown no sign of letting them down.

As he lifted his head to look for the fishing boat, Ira heard a murmur of anguish from Alix.

'Did they see us?' she asked.

He nodded, jerking a frozen hand at the fishing boat which was still heading agonizingly slowly towards them.

She was lying alongside him now and he was holding her on to the wing with one arm round her waist, trying to protect her from the cut of the water, and he could see that the gash on her head was deeper than he'd thought. She seemed to be only half-conscious and he could hear her muttering softly above the lap of the waves.

'Ira, I didn't let you down, did I?'

'No, by God, Alix! Never.'

'I didn't want to let you down,' she whispered. 'I wanted so much for you to succeed.'

He managed a shaky smile. 'We nearly made it.'

'I wanted you to. I wanted like hell for you to. I didn't want a single damn thing out of it but *that*.'

'We did all right, Alix.'

She became silent, and, as her head sank forward, he thought she'd become unconscious, but she lifted her head again and smiled with a brief show of her old spirit.

'Where's that lousy boat?' she said.

'She'll be here any time now.'

'I was just thinking. . . .' Her voice came slowly now, her words stumbling as though the cold were beginning to affect her. 'Whatever happens now, they'll know we *tried*.'

For a long time they were silent again and Ira could feel the thumping of the waves under the wing, producing a hollow booming sound in his ear. They slid into a trough between two waves, dropping down as though they were sinking out of life itself, and as the following wave caught them and lifted them, he saw the brown sail of the fishing boat again, nearer than he'd expected.

It was almost on top of them now, black against the sky, moving across the waves in a lumpy, lurching movement, a man in a blue jersey standing up in the bows, shouting words at them they couldn't understand. Behind him another man leaned over the tiller.

Alix's eyes opened again now and he saw her blinking away the tears, then she grasped his hand, lying her cheek on it, her lips moving in a little unselfconscious prayer.

The brown sail rattled down as the boat swung alongside, and there was a babble of shouting.

'The aeroplane,' Ira gasped as Alix disappeared from the wing across the gunwale. 'Can you get a line on her and tow her ashore?'

The fisherman jabbered at him in a thin high-pitched voice that sounded odd coming from his burly frame. His face was reddened and raw with the wind and his thin pointed nose was long and ugly, but there was a wide grin on his mouth that showed broken teeth, and it looked angelic.

'Sure, you're a long way off course, bhoy!' he said. 'Where yiz from?'

'America.'

The man stared, then grinned disbelievingly.

A flicker of a smile broke across Ira's face. 'That's right,' he insisted. 'We left New York at dawn yesterday.'

For a moment the two men in the boat stared at each other, then the red-faced one frowned. 'Sure,' he said again. 'You'll be pullin' me leg now, wouldn't yiz?'

Ira tried to explain, then the fishermen looked at each other and slowly the man in the bows began to grin. 'Be Jaysus,' he said. 'I thought ye wuz from Baldonnel or somewheres like that.'

He stared at Ira then impulsively thrust out his hand.

'Sure, I'm glad we wuz around,' he said. 'We'll save yer plane, misther. Where was ye headin' for?'

'Paris. Where's this place?'

'Castlegowan. That's Guinan Island. Twenty-five miles off Ballydavid Head.'

'And the bay over there?'

'Castlegowan Bay. Sure, wan of the luvliest in Ireland. Ye nearly made it.'

'Yes.' Ira nodded. 'We nearly made it.'

It was hard to realize they'd failed. As they were helped ashore some time later, stumbling stiff-legged, bruised and shaken, faces lined the stark stone jetty and they saw women with shawls over their heads peering down at them, their children peeping round their legs, raw-faced women in rough clothes who looked as though the battle with the elements on the wild Atlantic coast was as hard for them as it was for their menfolk.

As they climbed the weed-covered steps, the faces above them were sympathetic and there was a spatter of clapping and pats on the shoulder. Stumbling over the rough stones of the jetty, they passed more people arriving from the village to gape and grin shyly at them from among the lobster pots and fish boxes and strings of nets and piles of rotting rope and tackle. Then an ancient car drove up, older than anything they'd ever seen in America, and hands reached out to help them in. Blankets were thrown about them and curious welcoming faces stared at them, then a child in a ragged dress, pushed forward by a clucking woman, thrust forward a fistful of wilting blue flowers.

Alix looked at Ira, her expression a mixture of pride and humility, and he saw her throat work with emotion. There were tears in her eyes as she bent down to kiss the child's grubby face.

Castlegowan was too poor to boast an hotel, but a room was set aside for them in the local pub, by a bowing, scraping landlord who treated them as though they'd descended from heaven, and to the little wilting fistful of blue wild flowers were added bunches of crocuses and daffodils picked from the sheltered corners of the barren island.

Someone found a doctor, a big man who looked like a vet and smelled as though he probably doubled in the capacity. He slapped a plaster over the cut on Alix's forehead and bandaged her torn fingers, then, with an air of satisfaction, he lit a pipe and blew out clouds of thick acrid smoke.

'Sure, it looks very dashin' on a pretty face,' he said, blatantly admiring her. 'Ye were lucky! Ye'll be interested to know another one of your lot got off. They heard it on the wireless at the big house this morn. They told me when I went up there to dose the cook. I thought ye'd want to know.'

A change of clothing was produced, ugly and ill-cut but dry. The landlord dug out the elderly postmistress whose duties were shared with the responsibility of running a rope and paraffin store, and they managed, after a lot of difficulty and explaining, to persuade her to send telegrams to New York. It wasn't easy because she'd never had to send anything further before than Killyguinan, the only town on the island, or to Ballydavid on the mainland.

There was a surprising response. Within an hour they were called to the telephone to answer questions shot at them over a bad line by an awed reporter on the mainland whose accent was so thick he was barely understandable. Almost immediately, congratulatory telegrams began to come in, so that the postmistress had to shout for help to her relatives in the village shop, and they propped the buff sheets up on an old-fashioned dresser among the chipped pint pots and the portraits of the landlord's relations and a stuffed owl in a glass case. They were as full of praise and excitement as if they'd succeeded and there were offers from English and Continental newspapers for their story, the postmistress's nephew running along the village

314

street with them one after the other as they arrived. By the time it grew dark, they began to arrive from America, too, a jubilant one from Sammy and Mae saying, 'Well done. Come home. All is forgiven,' and others from Hal Woolff, Loerner and Boyle. There were more from the Wright Company and one from the people of Medway, to say nothing of dozens of unknown admirers in Dublin, Belfast, London and on the Continent.

When the flowers had first appeared, they had imagined it was merely the excitement of seeing something new and strange in the village, and they had never imagined that anyone would be interested in unsuccessful aviators, but then they'd caught the looks and realized that they'd come near enough to success to have aroused a surprising amount of admiration in Europe.

'It's almost as if we'd made it, Ira,' Alix said.

Ira shrugged. 'When someone *does* make it,' he said realistically, 'they'll forget *us*.'

She looked at him curiously. 'You disappointed?'

He grinned. 'I suppose so,' he admitted. 'But I'm grateful to be alive and I'm not ashamed. We know what let us down and it'll all come out in the wash. We'll still sell Courtneys to the airlines. Hal was dead right.'

The Courtney, still in one piece if a little battered by the handling it had received from fishermen unused to handling aeroplanes and the depredations of souvenir hunters, who'd come from Killyguinan in motor cars, traps and jaunting cars, was lashed down to stakes in a rocky meadow next to the pub, guarded by a policeman and covered with a tarpaulin borrowed from the harbour.

'Yes,' she agreed. 'Hal was right.'

They were discussing the imponderables of the trip when the landlord and his wife appeared. 'Ye'll be takin' a measure in the bar, I hope,' he said. 'Everybody wants to meet ye.'

He paused, somewhat embarrassed. 'Does the young lady feel up to a public appearance?' he went on, looking at Alix.

'I guess so. I'd like that.'

The landlord smiled, then he glanced at his wife and went on hesitantly. 'Because ye might as well make as much of the limelight as ye can get,' he said. He stopped awkwardly and looked again at his wife and they sensed that he was trying to tell them something as he shuffled his feet and his wife's eyes rested on Alix's tired white face.

'What's wrong?' Ira asked. 'Something is.'

The landlord managed a smile. 'Sure, nothin's wrong,' he said. 'Nothin' at all. But sure to God, they just sent the car down from the big house with a message. They'll be shoutin' for somebody else tomorrow. One of yer friends just landed in Paris. Them French turned out in millions, they say.'

Alix's eyes flew to Ira's face and the landlord nodded sympathetically. 'Just this minute they picked up a message, they say. It'll be in the newspapers tomorrow.'

Ira drew a deep breath. So someone had proved it could be done, after all! Despite his disappointment, he felt only pride at being associated, however indirectly, with success.

'Who was it?' he asked.

The landlord shrugged. 'Sure to God, I didn't catch the name. Lindbergh? Would that be it? Lindbergh?'

He had brought a bottle of Irish whiskey with him and they drank to the fair-haired young pilot from St Louis, then, as the door closed behind the landlord and his wife, Ira was silent for a while. They had been eager to get back to their customers and he suspected they were keen to hear more of the celebrations that would be taking place in Paris. The glory had gone from them already, he knew, as quickly as it had come, and as surely as if someone had turned out a spotlight. It was directed now on to another plane and they'd not even be noticed when they reached the mainland, because everyone—even the reporter who'd telephoned them—would be thinking of the tall young man with the Ryan.

Alix touched Ira's hand again, a small secretive confident movement. 'We can try again, Ira,' she said.

Ira smiled and shook his head. 'No. Not again. There'll be so many trying it now, they'll look like cabs along Fifth Avenue. There'll be hundreds now that Lindbergh's proved it can be done. Only the first one really means anything, Alix. The second one only proves the first one wasn't a fluke. It's time to turn to something else.'

She looked puzzled and he shrugged. 'We've hardly started yet,' he pointed out. 'This is only the beginning. This is only the first ocean. And there'll be other things to do besides break records. It's time now to look towards the next step.'

He reached out his hand and she took it without embarrassment. Outside, the night was dark now and they could see only an occasional star in the black sky above the line of the headland. The sound of the sea came to them on the breeze, surging and strong, bringing with it all the fears and anxieties of the previous night and all the agonizing moments they'd lived through. It wasn't hard to imagine it as the sound of the crowd swarming round the triumphant pilot in Paris.

They both knew that by the time they'd been ferried to the mainland and reached the civilization of Tralee or Killarney or Cork, the excitement attending their arrival would have died. By the time they'd reached England, it would have faded completely and by the time they'd got mechanics to dismantle the *Dixie*, had transported it to a ship and carried it back to America, they'd be quite forgotten in the hullabaloo that would have been raised round Lindbergh, and only Sammy and Hal Woolff and a few others would be there to greet them. What they'd done would have been unbelievable a year or two before, would still be unbelievable if Lindbergh hadn't succeeded in doing what they'd failed to do. But he had, and they were already probably forgotten in the capitals of Europe.

Ira jerked his head at the door and grinned at Alix. Outside, in the bar, they could hear the babble of broad-accented voices as the citizens of Castlegowan waited for them. Whatever was thought of them tomorrow, whatever was thought of them already, he knew that Castlegowan wasn't likely to forget in a hurry the excitement of their arrival. There'd never again be any transatlantic fliers arriving in the village and tonight might well be a celebration that would be remembered for a lifetime.

'Come on,' he said, opening the door so that the excitement outside rushed in at them in a surge of sound. 'Whatever happens tomorrow, *this* ought to be quite a night. When it's over we shall sleep for a week.'

Alix stared back at him. Her face was still pale and peaked but her eyes were merry.

'At least they haven't got Prohibition and the whiskey'll be worth drinking,' she said, and, grasping his hand, they went together into the smoke-filled noisy bar.